A DREAM COME TRUE

Garnet Winters had had dreams like this before, lying alone in her Boston bed. She was transported to a tropical beach, lying there with her sea-drenched dress clinging to her body and opening her eyes to see a tall, dark man kneeling above her, his strong tanned hands pressing her breasts through the flimsy lace of her chemise.

"I thought you would never come," she murmured, and she arched sensually against the man's warm palms.

"Come to me," she whispered, no trace of shame in her voice as she opened her arms to him.

It was only then, as naked flesh met naked flesh, that she realized this was no dream—and that it was too late to stop what already was happening.

Garnet Winters had arrived in St. Dominique. . . .

RAGE
TO LOVE

Great Reading from SIGNET

(0451)

☐ **SEASON OF DESIRE by Julia Grice.** (125487—$3.95)*

☐ **KIMBERLEY FLAME by Julia Grice.** (124375—$3.50)*

☐ **PASSION'S REBEL by Kay Cameron.** (125037—$2.95)*

☐ **THE DEVIL'S HEART by Kathleen Maxwell.** (124723—$2.95)*

☐ **JUDITH: A LOVE STORY OF NEWPORT by Sol Stember.**
(125045—$3.25)*

☐ **MOLLY by Teresa Crane.** (124707—$3.50)*

☐ **GILDED SPLENDOUR by Rosalind Laker.** (124367—$3.50)*

☐ **BANNERS OF SILK by Rosalind Laker.** (115457—$3.50)*

☐ **CLAUDINE'S DAUGHTER by Rosalind Laker.**
(091590—$2.25)*

☐ **WARWYCK'S WOMAN by Rosalind Laker.** (088131—$2.25)*

☐ **THE IMMORTAL DRAGON by Michael Peterson.**
(122453—$3.50)*

☐ **WILD HARVEST by Allison Mitchell.** (122720—$3.50)*

☐ **EMERALD'S HOPE by Joyce Carlow.** (123263—$3.50)*

☐ **THE BARFORTH WOMEN by Brenda Jagger.** (122275—$3.95)†

*Prices slightly higher in Canada
†Not available in Canada

RAGE TO LOVE

by
Maggie Osborne

A SIGNET BOOK
NEW AMERICAN LIBRARY
TIMES MIRROR

PUBLISHED BY
THE NEW AMERICAN LIBRARY
OF CANADA LIMITED

Copyright © 1983 by Maggie Osborne

First Printing, December, 1983

 2 3 4 5 6 7 8 9

 SIGNET TRADEMARK REG. U.S. PAT. OFF. AND FOREIGN COUNTRIES
REGISTERED TRADEMARK - MARCA REGISTRADA
HECHO EN WINNIPEG, CANADA

SIGNET, SIGNET CLASSIC, MENTOR, PLUME, MERIDIAN
and NAL BOOKS are published in Canada by The New American
Library of Canada, Limited, Scarborough, Ontario

PRINTED IN CANADA

COVER PRINTED IN U.S.A.

To Bill and Anne Prather
with love and appreciation

—1—

"WE'RE TAKING ON WATER. PREPARE TO ABANDON SHIP."

Garnet Winters stood at the ship's railing and stared blindly into the gray, wet dawn. Warm tropical rain pelted her face but she didn't feel the sting The knot of pale women beside her wailed and wrung their hands but she didn't notice. She heard only the creaks and groans of the breaking ship, and to Garnet the sounds were the same as those of a dream shattering.

For the *Commerce* to sink within sight of port was outrageous. The injustice brought angry tears to her green eyes, blurring the jagged mountaintops in the rain-washed distance. Another few hours and she would have disembarked at the foot of those mountains to claim her inheritance, an event she had impatiently awaited since the age of twelve. Nine long years of preparation—wasted. All the French lessons, the history lessons, the thick books on cane and rum and molasses . . . wasted.

Running feet pounded the deck behind her hem, but she didn't turn to observe the storm damage or the crew's frantic efforts to ready the longboats. The instant Garnet had emerged from belowdeck, her sharp eyes had inventoried the devastation caused by the storm. Immediately she had noted the frayed ropes where many of the longboats had been secured. As nearly as she could determine, three longboats remained to rescue nearly seventy people.

She glanced at the other women from beneath long, rain-wet lashes, wondering how long it would be before they guessed the crew would fight for space in the longboats and the passengers would be abandoned. Soon, she imagined as she listened to the snarls of a fistfight rising from the waist of the ship. She could almost taste the salty tang of fear in the hot, thick air. Or was it her own anger she tasted?

Garnet slapped at the slanting rain streaming from her face, transforming her skirts into a soggy mass weighing like lead, then she curled her fingers about the railing and stared hard at the distant peaks of St. Domingue. Within the saddle where the two mountain chains met lay the sugar plantation Garnet and her cousin, Simone, had inherited from Grandpère Philippe. Now Garnet would never see it.

"Damn!" Her fingers tightened on the railing as the deck slowly tilted beneath her slippers. One of the women shrieked and dropped to her knees, lifting clasped hands toward heaven and praying to see her husband and children again.

Garnet glanced at the woman curiously and then away. It never ceased to astonish her how death elevated husbands to the stature of sainthood when in reality she had never encountered one who could not be immeasurably improved upon. Thank God, Garnet had possessed the wit to break both her betrothals. Marriage, as she had observed the state, was the culmination of a brief period of insanity excused by the label of love. And love did not endure; in Garnet's opinion that temporal emotion proved about as substantial as the wisps of steam misting above the sea.

Land endured. Land was forever. Her eyes narrowed longingly on a shoreline she could not see, imagining sandy contours fronting a sweep of sugar plantations with rows of coffee trees climbing the mountainsides behind. Her fist smacked painfully against the railing before she dropped her eyes to the turquoise waves sucking at the hull. Bolts of cotton and crates of leather goods bobbed in the water, part of the cargo Boston merchants had hoped to sell in St. Domingue.

Frowning, Garnet attempted to read the water-blurred markings on the crates below, seeking Uncle William's company stamp, but the deep shadows blackening the waterline were too dense.

Thinking of her guardian raised images of that dear, good man in Garnet's mind. Perhaps it was true that a person's life flashed before his eyes in times of peril; the years following her parents' death unreeled before her eyes. She saw Uncle William's modest Boston home on Cupper's Lane and her own small room beneath the eaves; she remembered Uncle William praising her first, atrocious attempts at needlepoint, recalled his pride when she had first presided over his annual bachelor dinner. Countless carriage rides and Sunday suppers paraded through her memory. And a multitude of quiet discussions before the parlor fire, ending in a disharmony Garnet deeply regretted. Uncle William had wished her to marry; she had insisted on pursuing her inheritance. Marriage didn't interest her.

Her reverie ended with a jolt as the ship lurched drunkenly and the bow edged inexorably toward the waves. Men cursed and a bloody knife fight erupted near the longboats. The women clung to each other, weeping hysterically, and tore at their streaming hair.

Garnet blotted out the sight by closing her long lashes and breathing deeply of the hot, damp air. Then she turned to the wreckage behind her, presenting a slim column of calm amid the chaos and rising fury of emotion. A steady flow of shouting men rushed in and out of the hatches, screaming for patching pitch and buckets. A bailing brigade had formed, stretching from the hatch grids to the rails. The men might as well have attempted to empty the sea with a spoon. It was as hopeless a task as squeezing everyone on board the longboats, which swayed from the pulley lines, nearly ready to launch.

Those who claimed a seat aboard one of the boats might survive. "The rest of us will die." Garnet listened to the echo of her whisper and grimaced, her full pink lips pulling into a line of frustration and anger. What was she expected to do? Stand at the rail until the water and the weight of the ship sucked her to the bottom? No. A Winters didn't stand idly by and wait for disaster—a Winters fought to survive. Hadn't her father survived two British balls before a third killed him? And her mother, Marie Philippe Winters . . . if Marie hadn't contracted pneumonia, she would have survived the childbed fever that took her baby and finally herself.

Garnet spun back to the rail and narrowed her gaze, sweeping the horizon looming from the rainy mist. The ragged mountaintops serrated a drenched sky. Below them, in the faint dawn light, she could make out, barely, the curve of a distant shore.

Carefully Garnet gauged the distance, knowing the diminishing rain distorted her guess. The shore might be miles farther than she estimated. Still . . . what choice did she have?

Impatiently she tugged her shawl from her fiery curls and tossed it to the deck. "You can at least try," she admonished herself firmly. Her voice emerged low and breathless; a flutter of fear constricted her throat.

The women stared as Garnet tore open her bodice and ripped away her gown and heavy petticoats until she stood in the wind and warm rain wearing only her chemise and pantaloons. The eldest gasped. "What are you doing?"

Squinting, Garnet stared hard at the large island lying off the coast, fixing its position in her mind. The enormity of her plan squeezed clammy fingers around her heart, stopping her breath for a long moment.

The woman dashed rain and tears from her eyes and flung out a hand. "Don't be foolish," she implored. "The captain will save us. Any moment now."

Garnet swallowed a surge of dark panic. It was an impossible distance; the woman's fear clanged in her ear.

She kicked off her slippers, watching them catch in the

wind before they spiraled down, down toward the tossing waves.

Good God. She didn't stand one chance in a hundred of reaching the distant shore. Even if she could cling to a length of planking, she lacked the strength to go the distance. This wasn't Boston's placid Mill Pond; this was the ocean, disturbed and angered by the storm.

Ignoring the shrieks of the women, Garnet climbed over the railing and balanced perilously on a narrow lip of wood jutting high above the water. Behind her she heard the screams of the women and the shouts and curses of the men. Below . . . Eyes wide, she braced against the breeze and stared downward, far downward, where high waves flung bits of debris against the ship's side.

"My God," she breathed. Rain pattered her cheeks and pebbled the surface of the water. A dark fear trembled along her fingers. "I can't do this." It was sheer insanity to contemplate such a suicidal act.

The scrape and whine of machinery squealed above the noise and the first longboat put to sea. The bucket brigade faltered, then broke, the men rushing to the rail with screams of fury. Knives flashed and swords rang across the tilting deck.

Squeezing her eyes tightly shut, Garnet listened to the wild pounding against her rib cage, felt the ship shift and rise beneath her bare feet. Her shaking fingers tightened on the railing before she forcibly relaxed them. Her options diminished with each flying second; once the bow touched the water, the ship would pull everyone down with her.

"Please, God, let me live to see my land, my slice of forever."

Gulping, Garnet filled her lungs with the hot, humid air, pinched her nose, and, her free arm wheeling wildly, she jumped away from the railing, a scream trailing behind her as she dropped into the darkness.

A rush of waves closed over her head.

*   *   *

She was tired. Not the satisfying tired of a long day well spent, but tired as after a long illness. Her arms felt weak and rubbery against the plank she clung to; her legs trailed in the water, limp and drifting in the tug of the tide. A milky mist floating above the quiet waters blotted out the sky and all perception of time. Hours ago she had decided she was the only person alive in the world.

A vast loneliness assaulted her senses as Garnet roused herself from a peculiar state midway between waking and unconsciousness. With effort, she raised her cheek from the plank and peered into the damp swirls of mist, speculating detachedly whether she was dead or trapped within a damp white dream. Wearily she took stock by pinching the aching muscles in her upper arm. She winced but found assurance in the pain.

She wasn't dead; therefore she must be dreaming. An endless dream. A strange, disturbed slumber sunk in whispering waves and pale, choking mist. Her head ached with an attempt to remember, to sort out this eerie dream.

Frowning, she licked her lips and shoved at the tendrils of red hair sticking to her cheek. If this disorientation was but a product of her sleeping mind, if she had invented the sensual caress of water and mist against her skin, then where was the tall, intense man who electrified her dreams? Where was her dark companion of the fiery lips and strong arms?

Drowsily she returned her cheek to the wet plank and tried to remember when she had first dreamed of the man. Had she been sixteen? Seventeen? It must have been sometime after she had decided never to marry, after she had determined that if she was to have a lover, she must invent him. A manufactured lover wouldn't betray her, as her mother had betrayed her father during the war. And a dream lover wouldn't go away, as her father had, and never return. No, the man in her dreams understood "forever" as mortals did not. The man in her dreams would never betray her or mistreat her or die—he would be hers forever.

She shut her eyes, blanking out the sight of the splintered board, and she summoned the dream, conjuring her dark man in place of the water lapping against her waist. He would come to her soon now. And when he kissed her, she would forget her weariness and her loneliness and the fear climbing behind her eyes. In her dream his kisses swept all thoughts from her mind. His soft, intimate caresses aroused and soothed, and for a while she could believe in the existence of forever. For a while she could forget the mortal men who had made vows they couldn't keep, the men who had entered her life, then departed when her independent spirit had asserted itself.

Based on her stormy relationships with men, Garnet suspected she simply wasn't wifely material. Either that, or 1791 had proved a poor year for men. She concluded the former was more likely. Garnet stubbornly resisted becoming any man's echo. She refused to curb her tongue and nod pleasantly when a man voiced a stupidity. And she would not apologize for her intelligence or fade gracefully into feminine invisibility. All of which had far outweighed her beauty in the eyes of Boston's male population.

Therefore, as no man seemed capable of accepting her as she was, Garnet had planned her life around her inheritance. She had happily cast her lot with spinsterhood. She didn't need a man to provide for her future; she would do so herself. But now, right now, she urgently needed the comfort of her dream lover, the only man she could conceive of as a life's companion.

Squeezing shut her eyes, she wrapped her arms lovingly about the plank and willed his appearance, surrendering to her dreams, clinging to her fantasy as desperately as she clung to the shaft of wood. If she squinted just so, she could almost see his dark curls. Sighing, she drifted in time and misty space.

When her lashes again fluttered, a hard sand pack lay beneath her outstretched body; hot tropical sun beat against her face. She could almost believe the sand and the sun were genuine, so real did they feel. But part of her mind continued to register the treacherous hiss of waves, and distantly she felt the scrape of the plank stinging her cheek. Basking in imagined warmth, Garnet marveled at this new variation of the dream, astonished that her slumbering mind could create what she had only read about. And it was exotic and wonderful.

Lazily she opened her eyes and smiled invitingly at the tall, dark man kneeling above her, his strong, tanned hands pressing her breasts through the flimsy lace of her chemise. She had been waiting for him. A halo of sunlight shimmered around his dark curls, casting his face in shadow, but Garnet recognized him immediately by his touch, an intimacy as dreamily familiar as her own accelerating heart.

"I thought you would never come," she murmured, wetting her lips with the tip of her tongue. The sand heated her back and the soft tropical air caressed her skin with a touch as gentle as a lover's kiss. Her lashes closed, a sooty fringe against pale cheeks, and she arched sensuously, feeling her nipples rise up hard against the friction of the man's warm palms.

All movement ceased abruptly, and he murmured something Garnet didn't hear. Smiling a gentle protest, she reached to place a finger across his lips, tracing the firm, generous line of his mouth and halting further speech. He was not to speak until the moment he whispered "forever" against her kisses. She could accept this new location, but the remainder of her dream must proceed as always.

Lifting herself on her elbows, Garnet let her head fall backward, and her lips parted seductively. And she examined her creation shyly from beneath her lashes, slightly embarrassed to discover she couldn't remember his face. His features had altered through the years, taking on first one man's appearance and then another's. She didn't recall ever before observing him this distinctly.

She was thankful that he looked exactly as she wanted him to look, more rugged than classically handsome, a pirate instead of a poet. A feathery spray of laugh lines crinkled his eyes and rescued a sun-darkened face from hard, chiseled harshness. She peeked at black curls tied at the neck, dark sideburns hinting silver threads, a strong, stubborn jaw, a wide mouth, and thick-lashed eyes so warm and dark they reminded her of black velvet. Staring up at him, Garnet caught her quickening breath, and a rush of weakness swept the strength from her limbs. How could she have forgotten, from one dream to the next, a man this arresting, this compelling?

His curious expression, however, one that bordered on amusement, was a variation of the dream that surprised Garnet. And she didn't understand his hesitation. It was almost as if he didn't recognize her. But of course that was impossible; they had laughed and loved together through a thousand dreams.

"It's me," she assured him anxiously, feeling foolish. "Garnet." Now he would understand. Confident, she stretched back against the sand until the thrust of her breasts strained the stitching in her chemise. Overhead, puffs of cottony clouds dotted a hot blue sky. Gulls wheeled in wide, scenic arcs. Never before had she been blessed with so vivid a dream.

Slowly, seductively, she let her hands explore her breasts, then drop lightly across her stomach and to her thighs, reassured by his sharp intake of breath. Moistening her lips, she lifted her fingers to his shoulders, pleased by the consistency of her dreaming mind. His white linen shirt was as damp as her chemise and pantaloons. Which it would be, as they were actually drifting in the ocean, not lying on a beach.

"Come to me," she whispered, no trace of shame in her throaty voice as she opened her arms to him. Inhibitions

melted in her dreams; here she was accepted and cherished
no matter what she did or said. Her fingers tightened against
the sudden swell of muscle tensing along his broad shoulders,
and she slid her palms along a sinewy strength until she
found the opening to his collar and could touch the dark wiry
curls springing from his chest. She drew him nearer, smiling.
"Come to me . . ."

He reached to cup her face, slowly, as if awaiting a protest,
and his dark eyes posed a dozen questions. Feeling as if she
were drowning in the velvet intensity of his gaze, Garnet
smiled and again halted his murmur with her fingertip. Speech
would spoil the intimacy of the moment; they knew each
other too well to require endearments—and yet they were
strangers. The combination excited her, knowing but not
knowing.

Feeling her excitement build, as it had in countless yearning dreams, she offered herself in surrender, and it was like
the first dream. She felt his thumb caress her cheek as if he
had never done so before, breathed the warmth of his breath
on her lips as if the wine-scented sweetness were new and
unexpected. Her fingers slipped easily inside his shirt, and
she thrilled to the touch of his muscled chest as if she had
never known the firm texture of his skin.

And when his lips brushed a gentle leap of fire across her
mouth, she prayed she would not soon awaken to the water
and the fear.

"No, don't pull away . . . no." A tiny frown marred the
smoothness of her brow. She rejected his hesitation without
understanding it. She wanted her dream to unfold without
further alteration. The hot, shifting sand and the glorious
daylight were innovations enough. And the shamelessness of
making love on a noonday beach intruded a tension with
which she was not entirely comfortable. She wanted no more
surprises.

She caught his face between her palms, dismayed by the
questions in his eyes. Had she lost control of her dream's

direction? Must she seduce him for the dream to proceed? This new idea shot a quiver of excitement through her small frame. And a sense of urgency. Even as she experienced the lazy timelessness of dreaming, she felt the heaviness in her limbs, a deep weariness threatening just below the surface. At any minute she might open her lashes to the frightening solitude of mist and water.

Her lips parted and her eyes deepened to a smoky green, dropping to travel the firm curve of his mouth. Inviting, welcoming, beckoning. She stretched sensuously, arching her spine upward until her breasts swelled above her thin chemise, crying out for a man's caress. And a tiny moan issued from her throat as he slowly, ever so slowly, slid the strap from her shoulder, pausing to look into her eyes before he bent to brush a kiss where the strap had lain. And another kiss to mark the second strap. Slowly, skillfully, his palm caressed her bared skin, as moist and warm as the sun against her eyelids, as tantalizing as a whisper.

Trembling slightly, Garnet shyly slipped the chemise over her tangled mass of red hair, catching her breath against the sun's sudden heated embrace. And a breathless rush of weakness followed his hoarse groan. His voice was as deep and strong as she had known it would be. Closing her lashes, she twisted against the white sand and cupped her breasts, offering them to him, shyly proud of their youthful firmness and creamy beauty. The tips swelled like tiny rosebuds seeking the sun, rising in challenge and expectation.

His stare hardened from curiosity to desire. One hand pressed lightly against the hollow throbbing at the base of her throat, then he traced a burning pathway down, down through the tender cleft between her breasts, then around and around in ever-tightening circles until she wanted to cry out for him to touch her, to really touch her, to cover her breasts with his palms and love her.

When she could endure his hesitation no longer, Garnet reached up and drew his lips to hers in a fiery kiss of increasing passion. His mouth bruised against her own, now as eager as she remembered, as breath-snatchingly demanding. A wave of dizzying darkness clouded her vision as his ardent kisses swept her throat, descended to the swelling mounds she offered him. She gasped and caught her lip between her teeth as his mouth closed over a quivering pink tip, his tongue teasing, stroking, his hands warm and hard against her skin.

Her fingers wound through the black curls feathering against her throat, and she moaned in soft rapture and wondered at the smoldering realism of her dream. How could she possibly forget this ecstasy when she awoke? Or was each awakening a small death of memory? She writhed beneath his burning kisses and prayed to sleep forever.

"Please," she whispered hoarsely, "please . . ."

With one quick movement he removed his shirt and flung it aside, then dropped to the sand beside her, gathering her into his arms. The shock of skin against heated skin strangled her and Garnet gasped, fighting for each breath when his lips momentarily released hers. His kisses flamed against her shivering body, ignited liquid fire from forehead to toes, leaving her shaking helplessly in his arms. It was all so real, so rapturously *real*.

But in a corner of her mind she heard the whispering rush of waves and experienced the strange dislocation of mind and body. And suddenly an urgency tingled through her trembling flesh. Time was running out—hurry, hurry. Quickly, before she woke, he must deliver the last, frenzied kisses now.

Their bodies strained together. Dimly Garnet sensed his hard readiness, felt her own moist need; she heard the low murmur of endearments against her hair, whispering against her lips. And a cry of yearning scraped her throat. Her fingers curled into fists and pounded his shoulders until he released her, and suddenly they were shedding their remaining clothing, then reaching hungrily for each other when at last they lay naked and glistening upon the sand.

Passionately she surrendered to his mouth, her lips parting

willingly to the thrust of his tongue. And she stared at his closed eyes as his knee gently guided her legs apart and she felt the leap of his manhood hard and demanding against her inner thigh. Yes . . . oh, yes. A pang of regret, deep and biting, stung her eyes as she realized the dream would end now; it always did at this point.

She gazed at his lashes lying dark against his cheeks, seeing each lash in incredible detail.

And his hands continued to tease along her damp body, trailing a burning tremble of raw nerves in their path. He raised her knees.

A small stone pressed painfully into her tender nakedness. Unlike any dream she had previously experienced, in this one she could isolate pain. She stared up at him, not knowing what to expect, as the dream had never gone this far before.

His sure fingers slid upward along the insides of her thighs toward the crisp triangle of red curls, testing her readiness to receive him, and Garnet's breath burned. She felt dizzy and faint.

But she could feel the scratch of his ring along her trembling flesh—and it stung. Her green eyes flared in sudden panic. She could recall a dozen dreams in which pain had threatened, but this was the first time she remembered pain actually occurring.

"You are so beautiful," he whispered hoarsely. The words were French.

French. This, too, had never happened before.

Garnet's body went rigid with realization. Her pounding heart froze in shock. She stared at him from wide, flaring eyes. Oh, dear God! "Wait." A hand flew to her lips, and she bit down hard to stifle the scream clawing at her throat.

He thrust forward and a blinding heat of razor sharpness invaded her flesh, then the flash of white-hot pain was gone, only to return in waves of diminishing intensity as he pushed into her once, twice . . . then he halted abruptly and stared down into her ashen face, incredulous.

"You're a virgin." His tone registered disbelief and astonishment.

It was not a dream. Oh, God, it had never been a dream.

Garnet stared up at him, her eyes glazing with helpless shame. Horrified, she watched her pale fingers slide up his arms and twist into his dark hair. She wanted it to end; as God was her witness, she wanted it to end. But her shaking body arched into his hardness, lifting to meet him, sweeping her thoughts away in a blaze of fiery need. She could no more have wrenched away than she could have halted the rush of raw fire surging through her veins.

The man swore softly against her hair, hesitating as Garnet's traitorous body acted with a terrifying will of its own, beseeching him to continue. Only her wild, frightened eyes spoke of the shock numbing her mind.

"Shh," he murmured against her lips. "The worst is over."

As inexperienced as she was, Garnet sensed the alteration in his rhythms. Whereas before his passion had been a wild desire of sweeping urgency, now he kissed and stroked her with a gentleness that spoke more of responsibility than true passion. Theirs was no longer a duet, but a master coaxing a wild, crashing harmony from one quivering instrument.

"No!" She choked, her voice catching on a sob. Her fists rose to his naked chest, where he captured them easily, mistaking her protest.

"Relax," he commanded softly against her ear. "It's important that the first time be . . ." Whatever he had meant to say vanished in a kiss that snatched Garnet's breath away.

His mouth covered hers expertly, teasing, plundering, his tongue pushing into the sweetness within. Strong hands glided over her back, trailing shudders of delight in their path. Swiftly he returned her to a mindless state of trembling passion, to that soaring point where thought dissolves and flesh alone exists. His tongue drew circles of warmth and flame across her satiny breasts as his gentle fingers explored the moistness of her inner thighs. And she could no more resist him than she could resist the wild, urgent hammering of her heart. Her mind reeled and spun, and sensation washed across her damp skin in wave after rapturous wave until her body quivered like a drawn bow, until the pleasure was so intense it approached pain.

Only now did he increase the pace of his slow thrusts, watching her wild, pleading expression all the while, pacing himself to her pleasure. And his kisses no longer teased; he crushed her eager lips roughly beneath his own, catching her tossing head between his palms.

Carefully, skillfully, he guided her to the edge of a new and wondrous ecstasy, and when she thought she could not bear another searing breath against her raw throat, could not endure another caress along screaming nerves, when she thought her mind and body would surely explode . . . then and only then did he release her into a shattering eruption of unimagined rapture. The universe contracted sharply into fainting darkness, then exploded outward in a shower of color and sensation and melting heat.

She lay beneath him, gasping, her body limp and sated. And as the miracle faded, her shock returned. Her green eyes flared open and she stared up at him, at this stranger on the beach, this man who had plundered her body.

And she realized in horror that he hadn't finished with her. Once again his rhythm had altered, subtly increasing to keep pace with his own needs.

Revulsion and shame, shock and humiliation, crashed together in Garnet's head, the mix exploding outward.

Drawing back her hand, she slapped him with all her strength. And then again.

—2—

GARNET SLAPPED HIM HARD ENOUGH that her palm stung for
minutes afterward. His jaw dropped in amazement and he
lifted a hand to the fiery imprint flaming on his cheek.

"Get off me!" She thrashed beneath his weight like a
trapped cat, clawing and hissing. Hysteria shrilled her voice,
stifled her ragged breath. "Get away from me!" A spray of
sand shot from her kicking feet as she wrenched herself out
from under him, springing up to snatch her clothing from the
sand, clutching the pantaloons against her nakedness with
shaking fingers.

How could she have let this happen? Sunstroke? Fatigue?
A bump on the head? A sudden onset of insanity? She
blinked, hoping desperately that when she opened her eyes he
would be gone, the figment of her imagination she had
originally believed him to be. Please God, let it be so.

He hadn't vanished. He sat in the sand beside his sword
and leather breeches, his manhood swollen between his thighs.
Hastily Garnet averted her eyes, but she felt his hard stare,
sensed his astonishment becoming anger.

Face flaming, she turned her back to him and jerked on
her pantaloons and chemise as quickly as her trembling
hands allowed. She felt sick to her stomach. She'd seen the
rusty stains on her thighs, knew the damage was irreparable.
"How could you . . . Oh, God, how could you?" Furious

22

tears strangled her voice, blurred her vision. "What sort of brutish pervert are you?" Silently she prayed the earth would open and swallow him. She wished a bolt of lightning would strike him dead where he sat. With all her aching heart, she wished to open her eyes and discover herself in the sea clinging to the plank. Intact. Please God, grant me this one favor and I'll never ask for anything again, I swear it.

The request was futile and childish—Garnet's shoulders slumped. She waited until she heard him rise and dress before she spun to face him. The situation was ghastly; she had shamelessly surrendered her virginity to a stranger. Nausea boiled in her stomach. She didn't even know his name. Good Lord, not even his name.

Garnet's nails dug into her palms and she blinked rapidly at the sky, willing the hysteria to subside. Hysteria was the weapon of weak women; Garnet Marie Winters scorned hysteria. For one small moment, however, she envied those women able to faint at will. Gathering herself together with a forcible effort, she raised her long lashes.

"That was unforgivable, mademoiselle," he snapped coldly. He buckled on his sword.

Garnet's mouth dropped. "You attacked me." A wild, slashing fury cut through the numbness dulling her senses. If she could have snatched his sword from the scabbard, she would have run him through without hesitation. Her fists opened and closed at her sides.

Hard black eyes totally devoid of warmth raked across her body, his scrutiny a mocking insult. "I care too much for my comfort to attack women on gritty beaches, no matter how beautiful they may be. But neither am I immune to the temptations of the flesh. Particularly when a woman strips off her clothes and begs me to take her."

Crimson flooded Garnet's breast, shot to the roots of her hair. She wanted to die. "Surely you could see that I was confused, that I wasn't myself?"

"I have no way of knowing how your 'self' usually responds,

now do I? For all I know, you make a habit of seducing men on secluded beaches."

Garnet choked. Her father's New England ancestors were surely spinning in their graves. Shaking, she attacked from another angle. "Did you think I appeared by magic?" She waved a furious hand toward the bay waters sparkling in the sun. "I was drowning. My mind was affected."

"I'm well aware of that. Who do you think pulled you out of the water?"

"And I wake up with you mauling me like an animal." That much, at least, was true. Her lip curled in disgust. "Only a degenerate takes advantage of an unconscious woman." Accusation poured from her lips, fury diminishing her shock. Fury was easier to tolerate than truth and guilt. No matter the provocation, his actions were unconscionable, a violation of everything decent. "In Boston you would be strung up from the tallest tree."

"How else was I to pump the water out of you?"

"I thought I was dreaming—wasn't that obvious? I thought I was still in the water, more dead than alive . . ."

"Dreaming?" A slow, mocking grin spread a flash of white across his tanned skin. He faced her across a hillock of sand, amused by her angry gestures. "God help the man who encounters you when you're awake."

She stamped her foot in the hot sand. "Damn it. I *was* dreaming." He didn't believe her. Tears of anger and helplessness brimmed in her eyes, furthering her shame. What worsened the situation a thousandfold was knowing in her heart that she had accepted the experience as reality long before she had admitted she wasn't dreaming. She had wanted him. Savagely she chewed her lips and clenched her fists. She couldn't bear it. Lifting her head, she stubbornly clung to illusion. "You took advantage of me," she insisted fiercely.

His struggle to contain his anger was as obvious as the white shore and the blazing sun. "I think it remains a question, love, as to who took advantage of whom." His hand opened and clamped tightly about the sword hilt. "There are ugly words for a woman who takes her own pleasure but leaves a man painfully unsatisfied."

A small, bitter smile curled across Garnet's lips and she taunted him with it. She'd heard whispers that a man's unrequited arousal caused pain. Good. She hoped he suffered. She hoped he ached between the legs exactly as she did, only worse—much worse. His brief discomfort was hardly a fair exchange for her virginity, but it was something, at least. Not nearly enough, but something.

His admission of frustration wasn't as satisfying as having him beg her forgiveness, but she saw clearly that no apologies would be forthcoming. As incredible as it was, he had ravished her and now blamed her for the incident. With her defenses in position, her thoughts hastened swiftly past her own culpability. Instead she surrendered to the mantle of exhaustion bowing her shoulders and intensifying the tremble shivering through her body.

"Just go away and leave me alone." Resignation wove through her harsh whisper. "Just . . . go away."

"Nothing would please me more, love, but I'm afraid that wouldn't be wise." He shaded his eyes and gazed up the expanse of open beach.

Garnet looked up the shoreline, following his glance. A group of men approached at a rapid pace. Two were blacks dressed in ragged trousers and tattered shirts. The others wore the orange-and-white uniform of French soldiers. Garnet swallowed. Had they appeared five minutes earlier . . . Biting her lips, she slapped the sand from her chemise and pantaloons, deciding she might well have been naked for all the protection her undergarments afforded. Her eyes flicked along the beach searching out a clump of shrubbery, a large boulder, anything at all to use as concealment. There was nothing. The luxuriant growth fringing the upper edge of the sand was far too distant.

Uneasy now, she edged nearer the man who had ruined her, stiffly ignoring his infuriating grin.

The men halted before them, their eyes traveling slowly over Garnet's woefully inadequate chemise and pantaloons. Blinking, she focused on a distant yellow sail drifting in the bay, and her chin rose defiantly. She wouldn't show them her fear.

"We saw you pull her in," one of the soldiers said.

What else had they seen? Garnet's jaw tightened as scarlet flamed into her cheeks and her hands balled into fists. By sheer effort of will she resisted the urge to cover herself. The damp chemise molded her breasts; her pantaloons defined her hips and thighs, leaving little to the imagination. It was her worst nightmare come true.

"We were in the process of becoming acquainted." The man beside her hid a smile by bowing from the waist as elegantly as if they stood beneath a ballroom chandelier instead of on the scorching sands of a nearly deserted beach. "Colonel Jean Baptiste Belaine at your service." His eyes twinkled over her chemise as he straightened. Clearly he was enjoying her discomfort. "And who might you be, love?"

"I am not your 'love,' " Garnet spat through grinding teeth. Apparently he had decided this was a charade to be played for his soldiers' amusement. She slapped furiously at the sand and weed clinging to her hair. She would far rather have clawed the maddening smile from his arrogant face. Meeting his gaze coldly, she firmed her chin. "I am Garnet Winters, from the American brig *Commerce* bound for Port-au-Prince."

A glance at the knot of silent men abruptly informed her that her efforts to dislodge the sand attracted a dangerous attention to her breasts and hips. Scowling nervously, she folded her arms tightly over her chest, knowing it didn't help at all.

Every eye minutely observed her actions. The soldiers' stares narrowed in speculation. Only the two blacks regarded her with empty expressions. Their eyes focused on her flam-

ing hair and their bodies tensed. The stance of both men
indicated a preparation to flee, although their faces remained
deliberately blank.

If anyone had cause to fear, Garnet concluded unsteadily,
it was herself. She was half naked, surrounded by armed
men, and she didn't know where she was. Hating herself for
seeking his protection, she edged nearer Jean Belaine as her
eyes swept the men.

Belaine's hand curled pointedly around his sword hilt and
his voice roughened. "Need I remind you, gentlemen, that
French soldiers do not molest a lady seeking our protection?"

Garnet's lips twitched and her gaze flashed up at him.
Such noble sentiments had not concerned him earlier. She
swallowed a dark taste with difficulty.

"Should any of you gentlemen choose to forget your
manners, step forward and we'll settle the matter now." Belaine
unsheathed his sword and dug the point into the sand, leaning casually on the hilt, his cool gaze challenging. When no
man responded, he nodded curtly. "Then I suggest you return to quarters and make it known that any man occasioning
Mademoiselle Winters any discomfort during her stay in
Port-au-Prince shall answer personally to me."

Port-au-Prince. Relief loosened one of the knots in Garnet's
stomach. At least she had washed up in the right spot. Her
shoulders straightened, and she faced the men with returning
confidence, waiting for them to obey Colonel Belaine's
command.

They shuffled their feet, expressions sullen, looking from
Garnet to Belaine, then back again. Only the two blacks
appeared oblivious of her state of undress. They remained
transfixed by the sight of the wild red curls drying against her
back.

Neither reacted when Belaine addressed them in pidgin
Creole. "Hear me well. This be-me no sea woman, comprehend *oui*? This be-me no *loa*, say-me *oui*." The black men
stared impassively at Belaine's stern face. "Say-me *oui*?"

Garnet followed the bastardized language with difficulty, sorting the rhythms in her mind.

"Say-me *oui*," the black men muttered reluctantly. Eyes fixed on Garnet's hair, they slowly backed away from her, their bare feet dragging in the hot sand.

"She be-me no *loa*," Jean Belaine repeated emphatically. His voice had deepened into a growl of irritation.

The black men turned as one and sprinted toward the heavy stand of tall grass waving around the mango grove overhanging the beach.

Belaine cursed beneath his breath, contemplating the thick underbrush into which the Africans had disappeared. He jerked the sword from the sand with a short, angry movement as his gaze steadied on the soldiers. "Do what you can to stop the rumors," he commanded. "Now, move." A dark scowl dropped to Garnet. "I suspect you are going to be a great deal of trouble, Mademoiselle Winters."

Garnet's mouth opened and closed incredulously, and her eyes blazed as fiercely as the sun. He was despicable. Loathsome. He had performed the most shamelessly offensive act imaginable; he had not bothered to inquire if she was injured; he hadn't asked how it happened that she was in the bay and the *Commerce* was not; he had not offered her his shirt to conceal her near nakedness, as a man of honor would have done. And now he had the effrontery to suggest that *she* was a "a great deal of trouble." Green fire flashed from between her lashes and her weariness vanished in a stroke. "Perhaps you should have let me drown and spared yourself an inconvenience," she snapped.

Cool, dark eyes locked on hers. "The thought has occurred to me, Mademoiselle Winters." An appraising gaze swept the swell of anger quickening her breast, and his insolence returned with a grin. "Perhaps I'll feel differently if you ever wake up—or have you? It's difficult to judge. Tell me, love, do you remember your dreams?" He laughed at the furious color staining her throat, then turned to watch the soldiers until they dropped below the curve in the shoreline.

Garnet observed the soldiers' departure with a sinking heart, then gazed at the bay waters. There was no sign of the *Commerce*; not that she had truly expected there would be. Hastily she tightened her arms over her breasts, shivering despite the heat. How in God's name had she deluded herself into thinking this was a dream? When had she ever dreamed a heat this intense or a situation so ruinous? She suspected the questions would devil her for the rest of her days.

"What now?" she asked without looking at him.

"We leave, of course. Unless you prefer to remain here and fry in the sun."

His sarcasm made her feel foolish. Her chin rose as her eyes narrowed. "I'm not going anywhere with you."

Jean Belaine stared at her for a long moment, then he shrugged. "Very well, suit yourself." Spinning on his boot heel, he climbed a sandy incline leading upward to the lush growth edging the sand.

"Good riddance," Garnet muttered. First she would wash herself in the bay waters, scrub the sand and the ache from her body, then she would have a good cry, the first in years, and then . . . and then what? Slowly she scanned the area to her right and then to her left, seeing only sand and sea and sky. Emptiness. An alarming sense of disorientation distorted her sense of direction. What was she thinking of? She couldn't stay here—she needed clothes and food and shelter and . . .

Springing to her feet, she spun and shaded her eyes, watching Belaine mount the incline. A rush of panic exploded against her ribs. "Wait!" She threw out her hands, noticing the pink glow on her arms. In another hour she'd be crisped to a raw and painful red. "Belaine . . . Colonel . . ." Grinding her teeth, she struggled through the scorching sand, puffing hard. There was no choice, she would have to rely on him. Damn!

Jean Belaine waited, one hand on his sword, the other at his chin. He watched her as she stumbled, his eyes cool.

When she was nearly upon him, panting for breath, he pushed aside the grass and vanished. Immediately the tall stalks closed behind him, leaving no trace of an opening.

Garnet placed a hand on her heaving breast and blinked at the swaying green wall. A sob of fury lodged in her throat and hatred sapped her energy. Drawing a shuddering breath, she ducked her head and plunged forward, thrashing through the tall, spiny stalks with no notion which direction to choose. Broken stalks scraped her shoulders; nettles scratched her bare ankles. She heard nothing but the buzzing of insects, her own labored breathing, and the crash of falling stalks as she flailed forward. Panic returned, hot and choking, and she felt the threat of hysteria growing in murderous waves behind her eyes.

When he pulled her out of the green thickness and onto the road, she sagged with relief. The shore road was little more than twin ruts overlaid with a coating of drying mud, but she hardly noticed.

Belaine's hands covered her shoulders as he forced her to look up at him. "Are you ready to call a truce? I don't fully understand what happened back there," he said, his black eyes flickering. "But I'm willing to pretend it never occurred, as that seems to be what you want."

Garnet didn't answer. It galled her that he continued to treat the matter on the beach as if she owed him further explanation. Most appalling was the fact that she didn't understand her response herself. Nor did she wish to. If only he hadn't so closely resembled the man in her dreams.

"Like it or not, love, we're going to be together awhile." He waved toward a carriage waiting beside the road. "The journey will pass more comfortably if we declare a truce. Agreed?"

From the corner of her lashes Garnet examined the polished brass on the black carriage. If she was to find her cousin and her inheritance, she had no alternative but to agree. Unless she wished to walk. "Truce," she muttered sourly. An hour, two at the most, then she would never have to face him again. Please, God.

"Done." Strong, tanned fingers circled her waist before she could protest, and he swung her into the carriage.

She bit her tongue, determined not to thank the man who had ruined her. Instead she tested the thick upholstery of the seats. He had not exaggerated his enjoyment of comfort; the upholstery was as plump and comfortable as a pillow.

Belaine made a display of seating himself on the facing cushions without brushing the hem of her pantaloons, ignoring her equally exaggerated show of relief. Then he placed two fingers between his teeth and emitted a sharp whistle.

The grasses parted and a young black jumped onto the driver's seat and flicked the reins over the horse's back, guiding the carriage into the ruts. After one flaring glance at Garnet's red hair, he carefully paid his passengers no further attention.

"Put this on," Belaine said. "There's a hat in the carryall near your feet." He lifted his jacket and tossed it into her lap.

"I wouldn't wish to further inconvenience you, Colonel." Despite the promised truce, heavy sarcasm iced her tone. She didn't touch his jacket.

Belaine smiled. "You may stand on pride, love, and burn yourself to a cinder, or you can be sensible and protect yourself. I assure you it makes no difference to me." He spread his arms along the back of the carriage seat and gazed toward a sweep of coffee plantations climbing the mountainsides. "If you choose to ride through the streets of Port-au-Prince wearing your lace and ribbons, that is also your affair. Being seen on the Grande Rue with a half-naked woman will certainly do my reputation no harm." He grinned at the sky, his teeth white against his darkly tanned skin.

"You, sir, are despicable." Furious, Garnet shrugged into his jacket, rolling up the cuffs, which fell below her fingertips.

His jacket smelled of leather and sweat and spiced cologne, a
sensuous combination that made her feel sick inside. Being
surrounded by his smell was somehow worse than being
forced to look at him.

He waggled a finger at her and clicked his tongue. "You're
forgetting our truce."

The satisfied smugness of his superior smile set her teeth
on edge. Anger blinded her momentarily and she turned her
face aside so he wouldn't see her annoyance, pointedly directing her attention to new surroundings. At least she had
arrived in St. Domingue, not far from Port-au-Prince. It was
the single positive event in the last two days, and she clung to
it.

Beyond the cane fields covering the low hills to her right
rose an abrupt chain of blue-and-green mountains, their
craggy tops just visible behind a curtain of purplish haze.
Every shade of green carpeted the hills and mountains, splashed
by occasional streaks of riotous color where exotic flowers and
shrubs encroached upon the fields. Fragrant orange trees
shaded the roadside along with thick stands of mango, the
ripe fruit dangling from slender green cords. Tiny orchids
bloomed from the vines twisting about the tree trunks, and a
profusion of wild strawberries choked the road. With each
breath Garnet inhaled the heady sweetness of jasmine and
roses and wild honeysuckle. None of the books she'd read had
prepared her for the overwhelming beauty of St. Domingue.

Breathing deeply of the mingled scents, Garnet twisted her
hair into a tangled rope and coiled it atop her head, pulling
a thatched straw hat down to her ears. She passed a thought
of regret for the lovely new bonnets in her trunk aboard
the *Commerce*, and her shoulders dropped. "I must look
ridiculous."

She didn't realize she'd spoken aloud until Belaine nodded
agreement. "That you do," he commented pleasantly.

Garnet stared. Even if she had lacked previous reason to
dislike him, she would have done so now. He was arrogant,

selfish, and rude. His indifferent comment was an affront; she was not accustomed to men dismissing her so easily. At least not after so brief an acquaintance. Her cheeks colored, and her green eyes narrowed in stony judgment.

She knew this man, had deliberately avoided his type all her life. Jean Baptiste Belaine had nothing to offer but surface charm. Some women might have been taken in, but not Garnet Winters. Unbidden, her eyes swept the well-defined muscles hinted beneath his shirt, and she blushed at sudden, unwanted memories. Handsome? Yes, he was handsome. And he obviously knew it. Garnet would have wagered her inherited plantation that he collected women like beads on a string—and disposed of them as callously.

"I was making a statement," she snapped. "I was not soliciting your opinion."

He smiled. "Are you always this sweet-tempered, love, or do you tax yourself on my account because of some small sense of gratitude?" Reading her deadly stare, he hastily amended, "For saving your life, of course." Amused eyes swept her muddy feet, lingered at the thrust of breast against his jacket front. He relaxed against the seat, his voice teasing. One boot appeared at Garnet's side and he rested his forearm against an upraised knee. A light breeze feathered his black curls.

"I have no intention of explaining myself to you," she said.

"Good, because nothing you've said so far makes any sense. Further explanations would only confuse matters more."

She ground her teeth and felt like screaming. Leaning to one side, she held down her hat and peered up the stretch of empty road. "How far is it to Port-au-Prince?"

His grin widened. "About an hour's drive."

An hour. Garnet stared at the driver's back and wondered what she had done to deserve this. In the silence that followed, she seized hold of her mind and grimly adjusted her thoughts. What had happened, had happened. No amount of wishing or gnashing of teeth could change those awful moments on the beach. To state it delicately, Garnet Winters was now a spinster with experience. Her stomach lurched and her resolve weakened. She longed to leap on him and claw his eyes out. Instead she inhaled deeply and vowed to accept and forget what could not be altered. The circumstances of her arrival would become a blank space in her mind.

Feeling better, she nodded in her best Sunday-parlor manner and cleared her throat, determined to test her strength of mind. "I, ah, noticed you had a scar."

He laughed as if he understood perfectly what she was doing. Amused, he touched his side. "An old wound."

"Sword?" she asked with cool interest.

"Shot."

The scar had not been small, but an arc the size of a man's fist. She assumed the removal of the ball had required a serious operation, but as he didn't appear inclined to discuss the matter, she cleared her throat and gladly directed the conversation into more interesting channels, determined not to pass the journey in clumsy silence. "Would you know if the Habitation Philippe is near Port-au-Prince?"

"I believe you mean the Habitation du Casse, and it's perhaps an hour beyond the city."

Another hour. She studied the braid on his jacket cuff and concluded it would be prudent to observe the truce, no matter how galling. "I see." Two more hours, then she could dismiss him from her thoughts. In the meantime, perhaps she could put the time to good use. "Are you acquainted with Simone and Paul du Casse?" Garnet had met her French cousin years ago, when Garnet was five and Simone fourteen and both sets of parents were still alive. She remembered Simone's gentle smile and the scent of lemon, but little else.

"Of course." Withdrawing a silver case, Belaine extracted a thin brown cigar and lit it, expelling fragrant smoke toward the tree limbs passing over their heads. "I've known Paul and Simone for years. We met in Paris . . . in a different age . . .

when the world was young and innocent and so were we. A long time ago." He smiled. "The world is no longer young and innocent."

"And neither are you?" Garnet could have bitten her tongue for the acid remark.

He laughed. "And neither am I."

Lack of innocence was a topic Garnet definitely did not wish to pursue. She bit her lip and wondered what questions she could ask without revealing too much of her personal business yet at the same time learning more about Simone and Simone's husband, Paul. Paul du Casse had managed both his wife's inheritance and Garnet's for the past eight years. Curiously, he had turned a profit but twice, according to the annual report he rendered Uncle William on Garnet's behalf.

"I understand the plantation is doing very poorly—is that correct?" Garnet had agreed with Uncle William not to take possession of her half interest if, by doing so, she would deprive Simone and Paul of a living. If her presence strained the resources of the household, she would swallow her disappointment and return to Boston.

Belaine's amusement turned to surprise. "Whatever gave you that idea? The Habitation du Casse is the Cul-de-Sac's largest sugar exporter. In addition, Paul raises coffee and indigo and God knows what else—enough to feed one thousand slaves and still ship to market."

Garnet's eyebrows rose and she stared at him. One thousand slaves? The region's largest sugar exporter? This startling information required a moment to assimilate. "Ah, what exactly is the Cul-de-Sac?" she asked weakly, scarcely listening as he answered.

"It's the relatively flat area surrounding Port-au-Prince, an agricultural basin between the mountains."

Garnet wet her lips. "Are you certain the Habitation is as prosperous as you indicated?" she asked slowly. Belaine's description did not agree with Paul's annual reports. And the plantation was much, much larger than she or Uncle William had dreamed. Perhaps Uncle William had erred in agreeing with Paul that the plantation should be operated as a single unit, undivided until Garnet came of age.

"I haven't been invited to examine the books," Belaine answered dryly. He smiled and drew on the cigar. "I'm a friend of the family, love, not their financial adviser. It's hardly my place to question Paul about his plantation."

Pink flooded Garnet's cheeks. Each time he called her "love" she felt dizzy. "It isn't Paul du Casse's plantation. It belongs to Simone and myself, left to us by our grandfather." Belaine didn't seem as surprised as she would have expected.

"Which is to say that it belongs to you and Paul."

Not for the first time Garnet felt a grim stir of satisfaction in her decision to remain unwed. No man would lay claim to her property, by heaven. Thinking of property reminded her of her trunks, presumably lying at the bottom of the sea. Again shifting the conversation, she asked Belaine for any news of the ship.

"The *Commerce* sank. My men and I were searching for debris when I"—he examined the tip of his cigar—"found you."

"Are there any other survivors?"

Belaine appeared uncomfortable at the question. He glanced pointedly at his man, Jacmel, high on the driver's seat above them. "Not that we've found. The ship struck the reef—it's happened before. Many ships have cracked up in these waters." His voice struck her as too loud.

"It's a miracle I was saved. You see, I—"

He interrupted abruptly. "Are you comfortable, mademoiselle?"

His rudeness infuriated her. "I knew the ship was going down and I—"

"Is it too hot, or can you enjoy the breeze from your seat?"

His dark eyes were intense; he was trying to tell her something, but she had no idea what it might be. Exasperated, Garnet lifted her hands, stirring the scent of cologne in the folds of his jacket. "Colonel, if you don't wish to hear this tale, just say so."

"I don't wish to hear this tale."

She stared at him, deciding he was hopeless. "Very well," she snapped. "Then we have nothing further to discuss."

He leaned back, drawing easily on the cigar and smiling. "Suit yourself, love."

"I always do."

The smile broadened to a grin. "One couldn't possibly doubt it."

The temptation to insist on the last word was strong, but Garnet suppressed it. Golden flecks appeared in the depths of her green eyes, signaling anger to those who knew her well. She grasped the brim of the straw hat with both hands and jerked it low over her brow, directing her attention to the curve of the road as the carriage turned from the line of mountains, following the shore road.

Hillsides of cane and indigo opened beneath the distant coffee plantations, and more people appeared along the roadside now: tall, dark women balancing baskets of produce upon kerchiefed heads, barefoot men leading mules laden with wood and brush. Their quiet murmurs lapsed into silence as the carriage passed.

Garnet's natural curiosity suggested a dozen questions, but she refrained from voicing them. Each time she darted a glance toward Belaine and discovered him watching her, she was acutely conscious of being half naked, of her ears protruding beneath the straw hat. And of the scent of leather and sweat and spiced cologne.

She pressed her lips in a line of weary annoyance. Why must he bear such an uncanny resemblance to the man in her dreams? Why couldn't the dark hair tied at his neck have been light? If he had been short or fat or ugly, none of this

could have happened. But Jean Belaine was none of those
things; he was tall and lean and elegant in a controlled
manner. And when his velvety black eyes dropped to her lips,
her stomach wound into knots.

When the carriage topped a small rise and Port-au-Prince
at last popped into view, Garnet Winters released a breath of
relief and silently thanked God.

The city was considerably larger than she had expected.
Perhaps thirty ships jammed the piers jutting into the bay
waters. Church spires scratched the sky, and a multitude of
carriages and wagons spun along dusty broad streets, flashing
before rows of bustling shops and pubs and noisy street markets.
The young city was alive and thriving; its energetic din
reached the carriage well before they passed the outlying
markers.

Garnet chewed her lips and visualized her state of disarray,
and her heart plummeted. Fresh embarrassment scalded her
face. Stirring, she shoved ineffectively at the red wisps blowing about her cheeks, and she cast a miserable glance toward
her muddied bare toes. The ruffled hems about her ankles
were unmistakably pantaloons. She examined Belaine from
the corner of her eye, noting his shirt sleeves and open
collar. Anyone seeing them would immediately guess the
worst.

She swallowed, trying to control the crack in her voice as
she said, "Will we, ah, pass through the town?"

Jean Baptiste Belaine looked at her and grinned, his teeth a
flash of white. "Directly through the center." Amusement
twinkled in his dark eyes, and Garnet recalled her own
taunting smile when he'd mentioned his discomfort on the
beach.

Grudgingly she conceded that he had managed his disability
with discretion and, yes, a certain grace. She would do no
less. Her shoulders squared and her jaw set. She'd ride through
Port-au-Prince wearing nothing but a fan before she'd allow

Jean Belaine to witness Garnet Winters's mortification. Damn his smile, anyway.

She lifted her head high and stared straight ahead as the carriage bumped onto the dusty main thoroughfare of the city.

—3—

AS THE MINUTES STRETCHED INTO an hour Garnet's bravado sagged. A flush of sun and embarrassment painted her cheeks as fiery red as the limp strands dangling from the ridiculous straw hat. Silently Garnet cursed the day as a disaster from start to finish. She cursed the ship that had sunk with her clothing. And she thoroughly cursed Colonel Jean Baptiste Belaine, a cad and anything but a gentleman, for taking such obvious pleasure in her predicament.

Their carriage had stalled in a crush of horse-drawn traffic mired near the docks. Carriages, wagons, carts, and mounted riders were locked in a shouting, cursing melee. Despite Jacmel's vigorous efforts with whip and shouts, the gray mare could progress no more than a few feet at a time. Convinced that every eye censured her state of undress, Garnet fixed her eyes on her lap and listened to female voices calling to Belaine and to the angry frustration of passengers trapped in the jam. She did not raise her gaze until a rose plopped onto the carriage floor.

Stonily she watched Belaine place a smiling kiss on the rose, then toss it back across wagons laden with bananas and coconuts to the exquisite woman who had thrown it. The woman smiled provocatively and tucked the rose between ample breasts. She leaned to examine Garnet, then arched a brow and laughed before her carriage lurched forward and she was lost to view.

Garnet ground her teeth. "A friend of yours?" she inquired acidly. The suffocating jacket wrapped about her shoulders contrasted dismally with the elegant woman's light silk.

Belaine shrugged and smiled, stretching against the carriage upholstery. His gaze lingered where the woman had been. "Not as far as her husband knows . . . I hope." Tipping his hat over his eyes, he leaned back and lifted his face to the sun.

It was exactly as Garnet had predicted—beads on a string; that's all women were to Colonel Belaine, objects to be collected and used. A sound of disgust stuck in her throat. She had not been the first to fall prey to his seductive kisses and she doubted she would be the last.

Her hard stare examined the deep V of tanned skin showing beneath his opened collar, then dropped to the sweep of muscle flowing down to a lean, hard waist. And she swallowed furiously, angered by the slight tremble of her fingers. Forcefully she reminded herself, not of the incident on the beach, but that he was rude, insolent, uncaring, conceited, and probably had a dozen other unattractive qualities she hadn't yet discovered. And never would, thank God.

"Is the traffic always this deplorable?" She had no interest in Port-au-Prince's civic problems, but neither did she wish to continue staring at the sun-dappled shadows playing across his mouth and eyelids.

"Only when the slavers dock."

He pointed to the focus of the traffic congestion, a battered ship anchored close in. A line of blacks, some chained, some supporting each other, stumbled down a swaying gangplank, quivering in terror when they saw the crush below. Horses reared; people shouted and waved and jockeyed for closer inspection; half-naked children ran between the carriages selling oranges, limes, and sugar cakes.

Garnet's eyes widened as she stared at the ship. She had known to expect this, of course, but she hadn't anticipated how deeply upsetting the sight would be. Suddenly she placed the noxious stench pinching her nostrils; the odor emanated from the reeking ship.

"It isn't pleasant," Belaine commented, watching her reaction.

Indeed it was not. Many of the Africans emerging from the ship were seeing sunlight for the first time in more than a month; they staggered and rubbed watering eyes. Many appeared critically ill; all were malnourished. A large number bore scars and welts from recent whippings. They blinked at the blazing light and cringed from the sea of white faces and incomprehensible shouting. Many stared at the unfamiliar mountains rising behind the terraced buildings of Port-au-Prince, and tears streamed down their cheeks.

Nausea constricted Garnet's breast. Seeing what she had only read about, actually witnessing the fear and horror and abuse, shocked her. In a sobering flash she understood slavery was more than a vague concept of servitude. It was ugly, desperately ugly.

Bits of shipboard conversation returned to her mind, and she pieced the scraps into a disturbing whole. St. Domingue had earned a reputation as the cruelest of the sugar islands. Here the slaves were worked until they died of exhaustion, their owners believing it more economical to purchase replacement labor than to preserve the original stock. And here punishment in the form of torture had attained a level of savagery unknown in the civilized world.

Swallowing equal portions of revulsion and fascination, Garnet peered at the thick-set man wielding a whip at the top of the gangplank. And she grasped the fundamental truth of slavery: Slavery was desirable and economically profitable, a beneficial system in every way—unless one had the dire misfortune to be the slave. Then slavery became an atrocity.

"What will happen to them?" she whispered, her face chalky within the shadow of her hat brim.

"They'll be warehoused for about a week to determine who is healthy and who will die. At least twenty-five percent will die." Belaine didn't look away from her distress. "If a priest can be found who is willing to leave his rum and his mistress, the Africans will be baptized. Following the auction and the branding, the owners will fetch them. They'll be taught to speak Creole, a mix of French and African and English and Spanish and whatever else comes to mind. If they are servile and attractive, they may be trained for house duty. If they're sullen or if they look strong, they'll be assigned to the fields and worked until they drop."

"And they have no choice." As one who had valued independence and self-reliance all her life, Garnet thought the lack of personal choice the most appalling aspect of all.

"They have no choice. They are property—like a horse or a wagon."

She watched a pregnant black wench stumble, then cry out as the whip descended across her shoulders. "How did this horror happen?"

"This is neither the time nor the place to debate politically explosive issues." Belaine's seemingly careless glance directed Garnet's attention to the eagerness flushing the closely packed faces surrounding them.

But she couldn't let the subject drop. "Colonel Belaine, do you accept this abomination?"

He hesitated. "I'm a French officer, love. Currently assigned to Port-au-Prince to maintain order, which means upholding the laws as they now exist. The law supports slavery. This island is and will continue to be a powder keg awaiting a fuse. One thinks twice before voicing unpopular views."

He had answered her, but she still knew nothing of his personal persuasion. "Am I to understand that you are afraid to state an opinion, Colonel?" she snapped, her lip curling.

Belaine straightened against the upholstery. Knots rippled along his jawline and his fists clenched. "I have killed men for less of an insult." His voice sank to a dangerously soft tone. "In your case, love, I'm striving to recall that you are distraught from your recent misfortunes and therefore deserving of forgiveness for an obvious stupidity. I will assume that you are still, shall we say, dreaming." A tight smile curved his lips as Garnet smothered a gasp. "Others may not be so generous. You would be well advised to curb a hasty tongue."

A rush of scarlet suffused her cheeks. And a dozen scathing retorts stung the tip of her tongue, then were suppressed as she realized the futility of sparring with him. She was weary to the point of exhaustion, and hungry. And deeply humiliated by her scandalous state of undress. Too much had occurred in too short a period. Humbling Jean Baptiste Belaine could wait until she was rested and had restored her mental acuity.

Stiffening her chin, Garnet stared steadfastly at the plunging horses, at the shouting faces, at the slave ship—anywhere but toward Jean Belaine.

The blazing sun pounded restlessly against the top of her straw hat, and the dusty heat choked each breath. Garnet concluded dismally that she was doomed to endure eternity trapped in a web of traffic wearing her undergarments, sharing a scorching carriage with a vile despoiler of women, one who set her blood to boiling when she glanced at the firm, warm curve of his mouth.

Deciding her sanity was slowly melting, Garnet watched the impatient drumming of Belaine's fingers upon the top of the carriage seat, and she repented of all her past sins, imploring God to part the traffic and release them. The carriage lurched forward a few inches and rocked to a halt.

"Enough," Belaine muttered. Standing, he vaulted into the driver's seat, pushing Jacmel aside and taking the reins into his own large hands. He laid the whip across the mare's flank with an expert flick of the wrist.

Jacmel scooted obediently to one side, a wide grin of admiration appearing beneath his ragged hat as Belaine unleashed a thunderous string of curses, laying on the whip. The horse bolted forward, creating space where none had existed. Garnet gripped the edge of the pitching seat as the carriage jerked and plunged ahead amid a rising tide of threats, curses, and raised fists.

Enjoying himself hugely, Belaine prodded the horse onward until the carriage broke from the crush and its iron wheels shot into a nearly deserted street.

Refusing to relinquish his victory, Belaine retained the reins until Port-au-Prince lay in the distance, then guided the horse onto a packed dirt road identified as leading to Mirebalais. A stream meandered alongside the road; irrigation ditches drained toward waving fields of cane standing taller than a man. Brilliantly colored parrots cawed from the branches of leafy mango trees; velvet clusters of purple cockscomb crowded the roadside, along with stands of wild mint and begonia. A thick perfume of massed wild flowers and blooming shrubbery permeated the air.

Nothing was familiar, not the lavender-green mountains rising in the smoky distance, not the plants and fields encroaching upon the road, not the dark men and women bending to the solemn urging of the field drums. And yet, oddly, Garnet felt as if she had finally come home. Her roots lay buried in this land. Her mother had grown up amid this lush tropical beauty and had promised Garnet that one day this land would be hers. Now it was.

Swiveling on the seat, she gazed behind her, unwilling to miss anything. Rows of barebacked blacks bent in unison and hoes flashed near the ground. Behind them, women gathered the severed weeds and stacked them for burning. Field drummers maintained an unrelenting pace; hot, rapid, and excruciating.

Watching the Africans, sensing their stumbling fatigue, reminded Garnet of her own bone-deep weariness. A nervous edge had sustained her throughout her ordeal, but now she began to feel the strain of the last twenty-four hours. A tremor appeared in her tightly clasped hands. Events blurred in her thoughts. She swayed with the motion of the rocking carriage and imagined the seductive pull of water against her body. It would be so easy to close her eyes and slip quietly beneath the waves.

Belaine smiled over his shoulder. "Just a little farther, then I'll tuck you into bed."

She regarded him from fatigue-dulled eyes. Through the fog clouding her mind, she wondered how he had known where to deliver her. Had she told him? She was too tired to remember. Portions of her earlier experience were as vivid as his broad shoulders, but the rest blurred in a disordered spin. Narrowing her gaze, she speculated if he would actually have abandoned her on the beach.

The beach. Had Jean Belaine truly taken her in his arms and . . . Or had it really been nothing but a dream?

Garnet passed a hand across her eyes and forced herself to concentrate. "Like hell you will," she snapped. Had Uncle William been present, he would have glared over his spectacles and reproached her severely.

Belaine laughed and his velvety dark eyes locked on hers. "I'm not one to leave things half done, love. I mean to have you to the finish."

Her head swam, and he had spoken softly. Garnet promised herself she had misunderstood him. She dozed lightly until the carriage halted before a wooden gate upon which was nailed a painted gourd and the bleached skull of a mule or a horse. As Jacmel jumped down to push at the gate, Garnet roused herself to scowl at a fading sign announcing the Habitation du Casse. She would have to speak to someone about that. It should be the Habitation du Casse and Winters.

When Jacmel had returned to the carriage, Belaine turned the horse down a dusty lane overhung with feathery palms. Coffee trees scaled the nearby mountains rising abruptly to the north. Nearer in grew cane and cotton and low rows of indigo. A grove of banana and plantain trees surrounded a two-story house at the end of the palm lane.

Viewed from a distance, the house was impressive. Whitewashed pillars supported an upper balcony; a wide, vine-screened veranda wrapped about the front and sides. But as the carriage circled to a halt Garnet discovered sun and weather had peeled the paint to the wood in places, and here and there a shutter had pulled away from the wall. The house wore a neglected air, as if no one had noticed the hints of incipient decay, or cared.

Blinking back nostalgic tears, Garnet pulled the straw hat from her head and shook out a tumble of tangled curls. Marie Philippe Winters had grown to young womanhood in that house, had sipped tea in the shade of the veranda, had sat where Garnet sat now, watching a dozen half-naked small boys run forward to take the horse and carriage.

Hiding her eyes, Garnet allowed Jean to swing her to the ground, ducking her head as she tugged hopelessly at her pantaloons in a vain attempt to conceal her ankles and bare toes. And with all her heart she wished it could be her mother stepping from the veranda instead of strangers.

Belaine leaned into a bow. "May I present Paul du Casse."

Du Casse, dressed in fashionable cream-colored breeches and linen jacket, smiled from beneath the wide, flat brim of a planter's hat. "Titles have been abolished by the National Assembly. Otherwise it would be *comte*." He touched Garnet's fingers to his lips. "I don't suppose it's important."

His tone indicated the prohibited title was vitally important, a loss du Casse would resent to the end of his days. Behind him, a sultry, dark-haired beauty stepped from the shadow of the veranda vines, eyeing Garnet through half-lidded black eyes. Du Casse straightened, sipping from a pewter cup containing raw rum, and the woman was blotted from view. He smiled at the rumpled jacket hanging nearly to Garnet's knees.

With his prematurely white hair and vivid blue eyes, Paul du Casse should have been as striking a man as Belaine. Both were tall; both carried themselves with the natural confidence and hauteur of the born aristocrat. But whereas Belaine reminded Garnet of a pirate king bursting with energy and vitality, Paul du Casse had blurred about the edges. His eyes were reddened and slightly puffed; in a few years his jowls would be unpleasantly prominent. An aura of dissipation clung about him as tangible as the scent of rum.

Garnet directed a tired smile toward the dark-haired woman. She remembered Simone as light-haired and softer, but fatigue and the distance of years fuzzed her memories. "And you must be . . ."

Belaine's arm slid around her waist, the shock of his unexpected intimacy altering her words to a gasp. He interrupted smoothly. "May I present Tamala Philippe."

"*Cousin* Tamala Philippe," the woman corrected. Her dark eyes narrowed on the possessive arm circling Garnet's waist. Her eyes hardened as they flicked upward to Belaine and then to Garnet. "Your Uncle Émile was my father."

"Cousin?" Surprise swept the weariness from Garnet's startled expression. She forgot Belaine's hand at her waist. No one had mentioned Uncle Émile siring a child. But upon closer scrutiny, she guessed the reason for the secret. Tamala Philippe's skin was the rich, smooth color of coffee with cream. Her hair was as black as the ebony stare returning Garnet's examination. Africa lay in her high cheekbones and sulky lips.

Paul du Casse smiled into his rum. "Your Uncle Émile, though disdaining marriage, did, ah, enjoy the pleasures of the slave quarters."

Tamala's black eyes flashed. "Mama was more to him than that and you know it. Or Grandpère Philippe would never have freed me."

"It's true? We're cousins?" Garnet couldn't help staring. Tamala Philippe was as great a beauty as she was a surprise.

"Oh, yes. Like it or not, we are cousins."

"I didn't mean—"

"—that you're offended to claim an ex-slave as a relative?" Tamala's smile didn't warm her eyes. "Of course you didn't

mean that. It would be unworthy of you, wouldn't it?" She
boldly appraised Garnet's wealth of red hair, the full, rounded
thrust pushing at Belaine's jacket. Then her brow arched
toward Jean Belaine, shrewdly judging the intimacy of his
touch at Garnet's slim waist. A flash of unmistakable jealousy
sharpened her stare and Garnet involuntarily edged backward
from the challenge forming in Tamala's pouty lips and narrowed eyes.

The step molded her body against Belaine's solid warmth,
and she frowned and hastily moved beyond his reach.

"Garnet Winters, thank God you're alive!" Simone du
Casse ran down the veranda steps and clasped Garnet's hands
in her own. An exquisitely lovely face curved in a smile, and
clear gray eyes extended a warmth as natural as sunshine.
"You're exactly as I remembered you," she said as she embraced Garnet, surrounding her with the scent of fresh
lemon. "Only older and more beautiful."

Whereas Tamala's beauty was brash and vivid, Simone's
loveliness radiated from within, delicate and enduring. Flowing blue tulle revealed a slender figure, so slight as to be
almost boyish. She wore her masses of chestnut hair pulled
away from her face and coiled upon the crown. Garnet liked
her immediately.

Simone tilted her head and smiled at Jean. "I knew if she
was alive, you would find her. Thank you."

A surprising softness altered Belaine's arrogance, an expression of respect and admiration Garnet would not have guessed
him capable of expressing toward a woman.

"You said you were searching for debris," Garnet said
accusingly.

"You're the debris I was searching for." He grinned at her
anger. "She's half drowned at the moment, Simone, but I'm
confident your skills will restore her." He bowed over Simone's
hand. "Of course no woman in the Cul-de-Sac can compare
with Madame du Casse."

Simone laughed, and circles of pleasure pinked her cheeks.

But Garnet noticed Simone's small hand touched her husband's arm as Paul du Casse raised the cup of rum to his lips and regarded Belaine over the rim. "Such nonsense, Jean." The easy warmth of Simone's smile enveloped Garnet. "She's as beautiful as Aunt Marie. And she has no need of aid or artifice. Don't you agree, Paul?"

"Indeed." Paul du Casse drained his cup, his blue eyes shifting to Garnet's tumbled hair. "Yes, indeed."

Behind them, Tamala's gaze moved from Belaine to study Garnet, her sultry eyes sullen and uncompromising. Garnet, acutely aware of the dried mud between her toes and of her wildly unsuitable attire, returned her new cousin's stare. Something in Tamala's expression warned of a line that could not be crossed.

The undercurrents were too bewildering to decipher, at least for the present. Garnet's head ached with exhaustion. It was an effort to remain standing; she couldn't force herself to concentrate. Faces swam before her eyes, blurring.

"Please forgive us," Simone murmured. She tucked Garnet's arm through her own. "We're being thoughtless. Come inside, away from this dreadful sun." Concerned gray eyes lifted to Tamala. "Would you see if Fula and Josephine have finished preparing Aunt Marie's room? And please ask cook to heat water for a bath."

"I don't take orders, Simone," Tamala answered sharply. "You have thirty house slaves at your disposal. I am not."

Belaine grinned. "Our Tamala has perfected the art of luxurious living."

Black eyes flashed as pouty lips twisted. "You forget your place, Colonel."

Belaine lightly touched the pink blossom tucked behind Tamala's ear and his dark eyes dropped to the creamy breasts swelling above a low bodice. "My place is wherever I'd like it to be."

Tamala slapped his hand away from her hair, but the

annoyance in her eyes had softened to a smoky challenge. "And where is that, Colonel?"

He laughed.

Inside the house it was cool and dim, a blessing after the scorching carriage ride. Damask draperies shielded the rooms from the blazing afternoon sun. The ground floor flowed together, room after room, glimpsed through arched doorways that all appeared to open onto a central staircase leading to the second story. Garnet noticed a few heavy, carved mahogany chairs and chests, and settees upholstered in brocade and satin. But the interior was surprisingly bare, as if the residents were poised on the verge of flight, the bulk of their furnishings packed away.

Stumbling with fatigue, Garnet followed Simone up the wide, curving staircase, too weary to distinguish the pulse throbbing in her temples from the faint sound of drums drifting from the surrounding fields. The heavy perfume of flowering vines no longer seemed pleasant, but cloying and heavy. Her feet moved like granite blocks. Grasping the polished railing, she pulled herself up the remaining steps onto a waxed landing. A long, mirrored hallway opened before her.

"Your ordeal must have been dreadful," Simone murmured. A slender arm slipped about Garnet's shoulders and she led the way to a large, airy room as beautifully furnished as it had been when Garnet's mother had occupied it. Brilliantly colored straw hangings adorned the walls; an immense vase of cut flowers sat atop a polished mahogany bureau. A full-length, free-standing mirror reflected a settee and chairs upholstered in rose-colored satin.

"It's lovely," Garnet murmured. Two young girls clad in snowy aprons and kerchiefs curtsied, then hastened to tie back the yards of mosquito netting encasing a wonderfully inviting four-poster. Both gazed steadily at Garnet's flaming hair, their expressions a mixture of fascination and apprehension.

Simone addressed them in disjointed Creole. "Fula, fetch tub hurry-up-quick, and bring bath salts from Madame's dressing table plenty much." She glanced about the room, mentally listing what would be needed. "Josephine, fetch fruit platter, plenty big, and chocolate with cream hurry-up-quick." She touched Garnet's shoulder as Garnet sank to the edge of the bed with an enormous sigh. "Or would you prefer lemonade? Tea? Something cool? Wine?"

Garnet toppled back, nestling her head into the pillow, intending to rest her eyes for only a moment. "That would be fine," she murmured into Belaine's collar, inhaling the seductive scent of leather and sweat and spiced cologne. She had time to recall the fire of his lips and the hunger in his dark velvet eyes, then she was instantly asleep.

When she roused herself later, to shrug out of Belaine's heavy jacket, the room was dark and shadowed, the house quiet. She dropped the jacket over the side of the bed and sat up, rubbing at eyes drugged by the need for sleep.

"Good. You're awake."

"What?" Blinking into the shadows, Garnet searched for the voice. She sat a little straighter when she recognized Tamala standing just inside the door. Yawning, she fought against the urge to snuggle back into the pillows. "What do you want?"

"I want you to leave Colonel Belaine alone. He's mine." Long, slim fingers reached to the cord circling Tamala's neck, fingering what looked like a small bone dangling between her breasts. "Are you awake enough to understand? *Leave Jean alone.*"

In truth Garnet wasn't sure if she was awake or dreaming again. Her mind spun with dreams. Dreams of the storm at sea, dreams of a man on a beach, disturbing dreams of eager lips and urgently seeking bodies. Shaking her head, she rubbed her temples and blinked hard. When she stared at the door again, there was no one there. Sighing, she slipped back beneath the sheet and closed her eyes.

This time sleep brought her a memory instead of a dream. It was during the war and her father had been reported missing except suddenly he was home, bending over Garnet's small cot and laughing at her squeals of delight. Together they had tiptoed down the hall to surprise Marie, smothering their anticipation and laughter behind their hands. Garnet had opened the door and run into her mother's room, halting at her father's hoarse cry. Two heads had lifted from Marie's bed and Marie had screamed, a long, terrible sound of pain and shock. Garnet had chased her father down the hallway and into the dark street, but he was gone.

In the dream she ran from house to house, searching for someone, no longer her father now, but someone else. She pounded on a closed door and cried a name, her voice tight with unshed tears. If she could open the door she would be safe. And in the fashion of dreams, she knew the door was unlocked—all she had to do was press the latch. But she could not.

Perspiring and restless, Garnet rolled against her pillow and dreamed again. This time of a tall, dark man who whispered "forever" against her lips.

—4—

WHEN GARNET AWOKE, AFTER SLEEPING nearly twenty-four hours, a cool evening breeze drifted from the balcony, gently ruffling the gauzy draperies. Rustling fronds atop the banana palms glowed in sunset shades of pink and orange and gold.

Yawning, she pushed to her elbows and peered through the swaths of mosquito netting, her brows lifting in surprise and pleasure. While she'd slept Simone had provided for her comfort. The dressing table was covered with pots and crystal decanters; the wide, carved doors of the wardrobe stood open to reveal a generous array of silks and tulles and embroidered linen with slippers to match.

"You be-me wake up now." Josephine sat near the balcony windows, her hands folded patiently against the immaculate white apron covering her blue shift.

Garnet pushed aside the netting, her muscles feeling stiff and sore. "What time is it?" She halted when Josephine's chocolate eyes registered no response, then she tried again, imitating the Creole cadence. Her first effort failed, containing too much formal French and a smooth rhythm. She fractured her French and strove to catch the cadence and patterns of the language blends, not giving up until she'd made herself understood.

"Almost suppertime pretty much quick." The kerchief knotted about Josephine's head bobbed toward the dwindling light. "You want bath hurry-up-quick before eat time?"

"Say-me *oui*." A bath was a necessity. Garnet had never felt so gritty and soiled in her life. She smelled of sweat and seaweed, and itched everywhere from tiny grains of sand and salt. Reaching toward a fruit platter, she selected an orange to appease her growling stomach and watched Josephine swing toward the door, her wide hips swaying beneath the loose cotton shift.

Leaning into the hallway, Josephine slapped her palms together, calling inside two men carrying a shell-shaped tub. Fula arrived promptly behind them, leading several women balancing steaming buckets of hot water atop their kerchiefs. They filled the tub and Josephine added a generous stream of colored salts.

When Josephine had chased the women from the room, Garnet kicked aside Belaine's jacket with a sniff of distaste before stepping from her ruined pantaloons. She sank into the hot rub with a deep sigh of pleasure, inhaling the fragrant steam and closing her eyes.

"That Fula girl no be-me worth dirt—no, ma'am. Her be-me plenty good field hand, but no be-her plenty good house girl, say-me *oui*." Muttering, Josephine stacked an armful of towels beside the tub, then ran a bath brush briskly over her palm, continuing the tirade beneath her breath. "That Fula girl black as night, don't have no place in house. No, ma'am. Her have black name, no pretty good, and her full of Congo ideas plenty bad, say-me *oui*."

Garnet smiled. She suspected it had required a supreme sacrifice for Josephine to remain silent while Garnet slept. As the steamy water soaked the stiffness from her body, the sparkle returned to Garnet's emerald eyes and her spirits lifted. She was where she wanted to be; her life could truly begin now.

Josephine scrubbed a pink glow across Garnet's shoulders, clucking her tongue as the sand settled to the bottom of the tub. "That Fula girl say-me you be *loa*, you be Erzulie. Plenty dumb, plenty much. That Fula girl be-her 'fraid of red hairs, her plenty much stupid. You lucky pretty good you get Josephine. Josephine plenty good Catholic girl, no be-me stupid pretty much."

Garnet relaxed against Josephine's strong, kneading hands. "What be a *loa*?" Creole wasn't that difficult after all.

The hands paused before continuing. "*Loas* be like saints, *oui* and no, Missy Ga'net, powerful pretty much. But *loas* be good and bad, both plenty much, *oui* and *oui*. Not like saints who be-them all the time plenty much good. That Fula girl scared pretty much you be-you Erzulie in flesh. She see your hair all red and hear-her you come out of storm and sea."

Garnet laughed, trying to imagine herself as a saint. "That Fula girl be-her silly pretty much."

Josephine nodded vigorously. "*Loas* no be alla time in flesh, no and no." Pausing, she looked at the top of Garnet's head. "Missy Ga'net no be *loa*?"

"Of course not."

"Josephine no be-me stupid pretty much. Josephine no be-her 'fraid." To prove it, she pushed Garnet under the water none too gently and scrubbed her mistress's hair with hard strokes.

After toweling her tender scalp, Garnet rose from the tub, glistening with tiny soap bubbles, her skin pink and glowing from Josephine's brush and the earlier exposure to the sun.

Catching sight of her naked body in the mirror, Garnet stretched slowly, studying her full, firm breasts, the tiny waist flaring into smooth, curving hips, a sweep of long legs. Her small chin lifted as she remembered Belaine touching the blossom behind Tamala's ear. Her own figure was as lush and ripe as Tamala's, better in fact. She tossed her head and her gaze strayed to the open wardrobe. She wondered if the gowns within were as low cut as the one Tamala had worn.

Her expression tightened as she realized the focus of her

thoughts. Did she intend to compete for Belaine's dubious charms? Never.

Frowning, Garnet wrapped herself in a large towel and sat before the dressing table, berating herself for a fool. Whether or not she had dreamed Tamala's appearance last night, Tamala was welcome to Jean Baptiste Belaine. He was nothing to Garnet; he was the kind of man who . . . She clenched her fists and resolutely thrust his image from her mind.

When next Garnet examined herself, her lips curved with satisfaction. The enchanting creature in the mirror was not a vision of stuffy New England propriety. The image smiling back at her was naughty French sophistication. An impish twinkle appeared in her eyes; if Uncle William could see her now, he would clasp his heart and his bellowed outrage would be heard for a city block.

"You be-me certain I no need corset?" she asked, suddenly doubtful. When she least expected it, a streak of strong New England conservatism asserted itself.

Josephine asked for and received an explanation of "corset," at the end of which she shook her head emphatically. "You no need corset no how. You have itty-bitty waist and plenty good titties pretty much. 'Sides, it be-me too hot here plenty much for that corset contraption."

Garnet nodded weakly, then hastily rushed on, turning before the mirror. "And only one petticoat?" In truth, the lines of the high-waisted gown would have been marred by additional undergarments. The close-fitting flow of soft silk added grace and flatteringly emphasized the curves beneath.

"One be plenty much." Josephine brushed Garnet's thick hair into a smooth chignon, then teased curls out at the crown and pulled soft wisps free at the neck. The effect was stunning.

After powdering the light sprinkle of freckles bridging her nose, Garnet adjusted tiny puff sleeves and dusted the scent of roses over her breasts. Drawing on her gloves, she stared into the mirror and blushed at a lower-cut bodice than she would have dared in Boston, even as she decided the fashion suited her admirably. Simone's gown tightly hugged her breasts and fell a trifle short, but the sea-green color enhanced the sparkle in Garnet's eyes.

Flirting with the mirror, Garnet decided she had seldom looked as elegantly lovely.

After giving Josephine's hand a pat of gratitude, Garnet slid her feet into green satin slippers that pinched only a little and she descended the staircase in response to the persistent ringing of a dinner bell. And she smiled with pleasure at the whisper of fine silk about her body, anticipating Jean Belaine's expression. A frown creased her brow and she abruptly halted, her glove poised on the railing.

She had assumed Jean would dine with them but, upon reflection, it appeared more logical that he had rejoined his men. A surge of inexplicable disappointment drained the eagerness from her step.

"Idiot." The furious whisper tugged at her lips. "Have you forgotten what he did to you?" Impatiently lifting her skirt, she continued down the sweep of staircase, chewing her lip in irritation.

The dining room opened beyond a wide arch at the foot of the stairs. And the first person Garnet saw upon entering was Jean Belaine. His black hair was tied at the neck with a satin bow as richly dark as his jacket and breeches. A froth of snowy lace foamed about his wrists and throat, a stark contrast against his tanned skin. Garnet caught her breath at the leap in his eyes, at the smoldering stare sweeping her silken body. And when his gaze lifted to her wide eyes, her face paled at the hard intensity she read there.

"My God," he breathed softly. "I had no idea what a treasure the sea had yielded up." His eyes locked on hers and Garnet felt herself being drawn against her will into deep swirling velvet the color of warm shadows.

"Indeed," Paul du Casse agreed enthusiastically.

Garnet wrenched her gaze from Jean Belaine's stare and

smiled absently at the top of Paul's white head bending above her glove. As if in deliberate contrast to Belaine's black, Paul had chosen ivory satin opened to display a blue waistcoat shot through with silver thread. Next to Belaine's elegant simplicity, the ivory and silver seemed foppish and overdone.

"I knew green would be your color." Simone puffed Garnet's sleeves approvingly. She wore a dove gray, the quiet color matching her clear, smiling eyes.

"All this flattery and attention will go to my head," Garnet protested. She cast Belaine a hidden glance as Simone gracefully directed them to the table. She should have been embarrassed, distraught even, to discover Jean here. Instead she was appalled to admit a secret pleasure. To her surprise, she was insatiably curious about this man. She wanted to know more about him. She didn't want to think it had been a stranger who . . . No, nothing had happened, nothing at all, only a dream. She frowned uneasily at her gloves, confused by thoughts that wouldn't remain tidily arranged.

Responding to the curt commands of the head houseman, Rombo, barefoot men wearing white coats and trousers jumped to extend chairs and flick linen napkins across the diners' laps.

Simone hesitated, glancing toward the staircase beyond the dining-room arch. "Tamala is late."

"Isn't she always?" Paul reached for the cup of rum beside his plate. A wedge of lime and sprinkles of nutmeg had been added.

During the ensuing silence Garnet inspected the room. Although the table was laden with heavy silver and delicate English china, the room itself was distressingly bare of furnishings. Few paintings relieved the expanse of whitewashed walls, and the chandelier overhead could not be considered elaborate. In an age of overabundance Garnet had expected more, not less. The only furniture not absolutely necessary was a small table and single chair placed to one side of the major table. It was set for one.

Questioning eyes swung to discover Belaine watching her, an unreadable flicker in his dark gaze. As if reading her mind, he explained bluntly, "People of color do not dine at the same table as *grands blancs*."

"Not even family? A cousin?" It was the silliest idea Garnet had heard. She appealed to Simone's quiet distress.

"I'm afraid no exceptions are made."

"Tamala may be a cousin, my dear," Paul interrupted flatly, "but her blood is part black."

"Which makes me all black in the eyes of those present." Tamala spoke from the archway. A chill smile curved her pouty lips as she approached her table with head held high. The next words were directed to Garnet, but Garnet suspected they addressed a deep rift extending far beyond herself.

"Freedom in St. Domingue is a relative thing, cousin. At least for *gens de couleur*. The mulattoes"—Tamala spat the hated word—"are barred from competing with whites even at the dinner table. They may not enter the most lucrative professions, are segregated even in church, and are required to wear clothing that in no way detracts from that of the *grands blancs*." She touched the sash of a gown as elegantly designed as those worn by Garnet and Simone, but fashioned from muslin rather than silk. Smiling unpleasantly, she seated herself and leaned back as Rombo dropped a napkin across her lap. "Mulattoes must be indoors past nine in the evening and . . . the list goes on. Mulattoes may not inherit from a white. So you see, cousin, although our claims to this estate are equal, yours and Simone's are honored but mine is not. It makes one a little bitter. Had Grandpère neglected to free me, I would now, in fact, be owned equally by you both."

Garnet bit her lip and shifted from the hatred narrowing Tamala's eyes. The ugliness of the slaver returned full force to memory.

"My freedom, of course, is not equal to what you enjoy," Tamala continued, delivering her speech in a level, expressionless voice, more intense than anger would have been.

"You are much, much freer than I, cousin. You are free to eat at the large table, free to strike a white, free to dispose of your property however you choose. I am not. Yet I am called free in St. Domingue. Curious, is it not?"

Garnet kept her gaze averted from the malevolent glitter of the girl's eyes. The island's soft air and fragrant beauty concealed a simmering stew of ugly passions. She cleared her throat and prayed she was not expected to comment.

"What makes the situation even more curious is that in France mulattoes are welcomed as equals, but not in St. Domingue. Yet we are supposedly following French law here." Tamala's eyes swept the occupants of the large table. "Does no one think it remarkable that an American can inherit French ground, but I, a Frenchwoman, cannot?"

Simone released a sympathetic sigh. "It isn't fair." She shot a warning glance toward Paul as his brows furrowed in disagreement. "You have a home here, Tamala, for as long as you choose. You have servants and as many clothes as I do. You have—"

"And why not? My claim is equal to yours. If you expect gratitude, Simone, you won't get it. What you consider charity, I consider my birthright."

Paul's voice was as chill as his eyes. "The law says you have no claim whatsoever on our land."

Simone reached a hand to him and interjected quickly, "We all wish it were otherwise."

"Do you? Do you really?" Tamala's sneering laugh was harsh and disbelieving.

Both Jean and Garnet had remained silent throughout the exchange. Now Jean touched his cravat and leaned toward Simone. "Are you as hungry as I?" he inquired pleasantly.

"Of course." Simone cast him a grateful glance, then tinkled the small silver bell beside her plate. Immediately Rombo nodded sharply and a dozen liveried men appeared, bearing platters of spiced shrimp, pheasant in orange sauce, hearts of palm, creamed vegetables, several rice dishes, and a platter of fresh fruit so heavily laden two men were required to serve it.

After Rombo had filled the crystal goblets with a ruby wine, Paul rose from his chair and raised his glass. "To Garnet Winters. Welcome to the pearl of the Antilles, cousin. May your stay be pleasant and brief."

Belaine laughed at Garnet's startled expression. "Our host is not eager to be rid of you." Hastily Simone intervened to confirm the statement. "The toast is standard for St. Domingue. All native-born Frenchmen consider their sojourn here as a temporary curse, to be borne only until their fortune is assured. Only those of us born on the island refrain from counting the days until we can escape to France."

Tamala spoke from the smaller table. "Colonel Belaine speaks for the *grands blancs*, of course. Some native-born islanders are as eager to depart as the Parisians, believing France more hospitable than St. Domingue will ever be."

Paul squinted across the glow of the candelabra. "For Christ's sake, Tamala. Can't you pretend manners for one night? Garnet will be subjected to political issues soon enough. Let us enjoy our dinner without being subjected to your barbs—just once."

Tamala leaned back, her full breasts straining provocatively against a tight muslin bodice. Her tongue slid slowly over her lips, and she stared at Paul through half-lidded eyes. The sexuality in her pose was tangible, bold, a seductive invitation. "You don't insist upon silence when *you* are wielding the barb, do you, Paul?"

Simone coughed into her napkin, staring steadily at a point in space. Garnet caught her breath at the hard appraisal in both men's eyes as each contemplated Tamala's ripe curves and smooth, moist skin. Her New England propriety was shocked at the blatant display. Seeing Garnet's wide eyes, Tamala laughed and raised her wineglass in a mock salute.

The following silence was charged and uncomfortable, unbroken till Simone summoned a determined smile and begged Garnet to relate the tale of her survival. The conversation then turned to cane, as Garnet would discover it always did.

"Every life on this island revolves around the cane," Belaine explained. Garnet was thankful that nothing in his voice or gaze betrayed an intimacy beyond etiquette's limits. "There's nothing more exhilarating than harvest, and you've arrived in time to watch. In fact . . ." He glanced at Paul and broke off mid-sentence.

"Go ahead and say it," Paul said shortly. "Belaine insists we should already be cutting." He reached for the mug of rum, his expression sour.

"In view of the storm that sank the *Commerce*, it appears the rainy season is imminent," Garnet said. "The rains may arrive early this year."

Both men regarded her with sharpened interest. "You appear to have done your homework, mademoiselle," Paul commented. "Is cane grown near Boston?"

Garnet smiled. "No. But I've been reading about cane for years in preparation for accepting my inheritance." Paul looked at her strangely. "But book learning is no substitute for practical experience. When *is* the proper moment for cutting?"

Simone laughed and indicated both Paul and Jean. "No two cane men agree on the proper moment for cutting or striking."

"Oh?" Garnet kept her tone politely impersonal. "I thought the colonel was in the army."

"I am," Belaine said. "But not by choice. The instant my commission expires, I'll return to the fields."

"Working alongside the crews." Paul snorted. "I'll never understand owners who insist on working with the blacks. It's a bad precedent, Jean."

"I believe you can't ask a man to do more than you would yourself."

"A man?" Paul's voice rose in derision. "You think of the slaves as men?"

Simone regarded them both, her eyes troubled. She interrupted smoothly. "It seems a shame, Jean, that loving cane as you do, you decided to give your portion of the Habitation Belaine to André. Surely there was another solution?"

Belaine shrugged and turned to Garnet, explaining, "André is my half-brother, a mulatto." The words came easily, without apology. He ignored her slightly dazed expression. "André could never have owned a plantation if I hadn't given him my interest. He couldn't inherit from our father."

Garnet felt rather than saw Tamala's intense interest.

"In truth, the estate was not a gift, but an under-the-table sale. Everyone benefits. I've invested heavily in land outside New Orleans—good, rich cane land. When I leave the army, I intend to settle there."

Paul drained his cup and signaled to Rombo for the rum bottle. "New Orleans is Spanish," he said flatly. "If you dislike the politics in St. Domingue, wait until you experience Spanish rule. They're animals."

"The Spanish may foolishly believe they govern New Orleans, but the residents do not. New Orleans is as French as the Tuileries." Jean smiled. "I'm not concerned."

"You should be. I doubt the Spanish or the French will readily accept radical ideas supporting hired labor and owner participation. They'll burn your fields and hang you from the nearest tree."

The two men studied each other, both struggling to contain rising tempers. "Perhaps," Belaine answered levelly. "But others are succeeding in the area using hired labor."

Garnet examined him from beneath her lashes. So he didn't embrace the concept of men owning men. She lowered her gaze, confused by a surge of admiration. The mob scene in Port-au-Prince had convinced her of the courage required to voice dangerous opinions.

Belaine moved his wineglass in damp circles across the cloth. "Although you don't agree, Paul, I continue to believe owner participation is a vital element in the successful operation of a plantation. I think one ignores it to one's peril."

"The Habitation du Casse has not suffered from the use of an overseer," Paul insisted, frowning.

Immediately Garnet thought of the plantation's lamentable profit record and her attention sharpened. Ordinarily she would have interrupted to point out this fact, but for the moment she decided to exercise tact and learn all she could.

"I wonder," Belaine responded. "I noticed the ditches are still clogged. If the rains come earlier than you expect"—his expression clearly indicated that his prediction for the rains did not match Paul's—"your profits will rot under standing water."

"Not this year. I have every confidence in my own abilities and in those of Monsieur Lille, my overseer."

Simone rose gracefully. "Ladies, will you join me for coffee in the drawing room? We'll leave the gentlemen to politics and cane."

"I think not." Tamala stood, blotting her lips, then casting aside the napkin. "I'm not in the mood for the idle chatter of 'ladies,' thank you." For an instant her gaze steadied on Garnet, and Garnet was reminded of Tamala's midnight visit. Then the sulky lips smiled at Belaine. "Are you interested in a stroll, Colonel?"

Belaine swirled the wine in his glass. "A stroll?"

Tamala tossed back her long black hair and her liquid eyes extended an invitation. "A stroll up the staircase and along the hallway?" She looked at Paul and her sultry smile reflected enjoyment as she measured the tightness in his expression.

Garnet's jaw dropped, and her green eyes widened.

"I believe we do have a few things to discuss," Belaine said.

Speechless, Garnet watched him rise and bow to Simone and herself. He offered his arm to Tamala and escorted her through the archway and up the staircase. In a moment Tamala's low, husky laughter floated down the stairs.

A flush of shock climbed from Garnet's breast. She could not accept what she had just witnessed. "I can't . . . I mean, are they actually . . ." She couldn't voice the unthinkable. She shifted in her chair, reminding herself that this was precisely what she might have expected of Belaine. But she had not expected him to be so open, so unapologetic, so brazenly blatant. The man was an insatiable animal. And for a few moments she had forgotten.

Embarrassment etched Simone's gentle features. "It's the way of the islands," she murmured uncomfortably, not glancing at her husband. "If it eases your mind, tell yourself they are going to their own rooms."

Fresh color infused Garnet's flaming cheeks. "Belaine is staying here, too?" she asked, her anger rising; this was as disturbing as it was incomprehensible. The man was an insult to decent women. And fascinating. God help her, she thought him fascinating. Like a spider or a snake or any other deadly creature.

Paul's chair scraped back. He crossed his boots on the tablecloth near his empty plate and clipped the end of a thin cigar. "French officers don't share the common quarters of their troops—it would be unthinkable. Jean is our guest during his stay in Port-au-Prince."

"Normally Jean is assigned to Cap Français," Simone added quickly, "on the northern coast. But we had some trouble here a few weeks ago and the governor dispatched additional troops to calm the area." She read the alarm in Garnet's eyes, mistaking its origin. "It's over now. There's nothing to worry about."

Paul studied the glowing tip of his cigar.

"I see." Garnet watched the slaves moving past the open windows, lighting torches along bricked walkways circling the house and leading toward the stables and outbuildings beyond. There would be no escaping Jean Belaine. She would see him every day. She swallowed the last of an excellent French wine and absently waved Rombo aside as he stepped forward extending a fresh bottle. "Have you known the colonel long?" She knew the answer but some comment was surely expected. She could think of nothing else.

Simone nodded. "The three of us met in Paris about ten years ago." She sighed. "We were all so young—a lifetime ago."

Paul snapped his fingers and a dark hand filled his rum cup. Ashes dropped across his waistcoat from his cigar. His words slurred around the smile he directed at Garnet. "What my wife neglects to add is that she and my best friend were lovers. I didn't learn this until after we married, and then, of course, it was too late." He drank noisily. "Would you marry someone who had rutted with your best friend?"

"*Paul*," Simone gasped. Her fingers fluttered like pale birds. Quick tears filmed her gray eyes, and she dropped her head. "Please," she whispered. "Don't do this."

"Why not? Perhaps Tamala is right. Cousin Garnet will discover our nasty little secrets soon enough."

Small shocks piled atop one another more rapidly than Garnet could assimilate them. Acutely uncomfortable and embarrassed for Simone, Garnet laid aside her spoon and frantically searched for a polite escape.

Outside, the sound of a heavy drumbeat shattered the quiet darkness, and in a moment other drums joined, then the scratch of distant rattles and iron tapping rhythmically against iron.

Simone stroked her temples and squeezed her lashes against pale, high cheekbones. "Not tonight. Paul, can't you do something? Please?"

"You know I'd never find them," he replied flatly. "They could be miles away." He shrugged his shoulders in an indifferent gesture. "But if you insist, I'll order someone to ride out and—"

"No, no." Simone waved a hand. "You're right, of course."

She opened her eyes to apologize. "I can't sleep when the drums . . . The slaves are prohibited from gathering, but they do so anyway. Ceremonies," she added vaguely. "I don't know." Rising, she abruptly excused herself and, after touching Garnet's shoulder, fled up the staircase.

Garnet stared past the archway, listening to the rustle of silk and hurrying steps.

Paul smoked quietly, watching as Garnet looked uncertainly from the archway to the coffee untouched beside her plate, her unease apparent in her flushed face. "We're very different from the New England civilization you understand, aren't we?" he asked at length.

"*Oui*," Garnet responded faintly. The dinner was unique in her experience, not at all like Uncle William's stuffy gatherings. No one there departed before coffee to rush upstairs to the bedroom, nor had drums ever driven her, the hostess, from her uncle's table. Mary had served the dinner, not an army of men, and Mary had worn shoes upon her feet.

Garnet turned her spoon slowly against the lace cloth. She felt as if a giant hand had deposited her in a strange, exotic world where the veneer of civilization had worn intolerably thin, exposing all the turbulent passions polite society labored to conceal. Apparently no subject was considered too indelicate in St. Domingue. For the first time she wondered if her New England upbringing could adjust to this world.

Her mouth set and her shoulders squared. This world was what she had chosen. Of course she would adjust. She would, in fact, thrive on the island's sense of freedom. Here she could be herself without fear of censure.

"Civilization is dead in St. Domingue," Paul continued. The rum had dulled his expression, erased the life from his reddened eyes. "The climate and the cruelty crush any attempt at civility. It cannot exist in these damned islands." Candlelight burnished his hair to white gold. "Go home, Garnet," he advised, his eyes flickering with a sudden, intense emotion. "Go home while your spirit is fresh, while you can still be shocked. Go home before your innocence is destroyed."

She almost laughed at the irony. Instead she watched curls of smoke drift toward the open windows. Torchlight flickered beyond. The drumbeat halted momentarily, then resumed in another rhythm, the alteration subtle but evident.

"I'm staying," she said quietly. "In Boston I'm only my uncle's ward. Here I'm a property owner." She drew a breath, remembering all her hopes. "In Boston I'm censured if I express an opinion—the Bostonians hold very definite ideas of what is and is not proper. But here I can start fresh, without compromise." Her lips twisted wryly. "I can be myself, and who will disapprove?"

"It isn't that easy," Paul answered. "There are rules here, too."

"As a property owner I can make my own rules." She cleared her throat and decided to broach the awkward subject immediately rather than wait. "I do intend to assume the responsibility for my half of the estate, Paul." She met his startled stare levelly. "I thank you and Simone for tending to my interests, but I think the time has come to split the plantation in two."

Paul's boots hit the floor with a crash. "That's unthinkable," he stated flatly. "Women don't run plantations, particularly not women with a male relative present."

"Under the terms of Grandfather's will, Simone and I can share the single plantation as we've done to date, or we can split it into separate entities, or we can sell out." She glanced at his rum cup. "I prefer not to be dependent. When I've learned enough, I wish the plantation legally split."

He stared at her. "That's outrageous. Everyone in the Cul-de-Sac will think you found me incapable."

She glanced at him from cool green eyes. "Along those lines, I must ask myself why you've reported no profit for so long. I can't help wondering if perhaps you erred in your reports." She looked pointedly at his silvery waistcoat. "It would appear there was *some* profit. May I assume you are holding my share in a separate account?"

"Of course," he answered curtly, draining his cup.

"I'm relieved to hear it," Garnet responded, anger flashing in her eyes. "As I find myself temporarily without funds, I will expect a bank draft immediately. Agreed?"

He shrugged agreement and smiled apologetically at Garnet's stony features. His rum-addled face melted into a boyish vulnerability, and for an instant Garnet glimpsed the appeal he must have possessed years ago—for someone who found boyish men appealing. She did not.

"You're very lovely when you're angry," he whispered hoarsely. "Like a breath of chill mountain air."

Garnet gazed into his eyes, disturbed by what she saw. Hastily she rose from the table. "I'm still tired. If you will excuse me." She shot a quick glance toward Rombo, who maintained his position by the archway, his eyes fixed above her head. She wondered how much of the conversation, if any, he had understood.

Paul du Casse stumbled to his feet and leaned into a swaying bow. "Don't be stupid, cousin. Have a nice stay, then go home to Boston."

"This is my home now. And it will be forever." She felt his eyes on her back as she swept through the archway and up the staircase.

The heat and the heavy perfume of night-blooming jasmine drove all thoughts of sleep from Garnet's whirling mind. The pervading sensuality of the drums twisted through the darkness, invading her thoughts, quashing any hope of rest. She abandoned the effort with a sigh, throwing back the mosquito netting and stepping onto the balcony overlooking the grounds behind the house.

It was cooler outside, but the drums were more distinct as well; the wild abandon of music sounded nearby, as if it originated in the grove of banana palms swaying in the night breezes. Biting her lips, Garnet peered along the side of the house. Each room had an iron balcony; she wondered which one fronted Belaine's room.

Madness. Utter foolishness. Spinning away, she leaned heavily against the iron railing, lifting her eyes to a brilliant sweep of stars, so large and close she could have plucked them from the heavens. An enormous orange moon hung low on the horizon, illuminating a sea of cane fields and behind them a sweep of enclosing mountains.

Forcing her mind from the row of balconies, Garnet attempted to concentrate on the scented beauty of the darkness surrounding her, but the seductive throbbing of the drums overwhelmed her senses, pulsed along raw nerves. They reminded her that she was alone. Tamala had Belaine tonight; Simone would have Paul. But Garnet had no one and never would, by her own choice. Jean Belaine had been her first man, and her last.

The rhythm of the drums wound through her mind, stroked along her flesh. Her first man and her last . . . her last. She wet her lips and opened her light wrapper against the night heat. The drums teased primal memories as Belaine's lips had teased at her breast, hot and darkly seductive. Pounding like heartbeats, the pulsing sound washed over her and through her, calling to buried passions, calling.

Closing her lashes, she surrendered to the hypnotic music, unconsciously swaying, her thin nightdress molded to her body by the same breezes that brought the drums to her. The cadence built, tense and subtly demanding, weaving seductively in and out.

Her fingers had explored his broad chest; she had moaned as his kisses trailed low across her stomach.

Slowly she submitted to the heated stirrings awakening deep inside, primitive stirrings untouched and unknown until she had opened her eyes to a blazing sun and a beach deserted but for a man with eyes as velvety dark as the night and lips as fiery as a shooting star.

A small groan wrenched past her parted lips. She lifted the silky weight of her hair in both hands, letting it trickle through her fingers and whisper to her waist. Soft, warm air lay hot against her moist skin, and the insistent drums vibrated ancient rhythms through her racing blood.

She had caressed his face between her palms and tasted wine kisses. She had strained toward his hard, male body, had felt the satin strength of his manhood throbbing against her inner thighs.

Gasping, she gripped the railing and dropped her head.

"Oh, my God," she whispered helplessly. The moon hung suspended, a lovers' disk, and the drums throbbed to the pulse of blood tingling through her flesh. It was not a night to be alone: soft perfume scented each rapid breath; the drummer's bruising violation draped the darkness in deepening shades of passion.

Rushing inside, Garnet flung herself across the bed, thrashing from side to side, her hands clamped hard over her ears. "*Stop.*" A sheen of perspiration glowed on her skin, hot breath strangled in her throat, and she was more aware of a woman's secret needs than at any other time in her life. And more confused. Tamala's husky laughter echoed in her mind. She saw again Belaine's sea-wet breeches molding his thighs. A violent shiver racked her small frame at the memory of his hungry stare. And she knew that she was surely going mad.

A low, scraping noise cut across her despair and Garnet shoved herself up on her elbows, thrusting damp tangles of hair from her eyes.

The latch depressed and her door swung inward.

—5—

INSTINCTIVELY GARNET CURLED INTO A tight ball and pressed her cheek into the pillow. Her hands formed into fists and she held her breath until her lungs scalded.

A quick motion jerked the sheet from her bare shoulders, then warm fingers brushed her skin. A hand touched her hair before dropping to her throat.

Paul du Casse stood over her bed, swaying; he was very drunk. "Beautiful little cousin . . . saw that look in your eyes . . ."

Wrenching from his grasp, Garnet sat up, holding the sheet over her breasts. "You've made a mistake," she said stiffly. "I think you'd better leave. Now."

He wagged a finger beneath a drunken smile. "Cousin Paul knows what you want." The sour smell of rum bathed her face. "Together you and I could—"

"Paul." Simone spoke from the door, breathless, her long hair swinging down the back of a gauzy nightdress. She crossed the room quickly, wringing her hands against her breast. "Come away, Paul." Simone pried his fingers from the bedpost. She darted a quick, apologetic glance toward Garnet, then averted eyes moist with humiliation. "I'm sorry, he . . . he had too much rum."

"Too much rum," Paul agreed. He staggered and almost fell, clutching Simone's shoulder for support. "Just wanted to sample the last cousin," he muttered. "Before Belaine gets her."

Darkness covered the flush staining Garnet's throat. Everyone on this island was crazed, she was sure of it. "Do you need any help?" she asked Simone quietly.

"I can manage." Biting her lips in concentration, Simone draped Paul's arm over her small shoulders, wincing as his weight fell on her. A snatch of song broke from his lips. Before she coaxed him from the bedroom, Simone paused. "Garnet . . . may I return, just for a moment?"

"Yes, I . . . of course." Watching as they stumbled from the room, Garnet concluded this was not the first time Simone du Casse had put her husband to bed, nor was it likely to be the last.

After pushing her feet into thin slippers and tying a coral wrapper about her waist, Garnet stepped onto the balcony, listening to the beat of the drums. She moistened her lips and touched her temples, frowning.

She was disappointed.

There it was, the appalling truth. She was disappointed that Paul had appeared at her bedside and not Jean. Furious with herself, she tilted her head and stared up at the layers of bright stars spangling the night sky. The drums had bewitched her, she thought wildly. They had addled her senses, pounded morality and lifetime convictions into a mixed stew of frustration and confusion. And she understood none of it.

"Garnet?" Simone appeared from the shadows, hugging her arms about her shoulders as her thin wrapper rippled in the breeze. Her slight figure was as willowy as a reed. Moonlight smoothed the tired lines from her face. "I'm sorry," she whispered.

"There was no harm done." Not this time. Neither woman looked at the other as Garnet released a long breath. She had a feeling she hadn't finished with Paul du Casse.

"I . . . I don't know what to say." Simone rubbed her arms and stared upward at the sky. "It's this island, this terrible place." Closing her eyes, she cringed from the steady throb of drums and rattles. "I wish we could go home now. I wish we could turn back the years to happier times." A tremulous hand lifted to her forehead and she blinked at the moonlit shadows. "Please forgive him, Garnet. Paul wasn't always like this."

Garnet could think of no suitable response. She leaned against the railing and studied her fingers, embarrassed by her cousin's humiliation. "The drums . . . do they play every night?" Now she understood Simone's earlier outburst—the wild rhythms were profoundly disturbing. She couldn't imagine how anyone slept in St. Domingue.

"No, thank God. Usually it's only on Saturdays." The gauzy ruffles framing Simone's face shifted and fell. "But sometimes more often. Who can predict when the slaves will gather? Paul says the drums mean nothing, but . . ." Her voice trailed and she lowered her head, plucking at her wrapper sash. "Sometimes I think I'll go mad if they don't stop."

The seductive beat wove in and out of the night shadows, sensuous and compelling. Garnet inhaled deeply, grateful for Simone's presence and suddenly experiencing a wave of homesickness for dull, staid Boston. "You never mentioned the drums in your letters."

"There are many things I didn't mention." Simone sighed. "I apologize. I didn't dream you'd want to come here. I just assumed . . ." She looked at her hands.

A sea of moonlit cane rippled beneath the breeze like waves across a pale green ocean. Beneath the pounding of the drums, the banana palms rustled, each breath scented with the fragrance of jasmine and night-blooming vines. As quickly as Garnet's homesickness had appeared, it vanished. "It's lovely here, a paradise," she murmured.

Simone shuddered. "It's not. There's an ugliness and horror that you can't even guess. But you will." Her lips pressed into a thin line. "Before we came to St. Domingue, Paul had

problems . . . I'll admit it, but they're so much worse now."
She looked at Garnet, then hastily away. "This place brings
out the worst in people. Maybe it's the isolation or the
responsibility of ruling. I don't know." She lifted a slim hand
in a helpless gesture. "We do the best we can, but it's never
enough."

The conversation veered from one subject to another. A
hundred questions demanded answers, most of which tact
prevented Garnet from asking. Still . . . "Would you think it
amiss if I asked why you don't maintain the house?" The
peeling paint and sparsely furnished rooms assailed her sense
of order.

Simone plucked a blossom from the profusion of vines
curling about the balcony iron, turning it between her slender fingers. "We're packed to leave. We've been packed for
seven years." After a lengthy pause she sighed and continued.
"We promise ourselves we'll return to Paris after the next
harvest. But it doesn't seem to happen. Next year—it's always
next year. And next year never comes. The cost of operating
a large plantation is enormous—and there have been setbacks.
The profits seem to vanish." Her moist eyes found the huge
orange moon suspended in a pool of darkness. "Dear God, I
want to go home. I want to see the seasons change. I want to
feel a snowflake on my cheek." The yearning in her whisper
tugged at Garnet's heart. "I'm sorry. I shouldn't be talking
like this."

Garnet touched Simone's hand awkwardly, at a loss for a
reply. Then both women fell silent as a crunch of boots
scraped the bricks along the walkway curving beneath the
balcony. Jean Belaine appeared in the torchlight, dressed in
riding breeches and a dark jacket.

"No one can sleep tonight," Garnet said softly, watching as
he strode rapidly toward the path cutting through the banana
grove.

Hating herself for caring, she rapidly calculated the short
time he'd spent with Tamala against the moments on the

beach. And a gratified smile curved the corners of her lips.

"He'll ride out and investigate the drums," Simone guessed. "Jean doesn't believe the gatherings are as harmless as Paul insists." She tore the petals from the blossom and watched them flutter toward the hissing torches below. "What Paul said about Jean and me . . ."

"Please . . . there's no need to explain." Garnet did not want to know about Jean and Simone. Or Jean and Tamala. Or Jean and any other woman.

"It was a long time ago, in Paris. Before I married Paul, before we moved to St. Domingue." Simone's light touch begged understanding. "We were both nineteen. So young. And he was wonderful." She drew a long breath and looked steadily at the moon. "Everything a young girl could hope for in a first lover."

Garnet's cheeks heated. This conversation could not have occurred in Boston, not in a million years. What was it about St. Domingue that focused sexuality so sharply? The soft, seductive nights? The flowery perfumes? She thought of kisses where her chemise had lain, of the lazy timelessness of exploring hands and long, sensual touches. Yes, Jean Belaine had been everything a young girl could hope for in a first lover. Closing her eyes, she held to the balcony railing and felt her stomach tighten.

"Then my mother insisted it was time I married. Mama had married money, so she wanted a title for me. Paul had a title. And Jean had only money."

"I see."

Simone sighed. "It wouldn't have worked between Jean and me anyway. I want the comfort of predictability—slippers by the hearth, if you will. And Jean needs a woman who can challenge him."

"And somehow Paul found out?"

"He's never forgiven me." Simone passed a hand over her

eyes. "If it had been anyone but Jean, maybe . . . but there was always competition between them."

Simone's matter-of-fact tone astonished Garnet. She couldn't imagine a physical relationship without the cement of forever. Had she found herself in a similar situation, she would have refused to marry a title; she would have run off if necessary. "It appears Paul has forgiven Jean," she observed tartly. Although a tension undeniably existed between the two men, Paul had opened his house to Belaine and offered his hospitality.

"Only after a duel. Pistols."

"A duel?"

Simone stared ahead, looking into the past. "Jean refused to fire. Paul wounded him. And then it was over—all was forgiven."

The scar along Jean's ribs? Had Paul caused that? Garnet swallowed. "But Paul can't forgive you? That isn't fair."

"That, my dear, is the way of men." Sadness cracked Simone's whisper. "Friendship endures where love does not." Garnet nodded a hearty agreement. "But sometimes I wonder about their friendship. Paul has a way of . . . straining relationships."

Garnet wet her lips, choosing not to comment on Paul. "Will Jean be staying much longer?" Surely his presence was as painful for Simone as it was for Garnet. She suspected neither of them would fully relax until Jean Belaine departed.

"A few more weeks. The Cul-de-Sac has calmed now and there isn't much for him to do. But I doubt the governor will leave anything to chance with the harvest so near. He won't recall Jean until the cutting is over."

Garnet's heart fluttered and sank. The next weeks would be a test of patience and control. Impulsively she pressed Simone's soft hands. And wished she could unburden her own secrets as freely as her cousin had. But confessing a shared lover was more than she could stomach.

Moonlight shimmered across a film of tears as Simone

embraced her. "I'm glad you've come. It gets so lonely. And please forgive Paul—at heart he's a good man. It's just that there's nothing to do here but drink and gamble. It's this place, it . . ." She touched a lace cuff to her eyes and shook her head. "It's late and breakfast comes early."

Later still, frustratingly unable to sleep, Garnet punched her pillow, settled herself, and thought of the unanswered questions. Perhaps time would reveal the answers. Sighing, she tried to quiet a mind whirling with new impressions, with sights and sounds and smells so foreign to Boston. Pushing her cheek against the pillow, she allowed herself a rueful smile. She had scorned the traditional life in Boston in favor of an inheritance that had seemed exotic and compelling from a distance. She had longed for independence and adventure. It appeared she had found both.

For a brief instant her mind strayed into the forbidden area of her lost virginity and she struck the pillow with her fist. It shouldn't have happened that way. There had been no love on the beach, and no promise of forever. The shame of it would haunt her days.

When sleep finally closed her eyelids, the dream returned, this time to the accompaniment of wildly pulsing drums. And this time the tall, dark man had a face she recognized, and when he whispered "forever," his voice was rich and disturbingly familiar. And when he bent to her opening arms, he smelled of leather and the sea and spiced cologne. . .

Garnet awoke to the chattering of guinea hens and crowing cocks, and a shy, persistent hand shaking her shoulder. Below her balcony sounded shuffling feet and sharp, cracking noises, punctuated by muffled shouts and an occasional cry. Without yet knowing this was the daily march to the cane fields, Garnet shuddered, thinking it the remnant of a nightmare. Blinking and rubbing her eyes, she frowned sleepily at Josephine, fervently hoping the girl would disappear.

"What time is it?" She could have sworn her eyes had just closed.

"It be-me past five pretty much, Missy Ga'net."

Garnet gasped. Five? The abusive hour did not fit her image of plantation life. She'd cherished a vague conception of sitting peacefully on a veranda, embroidering maybe, and occasionally rousing herself to settle a dispute or to issue an important command. The early hour smacked painfully of her Boston regimen.

"Missy S'mone say Missy Ga'net go hurry-up-quick to breakfast then rounds."

The yeasty tang of fresh bread wafted from the kitchen, and a bell rang from somewhere behind the house. Garnet struggled to a sitting position, her shoulders drooping. Only madmen rose this early. Yawning and stumbling, she groped toward the water basin and splashed her face. At this hour the air was crisply cool and a crystal dew coated the vines twining through the balcony scrolls. A cloudless sky promised a day as hot as yesterday, and Garnet didn't object when Josephine chose a thin gown of yellow muslin.

"It no be white," Josephine said firmly. "Josephine no be-me stupid pretty much. Not like that Fula girl." Satisfaction brimmed over her round chocolate face.

The gown wasn't white, but neither did the pale color appear suitable for the baked dust coating the roadways. Smothering a yawn, Garnet wondered aloud at the state of her hem before the plantation rounds would be concluded.

Josephine regarded her sternly, shocked. "You no walk on you feet like a slave. You ride in Missy S'mone's fine carriage pretty much. You very grand white lady, mistress of big, big habitation, *oui* and *oui*." She thrust gloves and a wide-brimmed straw hat into Garnet's hands. "You go field hands' huts. Very bad, smelly bad. Field hands 'spect you be grand lady pretty much, *oui* and *oui*. You wear yellow gown very grand, pretty much."

Garnet smiled as Josephine pushed her gently into the mirrored hallway. If she experienced any doubts regarding her role, she suspected Josephine would set her straight.

Hurrying, she lifted her skirt and ran lightly down the staircase and through the dining-room archway. Nodding good morning to Jean and Simone, she reserved her brightest smile for Paul, hoping to indicate without discussion that last evening's incident was forgotten and forgiven.

Paul rose as Rombo stepped forward to seat Garnet. He touched a snowy cravat beneath an uncomfortable smile. "My wife informs me I owe you an apology, cousin." A long pull of rum fortified his speech. "My actions were unforgivable, made none the less so by the lamentable fact that I can't remember them. However, Simone informs me that I occasioned great embarrassment. I hope you will forgive my untimely appearance in your bedchamber."

An irritated blush shot to the roots of Garnet's hair. From the corner of her lashes she watched Jean's coffee cup pause in midair, and a wide grin began. He glanced slowly from Garnet to Paul and back again, amusement twinkling in his dark eyes.

She swallowed a knot of mortified anger. "Your apology is accepted, of course." Her eyes flashed toward Belaine. "After all, nothing happened." His accursed grin widened. "Nothing at all happened."

"Does it ever?" Jean smiled, his thick brow arching. "Don't be concerned, Paul. You probably dreamed the entire episode. Something similar happened to me recently."

Garnet's teeth ground. Her napkin balled in her fists, and she stared straight ahead as dishes of rice and banana pudding appeared on the table, followed by cassava cakes and slabs of roast chicken and boiled eggs and sweet figs in heavy cream. A dark hand placed pitchers of thick, pale molasses along the table and butter as creamy white as a new moon.

A crease lined Simone's smooth brow. "I hadn't realized how colorless breakfast is. Don't we usually have sausages and more colorful fruits?"

The absence of interesting colors did not occupy Garnet as much as the absence of Tamala. When Paul had irritably inquired if they would again be forced to wait, Simone had hesitantly informed them that Tamala had spent most of the night in a rage, smashing whatever came to hand. She had left orders not to be disturbed.

Jean directed a thoughtful glance toward Rombo, who supervised the meal service with a series of curt nods and low murmurs. "I suspect your cook may be laboring under the impression that Mademoiselle Winters is the human incarnation of Erzulie. White is Erzulie's color."

Garnet quickly surveyed the bland assortment of foods, then her head snapped up. She recalled Josephine's insistence that her gown should not be white.

"*Vodun*, Jean?" Paul smiled, adding a splash of rum to his morning coffee. "Come, now, are you suggesting *vodun* has crept into our kitchen?"

Belaine's wave indicated the array of pale foods. "Possibly. This could well be the cook's offering to Erzulie." He smiled at Garnet's frown. "You will, of course, be expected to grant the cook's request." His smile did not touch his dark eyes.

"What is the request?" Garnet found it annoying that she couldn't guess whether he was serious or teasing her.

"As a goddess, a *loa*, you are expected to know the request without its being stated."

In response to Garnet's irritation, Paul leaned back in his chair with a smile. His eyes were vividly blue after a night of rest, contrasting brightly with the white hair tied at his neck. "It's harmless, I assure you. Don't let Jean scare you with his tales of *wangas* and spirit possessions and strange doings. It's all superstition, tricks the *houngans*, the priests, use to keep the Africans in line."

Belaine's brows drew together in a thick line, and his voice was sharp. "Those of us who grew up in St. Domingue don't dismiss *vodun* that easily. It's a well-formed religion, a philosophy of ideas and beliefs. Some of which can be dangerous if ignored."

"You surprised me, Jean." Paul smiled. "Can you possibly

believe mumbo jumbo and a sprinkling of chicken blood can be considered a true religion? A mixed bag of magical nonsense originating in a faraway jungle? I rather think not."

"Unfortunately most of the planters tend to agree with you. They focus on the magical curiosities as an amusement and ignore the fundamentals."

"Which are?"

"A body of thought governing ideas and behavior."

Paul winked at Garnet and Simone, both of whom had laid aside their forks to follow the exchange. "More correctly, a body of sex-frenzied dances and the mutilation of sheep and fowl. The veneration of magic, nothing more."

Belaine's eyes met Paul's in the beginning of a challenge. "What of the magical basis of our own religion? Communion, for example. Are we not asked to believe the magical transmutation of wine into blood? Bread into flesh? But I think you'll agree that to concentrate on this ceremony alone would be to overlook the greater message."

Paul pretended profound shock, his hand covering his heart. "Surely you don't embrace the heresy that *vodun* in any way resembles Christianity?"

"Of course not," Belaine snapped. "Only in the seriousness with which it is regarded by its followers. And I assure you, the followers of *vodun* are deadly serious. If the *houngans* say 'jump,' the followers jump."

"Gentlemen," Simone interrupted faintly, one hand fanning her cheeks. "Must we discuss such weighty matters at breakfast?" A gentle smile of reproach curved her lips. "I haven't the stomach to discuss chicken blood and sex-crazed dancing at this hour."

"Forgive me," Jean apologized. "*Vodun* is, in my humble opinion"—he nodded at Paul, qualifying his statement with obvious reluctance—"not only a true religion but a potent political force as well. If I have allowed the strength of my convictions to cause offense, I beg pardon."

"Politics discussed by the beat of a drum? Carrying on the

wind from plantation to plantation?" Paul smiled, his contempt as evident as the steadily sinking level in the rum bottle.

"It happens," Belaine stated flatly.

"Gentlemen, *please.*"

Watching as Jean again apologized to Simone, Garnet couldn't help but imagine them as lovers, though she tried hard to resist the image. Had it been ecstatically wonderful? Had they thrilled to each other's touch? To secret smiles? Berating herself for a fool, Garnet covertly studied them for hints of a lingering attachment, all the while promising herself that the twist below her heart was curiosity and not jealousy. Never jealousy. Her sharp eyes could discern no trace of evidence suggesting that Jean and Simone regarded each other with more than the affection and respect of old, dear friends. But strangely painful scenes flickered out of control behind her eyes. She gazed hypnotically at Belaine's firm mouth as he spoke, remembering the hard rapture of his kiss. And she castigated herself for the sudden tension banding her breast. It was a decided relief when Paul addressed her, forcing her attention from areas she desperately preferred not to contemplate.

"I understand you wish to accompany Simone on her rounds this morning. I hope you have a strong stomach."

"Will I need one?"

Simone nodded unhappily. "I suspect the first time will be . . . unsettling," she admitted reluctantly.

Belaine added cream to his coffee and raised the cup to his lips, examining her above the rim. "Perhaps you should rest before viewing the estate. You've suffered a trying ordeal and the climate can be unhealthy for those unaccustomed to it."

Garnet frowned. At first he had displayed no concern for her welfare—now his twinkling eyes pretended an interest. He frustrated her beyond endurance. "My health is excellent, thank you," she replied tartly. "And my stomach is strong. I'll thank you not to offer unsolicited advice."

"What's this, Jean?" Paul smiled. "A woman who rejects your attentions? Simone, we are witnessing a miracle."

Jean Belaine shrugged and grinned. "Either I'm losing my charm or the poor child has suffered a sunstroke."

Garnet's lips thinned in anger. The man's conceit was beyond belief. "Is it so impossible to believe that not every woman falls senseless at your feet?" He brought out the worst in her, she thought, listening to the shrill petulance in her voice and despising it.

Laughing dark eyes contemplated the light muslin hugging her breasts, and Garnet's breath caught sharply at the cool speculation flickering in his velvet gaze.

"Occasionally I find a senseless woman at my feet, but I admit it doesn't happen often." Calmly he sliced into a cassava cake and smothered it beneath a flood of molasses. "My duty as a gentleman compels me to advise you, love, like it or not."

A gentleman? Garnet's spoon clattered against her coffee cup and she sputtered. Her self-assurance wavered beneath his confident smile. "First, you are not, and I repeat, you are *not* responsible for me." Fury fired her cheeks as he calmly continued eating. "I am responsible for myself, do you understand? I don't need or want anyone's advice." She was about to add that if he continued to address her as "love," she would scratch his dancing eyes out of his head, when Rombo spared her further embarrassment by ushering a man into the room.

Pausing, Garnet examined his dusty field clothes and a sweat-stained hat. She disliked the man on sight. His watery blue eyes skimmed her hair, then he bowed, a perfunctory gesture at best. His hard, greedy stare lingered on the heavy silver and china plate, and the man's envy was as tangible and sour as his strong, unwashed odor.

Paul draped an elbow over the top rung of his chair and sipped a rum-laced coffee. "Well, Monsieur Lille? What disasters have you brought us today?"

"Excuse me, Paul . . . ladies." Jean blotted his lips and stood, thrusting muscled arms into the orange uniform jacket Rombo had brushed and now held. "I'm expected at the fort, and I'm late as usual." He kissed Simone's fingertips and laughed when Garnet snatched her own hands away, hiding them behind her back and glaring. He strapped on his sword, then leaned near her ear, his breath disturbingly warm against her cheek. "You and I need to talk, love. Soon."

"Don't call me that!"

He settled his hat over black curls, and in a moment Garnet heard his boots outside on the veranda. His deep voice shouted for Jacmel. Only then did Garnet realize he had not addressed a word or a glance to Monsieur Lille, the plantation's head overseer.

Lille began his recitation in a nasal monotone, his watery gaze flicking from Paul to the women, swooping over their bodices like a tiny pecking bird. "Two of them new Ibos hanged themselves, and three Congos in the East village run off."

"Goddammit!" Paul's face darkened. He slammed a fist on the tabletop, moodily watching the glasses jump. "Do you know what a good Ibo costs?"

Simone withdrew a small book from her pocket. "Go on, Monsieur Lille."

"They's two females about to birth, Missy S'mone, one in the East Village and one in the manor village. Eight sick today—six in the West village and two in the East village."

"Did you finish clearing the ditches?" Paul demanded.

"Yes sir, Mist' Paul."

Paul cast a triumphant look at Simone. "We'll start cutting the North carrys the week after next. Check the equipment in the boiler houses and hire that Ashanti away from Villier. Kotu, I think he calls himself. They say he's the best sugar man on the island."

Lille spit, the globule splattering a few inches from Garnet's hem. She stared in shock, then gathered her skirts about her ankles. Rombo hissed and a man in white livery hastened to clean the floor at Garnet's side.

"You gonna pay a freeman, Mist' Paul? A *black* freeman? We got whites as good as that Ashanti, better in fact."

"Not that I've heard of." Paul's eyes chilled to blue ice. "I don't want to lose another harvest because the idiots in the boiler house don't know when to strike . . . like last year."

Lille's sullen stare darted about the room. "How much you willing to pay that Ashanti?"

"Offer whatever it takes to hire him away from Villier."

Lille considered, peering at his shoetops, his straw hat turning in his hands. His voice whined. "You gonna pay him as much as me?"

Paul added more rum to his coffee with an impatient twist of the wrist. "Can you endure the boiler house heat, Lille? Can you draw a thread of sugar between your thumb and forefinger and judge the right moment to strike? I can always hire an overseer, I can't always find a good sugar man. You would do well to remember that."

Lille didn't respond. His mouth twisted. "What you gonna do about that hitter, Muboto? We had him strung up in the cage three days now. One more day in the sun and his brain is gonna be fried."

Paul raked a hand through his hair, pointedly ignoring Simone's pleading glance. "He actually hit you?"

"Yes sir, Mist' Paul."

"Give him the four post. Don't wait until Friday, do it today. Make sure the field crews see it."

A satisfied gleam appeared in Lille's small eyes. "How many strokes?"

"Twenty."

Disappointment pushed at the satisfaction. "Yes sir, Mist' Paul. And that woman what tried to run off?"

"Leg chains for a month. And put the collar on her."

When Monsieur Lille had departed, Simone released a sorrowing breath. "Oh, Paul . . ."

"Simone, dammit, it has to be done. The woman will run if she isn't chained. And Muboto struck a white man—letting him live is a mercy. Today it's Lille. Tomorrow it could be me. Or you. You have to show them who's superior. Force is the only thing an animal understands."

"But the four post? Pushing his face into the dirt like . . . like . . ."

"Are you affronted when a man whips his mule? It's the same thing exactly. Both are stupid animals and have to treated as such."

Simone gazed steadily into her coffee cup, her eyes and mouth pinched.

Garnet also looked away, shifting toward the open window, her gaze seeking the dark figures moving through the banana grove with hoes and carts. Trained animals? Her frown intensified at the image. When she considered the man called Kotu—the "best sugar man on the island"— she wondered uneasily if Paul recognized the contradictions in his viewpoint. One glance toward his brooding countenance convinced her that now was not the right moment to voice the protests rising to her lips.

But the moment would come. Standing, she looked down at his white head with a grim expression. The sooner she took control of her half of the plantation, the better.

"Show me the villages," she said to Simone. There was much to learn before the Habitation Winters became a reality. "I'm in a hurry."

—6—

NOTHING IN SIMONE'S LETTERS HAD prepared Garnet for the awesome size of the plantation. The miles of coffee trees sweeping up the mountainsides grew on Philippe land. As did field after field of cane and cotton and indigo stretching as far as the eye could perceive.

"You can ride for a day and a half and not leave our property if you ride north," Simone explained with quiet pride. "The Habitation occupies most of the area between Port-au-Prince and Mirebalais."

"I had no idea it was this substantial." Garnet adjusted her parasol against the climbing sun and gazed at the rippling fields passing on either side as the carriage rattled down a long green tunnel of waving stalks. It occurred to her that had Paul's annual reports been accurate, she would not now be experiencing this sense of surprise.

"There are five support villages on the plains and three in the mountains. We can't possibly visit them all in one day. They're alike, anyway. You'll be more than a week seeing everything you should see."

The news was puzzling. "Then how will we call on all the sick?"

"We can't," Simone admitted with a sigh. "We'll tend to the birthings. I've asked a *mambo* to care for the others." She looked acutely uncomfortable.

"A *mambo*?"

"A priestess. Paul wouldn't approve, I'm afraid." Avoiding Garnet's stare, Simone ducked her head beneath the brim of her hat. "Much of the Africans' illness isn't physical. A *mambo* will be more useful than we can be."

Garnet's eyebrow arched. "Is this the *vodun* the men were discussing?" Despite her skepticism, she thought of the wild night drums, and a prickle rippled across her skin.

"*Oui.*" Uneasily, Simone darted a quick glance toward the broad back of the carriage driver. She lowered her voice to a whisper. "There's no escaping it, Garnet. *Vodun* is very real to the Africans. I can't begin to explain it, but a spell can make them very ill, sometimes deathly ill. Only a *mambo* can find the *wangas* and remove them. I wouldn't know where to look."

Garnet was amazed that Simone would even consider seeking the source of a spell or a charm. "How in the world do you contact a *mambo*?" The entire subject both repelled and fascinated. Any "religion" that could create a goddess from red hair and a storm could hardly be taken seriously in her opinion.

Simone hesitated, her answer emerging reluctantly. "Tamala is a *mambo*."

Garnet might have guessed. She sighed. "I don't think Tamala and I will ever be friends."

"Poor Tamala was born hating the world. We shouldn't judge her too harshly; you and I can't even imagine what it's like to wear the brand."

Shock widened Garnet's clear gaze. "Tamala Philippe is branded?"

"She tried to remove it. There's a nasty scar on her breast." Simone twirled her parasol and her troubled gray eyes fixed on the thick fields of cane. She continued quietly. "And I've seen the scars of whippings on her back." Simone bit her lip and her soft eyes brimmed with sympathy. "Is it any wonder she's bitter? That she strikes out at the world around her?"

Garnet released a stunned breath. But try as she might, she lacked Simone's empathy. In Boston a person was judged not by his yesterdays but by what he made of today. "What exactly does a *mambo* do?" Garnet asked, curious how Tamala spent her time.

Simone's pleading glance indicated the driver. "It will be hot today, I'm glad you remembered your gloves. It's so easy to burn before one notices."

"Yes, but . . ."

"This afternoon we'll make up a list of materials and send a rider into Port-au-Prince to fetch bolts of cloth. Our plantation seamstresses are skilled and quick—you'll have your own clothing sooner than you can imagine."

"Simone . . ."

"I believe Cook sent along a jar of lemonade, would you care to share a cup?" Simone's unhappy glance focused briefly on the stiffened shoulders above them.

"Oh, very well." Would the questions ever be answered? They piled atop one another at an ever increasing rate. Releasing a frustrated sigh, Garnet forced herself to relax against the upholstered seat. She wouldn't be stalled forever; she would have her answers, and she informed Simone as much by maintaining a cool silence as the carriage turned onto a rutted road leading into an uncleared section of the estate.

Here the vegetation ran riot. Mango trees intermingled with the giant leaves of the tannia plant; loofa vines strangled the ground and wild honeysuckle choked the tree trunks. Bananas and tall waving plantains crowded the perimeter of a village formed in a square, composed of dilapidated wattle huts roofed over with plaited palms. A sluggish brook cut through the center of the square but its questionable freshness did nothing to dispel a heavy noxious stench.

Simone pressed a lemon-scented scrap of lace to her nostrils. "Cooking refuse, animal and human waste . . ." A wince of pain wounded her gray eyes. "I beg them to bury it, but . . ."

Garnet's face paled at the appalling squalor. Scrawny chickens scratched listlessly at ground sun-baked to the consistency of brick. A thin, hairy pig rooted in a fly-blackened hill of waste piled as high as a man's chest. Naked children ran shouting through the village, falling silent before the horse and women. Along the banks of the brook, two dozen kerchiefed women beat laundry against flat rocks. Others labored above outside fires, preparing the noonday meal for the field crews. At least two hundred people lived here, Garnet guessed, and, from the look of it, in wretched misery.

Simone gently took her cousin's hands and gazed into Garnet's shocked face. "I know you have many, many questions. I beg you to wait for a moment of privacy. And then I'll do what I can to answer."

Garnet nodded doubtfully. Already she had observed that privacy was a scarce commodity on a large plantation. Always someone hovered nearby. But she saw no choice. Slowly she descended from the carriage, trying not to breathe, and she followed Simone, at the same time examining the children who clamored about their hems. Many had patches of scaling white skin, a sure sign of gusarola, a disease common to the locale; others coughed incessantly. None appeared fully healthy. Garnet observed a range of disorders, everything from goiter to an old woman, groaning beneath a cotton awning, her painful legs hugely swollen.

Simone paused to touch Garnet's icy fingers. "There's nothing we can do." She bit her lips. "I wish Paul would . . ."

Garnet waited, but Simone turned, holding her skirts close and hurrying through a scraggly garden scratched out of the hard dirt. Garnet followed reluctantly, ducking to enter a darkened hut and catching her breath against a wave of sour air. There were two rooms inside, small and close; the windows were heavily shuttered, as they always were during childbirth. The only light shone from the door and this was quickly closed behind them, leaving only the smoky flicker of candles cast from stinking animal fat.

Garnet's eyes adjusted slowly, and she blinked at three of the pregnant woman's friends as they curtsied. They stared at Garnet's fiery curls with the same mixture of fear and fascination she was becoming resigned to inspiring. She wondered curiously what lay behind their carefully blank faces. Did they, too, see her as a—what was it?—as a *loa*?

"What do we do?" She hung back, standing near the door and feeling totally inadequate for the task ahead, whatever it might be. She hoped the women did not notice her repugnance at the strange, noxious smells, the packed-earth floor, the sour darkness, and the lizard skittering up the wall. And she admired Simone intensely for her apparent ease.

"What little we can." Simone laid aside her hat and gloves, and rolled up her sleeves as she smiled gently at the groaning woman on the ground. "We can't do much, unfortunately. They won't allow it."

The woman, sweat beading in crystal pearls against her ebony skin, was Senegalese, a tribe noted for dignity and bearing. She rested in a depression in the dirt, her knees drawn up and her spine supported by mounded straw pillows.

Simone knelt beside her. "She be-her ready hurry-up-quick," she announced softly. She blotted the woman's forehead with the lemon-scented handkerchief.

One of the women moved to the door and placed a lighted candle in the center of a pattern drawn with lines of white cornmeal. She poured a libation of water across the threshold as Garnet hastily stepped backward, her eyes wide. She thanked God that little would be expected of her. And she wished she had paid more attention to women's doings in the past instead of always burying her nose in a book.

"Everything must be done exactly according to their customs," Simone murmured, using formal French. "Watch what I do, and you can help with the next one."

Garnet swallowed hard. She had never witnessed a birthing and wasn't certain that she cared to.

At Simone's nod, one of the women lifted the head of the

mother-to-be. The pregnant woman drank three sips from the cup in Simone's hand. "It's stewed mango leaves," Simone explained. "What be-me you name?" she inquired gently when the mango ritual had been completed.

Gasping, the woman looked from Simone to Garnet. "Caco," she said, panting heavily. Garnet didn't know how the woman breathed at all; the air was thick and choking.

Simone dipped her fingers into a cassava gourd, wetting her hands with palm oil. "Caco be-you nice name, plenty much good." Carefully she raised the woman's cotton shift and ran her oiled hands lightly across the distended stomach, massaging gently. "Soon now, plenty much soon. You have big, plenty good baby."

The woman groaned and tried to smile.

Then there was nothing to do but wait. Caco's friends silently served fried balls of cornmeal and cassava, which Garnet and Simone dutifully sampled, offering polite murmurs.

"These are awful. Is this what they eat?" Garnet couldn't believe it. The balls were the consistency of paste and tasted worse. How could people live and labor on such a diet?

"They honor us." Patiently Simone explained the monthly rations, gone before the month ended. She didn't look at Garnet. "They've saved the cornmeal for the birthing. They seem to believe your presence is a good omen. One of them said you were a powerful *wanga*." Simone's smile was weak.

Garnet swallowed with difficulty, the food and the anger sticking in her throat. More questions stacked on the pile, questions she would soon, by heaven, demand answers to. She looked at the wide palm leaf in her hand and the half-eaten paste ball, and she thought of the breakfast table in the manor. Injustice grated across injustice.

"Will you perform the actual delivery?" Garnet asked, pushing aside her questions for a better moment. Caco stared at the smoke-blackened roof and bit her lips to hold back a scream. Surely it wouldn't be much longer.

"No. The women will do it according to custom." Drawing a breath, Simone finished the fried cassava ball. "I wish they'd allow our assistance, but that would jeopardize the mother." She nodded unhappily at Garnet. "*Oui, vodun* again. Our presence honors them, but it could become an offense if we insist on participating. We might unwittingly open the door to an evil charm."

Incredulity weakened Garnet's knees. She wished she could step outside for a breath of air, but it was clear that to do so would breech the uncertain etiquette of the occasion. Or open the way for an evil spell. There was nothing to do but wait and watch. She paced before the doorway, from the corner of her lashes observing the ongoing struggle unfolding upon the ground.

And without intending it, she began to experience an unexpected kinship with the laboring woman. Such was the fate of all women, to give of their pain and suffering to produce glorious new life. Perhaps someday . . . Garnet swallowed hard and her nails dug into her palms. She had relinquished the honor of motherhood when she chose independence over marriage. With all her heart she wished she could be fully comfortable with her choice. Perhaps in time . . .

Finally the miracle began. And tears sprang to her eyes as a small, dark head appeared between the woman's straining thighs. Garnet wept joyfully into her handkerchief, as did Simone, and she did not think until much later of the barbaric practices of severing the umbilical cord with a splinter of sharp glass and cauterizing the stub with a glowing hot iron. The small wound was then oiled and bandaged, and the infant quickly laid on a palm mat, where it was covered with a large iron pot.

One of the women motioned Garnet forward and thrust a wooden spoon into her hand. Frantically she looked to Simone as the women regarded her expectantly, a sense of urgency in their shiny faces.

"Beat the pot."

"*What?*"

"Beat the pot. Quickly. They are giving you the honor of summoning the child's spirit."

Garnet thought it more likely she'd deafen the child. Feeling foolish, she hammered the spoon atop the overturned pot, beating it loudly until the infant protested with a lusty cry. The women broke into wide smiles and rescued the child. Next they washed the bloody smears from the infant's body using the liquid from steeped calabash leaves, then fed her a teaspoonful of muscat and palm oil. One of them then wrapped the baby in loose cotton.

Garnet smiled widely, foolishly pleased that she had performed well. "What be-me you baby's name?" she asked.

The women froze, then silently continued washing the mother in the calabash broth. They didn't look at Garnet.

"The father will name the child," Simone explained hastily. "He'll give the child her true name, which no one will ever know, and her public name, which won't be known for another week." She switched into Creole. "It be-me a girl name, say-me *oui?*"

The women relaxed, nodding vigorously. "She be-her girl child, plenty good." They bound the mother's abdomen with a stout band of folded cotton to provide support. Then, to Garnet's astonishment, Caco immediately sat up, talking and laughing shyly with her friends, watching carefully as one buried the placenta before the threshold, adding a heavy sprinkling of salt before she packed the hole with dirt and stone, saying, "So evil eye no take it, plenty bad."

Another woman gathered the cloths and rags used in the delivery and burned them in the corner, watching sharply to see that all were reduced to ashes, which she buried in the second room lest the ashes be stolen by evil persons to cast harmful spells against the mother or the baby.

Simone touched Caco's shoulder and offered congratulations. "You baby be-her fine, plenty fat girl." She rummaged in her reticule, producing two tiny gold earrings. "This be-me for you fine, good girl. Outside be a bolt of cotton for you."

Caco nodded, her bearing dignified and solemn. "Thank you, Missy S'mone, Missy Ga'net." With the creases of pain eased from her brow, Caco was a fine-looking young woman.

Garnet smiled and murmured something she hoped was appropriate, then stumbled after Simone, following her to the carriage through the crowd of children. It surprised her to note the sun high overhead—she could have sworn they had been in the hut all day. She shook her head, clearing the smells and tightness, inhaling the hot, dusty air. Nothing she had witnessed since breakfast seemed entirely real.

Simone touched her hand as they settled gratefully against the carriage cushions. "Is this the first birthing you've witnessed?" she asked. Sympathy vied with gentle amusement in her tone.

"Yes." Garnet blotted the dampness on her pale, smiling face. Throughout the last hours she had run an exhausting gamut of emotions, ranging from anxiety to fear to curiosity to heart-wrenching joy. Her yellow muslin was soaked through. "Do you do this sort of thing every day?"

Simone laughed and pushed open her parasol. "Not every day, only when needed. You become accustomed to it." The carriage turned onto the main road and proceeded toward the manor village.

"It was wonderful. Amazing." Garnet fanned her face and sipped from the cup of lemonade Simone poured. After a moment her eyes clouded. "Will that infant be branded?"

Instantly Simone's expression sobered, and sadness paled her eyes to the color of driftwood. "Yes," she answered, so quietly Garnet almost didn't hear. "When she is a month old."

A momentary darkness blotted out the relentless sun blazing overhead; a rush of dizziness blurred Garnet's vision. She lapsed into silence as terrible images whirled in her mind. She was almost grateful for the appearance of the next village square. Almost. Until she entered a dark, foul-smelling hut where a sweat-drenched girl no older than thirteen thrashed on the ground and screamed and clawed the dirt beneath her fingers. Her eyes rolled toward them and she begged Garnet to find the *wanga* that was killing her.

Dry-mouthed, Garnet followed Simone's instructions and gently rubbed palm oil on the girl's hot stomach. The girl screamed in agony.

The girl's friends stared at Garnet's hair, and they shrugged and looked away when Simone questioned them. They had searched the hut, but they had not found the *wanga*.

Three hours later, the girl gave birth to twin boys, both born dead. And Garnet wept in Simone's arms as the girl bled to death before their eyes and the women would allow them to do nothing. The women stared, and Garnet imagined she read accusation in their dull eyes.

The previously joyful event fled from her mind, and she stared at the dead girl and her babies. The risk of loving was even more terrible than Garnet had dared to suspect.

She and Simone spoke only once during the short ride to the manor. Each was exhausted and emotionally drained.

"Did you see the babies?" Simone asked, her lips a thin, hard line.

"They were beautiful."

"They were nearly white."

Garnet's eyes widened.

"*Damn* Lille." Simone's fist struck her knee and her head dropped. "Damn him to hell."

They said nothing more until they reached the house, then Garnet embraced Simone wearily and fled to her room, pleading a sick headache. The idea of idle conversation around a dinner table was more than she could face. Instead she curled up in her bed and wished she could go home. She didn't want to be a plantation mistress at this moment; the ugliness of it cut like a blunt knife. She dreaded tomorrow, and seeing Lille, and accompanying Simone on her rounds.

But she would. She stared at the mosquito netting and her jaw set. She would do her duty and she would learn. And when she was prepared, she would claim her portion and make changes.

"You be-you wake up?" Josephine called softly from the door. When she saw Garnet sit up on the bed, she bustled inside the room and placed a dinner tray across Garnet's lap. "No plenty much good, not eat." She flicked out a linen napkin. "Grand white ladies no have-you plenty much strength. Got to eat."

Garnet shoved back her hair and examined the food listlessly. "What's this?" She lifted an exquisite blossom from a bud vase and inhaled a light, tender fragrance.

"That be love flower. Very rare, plenty much. Him grow only in big and big mountains, *oui* and *oui*."

Garnet frowned into the velvety heart of the flower. "If it only grow in mountains pretty much, then how be-it come here?"

Josephine grinned and her brown eyes sparkled. "Colonel B'laine, him ride far pretty much to get love flower. Colonel B'laine bring him back hurry-up-quick for you."

"Colonel Belaine sent this to me?"

"Him say-me tell you, Missy Ga'net be missed plenty much, *oui* and *oui*." Josephine put her hands on her broad hips and smiled down at Garnet.

The action caused her cotton blouse to gap and Garnet could see the small dC puckering the upper slope of Josephine's ample breast. She pitched forward and vomited into the chamber pot.

Later, when Josephine had cleaned the bed linen and taken away the untouched tray, Garnet finished listing the materials and colors she wanted for her new clothes, then she slipped into her nightgown and wandered onto the balcony, seating herself and listening to the night sounds.

And she stroked the rare blossom along her cheek and inhaled its delicate perfume and wished with all her heart that her pride would allow her to share this lonely, solitary night.

—7—

BY SPENDING LONG DAYS IN the saddle, Garnet managed to tour the kitchen and the smokehouses and the manor village by the end of the following week. She examined the smithy, the carpenter shop, the ironworks, the stables, and the laundry. Each night she returned to the manor exhausted, smelling of horseflesh and aching in every muscle. She bathed, ate her dinner on the balcony, then allowed Josephine to smear sunburn ointment across her nose before she fell into a deep, dreamless sleep. Then she rose at dawn to ride out once more.

She saved the best for last, reserving the sugar mills and boiler houses until she understood the daily workings of the plantation. Only then did she give way to an enthusiastic curiosity and inspect the huge stone rollers and lead-lined gutters leading to the curing tanks, discovering them to be as she had expected from the books she had read.

But no book could adequately describe the sharp, syrupy odor, an odor one immediately recoiled from or loved. Standing inside the boiler house, watching avidly as sweating men scoured enormous copper caldrons in preparation for the harvest soon to come, Garnet decided instantly that she loved the ripe, rich scent that no amount of scrubbing could remove from the floor and walls.

Inhaling deeply, she again experienced the soaring joy of

coming home to a land at once strange and familiar. Rich,
fertile land she could call her own. Reluctant to leave, she
finally gathered her dusty riding skirt and stepped from the
sugary gloom of the boiler house into the blazing noonday
sun, concealing her joyous smile of pride from the men
laboring behind her. She would raise the finest cane the
Cul-de-Sac had yet seen. Her rum would be the smoothest,
her molasses the thickest.

"You've been avoiding me, love."

Every nerve jumped and she halted abruptly, shading her
eyes against the glare. Belaine sat on his horse beneath the
shade of a spreading mulberry tree, his arms crossed on the
saddle horn.

Recovering her composure, Garnet strode toward the mare
tied in the shade beside Belaine's mount. And she thought of
taking her dinner alone in her bedroom instead of descending
to the dining room. A flush of color spread across her cheeks.
"I see you every morning at breakfast. That can hardly be
construed as avoidance."

"In the morning everyone is hurried. Where are you in the
evening, when there's time for a private word?"

"You flatter yourself, Colonel, if you believe I'm interested
in conversing privately. And I'm not avoiding you—I don't
think of you at all."

Belaine's infuriating grin implied he didn't believe her.
"Well, I've been thinking about you, love."

"Whatever for?" She paused beside his horse and frowned
up into a face better suited to wars and sword battles than to a
cane field. "Doesn't the army provide you with enough to
think about?"

He laughed. "Not at this point. The area commander has
everything well under control. My men and I have little to
do."

"Then why don't you return to Cap Français?" The best
thing that could happen to Garnet Winters was the immediate departure of Colonel Jean Belaine. Then perhaps she

could sleep at night, could hear the damned drums without his lips swimming into her vision. She needed no distractions if she was to learn what was necessary to produce the best sugar cane ever. And Jean Belaine was a troubling distraction despite all her vehement protests to the contrary.

"We'll do just that the minute the governor recalls us," he answered lightly. "Now that we've exchanged pleasantries"—his teeth flashed as he grinned—"I have in this basket a lunch fit for royalty. Josephine sent it along with instructions that puny white ladies must eat. I am not to return unless I can swear I have personally witnessed you eating this lunch."

"Then you are homeless, Colonel, because I'm not hungry." The tantalizing aroma of roast chicken wafted from the wicker basket tied behind his saddle, and Garnet's stomach growled audibly. Cursing the betrayal of her body, she swung into her saddle and tipped her hat to him, preparing to leave.

"Are you afraid to lunch with me, love?"

The lazy challenge in his tone pricked her pride, exactly as he had intended. Golden flecks of anger shimmered in her stare. "Of course not," she snapped, knowing he had backed her into a corner. His infuriating slow smile indicated he knew exactly that her choices were lunching with him or appearing to be a coward.

"Well, then . . ."

Wheeling his stallion, he cantered north toward a stand of oak, leaving Garnet to inwardly rage. Against her will and better judgment, she jerked the mare's reins and followed him, muttering beneath her breath.

When she found the clearing he'd claimed, he had already dismounted and spread a checkered cloth over a floor of grass and wild flowers. Nodding pleasantly, he cast aside his uniform jacket, then dropped to the ground, lying back and crossing his arms behind his head. "You may serve."

"And you may go straight to . . ." Biting her lips, Garnet halted in mid-sentence. There was no point in sparring with him—she had already learned that. She was here and she was hungry. And marvelous scents drifted from the basket. Dropping to her knees, she opened the basket and removed a platter of crispy chicken, a wheel of cheese, a crusty loaf of bread, and a bottle of sweet white wine. She would satisfy her hunger, then leave immediately.

"Much nicer. I like you best when you remember our truce." His velvety eyes twinkled over the hat shading her brow. "Aren't you going to remove your jacket and hat?"

"I won't be here that long," she snapped, shooting him a warning glance. After pouring the wine, she bit into a chicken leg with an involuntary sigh of pleasure.

In one flowing motion, Belaine swung to a sitting position and reached for a piece of chicken, tearing it easily between his hard brown hands. "Much as I'd like to consider this a social event, love, it isn't entirely. You and I need to talk."

Her green eyes turned instantly wary.

"In your travels about the plantation, have you noticed an abundance of heart shapes with scrolls extending to the sides? Drawn with cornmeal?"

Curiosity overcame her suspicion. "Yes, I have." The cornmeal shapes appeared on the veranda in the mornings, along the manor pathways, and by the roadside. In fact, now that she thought about it, wherever she went, the heart shapes seemed to follow. "What are they?"

He swallowed his wine, noting with pleasure that Garnet had slowed the pace of her eating to follow his words. "The drawings are *vèvès*. Each *loa* has a unique *vèvè*."

"*Vodun* again?" Smiling, she asked for his knife to slice the cheese, beginning to relax. The seriousness in his dark eyes indicated she needn't fear a repetition of the scene on the beach. And, no, she was *not* disappointed.

"You can't live here and ignore it, love." He accepted the sliced cheese and placed it on a piece of bread. "Have you also noticed drawings of a knife blade pointing left, with what seems to be a fence positioned above it?" When she nodded, he added soberly, "The knife drawing is Ogoun's *vèvè*. Ogoun is an African war god, a very powerful *loa*."

Garnet's head came up sharply, and her amusement faded. If someone was drawing signs to a war god, then it followed that someone was thinking war. Her lips tightened. She had given two parents to a war, and wanted no more of it.

"One of Ogoun's lovers is Erzulie," Jean continued. "The heart shape is Erzulie's *vèvè*." When he paused to study her, his velvety gaze reminded Garnet of the secret inner heart of a flower, dark and warm and intimate. "Unlike most *loas*, Erzulie has a human counterpart in this area." His gaze slid to the red tendrils falling from beneath her hat brim. "You, love. By now every African in the Cul-de-Sac believes you are Erzulie visiting the island in human form."

"That is utter nonsense."

"What they haven't yet decided is the purpose for your visit." The intensity in his eyes made Garnet suddenly feel dizzy. She laid aside her plate and drank heavily from her wineglass. "When the priests discover you are not Erzulie, there are going to be a great many furious Africans, my love. And you are going to be in great danger."

She removed her hat and used it to fan the flush of disbelief heating her cheeks.

"As of now, the Africans worship you, hence the heart *vèvès*. But eventually their beloved Erzulie is going to prove all too human."

"Jean, you *can't* believe all this."

His eyes met hers squarely. "The point, love, is that the Africans do."

Garnet wet her lips. The fragrance of sunshine and dusty green cane fields invaded her senses. A tiny hummingbird thrummed about a tangle of honeysuckle climbing a tree trunk. War? Danger? She looked about the drowsy clearing and couldn't imagine any peril disturbing the timeless beauty of the island. "I'm not a goddess or a *loa* or whatever you call it. Sooner or later, they'll realize that." Unwillingly her eyes strayed to his mouth, the same mouth that had flamed across hers in a thousand dreams, the same mouth that had awakened her on the beach. She pressed her fingers to her lips and wondered wildly what chemistry existed between them that drew her so powerfully. She looked at the tanned V below his throat and the black curls beginning there, then hastily averted her eyes.

An effort toward patience deepened his tone. "Aren't you listening to what I'm saying? When they realize you are human, love, the Africans will feel betrayed."

A tension stretched between them that Garnet preferred to attribute to the subject they were discussing. In an attempt to lighten the mood, she shrugged prettily, her hair catching a shaft of sunlight and glowing red and gold. "Then perhaps it's better if they continue to think I'm Erzulie."

"Garnet, sit still and listen!" His thunderous tone startled her and she frowned. "Do you recall the girl and the twin boys who died in childbirth?"

She would never forget. Nor would Lille set foot on her property once she formally received it. "Of course."

"The Africans believe you killed that girl and her babies."

"*What?*" She sat bolt upright, her spine rigid and her eyes pale with shock. "I didn't—"

"I know that," he replied softly. "But they think you did. The Africans don't expect their *loas* to act as saints. But neither do they expect wanton killing."

Garnet's mouth was as dry as cold sand. "What will they do?" Her skin crawled as if a dozen eyes spied on them from the bushes. Every word he spoke made it harder to convince herself that *vodun* was a harmless conglomerate of nonsense. She thought of the hundreds of blacks she'd passed in the last week, and suddenly every sidelong glance became suspicious. "What will they do?"

"Nothing for the moment. They will wait."

God help her, she couldn't lift her gaze above the firm, hard line of his lips. She wanted to, but she couldn't. Helplessly she watched him withdraw the silver case from his jacket. He lit a thin brown cigar and exhaled slowly, the smoke drifting about his black curls. He spoke of dangers she didn't fully understand, warning her, and all she could think of was his mouth, his strong, warm mouth. If she had been standing instead of sitting on the checkered cloth, her knees would have buckled.

"Jean, please—I don't want to talk about this anymore."

"All right. But it isn't going to go away, love. Eventually you'll have to take a long, hard look." He stretched out on the ground, one knee raised, his head in his hand. "Tell me about you."

And Garnet looked away from the stretch of cloth pulling across his thighs, from the flow of muscle and sinew, and wondered uncomfortably what on earth was wrong with her. Had she contracted a fever? A sunstroke? "There's nothing to tell."

"How did you parents meet?"

She sighed. When he wasn't laughing or teasing, his face settled into lines that brooked no argument. Surrendering, she removed her jacket and laid it beside her hat, feeling a rush of relief as a breath of air cooled her ribs. Then her eyes flashed a warning as she saw his velvety gaze sweep the thrust of her breast. He grinned and repeated his question.

"My father and his brother, my Uncle William, inherited a shipping company. My father came here, to St. Domingue, to establish a new route for the company. He met my mother in Port-au-Prince."

"Ah, love at first sight."

She looked at his sprawled figure over her wineglass. "Surely you don't believe in love at first sight."

"Of course I do. I'm a hopeless romantic."

Garnet laughed. "Maybe you are at that." Only a romantic would have ridden into the mountains for one perfect blossom. And only one who believed in love at first sight could pursue as many women as she suspected he had. Beads on a string—

that had been her initial assessment and nothing had altered her opinion.

"Let me guess what happened next. Monsieur Winters swept your beautiful mother off her feet and took her back to Boston, where they lived happily ever after."

Until the war. Garnet frowned at the fingers intertwined in her lap. "It was hardly 'happily ever after.' " The bitterness in her tone embarrassed her. "Have you ever known a marriage to end happily ever after?"

"Yes. My own father and mother had such a marriage."

Garnet's eyebrow arched in derision. "May I remind you of the mulatto half-brother you mentioned? Or did he arrive by stork?" The question was too personal and she regretted it instantly.

Belaine smoked in silence for a moment, watching the drift of smoke dissipate toward the treetops and blue sky above. "My mother was paralyzed from the waist down after giving birth to me. When it became clear she could no longer, shall we say, perform her wifely duties, she bought and freed an educated black named Claudette, whom she then gave to my father as a gift. Claudette is André's mother, a fine and gracious woman."

"Jean, I apologize. This is none of my business, I—"

"André and I were fortunate. We grew up with two mothers." He rolled on his side to look into Garnet's eyes. "My father adored my mother until the day he died."

"And Claudette? Did he adore her, too?" Garnet whispered. The situation was unimaginable.

"Not adore, but I think he loved her, yes."

Garnet stared at him. The conversation had shifted into areas of intimacy she couldn't have predicted. She didn't want to know his family history. And she didn't want to be alone with him any longer, speaking of love and marriage. Hastily she threw the remains of their lunch into the basket and stood, pinning on her hat, escape uppermost in her thoughts.

Belaine sat up and watched her thoughtfully. "Whatever happened between your parents—that's why you're here instead of warming some Yankee merchant's bed, isn't it?"

"I find that remark offensive, Colonel." Hurrying now, she shrugged into her jacket and straightened her skirts.

"It's puzzled me from the first why you don't have a husband to run the plantation for you. Were the men in Boston blind?"

She whirled on him. "I don't need or want a husband. I'm capable of handling my inheritance myself."

"I don't doubt it, love." He smiled up at her angry face. "I've merely wondered why you would prefer it that way."

Something exploded inside. "Because I don't want a Paul in my life, a drunken incompetent who has ruined Simone's inheritance by gambling the profits away and by spending his days at his club in Port-au-Prince instead of riding the carrys and tending the land. Because I want a marriage that lasts forever, not until a prettier face comes along or boredom sets in. But a lasting marriage is impossible. Because men think below the belt instead of above the eyebrows. They don't understand forever—they only understand urges of the moment." She paused for breath, her green eyes flashing fire as her fears spilled forth. "And because I will not conform to someone else's idea of what I should or should not be." She jerked on her riding gloves. "That's why." Spinning on her heel, she strode rapidly toward the mare and swung up into the saddle.

Belaine watched her jerk the horse's head toward the boiler houses. "It's a pity you aren't more definite in your opinions, love."

Grinding her teeth, Garnet rode away from his smile, leaving him sitting on the edge of the checkered cloth. And against all reason, she wished he had kissed her when he had told her of his parents' love. "*Idiot.* You stupid, crazy idiot." Leaning low over the mare's coarse mane, she dug in her spurs and rode until the hot air rushed across her face, drying the strange moisture rising in her eyes.

And that night she again ordered dinner in her room and told herself that she didn't care in the least if he thought she was avoiding him.

In the morning, when she was certain Belaine had departed for the fort and Paul had left for his club, Garnet ordered breakfast in the drawing room and began a letter to Uncle William, feeling guilty that she hadn't done so before. She explained the circumstances of the loss of the *Commerce* and its cargo, and she heavily edited the version of her eventual arrival at the Habitation du Casse.

"Have you finished your letter?" Simone leaned into the archway, faint violet circles ringing her gray eyes. Drums had kept everyone awake the night before. "We'll post it in Port-au-Prince if you finish in the next few minutes."

"I'm nearly through."

"Good. I'll fetch our hats and parasols, and order up the carriage."

Concentrating, Garnet reread her last paragraphs, aghast to realize how often she had quoted Jean's opinions and how often she agreed with him when the subject was cane.

Colonel Belaine believes the rainy season is hard upon us and the Habitation unprepared. In his view, cutting should have commenced last week. As Paul vehemently disagrees, the breakfast conversation is uncomfortably argumentative. I would prefer to believe Paul is correct and Colonel Belaine in error, as the plantation would profit. However, the colonel's family plantation is, I understand, consistently profitable and this one is not. It appears, Uncle William, that your estimate of something amiss here is correct. And I suspect the something is Paul du Casse. If he possessed the colonel's expertise and experience with cane, all would be well, but he does not. We begin cutting tomorrow; I suppose the next few weeks will tell the tale. Simone and I are driving into Port-au-Prince today to buy material for the gowns we'll need for the harvest ball she is planning. I'll describe the town when next I find a moment to write.

Garnet dipped her quill and added a few lines hoping her guardian was both prosperous and healthy, then she sealed the letter and released a sigh. Her letter had omitted more than it had revealed. She had deliberately neglected to mention Paul's excessive fondness for rum, and she hadn't so much as hinted at a subject that froze her blood. The punishments.

The punishments were without question the most horrifying events she had witnessed in her life, and were the single most compelling reason she fled to her room each night rather than remain below. Scarcely a night elapsed that didn't see an act of barbarous savagery. Each evening, when the field hands had returned, the punishments for major infractions were executed in an earthen circle to the side of the manor, punishments discussed and decided upon by Paul and Lille over breakfast.

During her first week in St. Domingue, Garnet had watched as men were forced to eat their own excrement. She had seen scalding wax poured on a black arm that had lifted against a field overseer. She had wept in futile rage as men were buried to the neck, then smeared with molasses and abandoned to flies and murderous insects. And she had aided Simone in applying salt and herbs to black flesh mutilated by the whip.

One glance was enough to see that Simone's soft heart bled for the ugliness and cruelty. But Simone could only bite her white lips and turn away; the matter lay outside her control. By law, Paul was absolute master. The clash brewing in Garnet's horrified mind would be with Paul.

She folded her letter and sealed it, thinking about Paul du Casse. Rum and greed did strange things to men. In truth, Garnet could not find traces of the good man Simone insisted

Paul was. The rage motivating the punishments surprised and frightened her. And his obstinacy in delaying the cutting made no sense whatsoever.

It seemed almost as if Paul deliberately defied Jean's expertise, as if he believed it vital to prove Jean wrong. Perhaps it was. The competition between the men was not so subtle as Garnet had first supposed.

"Ready?" Simone called from the doorway. She entered the drawing room with Tamala a step behind. "Tamala is coming with us," she announced brightly. "Isn't that nice?" Her gray eyes pleaded with Garnet to agree.

Garnet suppressed a grimace. There was nothing nice about Tamala Philippe. Her sultry form haunted the plantation, drifted along the torchlit pathways after the manor had darkened and quieted. And always her sly ebony gaze seemed to watch, judge, plot. Her hatred was a tangible force, its weight crushing any gathering she attended. And Garnet had noticed that every other person on the plantation could be rigidly accounted for at any given hour, but Tamala came and went as she pleased, telling no one of her whereabouts or when she would return.

Tamala's cautious smile curved above Simone's shoulder. "I need a gown for the ball."

This hardly seemed credible to Garnet, as Tamala had not appeared twice wearing the same ensemble. Garnet had not seen the smoky rose muslin Tamala had chosen today, matched by a stunning wide hat and a rose parasol trimmed with blue fringe.

"New gowns for everyone," Simone announced gaily, leading the way to the carriage. "It will be the grandest party I've ever given." She pulled on pearl-blue gloves complimenting her eyes and pale gown, then settled against the carriage cushions. Pulling a list from her reticule, she scanned it carefully. "We'll need fans and slippers, too, and . . ." She blinked at Garnet. "You have no jewelry. It was all lost in the wreck."

"It doesn't matter." Garnet seldom wore more than pearl eardrops anyway; Uncle William hadn't approved of lavish adornment. Smiling impishly, she glanced at the daring bodice of a cinnamon-colored silk and was glad Uncle William was not present to see her. French fashion extended far beyond the boundaries of New England propriety.

"Of course it matters," Simone insisted. "Tamala and I will lend you whatever you need for the ball." She nodded to the driver and unfurled her tiny parasol against the morning sun as the carriage rocked forward.

"I don't lend my possessions," Tamala said. As always, her half-lidded smile suggested disdain. "What is mine, I keep." She looked pointedly at Garnet as she spoke, and her steady gaze suggested more than the subject at hand.

Belaine, Garnet mused. It had to be Jean. Or . . . Coloring slightly, she dipped her head and straightened the ribbons tied about the handle of her parasol. Three days ago she had returned early from her plantation explorations and discovered Tamala and Paul in a dim corner of the drawing room. Tamala had been naked to the waist, Paul's lips at her breast. Garnet didn't think Paul had overheard her shocked gasp, but Tamala had. Their eyes had clashed over Paul's white head, then Garnet had spun and fled, Tamala's husky laughter following her up the stairs.

"You are welcome to borrow anything of mine," Simone offered quietly.

Lazily Tamala pushed at the glossy black tendrils curling across her brow. She smiled. "We all know you don't object to lending anything." Her dark gaze held Garnet's. "Simone prides herself on acts of kindness. Have you noticed? She's the benevolent one in the family. Our little mother. It's so very, very touching."

When Simone had first related Tamala's story, Garnet had promised herself to expend every effort toward understanding. To be branded and denied recognition by one's own family might burn an indelible rage into anyone's spirit. This Garnet could understand. Tamala's hatred of black and white alike simmered as a hot fire ever on the verge of violent eruption.

But the fire scalded indiscriminately, and this Garnet could not forgive, not when the target was Simone. Nothing in Simone's gentle, giving nature merited Tamala's attack. Garnet deliberately met her cousin's ebony challenge. "I don't like you," she said slowly. Tamala had rebuffed each effort toward friendship. And Garnet no longer cared to continue the effort. "I don't like listening to you beat your maids, I don't like how you . . . *borrow* things that don't belong to you. I don't like your sarcasm or insinuations, and most of all, I don't like the venom that spews out of your mouth."

"Well, cousin." Tamala smiled, her narrowed gaze negating the deceptively pleasant tone. "We're finally beginning to understand each other. I don't like you, either. I don't like your coming here uninvited and strutting around as if you owned everything you see."

"I *do* own it," Garnet snapped.

"The slaves laugh at you behind your back for all your pretty 'pleases' and 'thank you's.' " And you think your red hair and tiny waist and lily-white skin have every man swooning at your feet." Her ebony eyes glittered like black stone.

"If you mean Paul and Jean—"

"You're nothing but a tease, a spinster virgin drying up, an exhibitionist. There are unpleasant words for what you are."

"Please," Simone begged. The sunlight washed her eyes of color, leaving them pale with distress. She reached a glove toward both of them. "It's harvest time, a happy time. Don't let's spoil it by quarreling."

Hastily Simone fumbled in the hamper at their feet, ignoring the glares above her head as she searched for the jug of lemonade and the cups.

Garnet seethed. A tease? A spinster virgin? An exhibitionist? She constructed a dozen scathing retorts, then glanced at Simone's imploring expression and bit her tongue instead. Tamala was jealous of Garnet's inheritance; that was the basic problem. And jealous of Jean's attentions, too, no doubt. Tossing her head, Garnet labored to rise above the petty exchange, deciding generously that it was a pity Tamala spoiled a vivid beauty with a viper's tongue. From the corner of her eye she noted Tamala's lush, ripe figure and flawless, creamy skin. All the mulatto women were lovely, the mixture seemingly taking the best from both races. But not all viewed the world through poisoned eyes.

Simone filled a lengthy silence by detailing the party she planned, anxiously attempting and failing to involve her flinty cousins. "We'll open the ballroom and bring out the good silver." She chattered on, desperation shading her tone as the staring faces didn't soften. "As soon as the harvest is in, we'll dispatch the invitations."

It would have been difficult to determine which of the women was more relieved when the carriage bumped onto the packed-dirt lane leading into Port-au-Prince. Even Tamala appeared to relax enough to pretend an interest as Simone described the sights. After a few moments Garnet cautiously lowered her guard and gave in to her curiosity about the town.

There was much to see. Their route took them along the outskirts of the Bel Air slave quarters. A pall of smoke overhung the area, drifting upward from cooking fires and burning dumps. Many of the shacks still lay in ruin from last year's earthquake. An old man leaned against a sagging stoop casting seeds in the dirt between his bare feet, divining a future as dismal and as preordained as his surroundings. Garnet viewed the tumbledown quarters with sorrowing eyes, smelling the despair and hopelessness in the smoky overhang, seeing it in the dulled eyes of gray-brown faces.

Farther in, the houses became more respectable. Most were small but lush, with pink coralilla clusters hanging gracefully from window boxes and running wild to climb the surrounding shrubbery. Explosions of crimson bougainvillea burst from overhead balconies, occasionally mixing pink and

purple and scarlet and violet in a triumphant statement.
Beneath the blazing tropical sun, the colors sparkled with a
vivid brashness that drew the eye from offending sights, of
which there were many.

Packs of scavenging dogs ran wild in the lanes. The rotting
carcass of an abandoned horse released a buzzing black
cloud as the carriage passed. A group of women listlessly
washed baskets of soiled linen in the spring that was the
town's only source of fresh water. Alongside the dark
laundresses, men and boys soaked manioc and still others
diligently made indigo from pilfered plants. The stink rose in
waves, engulfing the area for blocks. Garnet swallowed hard
and vowed to drink raw rum before daring to sample a cup of
city water. No wonder visitors sickened.

"It isn't Paris," Simone sighed. Without much interest she
pointed out the cathedral and a tiny square that had been a
park but was now a sun-scorched patch of yellowish growth.
"This," she said finally, displaying the first faint hint of pride,
"is the city's crowning glory, Monsieur Acquaire's repertory
theater." With the tip of her parasol she indicated a substantial whitewashed edifice. "It seats eight hundred. We saw
Othello last season."

"I, of course, sat in the back with the other undesirables,"
Tamala commented. She twirled her parasol negligently,
losing patience with Simone's determined tour until the carriage turned onto the Custom House Road, which afforded
an excellent view of Port Royal and the twelve-gun battery,
Fort Ilet.

"Is this where Jean goes every day?" Garnet asked, leaning
forward to inspect the fort. It sat at the end of a thin strip of
land jutting into the sparkling bay. Seeing the sudden, malevolent flash in Tamala's eyes, she instantly regretted the impulsive question. Then, deciding she had every right to inquire,
she tossed her head and met Tamala's glare with a challenging smile.

"*Oui*," Simone answered. "Or at least he did. Now I think

he spends most of his time in the cane fields." Distressed by the animosity within the carriage, she leaned forward and ordered the driver to proceed immediately to the Rue du Center and Madame Racine's shop, where they would purchase the bolts of cloth for the plantation seamstresses.

The Rue du Center was the main artery of a city unlike any city Garnet had encountered. Toads croaked from clogged drainage ditches running under sagging wooden walkways. Men in fine clothing caned their slaves in the streets without regard to stalled traffic. Tall, stately black women glided beneath the balconies, balancing awesome loads upon their kerchiefed heads. On every corner hawkers screamed the value of goods spilling from stalls beneath striped cotton awnings. One could buy produce, fried shrimp, straw goods, herbs, leather goods, exquisite wrought-iron objects. Whatever one could possibly desire, someone was selling it. The street bustled noisily with horses and carriages, the congestion as thick and colorful as that along the walkways.

"Visiting Europeans call this a Tartar camp," Tamala observed with a sniff. "Primitive and rustic and dirty." Her black eyes settled on a young blond man who tipped his hat to their carriage and grinned appreciatively. Tamala's lip curled in a sneer and the young man's hopeful expression dissolved in disappointment. In a flash he was lost in the jostling crowd.

"Here we are," Simone announced, mustering flagging spirits. She extended her glove to the driver and stepped to the wooden boardwalk before a row of shops hidden by the throngs of people. She waited at the edge of the crush for the others.

Garnet was last to descend. She paused a moment to brush down her skirts, and when she looked up, Simone had been swallowed by the shifting stream of people. A hand tugged her elbow sharply, and she stiffened as Tamala's throaty voice hissed in her ear.

"You leave Belaine alone. He's my passage out of this

pigsty town. You hear me? When he finally leaves for France or New Orleans or wherever, I intend to be on his arm. I'm warning you for the last time—*stay away from him.*"

They formed a silken island as the crowd swirled around them. Garnet stared into glittering twin points of hatred as she righted her hat and her jaw firmed stubbornly. "I don't take orders from you or from anyone else. If I decide I want Jean Belaine, then I'll have him." The angry declaration offended her own ear as much as Tamala's. She couldn't believe she'd made such a ridiculous statement. On the other hand, she refused to be intimidated by the likes of Tamala Philippe. Their eyes clashed, and black and green sparks flashed.

Tamala's voice harshened into ugliness. "Events were proceeding nicely before you came. You've gotten in the way, cousin."

"I belong here as much as you do. If I've disturbed your plans, that's just too bad."

"Either you leave Jean alone, or you'll live to regret the day you were born."

"Threats? How charming and how typical of you." Garnet smiled sweetly, her lips curving in an enormous effort. "But I don't respond to threats, cousin. If Jean finds me more attractive than a viper like you, it's hardly surprising, is it?" Her voice purred, disguising her anger. "Let's leave the decision to the gentleman, shall we?" It was a measure of her emotional state that she bundled Belaine's assurance and irreverence into the term "gentleman."

Tamala's fingers bruised her arm. "I leave nothing to chance, bitch. Remember that." She smiled nastily as Garnet jerked her arm free. "Tell the little mother that I'll find my own way home." Spinning away, she pushed into the crowd, trailing the heavy scent of musk.

Rubbing her arm angrily, Garnet watched until Tamala's rose-colored parasol vanished around the corner stalls. Her lips set in a determined line of concentration. It appeared

Belaine was the prize in a strange game of tug-of-war. She suspected nothing would please him more.

Good Lord, what on earth was she thinking? Belaine meant absolutely nothing to her. She was counting the days until he departed for Cap Français. The sensible course was to step aside and let Tamala have him, and good riddance to both. For a brief instant Garnet seriously pondered backing away from Tamala's childish challenge.

But Garnet Winters did not submit to idiotic threats; she did not bend to intimidation. Lips tightly pressed, she charged forward and burst into Madame Racine's tiny shop, selecting the first bolt of silk her fingers touched.

Only later did she remember that Tamala was a *mambo*, and wondered what part, if any, that role would play in her cousin's threats. She finally decided it wasn't important.

—8—

WHEN GARNET JOINED SIMONE AND Paul on the veranda
before dinner, her mood hovered about her hemline. She
accepted a rum punch she didn't really want from the silver
tray Rombo extended and silently pushed a sprig of mint
around the rim. Pride, she told herself grimly, was a curse.

Since returning from Port-au-Prince, she had paced her
room and pitted pride against a strong New England streak of
good sense. Good sense counseled avoiding Belaine—he awakened strange, heated emotions; he called into question the
values upon which she had based her future. Pride, on the
other hand, insisted that she not appear to fear him and that
she not shrink from Tamala's threats.

Pride had emerged victorious.

Her brooding green eyes glared at a magnificent sunset
panorama. And Garnet sourly reflected that the tropical sun-
sets were all depressingly alike, all glorious, all the work of a
master painter. But after her first week she had ceased to
notice them, discovering that perfection dulled the senses.
She frowned at the breathtaking sweep of crimson and violet,
and wished for an obliterating black cloud. Her mood demanded it.

Jean and Tamala had not returned from the city.

"Why so glum, cousin?" Paul toasted her with a mug of
undiluted rum. "It's a time to rejoice. Tonight will be our

last quiet evening for the next three weeks at least. Cropping begins in the morning." The slurred speech and the puffiness about his eyes suggested he had begun the celebration early. As usual.

Paul's ability to consume raw spirits with no impairment of his capabilities was impressive. Another man would have been senseless before midday. Garnet was continually surprised that Paul managed to remain on his feet until Rombo pinched the candles and helped him upstairs. In addition, although his reasoning undeniably suffered lapses, his bearing seldom did. Drunk or sober, Paul du Casse was the aristocrat, unassailably confident in the superiority of noble birth, unquestionably the master of all he surveyed.

Simone peered at them above the rims of small reading spectacles, then ran a slim finger down a page in her notebook. "I've decided to invite the mulatto planters," she said in a quietly determined voice. "It will do no good to protest, Paul. I've made up my mind." Even so, the following pause subtly begged approval. "Jean agrees it would be a conciliatory gesture, and the area *is* calmer now."

Paul's silvery eyebrows snapped together and he focused a glare over the candle flickering on the small wicker table between them. "I won't have blacks in my house, not as social equals," he stated flatly.

"Not blacks, Paul, mulattoes." Simone tasted her rum punch and made a face. "And not as equals, of course. They will have separate tables and a separate area for dancing. Jean says if a revolt comes, the mulattoes will be the deciding factor. We could do worse than to mend our fences."

"I'm damn sick and tired of hearing 'Jean says' every goddamned time we have a conversation." Paul slammed his mug on the table and Rombo stepped forward to fill it.

"I think we should listen on this point," Simone insisted stubbornly. The glasses slid down her small nose and she folded them away into her pocket. "Paul, there are fifteen thousand inhabitants in the Cul-de-Sac area, only three thousand of whom are white. If the slaves ever rose against us . . ."

Garnet drew a sharp breath. "Is a revolt possible?" Immediately she thought of the punishments, suspended now for harvest, and the dark, sullen faces ringing the earthen circle. And she remembered the *vèvès* drawn to Ogoun, the African war god. On this plantation alone there were nearly a thousand blacks—and only six whites, counting Lille. A light shiver chased up her bare arms, intensifying when she glanced up to discover Rombo's shrewd black eyes watching her. Without understanding how she knew, Garnet realized suddenly that Rombo understood French. Her eyes flared and she swallowed hard.

"Of course not," Paul answered, draining his mug and extending it to Rombo. "Oh, an incident occurs here and there, but an organized revolt? Never. That requires intelligence and leadership."

Garnet darted an uneasy glance toward Rombo's impassive dark face. Nothing showed in his expression. But the blacks were masters of deception—they had to be; their survival depended upon it.

"The British thought the same about the Yankees before the war," she commented thoughtfully. Rombo stood away from the veranda candlelight, hands clasped behind his back, his gaze on the final glow of sunset. "But when leadership was required, leaders emerged. The same thing is happening in your own country now. The French king is no longer the power he was. New leaders have arisen to form the Assembly . . ."

Her voice trailed as Belaine's horse loomed from the dwindling light; he reined to a halt before the slaves lighting the torches along the pathway in front of the veranda. Seated on the saddle behind him, Tamala lifted her head from his shoulder and slowly, very slowly, unwound her arms from about Belaine's waist. When she was certain they had been seen, she allowed Belaine to assist her to the ground in a tumbled swirl of rose-colored muslin.

"It's about time," Paul muttered. Returning to Simone, he conceded without grace. "With the harvest on us, I don't have time to concern myself with frivolous items. Do whatever you like about your damned party. Just don't bother me with it."

"Then I may invite whomever I choose?"

"Whomever you choose." Standing, he bowed to Tamala as she stepped onto the veranda. "Even the mulattoes."

Tamala ignored the reference. "I'm sorry you waited dinner." She smiled. "We dined at Jean's club." Whether the information was designed to sting Paul or Garnet was of little consequence. Both stiffened. Stretching, Tamala yawned elaborately, pretending to be unaware that the action provocatively molded her bodice tightly across her breasts, drawing Paul's eyes. "I'm too exhausted to eat another bite. It's been such"—she arched a coy look toward Belaine, who followed her up the veranda steps—"such an energetic day."

"How interesting." Garnet lowered a sweep of lashes, then opened them wide. "I thought only whores and street tarts were allowed in the men's clubs . . ." Her pause added the unspoken "Which are you?" but her smile was all innocence. "Is there really a bordello upstairs, cousin? And is it true they have silk sheets?"

A choking sound strangled Tamala's reply, and her face twisted. But Garnet saw only Jean's quizzical grin. A smoky speculation entered his gaze as he accepted a rum punch from Rombo's tray before explaining. "There's a ladies' section. Quite respectable. I'd be happy to show you one day if you like." The grin returned, exposing a flash of even white teeth. "As to the bordello, the entrance is off the alley, and I've been told the silk sheets are greatly overrated."

Tamala's laugh was short and harsh. "I doubt Mademoiselle Winters is an authority on bed linen." She untied her hat and shook out hair that was clearly disarranged from the morning's perfection. "I'm so tired." She yawned, managing to invest the words with an intimacy that turned Garnet's stomach. "Good night, all." Her sultry black eyes swept Garnet triumphantly as if to say, "I've won." Then her gaze narrowed into a warning before she lifted her skirts and swept victoriously into the house.

"Jean, would you come inside, where the light is better, and help me with this guest list?" Simone lifted her head from her notebook, her brow furrowed.

"Of course." After bowing to Garnet, Jean followed Simone into the house, leaving Garnet and Paul alone on the veranda.

Garnet stood uncertainly beside the screen of twisting vines, her narrowed gaze on the door. Somehow she felt she'd been bested. And Garnet Winters didn't like being bested. Angry, she didn't notice Paul's boots sprawled in her path and she stumbled as she turned, falling into his lap before she could regain her balance.

"I'm sorry, I wasn't watching where—"

"Well, now." Paul smiled at her and his arms tightened around her waist, holding her firmly on his lap. "This is more like it, cousin." The strong scent of raw rum sprayed across her cheeks and she turned her face aside, struggling to rise as she read the interested flicker in his blue eyes and heard his voice deepen.

"Let me go, Paul."

"Why the hurry, cousin?" His hands moved on her waist, caressing. "You don't know how many nights I've lain awake wondering if you're as fiery in bed as I think you are." One hand moved up and squeezed her breast.

Garnet gasped, then she slapped him and wrenched free. In a rage of humiliation she realized Rombo had observed the entire episode. Face flaming, she presented her back to him and faced Paul, keeping her voice low. "Since I've been here, I've come to respect and love Simone. For her sake I'll say nothing about this." Her voice shook. "But if you ever touch me again, I'll scream."

"I like women who scream, cousin. I don't like the quiet ones like Simone, who just lie there and endure." Paul sprawled in his chair, grinning up at her.

"I mean it, Paul."

His reddened eyes regarded her closely and the smile faded from his lips as he understood her rejection was final. Hurling his rum mug to the veranda floor, he pulled unsteadily to his feet and swayed over her. "Is it Belaine? Did he get to you before I did?" He reached for her, his hands bruising her shoulders.

"I think you're disgusting." Her lips thinned. "Incompetent and disgusting."

He released her so violently she almost fell. "Who are you to judge me?" he shouted. Droplets of spittle sprayed from his lips as he drew himself to his full height. "I am the Comte du Casse, and you are my guest."

"I am not your guest. I own half of this plantation."

Magically Belaine appeared at her side, his hand on her elbow. "Is there a problem here?" he asked quietly.

"Mademoiselle Winters has forgotten her obligations to her host," Paul snapped. He lashed out at Rombo, sending the man hurrying into the house for another mug and more rum.

Garnet's lips opened, then clamped shut in a hard line. Trying to reason with a drunk was like arguing with the wind. Without a word, she gathered her skirts and jerked free of Jean's hand, storming down the veranda steps to march along the torchlit path, her head down and her teeth grinding. Other than Simone, she had yet to meet a single rational being in St. Domingue.

She walked to the point where the pathway cut through the banana grove, leading toward the stables, then she paused and drew a long, steadying breath, inhaling the sweet night perfume of jasmine and cerese. Then she turned slow steps back toward the manor.

Before she saw the white sleeves of his shirt ruffling in the gentle evening breeze, Garnet smelled the scent of Belaine's thin cigar. He waited for her with one boot lifted against a bench positioned at the edge of the banana grove, his forearm resting on his raised knee.

Garnet almost laughed. The only thing needed to make the scene perfect was to know that Tamala watched from an upstairs window. Reminded of her cousin's challenge, she didn't brush past Belaine as she might have done yesterday. Instead she halted beside him, glancing at muscles defined by the breeze ruffling his shirt and wishing he had worn his jacket. She also wished she possessed more good sense and far less pride. In the back of her mind she admitted the foolishness of playing games with Tamala. On the other hand, since Belaine would be leaving soon, what harm could there be in enticing him just enough to prove a small point?

And if he should emerge somewhat humbled, so much the better. Imagining a humble Jean Belaine prompted a secret smile and firmed her resolve to play the game. Perhaps it was time he discovered a woman he couldn't have.

"What happened back there?" he asked, looking down at her.

"A misunderstanding, it was nothing." She smiled, tilting her head to catch the moonlight in her hair. "Speaking of misunderstandings, I don't believe I thanked you for the flower. I've been so busy that, unforgivably, it slipped my mind. But I do want you to know I appreciated your thoughtfulness." Her long lashes feathered against her cheeks, then swept upward as she gave him a dazzling smile.

Belaine stared at her for a moment, then threw back his head and laughed. "My dear Mademoiselle Winters, this unsolicited sweetness scares me to death." A hand covered his heart in mock fear. "Forgive my suspicious nature, love, but when a tiger suddenly becomes a pussy cat, one should definitely ponder the reasons."

Grimly Garnet reminded herself that she hadn't expected to beat Tamala easily. And she had, after all, consistently kept Belaine at arm's length. Suppressing the sharp reply that leaped to her lips, she formed her mouth into a charming pout, and bent to pluck a sprig of jasmine, tucking it conspicuously between her breasts, her movements slow and seductively deliberate. The heady fragrance filled her nostrils.

"I deserve that remark," she lied. "And I apologize for not always respecting our truce." The words gagged her. But she wasn't one to renege on a decision. The game was on. "I've been so busy learning about cane . . . Everything is so new and different . . ."

She let each sentence trail, a calculated invitation to respond. And she hated herself for sounding like a simpering, brainless woman, the type who played to a man's inflated opinion of himself, the type she had always despised.

Jean grinned, the moonlight carving shadowed hollows beneath his cheeks. "I'm growing more and more alarmed by the minute. Is this Garnet Winters? *Our* Garnet Winters?" He inhaled on the cigar and blew a fragrant stream toward the moon. "I'll grant that you've been busy, but learning about cane? You knew more about cane the day you washed up on this island than some men know after living here for years."

The compliment raised a flush of pleasure to her cheeks. "Book learning isn't the same as actual experience," she murmured, seating herself on the bench and arranging her skirts prettily. She glanced up at him and then quickly away, moistening her lips. Why did he have to be so handsome? It was impossible to look at him without feeling her stomach tighten and her breath quicken. Or were the hard lines of his face and the crinkles about his eyes merely a trick of the moonlight?

All her habitual defenses leaped into position, banding her chest in a viselike grip. How easy it would be to forget this was merely a game.

"Have you thought about what we discussed yesterday, love?"

The amusement in his eyes contrasted with the subject,

and Garnet wondered uneasily if he saw through her. She would have to remember he was not inexperienced. Unless she was careful, he would guess her insincerity. Thinking of the unspoken contest between herself and Tamala reminded her of silk sheets. Had Belaine actually taken Tamala to the upper floors of his club? Garnet wished she knew for certain. She doubted the most flattering conversation could adequately compete with silk sheets. And conversation was all she was prepared to offer. She started when he seated himself beside her and stretched his arm along the back of the bench, then repeated his question.

"What is there to think about?" she replied. She looked at him above the painted edge of her fan, steadfastly resisting a glance toward the dark hair at his collar. This was not easy, attempting to entice him yet keep him at bay. "I'm in danger if the Africans continue to believe I'm Erzulie, and I'm in danger if they decide I'm human. What I can I do?"

"You can leave St. Domingue," he said quietly.

She felt the warmth of his arm along the back of the bench, knew when she turned to gaze at him that her curls lightly brushed his sleeve.

"I can't do that, Jean." She frowned at her hands, watching them open and close her fan. "I won't be chased away."

His hand opened and closed near her shoulder as if he wanted to shake her. When she dared a quick look into his eyes, the amusement had been replaced with an intensity that stopped her breath. "I can't seem to make you understand the extent of the problem here. You could be in real danger, love."

"What do you want me to do?" She pulled away from his arm and lifted her hands, forgetting the game for a moment. "Return to Boston? Return to living on Uncle William's charity?" Uncle William would have been hurt and horrified to hear what she had just said. "He loves me like a daughter, but I'm not his daughter. I want a future of my own making. I can do that here."

"You would be safe in Boston."

Jumping from the bench, she paced in front of him. Torchlight shimmered across her silk gown and raised gold flecks in her eyes. "I know you mean well . . . but I have all my school primers stacked in my closet in Boston. I kept them because they were mine. Can you understand that?" Her brow knit with the effort to make him grasp how important this was.

He stretched along the bench, his eyes sober.

"And this land is mine. I can count on it. I can trust in my future here. And I can build a good future, Jean—I know I can." She wet her lips, already regretting the outburst and how much she had revealed of herself. The heavy scent of jasmine rose from her bodice and invaded her senses. She wished she could discard the silly sprig without appearing foolish.

"This isn't the only land in the world, Garnet. Sell it and buy more in Boston, or in New Orleans if you want to grow cane, or anywhere you choose. But leave St. Domingue."

His hard tone drew her stare to his rugged features. And suddenly she thought how wonderful it would be to have someone with whom to share the burdens. How wonderful to simply surrender to the sultry night and to a man's arms.

And the sand had been so hot that day, and his kisses had tasted of wine and the sea and passion. Oh, God, she didn't want these thoughts.

"I'm not leaving." Against her will, her eyes traveled to his lips, hard, firm lips that commanded soldiers and women. Where were these thoughts coming from? she wondered helplessly. Why couldn't she have a simple conversation with this man without thinking about what she wanted to forget?

"I didn't think you would." Sighing, he stood and looked down at her.

And for a moment she thought he would kiss her, knew he would kiss her. Instantly she returned to the game and prayed

Tamala watched from a distant window as she closed her eyes and lifted her mouth.

"It's late, don't you think? The others will be concerned by your absence. May I offer you my arm?"

Garnet's eyes flew open and she hastily lowered her head, staring at him as her cheeks flushed as fiery rose as the ribbons quivering on her bodice. He had known she expected to be kissed and he had chosen to humiliate her instead. The amusement in his level gaze was confirmation.

Mustering her dignity, Garnet lifted her skirts and, gritting her teeth, exercised the Winters control to force her pace to a walk, judging the distance to the veranda an endless span she would somehow endure. Furious and embarrassed, she concentrated on willing him to silence. She couldn't bear it if he spoke a single word.

Foolish pride had made her believe he would rush to kiss her if provided the least hint of invitation. Well, he wouldn't have another chance, by God. Tamala could have him and welcome. She wouldn't be humiliated again by focusing on Tamala's challenge instead of Belaine's arrogant conceit.

At the bottom of the veranda stairs, she quickened her step, hurrying forward in silence, but his hand shot out and he spun her to face him. Shadows darted along the chiseled planes of his face, and his eyes were not velvety soft but hard and piercing as he stared into her flashing glare.

"I don't know what that was all about, love." His voice growled, low and hard. "But a kiss should be honest, and what you offered was not. A kiss is an expression—it says something and should mean something." Before she could voice the furious protests scalding her throat, he pulled her roughly into his powerful arms, molding her hard against his body. "Like this."

His mouth covered hers, firm and bruising in an expression of a savage desire that swept her breath away and left her deeply shaken. Her breasts crushed against his broad chest and the perfumed scent of jasmine drifted to envelop them. Garnet's fists rose and she struggled violently in his embrace, but his lips held hers and the strength rushed from her limbs as his tongue invaded her mouth, ravaging the sweetness within. A terrifying weakness robbed her of her senses as his strong arms bent her body into his, and she gasped at the powerful leap of passion she felt against her thigh, at the urgency of his need and desire.

Panic hammered against her ribs, a deep, swelling panic as she battled surrender and the blaze of heat between them. A deluge of memory and sensation transformed her limbs to water. And when his mouth released hers, she stared at him through a veil of confusion, too weak to wrench away. She felt uncharacteristically helpless, struggling to grasp what was happening to her rebellious flesh. His lips gently brushed her cheeks, her eyelids.

"That is as honest a kiss as you will ever receive, love," he whispered against her hair, his voice hoarse.

She stared up at him, trembling in his arms.

Warm, strong hands slid to her shoulders. "I'll have you, Garnet Winters," he promised softly. "To the finish." His dark eyes held hers and now they were velvety and deep. "But I want it honest, do you understand? The stakes are too high for foolish games."

A shaky laugh passed her bruised lips, scorning his hypocrisy. "What do you know about honesty, Colonel Belaine? Don't speak to me of honesty when you ride in here with your mistress's arms around your waist, when you rush from the dinner table directly to her bed." She wrenched free of his hands and stepped back, her green eyes blazing.

"What the hell are you talking about?" Belaine stared at her, a mixture of anger and bewilderment intensifying his steady gaze.

"Tamala, of course," Garnet snapped. "I know you're"—a fiery blush deepened her embarrassment—"sleeping with her."

This time her tongue had truly run away with her. She thanked God for the darkness.

To her astonishment, Belaine threw back his dark head and laughed. He passed a hand across his eyes and smiled at her through his fingers, his black eyes twinkling. "Is that what this is all about? Tamala?"

Garnet's teeth clenched. She had stumbled into this; she would see it through to the end. "How many women does it take to satisfy you?" she inquired acidly. "Tamala and me and who else?"

"Just you, love. I think. You won't give me the opportunity to find out." He caught her shoulders again, holding her despite her struggle to twist free. His face sobered, he captured her chin in his hand and forced her to look at him. "Listen to me, Garnet, because I'm going to explain this only once." She lowered her eyes and he shook her slightly, his grip tightening until her flashing eyes lifted to his. "What happened between Tamala and me before you came is none of your business. All you need to know is that nothing exists between us now."

"But you took her upstairs that first night," Garnet insisted hotly. She wanted to believe him, but . . .

"To tell her it was all over."

"But today, when you . . ."

He sighed, as if explaining basic principles to a child. "What would you have me do, love? Cast her aside like a book that's been read? Never talk to her again? Never look in her direction again? Or would you agree these matters can be handled in an adult and friendly manner?" His eyes bored into hers in a pointed stare. "By all concerned."

Garnet stared into his eyes and tried to read beyond the velvety warmth. She bit her lip uncertainly. If he was telling the truth, then Tamala's jealousy was explained. No wonder Tamala hated her. But if she were to trust him and then discover she was just another bead on a long string of women, could she bear the heartbreak? And what of her land and her future and all her high-flown beliefs about marriage and love? A headache began at the base of her neck as her emotions spun in winds of turmoil.

Belaine drew her gently against his body, cradling her loosely in his arms. "Would you like to begin the evening again, love?" he asked softly. "And this time we'll play it honestly?"

She was honest enough to concede the game. She hadn't the fortitude to play. "Please, I . . . I really thought that you and . . ." She felt like a fool. And she was incapable of thinking with his powerful arms around her. Belaine possessed an uncanny talent to penetrate her defenses and touch something she didn't want disturbed. The knowledge shocked her. Did all women fixate on the first man to awaken them? Did all women dream the experience again and again? Or was there something dreadfully wrong with her?

Her future had been so clear-cut and satisfactory. Then Belaine had intruded into her thoughts, both waking and asleep, and suddenly nothing seemed absolute anymore.

She pulled away from him, gathering her skirts for flight. "Jean, please. I've been a fool tonight and I ask your forgiveness. But . . ." Minutes ago she'd been cursing him; now she was apologizing. Something in the island air sent emotions swinging like a pendulum. "I'd rather be alone for a while."

His eyes flickered with momentary disappointment, then he bowed. "As you wish."

Garnet stamped her foot. "Damn it, Belaine. Why must you always make me feel like a bad-tempered child?"

He straightened from his bow and, grinning, said nothing.

Head down and teeth grinding, Garnet dashed into the house, rushing past Paul and Simone and up the staircase. Safely inside her darkened room, she flung herself across the bed and covered her face with shaking hands. If only she knew whether to believe him. And if what he said was true, then what did it mean? Nothing? Everything?

When the drums sounded their seductive throbbing, she cried out and wept tears of confusion and frustration into her pillow, knowing she would not sleep tonight.

—9—

NO ONE ESCAPED THE EXCITEMENT or the rigors of cropping. Rombo pared the house staff to a skeleton crew, ordering the men into the carrys and the women to the field kitchens. All worked except those too ill to move and children too young to walk, and the slave villages emptied before sunrise. Double shifts rotated in the fields, mills, and boiler houses. The pounding of field drums was as constantly pervading as the pungent sweet-and-sour smoke puffing from the boiler-house stacks. The smoke clung to hair and clothing, and even the harsh lye soap used by the slaves couldn't obliterate the syrupy odor.

Toward the end of the first week, exhaustion dogged everyone's steps and Garnet couldn't conceive how the next two weeks would be endured. Then she inhaled the sugary odor and listened to the clatter of laden wagons rumbling toward the mills, and the excitement returned, lifting weary spirits.

Her spirits had suffered a battering at being banished from Paul and Lille's morning conferences. But she wasn't really surprised by her exclusion. From the first, Paul had strenuously objected to a woman's presence.

"But how will I learn if I can't watch what you do?" Her request had seemed undeniably reasonable, and she had kept after him until he reluctantly conceded.

"Very well, but stay out of the way. Agreed?"

"Agreed." Careful not to flaunt her victory, she had eagerly followed Paul into his study, where Lille waited, examining a map of the plantation unrolled across the top of Paul's mahogany desk.

Paul's study was a large, dim room paneled in orangewood; the odor was that of moldering books and musty draperies. Had the study been hers, Garnet would have encased the books behind protective glass, burned the aging draperies, and added a wall of windows to admit more light. The only items worth salvaging were chairs dating back to her grandfather's time, upholstered in buttery soft leather. Choosing one, she sat demurely and folded her hands in her lap after nodding coolly to Lille. And she listened sharply as Paul and the overseer planned the day's strategy, deciding which carrys to cut first, where to locate the field kitchens, how many people and wagons would be required and in which fields. A smaller crew was needed to hone the machetes, repair the carts, and replenish water supplies. And everything must be accomplished without interrupting the cutting, for once the harvest began, it was a race against time. And the weather.

As the men talked Garnet had quietly risen and gradually edged nearer until her skirts brushed the desk and she, too, could see the map. Her eyebrows arched in surprise.

"Why are you beginning near the mill?" A slim finger touched the X's drawn on the map. "If we're trying to beat the rain, why not begin out here?" She touched the outlying fields with her fingernail. "Then, if the rain does come, the farthest fields are finished. The crews would have less distance to transport the cane if we work toward the mill rather than away from it."

Both men had stopped talking. They stared at her.

"That seems far more sensible to me," she said stubbornly, resenting the censure in their expressions.

Lille covered a snort behind a dirty hand and his watery blue gaze slid to Paul.

"We have always done it this way, cousin. Call it tradition if you like." He turned back to Lille.

"If a tradition is foolish, it should be changed."

Paul lowered the papers in his hands, flushing at the sly amusement in Lille's hunched shoulders. His jaw tightened. "It was my impression, cousin, that you wished to observe. I didn't realize you considered yourself competent enough to issue directives."

Warm pink climbed from the ruffles of Garnet's morning gown. Her chin lifted and she returned his level stare coldly. "I'm entitled to an opinion, I think, as half the profits—or half the loss—is mine."

"A state of affairs you are continually reminding me of, cousin," Paul snapped.

Garnet ignored Lille's darting eyes. The loathsome little man was clearly enjoying this glimpse into the inner stresses of the manor. Though she suspected the conversation would be reported along the dockside pubs in Port-au-Prince, she refused to curb her tongue. "It appears you need reminding, Monsieur le comte. Occasionally you seem to forget that you are not the sole owner."

Anger flushed Paul's face, then paled it to the color of his hair. "Your opinion has been duly noted, mademoiselle. Now pray allow us to continue."

"Am I to understand the threat of rain does not concern you?" Garnet's hands gripped the edge of the desk.

An irritated explosion of sound puffed Paul's cheeks. "You've been listening to Belaine, haven't you?" He glanced at Lille's averted eyes and strove for patience. "The Habitation Belaine is near Cap Français, a hard three-day ride from here, with a chain of mountains between. The weather is much different there from what it is here. I suggest you bear this in mind when judging the colonel's expertise."

"I hope you are correct, because the ditches are still clogged." Cold green eyes regarded Lille with contempt. "And because you appear to be conducting this operation"—her finger tapped the map—"as if you expect hot, dry weather for another month. For the sake of my purse and your own, I pray you are right."

Paul drank heavily from his rum glass as she gathered her skirts and, head held high, swept from the study. "I proceed with full confidence," he insisted loudly before the door closed behind her.

Garnet sought refuge in the drawing room, unwilling to face Simone until her heart had ceased its angry hammering. Not for the first time she questioned the wisdom of waiting until the harvest was over before she laid official claim to her estate. From the look of it, she could have organized the cutting as efficiently as Paul—possibly more so. She was preparing to run upstairs and change clothing when Paul charged into the drawing room.

He grabbed her wrist and spun her to face him, his features tight with fury. Bending so near her face that a fine mist sprayed across her cheeks, he hissed, "If you ever again embarrass me in front of my subordinates, I'll . . ."

"You'll what?" Resolutely she faced him, overcoming the urge to wrench away. They stood close enough that she could see the tiny broken veins fanning out across his cheekbones.

"I'll . . ." He stared into her blazing green eyes, then his gaze dropped to the rapid rise and fall of her breast and his expression changed. "God, you're beautiful when you're angry," he breathed. "A goddess."

"Let go of me." Disgusted, Garnet jerked at her hand, but his grip only tightened. Suddenly he yanked her forward, pressing her hard against his body so that she could feel the hot thrust of his desire.

He spoke against her hair and his words were thick and husky. "I know what you want. I could make you scream and scratch." His fingers clamped around her wrist and pulled her hand down, pushing it between them until she was forced to touch him.

Garnet's lips curled in revulsion. She kicked him as hard as she could, at the same time twisting her hand free and jumping back from him. The kick had done no more than startle, her slipper no match for his heavy leather boots. "Rombo," she called loudly, stopping Paul's forward step. "Rombo, I need you."

Rombo appeared so quickly that Garnet uneasily suspected he had been standing just beyond the arch. "*Oui*, Missy Ga'net?" His expressionless gaze moved from Paul's flushed face to Garnet's wary frown.

"Order up carriage plenty much quick for Missy S'mone and me, *oui* and *oui*." She turned to Paul, her body stiffening, and her tone glacial. "You do remember Simone, don't you—your wife?"

Paul's smile was ugly. "Isn't she the one with the figure like a boy and the smile of an angel for everyone but her husband?" A hand rose to straighten his cravat. "Ice does not interest me, cousin. Fire does."

A flash of insight steadied her shaking hands. "Or perhaps control is what interests you." She met his stare. "Perhaps your interest in me extends no further than my land."

Again his blue eyes raked across her body. And Garnet swallowed, believing that if Rombo had not stood beside her, Paul would have crossed the room and taken her forcibly in his arms.

"With a little encouragement, cousin, I could prove otherwise."

"You won't receive it," she had snapped, whirling from the room.

Now, sitting at the breakfast table and listening to the murmuring voices in Paul's study, Garnet wondered if she would have been wiser to remain silent that first day. Had she held her tongue, the scene with Paul would have been avoided, and she would now be in the study learning about cropping instead of brooding over her plate.

Lifting her head, she looked at the sunshine gleaming through Jean's dark hair. She'd scarcely seen him since the cropping began. And perhaps that was best. She needed time to realign her defenses, to convince herself nothing had happened between them worth altering her future for. "Will they finish cutting before the rains?" she asked him, leaning to one side as Rombo filled her coffee cup. Rombo performed the menial duties as his staff worked in the fields or scrubbed the ballroom in preparation for Simone's celebration.

"I doubt it." Jean Belaine extended his cup to Rombo and his dark eyes strayed to the window, contemplating the long lines of women departing for the carrys, pots and produce balanced atop their snowy kerchiefs.

"I hope you're wrong." Garnet shredded a raisin bun between her fingers. Today Jean wore dove-colored breeches and a pale linen shirt instead of his uniform. At cutting time the streets of Port-au-Prince were as quiet as a tomb; the regular militia strolled the lanes in boredom. Jean had granted himself and his men an extended leave.

"Of course he's wrong," Simone commented gaily. "This year is going to be the biggest harvest ever—I just feel it. And when it's over, we'll go home to France. This year—we'll go home." She watched Belaine's unwavering gaze focused on the departing women and her gaiety clouded with sympathy. "You miss being part of it, don't you?" she asked softly, reaching to cover Belaine's hand.

"God, yes." His jaw tensed and his fingers formed into a fist beneath Simone's hand. "The drums in your ears, that peculiar sweet, dusty smell, the swing of a machete." A crooked smile curved his lips as he looked at the women. "Once a cane man, always a cane man."

Paul spoke from the archway. "What a charming scene. My wife clinging to my best friend. Again." His eyes narrowed as he toasted them with his mug. "Don't break apart on my account." When he'd seated himself and drained his rum cup, he rubbed at the weariness in his eyes, then snapped his fingers for breakfast. "Someone should receive the benefit of her favors—God knows she doesn't grant them to me."

Simone's fingers trembled as she smothered a gasp, and a rush of crimson stained her pale cheeks.

Jean laid aside his napkin. "That was uncalled for, Paul."

"Do you propose to lecture me on domestic affairs, too, Jean?" Fatigue and rum honed Paul's temper to a razor edge. "Or shall we confine our discussions to the haphazard management of this plantation?" His stare made Garnet think of an arctic lake.

"As you wish." Jean's black eyes assumed a granite bluntness. "If you spent less time at your club and more in the fields, you might notice the ditches are still clogged."

"I am damned sick and tired of hearing about the ditches. Lille says they are clear."

"Has Lille also told you that his men cut the wrong field yesterday? Most of the stalks arriving at the mill were sour, coming from young fields that needed another six months to ripen."

"Christ!"

Jean leaned back in his chair, relaxing. "And if you'll trouble yourself to glance into your boiler house, you'll discover vats of juice about to ferment—you're going to lose them. Damn little juice is running into the curing tanks because the temperature is wrong."

Garnet studied him soberly. Whatever else Jean Belaine might be, he knew cane. Now she understood where he'd been during the last hectic days, inspecting the harvest from field to mill to curing house. A task Paul seemed to disdain.

Paul's lip curled. "Boil the juice and you ruin it."

"And if the temperature is too low, the best you can hope for is low quality—if it sets up at all." The men regarded each other across the breakfast table. "Your scummers face an endless job. Unless the temperature comes up, the bubbles are never going to clear."

Paul shoved his plate aside. "Is this true?" he asked bluntly.

Belaine's eyes flickered a warning, then his shoulders flexed and he raised the hand that had dropped to his scabbard.

"Before you question any further, I suggest you ride out and see for yourself."

"By God, I will." Paul filled his mug and slammed the rum bottle against the tabletop. "Nothing is going to jeopardize this harvest. Not this year." His glare dared Simone or Garnet to refute his statement. Neither did. After a moment he swung toward Garnet, his mouth an unpleasant twist. "You agree with Jean, don't you? You think I'm mismanaging this plantation."

Garnet felt the eyes of the men on her. But this wasn't a propitious moment to voice her objections, not when everyone was tired and upset. She exchanged a quick glance with Simone, reading the plea in her cousin's eyes. Slowly she added cream to her coffee, considering her answer. "In truth, Paul, I don't know what to think." She felt rather than saw Jean's frown. "I know you want a good harvest, as we all do." Attempting to smile, she maintained a light tone. "I guess time will tell."

"You're goddamned right it will." Disgusted, Paul hurled his empty mug to the floor. Expressionless, Rombo bent to the mess as Paul's moody gaze swept the table. He chewed the edge of his thumbnail. "Perhaps it will put your mind at rest if you see for yourself what's happening in the fields."

"I intend to."

"What better time than right now?"

Garnet considered for a moment. "I accept. But," she added hastily, "only if we all go." Under no circumstances would she be alone with Paul.

"Agreed." Simone rose from the table. "If you'll order up the carriage for Garnet and me, gentlemen, we'll be only a moment." She led the way to the staircase. "We'll need wide hats and our long gloves. The sun is hot."

Upstairs, Josephine resisted, her fists on plump hips, her broad face tight with disapproval. "Cane field no be-me plenty good place for fine white lady, no and no."

Josephine would have been laboring in the fields had

Garnet not firmly countermanded Rombo's orders. The experience had been a heady one. Rombo continued to unnerve her with his carefully blanked eyes, which, Garnet suspected, concealed a shrewd, quick mind.

"Missy Tam'la go fields, *oui* and *oui*, but you be-you white, sun and dust no plenty much good for you skin."

Garnet looked at Josephine in the mirror. "Missy Tam'la be-her in fields?" She hadn't thought about Tamala's whereabouts until this moment. Thinking back, she tried to recall when last Tamala had appeared at the dining-room table.

Josephine adjusted Garnet's hat to a saucy angle, surrendering grudgingly. After casting a careful glance over her shoulder, she leaned to Garnet's ear. "Missy Tam'la placing powerful plenty much spell for big good crop." She nodded conspiratorially. "Bad spells no be-me worth dirt, no and no. Josephine no believe bad spells, no be-me stupid plenty much." Her white kerchief bobbed. "But good spells work plenty much, *oui* and *oui*. Missy Tam'la make good spell to stop rain hurry-up-quick."

"I see." Garnet had previously tried and failed to convince Josephine of the inconsistencies in her reasoning. Josephine patiently insisted there was nothing contradictory in her thinking.

But of course there was. Josephine constantly disavowed any interest in *vodun*, yet clearly she lauded Tamala's talents as a powerful *mambo*. Garnet thought the girl too sensible to be taken in by cornmeal drawings and the peculiar burned bags containing heaven knew what that occasionally appeared on the veranda steps.

On the other hand, if Tamala wished to ride over the plantation nailing up painted gourds and burning twigs at the base of rock formations, at least it kept her away from the manor and the dinner table. Anything that accomplished that feat was a blessing in Garnet's view.

Dismissing Tamala from her mind, Garnet pulled on her gloves and ran downstairs to join the others.

*   *   *

A ceiling of dust overhung the road, thrown up in hot, choking clouds by the wagons rushing back and forth between the carrys and the mill. Naked children darted between the spinning wagon wheels, shouting happily and sucking on stubs of cane. The juice cut tracks across their dusty grins. A steady stream of women hurried from the field kitchens and into the fields, pots of stew balanced on their heads, pails of cool water swinging from the yokes bowing their shoulders. Twigs cut from the sour-orange tree protruded from the women's mouths, brushing the taste of cane from teeth and tongues. The steady pounding of field drums rose from both sides of the road, as driving and relentless as the blazing sun overhead.

Garnet watched it all with a golden glow of excitement sparkling in her eyes. Noise deafened her ears, the shouts and drums and cracking whips. And the pace was exhausting, a pace that left men shaking. They fell to the ground in crumpled heaps when finally the next shift appeared, not stirring until the women propped them up and goaded them toward the pallets along the road, provided for those too fatigued to endure the walk to the villages.

She watched everything through wide green eyes and she vacillated between excitement and pity for the weary creatures moving through the fields.

Simone placed a hand on her arm, and when Garnet shifted on the carriage seat, Simone smiled and nodded at Jean, whose white stallion pranced alongside the carriage.

Jean studied the field operations with a sharp, hard expression midway between yearning and frustration. One hand gripped the reins; the other slapped lightly at his thigh.

In contrast, Paul seldom glanced toward the fields. He rode on the opposite side of the carriage, coiled in silence.

Garnet shaded her eyes and followed the direction of Jean's gaze. Rows of shirtless men swung heavy machetes near the ground, then, grunting in unison with the field drums, they topped the stalks with two quick strokes before stepping forward in a half shuffle to repeat the process. The strongest women followed behind, bunching the severed stalks, then carrying them atop their heads to a line of wagons waiting to rush the cane to the mills before the juice soured to acid in the stalk.

The harvest was nearing the end of the first week; movements had become mechanical, the men dulled by heavy fatigue. Bare feet dragged, machetes dropped rather than swung. The mounting exhaustion from days of fourteen-hour shifts showed in sweat-drenched faces and stiff, bowed backs.

Garnet ached, watching the intense effort before her. But she also experienced a sudden understanding for Belaine's yearning to be part of it. She peeked at him from beneath her hat brim, and her heart turned over in her breast. If he ever directed such a hard look of smoldering intensity at her, she doubted she could have resisted him. She read the longing in his tight expression.

Paul threw out his hands. "Oh, for Christ's sake, Belaine. Go ahead—go out there like a common piece of white trash. Swing a machete, sweat until you drop, and enjoy yourself."

Belaine grinned at Paul and then at the women. "By God, I will." His velvety eyes gleamed with anticipation as he jumped from his horse and stripped off his shirt, flexing bared muscles until they swelled and rippled. He started to tie his horse to the back of the carriage.

"Never mind, I'll ride him back to the manor." Garnet stepped from the carriage, laughing at Simone's gentle expression of reproof. But her smile faded abruptly as Jean's strong hands circled her waist, holding her a fraction too long before he swung her past his broad, naked chest and up onto the saddle. Swallowing, she looked down at his grin, her eyes dropping to the scar at his side. She had forgotten how large the old wound was.

Simone was staring at the scar as well. Her brow tightened in concern. "Do you think you really should?"

Jean laughed, his thoughts already on the cane. "Don't worry, little mother, I'm doing what I want to do." He jumped the ditch then and lifted a machete from a supply cart, hefting it in his hand, testing the weight and balance. And because he was Belaine, not a man failed to respond to his presence. Shoulders straightened and eyes sharpened. Belaine strode into the field, the sun hot and glistening on his bronzed back, and he took his place in the first row, where the pace was set. "A gold louis to the man who can cut more cane than I can before the sun sets."

A shout rose in the field, then drums rolled and machetes flashed. New vigor quickened the steps of the men behind Belaine.

Garnet shaded her eyes against the glare and watched his arms swell as the machete rose and fell and the line of men crept forward. A lump of sentimentality lodged in her throat at the beauty of the scene, the pageantry and color. She watched until Belaine's black curls plastered wetly to his brow, until sweat oiled his chest and back, until the joyous concentration in his face released nervous butterflies in her stomach. Only then did she bite her lip and hastily urge the stallion after the carriage.

When they next stopped, Garnet's gaze followed the drainage grid leading away from the road. Nearly all the ditches were clogged with brush and debris. Many of the women threw the toppings into the ditches rather than stack them near the road for burning. If the gullies weren't cleared before the rains, the fields would be flooded.

Angrily Garnet pointed to the ditches with the tip of her parasol and glowered at Paul. "Are these the ditches Lille swore were clear?"

"Damn it." Paul removed his hat and wiped the back of his glove across his brow, then waved aside the cup of water Simone extended from the carriage.

Garnet was about to demand that men be pulled from the cutting and reassigned to the ditches. But she glanced at

Paul's face and bit back the words, deciding on discretion instead. Silently she accepted a cup of water from Simone, and both women regarded the field, hoping to avoid becoming targets of Paul's rage. Cursing steadily, Paul spurred his mount along the side of the road, glaring at the ditches.

Simone looked at the sky, then blotted her brow with a scrap of lemon-scented lace. She drew a breath. "This will be a fine harvest, a bigger harvest than ever before." She spread her skirts over the carriage seat and adjusted the ribbon tied beneath her chin to secure her hat. "The very best harvest ever." If she said it often enough, it would be true.

Unaccustomed to curbing her tongue, Garnet stared into the ditches and silently voiced the tart comments pushing at her lips. She swiveled on the saddle when she heard Paul's furious shout.

"*You* there. What do you think you're doing, leaving the field?"

Garnet inhaled sharply and, behind her, heard a gasp as Simone rose to her feet in the carriage.

Moving awkwardly, four of the field slaves negotiated the ditch, carrying a man strapped to a board. One of the man's legs was opened to the bone beneath his knee; blood soaked his trouser leg and dripped into the dust.

"Machete slip, massa." The men laid their companion on the side of the road and swept their hats from sweat-soaked heads. "Leke be-him need help plenty much bad, hurry-up-quick, massa." The man who spoke waved a hand behind him, indicating the black field overseer. "Nesta, him say-us take Leke hurry-up-quick to village, say me *oui*."

Paul cursed beneath his breath, then clenched his teeth and glared at Garnet. "See what we're up against? We'll never finish in time if four men leave the fields every time some little thing happens."

Garnet stared at him, unwilling to believe what her ears registered. Then she stifled a scream as Paul slid from his horse and stalked toward the fallen man, probing roughly at the man's leg with his boot tip. The man shrieked. When Garnet opened her eyes, Paul had jerked his musket from the holster on his saddle. He walked to the man on the board, lowered the barrel, and squeezed the trigger.

"*No.*" Garnet and Simone screamed in unison, their shock lost in the noise of the explosion.

Red dots sprayed across Garnet's vision. A spasm of violent shaking swept her body and she gripped the saddle to prevent herself from falling. From the corner of her lashes she saw Simone drop limply to the carriage seat and cover her eyes. Gasping, Garnet raised her face to the hot, empty sweep of sky, then lowered her lashes slowly. It was not a nightmare, not an aberrant fantasy.

The field drums faltered, then steadied, and the dark spines bent, machetes flashing in the blazing sunlight. The work continued as if nothing had occurred. The men who had carried their friend to the roadside stared at their bare toes. Nostrils flared and hats were crushed in squeezing fingers, but no one spoke. And their blank, blank faces were the worst of all. Garnet swallowed hard, battling a scalding nausea.

"Back to work," Paul shouted.

They stared at the musket, then turned as one and jumped the clogged drainage ditch, shuffling toward the lines of men swinging through the cane.

"That was . . ." Garnet stuttered, shock tumbling the words in her head. Her lips moved like chips of wood. "You . . . you *murdered* that man." She couldn't believe it, could not bear to glance at the bloodied man sprawled at her horse's feet. Her stomach burned and knotted, shudders of denial clawing along her spine.

"Oh, please, cousin. No melodramatics. I ended the misery of a wounded animal." Paul's angry glance scanned the fields as he swung onto his saddle and smugly holstered the musket. "And sent four slackers back to work. You wanted efficiency? I gave you efficiency."

"Oh, Paul." Simone looked at him from between the fingers of her gloves, her face ashen.

"What the hell is the matter with you two?"

"You really don't understand, do you?" Garnet whispered. A loaded wagon spun out behind them, spraying small rocks and dust over the dead man. Already flies had gathered. She couldn't understand why no one took away the man's body. Then she realized that no one would, not while the masters looked on. Yanking on the reins, she jerked the stallion's head toward the manor, departing without a word.

But Paul refused to leave the matter alone. He spurred his mount to catch her, his face as red and furious as her own was white and sickened.

"What I've done, cousin, is save precious time." The words were spaced evenly, an effort to control his temper before the blacks. "It's a simple problem of economics."

Economics? God in heaven. Garnet chose the only weapon she believed he might understand. "Ah, yes, economics. And is it a wise practice to destroy your labor force? What did that man cost? A thousand livres? Two thousand? How many sacks of sugar must we refine and sell to pay for him and for his replacement? How many gallons of rum?" Revulsion shadowed her flashing eyes. "No wonder profits vanish. You murder them." She swung her leg across the saddle, riding astride despite her frothy skirts, and dug in her heels. She couldn't stand the sight of Paul's rum-ruined face another instant.

Wagons careened in the dust and cane spilled onto the roadside as the drivers attempted to avoid colliding with the two dodging horses.

"Bleeding hearts," Paul hissed when he overtook her. "You and Simone—nothing but goddamned bleeding hearts. Don't you know the Africans would slice your throat in an instant? And you think they're human. *Christ.*"

Garnet cracked her parasol across the horse's flank and

swore under her breath as a wagon veered in front of her and the stallion reared.

"You haven't been here a month, but you know all there is to know about running a cane plantation. Well, let me tell you this, cousin. I've been here eight long, miserable years and I don't have all the answers. What in bloody hell makes you think you do?"

She knew she was being goaded and she vowed not to respond, but the answer came anyway. "I have eyes in my head," she shouted. "I know when a house needs paint. I know men and women can't live productively on what you feed them. I know they can't survive long in the middle of filth and despair and torture." She ground her teeth against the clouds of dust, wishing the road was clear, wishing the blank faces driving the wagons were not so silent. "And I know you take a sick pleasure in these people's torment. It makes you feel superior, doesn't it?" She shouted above the noise, her lips pulled back from her teeth. "Of course they'd slice your throat. Wouldn't you do the same?"

His offensive laugh belittled her. "Wisdom from the distaff side." He licked his lips and wiped his chin, and the need for a drink narrowed his eyes. "You don't understand a damned thing."

She eased up on the reins and looked at him fully, her eyes cold chips of emerald stone. "I understand you aren't fit to manage a plantation." She didn't care what he thought; the moment for truth was long past.

Both had slowed nearly to a halt. Neither was aware of the wagons blocked in a long line behind them.

"Well, then, cousin, the problem becomes simple, doesn't it?" he snapped. "You manage your own plantation and good riddance."

"That suits me fine."

His eyes glittered and Garnet sucked in her breath. Her anger aroused him, the flush in her face, the hard pinpoints of fury flashing in her eyes.

"The minute the cutting ends, I'll have a solicitor draw up the papers." He licked his lips hungrily, his bloodshot eyes savaging her heaving breast.

If she'd had a longer parasol, she would have slashed it across his face. "Agreed. In the meantime . . . until we decide what belongs to whom . . . don't murder any more people." Each word emerged like a crack of a whip.

He laughed and patted his horse's neck. "Look at it this way, cousin. I killed only my half—your half is still good, except for a machete wound." He shrugged, his laugh ending in a wide grin.

She stared at him and gagged. Then she bent low over the horse's mane and raced toward the manor as if the devil nipped at her heels.

—10—

"I NEED TO TALK TO YOU." Garnet had chosen the moment carefully, appearing in the dining-room archway as dinner concluded. A hasty glance revealed her precaution had been unnecessary. After the morning incident Paul had departed for his club in Port-au-Prince and hadn't returned yet.

"I rather thought you might." Jean blotted his lips and rose from the table. He bowed to Simone. "Will you excuse me?"

"Oh, Garnet," Simone sighed. Distress misted her large gray eyes as she pushed distractedly at the mass of chestnut hair. "I'm so sorry for the ugliness—I wish there was something . . ."

Garnet touched her cousin's satin shoulder and felt Simone's warm fingers move to cover her own. "I wish so, too, Simone." It would be unjust to place Simone between her husband and her convictions by railing against Paul. Garnet drew a breath and looked up at Jean; there was no one else.

"Outside?" he asked, lifting a dark eyebrow.

"It would be more private." A flush of pink colored Garnet's cheeks and she pressed her lips together, waiting for a teasing remark that would twist her comment into an innuendo.

Instead he offered his arm in silence and neither spoke until they had followed the pathway to the entrance of the banana grove. To distract her thoughts from the warm strength beneath her fingers, Garnet counted the torches flickering

151

along the path, absently noting a misty halo surrounding the flames. She listened to the hiss of the fire and to the whisper of her skirts brushing across the bricks.

"You've had an eventful day." Jean paused before the wrought-iron bench positioned just off the path. Leaning against a tree trunk, he withdrew a cigar from his dinner jacket as Garnet seated herself and arranged her skirts.

"You know what happened, then." A distant glow of torches illuminated the fields, flickering along the western horizon like an afterglow of sunset. The relentless heartbeat of the field drums throbbed beneath the buzz of the insects flitting about the torches. The harvest continued.

"Yes."

"Is that all you can say?" Garnet's fan opened and snapped shut across her breast. She felt like a volcano building toward explosion, all strange rumblings and fire. Removing a handkerchief from her lace cuff, she blotted her forehead. The air was heavy and still tonight, the heat oppressive.

"What is it you want, Garnet? Do you want me to say you were right to make a scene?"

"It's the principal—Paul murdered that man." She wished he would stand out of the shadows; she wanted to observe his expression. The tip of his cigar glowed, then faded. "Well, *was* I right?"

"Yes . . . and no."

"That's no answer. Damn it, Belaine." Biting her lips, she glared at a pale blur above the snowy outline of his cravat.

"Yes, because your instincts are admirable. And no, because St. Domingue exhibits no esteem for admirable instincts." He crossed his boots at the ankle and smoked in silence. "There's no point in debating morality, as we view it the same way."

She had guessed as much from the moment she'd learned his plans for the estate he had purchased in New Orleans.

"This economy is dependent upon slave labor, Garnet."

"I don't want to discuss economy."

"And that isn't going to change. Not without violence. If Paris orders St. Domingue to free the slaves, St. Domingue will secede from France. It's that clear-cut."

"But what's happening here is wrong." Her hands lifted. "Murder, torture . . . ." Everything Simone had said was correct. St. Domingue was ugly, a poisoned paradise. Garnet blinked back the moisture springing into her eyes and raised her face to the dark sky. A flash of heat lightning opened and closed the night.

"If you're thinking about experimenting with emancipation, I'd strongly advise you to reconsider, love."

It was exactly what she was planning. Startled, Garnet shifted on the bench, her jaw set in a stubborn line.

"It won't work, Garnet."

"You plan to employ free labor in New Orleans."

"We're not discussing New Orleans. We're discussing St. Domingue, and emancipation won't work here."

"Why not?"

A tiny glowing point arched over the nearest torch and spun into the banana grove. Belaine stepped from the shadows, placed his boot against the bench, and leaned his forearm on his raised knee, looking down at her.

Another crack of lightning splintered the sky. "The planters will kill you less than twenty-four hours after you announce your intention." The hard edge of truth roughened his voice.

She pressed a hand to her forehead. "But why? You employ free blacks at the Habitation Belaine—you told me so."

"André's actions are not a threat because he's a mulatto. As such, he's setting no precedent. Also, André has freed his people over a period of years. And he's not a stranger to this island."

It was pointless to argue. "It isn't fair. None of this is right."

"No. It isn't."

The exhaustion of long, tiring days overwhelmed her. She surrendered momentarily to the weary succession of crowded days and late nights, to emotions that soared one minute and shrank the next. Her head tilted back and the long fringe of dark lashes closed. Everything had seemed so simple in Boston, so uncomplicated.

In a short span her life had utterly changed; nothing was simple anymore. The blacks worshiped her as a goddess— and that was dangerous. Tamala hated her—and Tamala was a *mambo*, both revered and feared. Paul was furious with her. And she didn't know if she was truly prepared to assume the management of a large plantation.

When her green eyes blinked open, she discovered Jean staring at her with a thoughtful expression. "Did I tell you that I came here seeking adventure?" A tiny smile tugged at her full lips. The idea seemed ridiculous and adolescent. A frothy little bubble formed in her throat. "But it's so dull in St. Domingue—have you noticed?" She pressed her fingers against her lips, smothering a rush of ironic laughter. "Nothing ever happens."

"Nothing at all." He grinned.

They looked at each other and smiled, and suddenly both were laughing. Garnet clamped a hand to her ribs and then to her lips, but it was hopeless. The laughter emerged in choking gusts. Tears streamed down her cheeks. "So terribly dull and uneventful." She gasped. Struggling from the bench, she held to his arm; nothing helped. The laughter welled up from deep inside, cleansing and wonderful.

She wiped her eyes and held her breath, blinking at the sputtering torches, her tears of laughter spreading rainbows across the strange halos.

Still smiling, Jean grasped her lightly by the shoulders. "Surely you didn't spit on me just now. Did you, love?"

"There have been times when I've wanted to, but no, I didn't." A splash of water struck her cheek and she touched it with surprise, blinking foolishly at the dampness on her fingers.

They froze as a boom of thunder rolled over their heads.

"My God," Garnet breathed. Her heart lurched in her breast. Spinning, she stared at the glow along the horizon, watching as the torches dimmed. She could no longer hear the field drums.

A monstrous clap of thunder exploded across the sky, and she jumped. The ground vibrated; the air quivered, hot and still. A brilliant fork of lightning speared the sky, and the smell of burned wood lingered behind. A droplet the size of a child's fist slapped the bricks near Garnet's hem. And then another, falling like fat stones.

"Rain," she whispered. Her thoughts shied from the fields as she lifted her skirts in dismay. Before she could dash back to the house, her gown would be soaked.

"Over here," Jean ordered. Catching her hand, he pulled her into the banana grove, seeking the protection of the thick overhang. "Sometimes the first storm passes quickly."

They waited beside a thick, twisted trunk, watching as the torches sputtered and died out. "I think this storm will last awhile," Garnet predicted uneasily.

The storm broke around them with the sudden ferocity of a tropical downpour. In a blink, the bench was obscured by a curtain of hard, slanting rain. Water gushed over the bricks and gouged rivulets into the floor of the grove.

They retreated deeper into the sheltering trees. The feathery fronds overhead filtered the largest drops, but a constant chill spray showered down on them.

Garnet pushed at tendrils of wet hair curling about her face and sticking to her cheeks. The curls on her crown sagged, then toppled down her back, showering hairpins around her slippers. Slowly her silk bodice darkened and molded damply against her skin; her nipples protruded like small buttons. Self-consciously she crossed her arms over her breast and shivered. A chill rippled along her flesh as the temperature steadily dropped with a rapidity that surprised her.

"We should have made a run for the veranda," she said dismally. "My gown is ruined anyway." The earth had dissolved to mud. Her wet gown lay cold and clammy against her skin.

Jean sank to the ground, his back propped against a tree trunk. "We'll have to wait it out. Are you cold?"

Her teeth were chattering. The abrupt change from hot to cold had taken her unaware. She rubbed her arms and stamped her feet, hoping to restore the warmth of circulation. Mud seeped into her silk slippers.

"Here." Shrugging out of his satin dinner jacket, Belaine handed it to her.

She accepted with alacrity. "Thank you." It smelled of spiced cologne. And it was damp. She lifted her wet hair over the collar and glanced upward, squinting. Water poured from the blackness in a torrent; the spray filtering past the banana fronds seemed heavier, colder.

"Come here, love." Jean opened his arms.

Delaying, Garnet held her breath and shivered. She remembered the last time she had lain in his arms. A weakness stole through her limbs. "I . . . I don't . . ."

"You don't have to be afraid." He smiled. "I like comfort, remember?" Water dripped down his sunburned face, and black curls lay plastered against his broad forehead. "I've never yet ravished a woman in a mud hole."

She returned his smile. "Well, you counseled honesty—and I'm honestly cold."

He laughed. "Then come here and get honestly warmed."

Good sense warned against complying, but she was thoroughly chilled. After hesitating only a moment, Garnet sighed and dropped to the ground, burrowing into the shelter of his arms with embarrassing eagerness, clamping her teeth to prevent them from chattering in his ear. He gathered her tightly against the hard, solid warmth of his chest.

"Better?"

She nodded, her face pressed into the damp hollow of his neck. There was no help for it; she would have to trust his intentions.

"Liar. I can feel you shaking." Before she could protest, Jean lifted her onto his lap, the mud from her gown smearing across his white breeches.

"I'm fine where I am." But she adjusted herself gratefully against his firm body, snuggling into his warmth and shivering, smelling the rich, disturbingly good male scent.

His arms tightened, and he pressed her head against his shoulder. His lips brushed her hair.

Garnet froze, listening to the strong, steady pulse beneath her ear. Had it been accidental? She didn't dare move lest he interpret her adjustment as encouragement. She wanted to jump to her feet and run. She told herself so. Even considering the distance to the veranda, she doubted the rain could do more damage than it already had. But she didn't move from his arms.

A damp carpet of dark hair lay beneath her fingertips where her hand touched his opened collar. And as she felt the warm, firm flow of muscle and bronzed skin, she wondered where his cravat had disappeared to. Her stomach tensed and she was suddenly aware that her breast thrust against his chest with each strangled breath. Face flaming, she silently questioned if he could feel her nipples rising hard against her bodice. As she could. Desperately she decided to run for the veranda. This was sheer madness.

He murmured something against her hair that she didn't hear. The rain pounded the banana fronds like drumbeats, blotting sound and blanketing the night. Heavy drops battered the pathway bricks, rattled the fronds above their heads, hammered into the earth. Wind hurled the rain like pebbles.

She lifted her face, wiping at the water clinging to her lashes like diamonds. "What? I didn't hear."

Her movement brought his lips within a heartbeat of her own, and their breath mingled, sweet and intoxicating. And his eyes were deep and warm and velvet. Gently he brushed the raindrops from her cheeks, and shadowed dark velvet embraced her as his hand brushed fire along her face.

"Please, Jean . . . don't!" Something was melting inside, dissolving. A dizziness blurred her vision. And she was suddenly, agonizingly aware of his hard warmth molded against the pressure of her breasts, of his powerful arms enfolding her, of his mouth—oh, God, his mouth—teasing softly along the curve of her lips, almost touching but not quite. His smoldering velvety eyes made love to her, challenged her, invited her to dare forbidden portals, reached into secret spaces and invaded the aching emptiness.

"Oh, please." A tiny sob scalded her throat. She didn't want this. What magic did he have at his command? Those velvet eyes looked into hers and her defenses shattered; raw sensation overran her intellect, and she could no longer think clearly. She could only feel and respond to the dark intensity of his desire.

"Beautiful Garnet . . . witch woman . . . goddess." His breath caressed her lips, as soft and warm as a whisper. Her lashes closed and her head fell back as she moaned. Wind and rain tossed the red hair spilling across his shoulder.

Rain hung from his lashes and from the black hair curling around his face. One strong arm pressed her tightly against him; the other hand slid beneath her breast, not touching her breast, no, and the firm warmth beneath her breast raised a crest of need that swept her breath away. She fought a yearning tremble stealing upward from her thighs. And felt his hand like a searing imprint burning past her wet gown and deep into her flesh.

"Jean . . . don't." Her fingers dug into his shoulders as a stirring rose between his thighs and she felt the thrust of his passion. A small cry of fear and confusion cracked in her throat. This was insanity. The storm raged above and around her, and the rain and the wind penetrated her mind and savaged her emotions. Blood pounded in her head.

"Don't be afraid," he whispered, his voice deep, rich, heavy with emotion.

But she was terrified. Everything she was, everything she

planned to be, was swept aside by a man's touch, by her own body's betrayal. The loss frightened her even as an instinct as old and primitive as the primal storm possessed her body, and she responded helplessly, arching against his fingers, leaning the weight of her breast on his hand, silently begging him to touch her, to end his hesitation. She wanted his hands on her, wanted it with a raw, scraping need, and all the while a corner of her mind urged her to run, to run as far and as fast as she could.

She stared into his face, her eyes as wild and stormy as the black skies. "I don't understand . . . I don't want this . . ." But she did. She wanted his kiss, needed his kiss, and please, please, she wanted it now.

He brushed the streaming hair from her face. "Don't be afraid. You know I won't hurt you." He spoke against her open lips, murmuring soft fire along the rain-wet contours of her mouth.

Her fingers bit into his shoulders and she wanted to scream at him, wanted to strike out at him, wanted his mouth on hers, hard and crushing and as urgent as the wild tides rushing through her veins.

His large hands lifted to cup her face, and he stared deeply into her wet eyes as if searching for something. Then he kissed her softly, stopping the sob in her throat. His tongue explored her eager mouth, and his arms tightened.

Her arms circled his neck, and she returned the increasing pressure of his kiss with a fiery wildness that frightened her.

She wanted him. And the realization shook her to the core of her being. Her shaking flesh wanted him, craved him. His hard lips, rough and demanding on her own, severed her vow not to surrender as surely as a machete cut through cane. Gasping, she let her head fall back as his kisses slid down her throat and found her breast. And she could have stopped him; she could have jumped up and run away. But she didn't.

Instead a low, throaty moan wrenched from her lips and

she pressed his wet head to her panting breast and heard him murmur and thrilled to the deep, hoarse rumble of her name groaning from his hot mouth. And his lips seemed to be everywhere, rain wet and warm and teasing her into a wild urgency she had never dreamed, never felt. The rain no longer chilled her, but sprayed over her face and arms like a warm caress, as if the heat of her body had the power to alter the elements themselves.

He kissed her streaming hair, her eyelids, her parted lips. And she held him so tightly she felt his heart hammering against her own, the rhythms catching, matching in a wildness that swept aside sanity and thought. The storm crashing above their heads dimmed as a furious storm of passion exploded between straining bodies and frantic hands and bruising lips.

"Yes," she whispered hoarsely, helplessly, as his fingers fumbled with the drawstring of his breeches. She flung her arms around his neck, her fingers tangling in his wet hair, his kiss drowning the sob in the back of her throat. She surrendered wildly, refusing to think, refusing anything that extended beyond the commands of her trembling flesh. "Yes, yes, yes . . ."

And then she was raising her skirt, frantically positioning herself above him, her knees sinking unnoticed into the mud on either side of his thighs. He caught her face and kissed her as she had never been kissed, drinking her loveliness, consuming the raw, flaming passion she offered so blindly. His hands cupped her breasts, slid over her bodice and the rain-wet nipples, and found her hips, guiding her onto him.

A small scream of pleasure broke from her lips, snatched away by the wind and wet, and she shuddered deeply as he thrust into her, her fingers digging into his shoulders. He knew, somehow he knew exactly what she needed, what her body quivered to receive and how. Strong fingers rocked her, guided her, led her in slow, agonizing strokes of rapture so deep and pleasurable it seared her mind of all thought. And when she feared she was lost on a tide of stormy emotion, his kisses brought her back, eased her from the edge of explosion only to lead upward again, nibbling and teasing until her groan became a cry for release.

Finally his hands slid up to either side of her breasts, and he rocked her faster, faster, his breath hot and rapid against her lips, and she felt him tense beneath her and she heard the storm howling above and blackness and heat and . . . and . . . oh, yes, and . . . and her body and mind rushed suddenly together and melted into blinding ecstasy.

She leaned her forehead against his, gasping for breath, feeling his hands light and warm on her back, listening to the sounds of hearts gradually quieting.

As her breast stilled she listened to the storm above still raging against the earth. And the chill of the cold rain crept over her skin, a chill not nearly so sharp as the chill frosting her mind. Slowly her eyes opened and she drew slightly away, awkward now as she moved from his lap. Her knees wore a coating of cold mud. And the mud horrified her. She covered her face and wrenched aside when Jean gently attempted to pull her hands down and away.

"Garnet?"

They had rutted in the mud like two wild animals, oblivious of the rain or of the need for privacy. Like animals. The thought sickened her. Like crazed animals, aware only of their need for each other.

"Garnet?"

"Don't touch me." She couldn't look at him. Shame pierced to her soul. Her hair streamed down her back; her sodden gown hung in ruin. And there was mud on her knees.

Water streaked her cheeks, whether tears or rain she didn't know. "Oh, my God," she whispered, her voice wild, hoarse, frantic. "What have we done?" Scrambling, responding to a primitive need, she pulled to her feet, recoiling from the icy mud in her slippers.

Panting, she trembled before him poised for flight, her

breast heaving. And she shoved at the hair falling past her
eyes, painting muddy streaks where her fingers touched.

Jean sat against the tree trunk, looking up at her. His dark
eyes locked on hers, puzzled and expectant.

"Please . . . I . . ." She struggled from his jacket and flung
it near him. Rain dripped from her hair, her lashes. "You
promised you wouldn't hurt me," she blurted. Thunder exploded above her head and she covered her ears, believing it
was the sound of her pride shattering. Or her honor. Like
animals—oh, God, she couldn't stand it, couldn't bear the
images pounding at her brain.

"Did I hurt you?" he asked quietly.

She stared at him through her fingers, at the softness in his
dark velvet eyes, and a sob broke past her lips. He didn't
understand, he couldn't. Her fists clenched over her eyes
before she could look at him again.

"I wanted forever—I didn't want a mindless coupling in a
mud pit," she cried harshly. She felt like a whore trading her
favors wherever the client demanded. "I didn't want this."

He regarded her silently, then he responded. "Nothing is
forever, Garnet. Not the way you mean."

She flinched as if he had struck her. Sobbing wildly, her
hair swinging in limp wet tendrils around her shoulders, she
clutched her skirts and staggered blindly through the mud and
rain until she tripped at the edge of the bricks. And she
wished to God that he had lied and promised her forever, that
he had given her something to take from this night besides
the mud on her knees.

She awoke with a raging fever and spent the next two days
huddled in bed, sipping tea brewed from wild-plum leaves
and shivering beneath a heavy quilt when the late-afternoon
rains abruptly cooled the scorching midday heat. Her body
succumbed to the flush of fever and her head ached from the
inner lashings of shame. Once again Belaine—damn his
velvety eyes—had taken advantage of her helplessness. That

he had seduced her she didn't doubt for a moment. Left to her own preferences, she would have dashed for the safety of the house. But, being an opportunist, he had led her into the banana grove like a lamb to the slaughter.

One could dress a wolf in silk and teach him manners and style, but one could not eliminate his predatory nature. Belaine was Belaine. What Garnet struggled to deny was the shameful memory of her own wanton response.

Hot crimson flooded her cheeks. She had thrust her body against his until her muscles strained and her heart had pounded as if it would fly from her breast. Her mind had screamed in yearning frustration that touching was not enough; she had demanded more. *Dear God.*

She pummeled the pillows and gnashed her teeth, and wished with all her soul that she could turn back the clock. The thought of facing him sent her into spasms of mortified despair.

Although she reviewed those stormy hours a hundred times, she couldn't account for the insanity that had gripped her emotions. Belaine had touched her and something had snapped in her mind. Something that still refused to heal. Whenever she recalled his hard, insistent lips crushing hers, she squirmed on the bed and groaned aloud at the strange, heated sensations racing through her blood. And her shame was compounded by the awful suspicion that if she could indeed spin back the clock, events would unfold exactly as they had.

"Missy Ga'net be-me wake up now?" Josephine entered the bedroom tentatively, her chocolate eyes wide with concern.

"*Oui.*" Irritation sharpened Garnet's response, instantly regretted. The household was in an uproar, everyone on edge. Deep purple shadows ringed Simone's weary eyes when she came to sit by Garnet's bed, Paul's drunken rage bellowed through the house at all hours, and the slaves crept about as if they tread on hot embers. Garnet rubbed her temples. "Did you bring something for my head?"

"*Oui* and *oui.*" Josephine placed a basin beside the bed,

filled with stringy pulp ground from the fleshy leaves of the wonder-of-the-world plant. As Garnet held her nostrils against the odor, Josephine plastered a coating of the mash across her mistress's forehead and tied a band of cloth around her head to contain the pulp and prevent the pungent juice from dribbling into her eyes.

"This be-me help plenty much?" Garnet asked doubtfully.

"Make you bad head go away hurry-up-quick." Josephine seated herself near the balcony doors, folding her hands in her apron lap, watching the steady drumming of rain against the balcony floor. She moistened her lips, dared a glance toward Garnet, then clamped her mouth in an uncertain line.

"If you have something to say, be-you *say* it," Garnet snapped, her tone harsher than she had intended. Her head ached, her conscience smarted, she felt the chill of the rain. Her thoughts were as gray as the dripping skies.

Josephine swung her bare toes back and forth. Her hands plucked at her apron. When an explosion of exasperation erupted from Garnet's bed, she drew a breath. "Rombo say you be-you plenty much mad at Mist' Paul. Rombo say you bring plenty much rain to flood crop and punish Mist' Paul hurry-up-quick."

Garnet wondered if the poultice stinging against her forehead had curdled her brain. She stared at Josephine.

"Rombo say-me to say-you that he give plenty big dance in you honor and make plenty much big, big offerings." Josephine swallowed and lowered her gaze from Garnet's frowning bewilderment. "Rombo say you stop rains now, hurry-up-quick. Him say he give blood feast if Erzulie stop rain plenty much quick, hurry please."

Garnet's eyes widened in disbelief and she sat up against the pillows. "You want *me* to stop the rain?"

Josephine's kerchief bobbed. "If rains stop hurry-up-quick, Mist' Paul be-him calm down and stop bad trouble." A hood dropped over her dark gaze. "Him punish enough, say-me *oui*?"

Garnet touched the seeping band of cloth crossing her brow and lifted a palm. "Rombo thinks that *I* . . ." She bit her tongue and listened to the beat of the rain, feeling its gray weight deep in her head. Until this moment she had not connected Rombo with the tales of *vodun*.

"Many much offerings be give to you, but do no good, no and no. Rombo say you-be want blood feast hurry-up-quick."

Above the monotonous pattering of rain came the sound of persistent knocking. Frowning, Garnet called irritably, "Come in." To Josephine she added, "Don't go. We get to bottom of this plenty quick, say-me *oui*."

Her cheeks flushed, then paled, as Jean Belaine pushed open the door, strode to her bedside, and dragged a chair near her pillows. Vitality snapped through the room and suddenly her bedroom appeared very small. He scanned the greasy cloth tied across her forehead, the wild tangle of hair exploding about her head, her hurried attempt to close the collar of her nightgown.

"I hope you're feeling better than you look." He laughed.

"State your apology and leave me alone."

"Apology?" Velvety amusement danced in his eyes.

Dots of scarlet flamed on her cheeks and her chin firmed angrily. His obstinacy infuriated her as much as his lack of manners. He knew what he'd done; a true gentleman would fall on his knees and beg forgiveness. "You took advantage of me."

He laughed. "Like hell, love. We're not going to play that game again—this time you were wide awake."

The scarlet shame deepened in her cheeks and embarrassed fury sparked from her green eyes. "There's nothing more to say, is there? Please leave."

"We need to talk." He pulled the chair nearer, disregarding her cry of anger and protest. "Get out," he ordered Josephine, "now. Hurry-up-quick."

"You stay," Garnet demanded, aghast at his audacity and at the idea of being alone with him. She looked at his broad shoulders and hard mouth, and her voice dried in her throat. "Josephine be-her *stay*."

"Now," Jean repeated. His hand dropped to his sword.

Josephine scuttled out the door, slamming it firmly.

"You wouldn't hurt one of my servants," Garnet gasped.

"Of course not."

"How dare you march in here and . . ." She drew back from his grin, pressing into the pillows. And she jerked the soiled band from her forehead, scrubbing at the mess dripping from her brow. Her hair was tangled and matted, her skin as pale as milk, and she knew she smelled of sweat and fever. Her teeth clenched and she drew a breath. "What do you want?"

Jean waited until she'd cleaned the mash from her skin and had flung the cloth across the room before he leaned back in the chair and lit a thin cigar. "I want you to listen quietly like a good little girl." He smiled at her stifled shriek. "Agreed?"

Garnet felt as if she was choking. "Say what you came to say, then get out." Clumps of quilt balled in her fists. She longed to fly out of the bed and assault him with her nails. Her initial embarrassment had clotted into a burning anger evident in narrowed eyes and a furious mouth. And the anger was safe, a comfortable defense.

Jean exhaled slowly, watching the smoke drift toward the wet, gray mist steaming outside the balcony doors. "At this moment every African in the Cul-de-Sac believes you are Erzulie, a human *loa*."

"We have established that," she snapped.

"And most believe Paul seduced you and then seduced Tamala, so you turned against him."

"*What?*" Garnet bolted upright on the bed, staring.

"The story apparently originates with Rombo. As the Africans believe Erzulie is a jealous *loa*, they believe you hurried the rains to punish Paul for his dalliance. Thus destroying the major part of the harvest."

"That is utter nonsense."

Jean nodded. "But what's happened since is not. Paul has been in a rage—perhaps you've heard?"

She had. She considered it likely that people for miles around had heard Paul's shouts and fits of rage.

"From Paul's viewpoint the problem lies in who is to blame for this year's disaster." Belaine stubbed out the cigar and leaned forward, his hands clasped around a lifted knee. "We always need someone to blame, don't we?" he added evenly, watching the color flood into her face. "In this case Paul blamed Lille, and Lille shifted the blame to the Africans— they're lazy, they sabotaged the harvest, and so on."

"What does this have to do with me?"

"Have patience, love. I'm coming to your part." He looked at her lying against the pillows, the flush of receding fever warm on her cheeks and breast, and his dark eyes flickered. "The slaves have no one lower to blame, so the rain is their fault. It's their fault that the profits are rotting under a foot of water." His voice stiffened. "They must be punished."

Terrible apprehension prickled along Garnet's skin. She frowned at her hands twisting across the top of the quilt.

"The foremen of the field gangs were forced to swallow gunpowder and then they were blown up."

"Oh, my God," Garnet whispered, covering her eyes. She had heard the explosions yesterday, not realizing what they were.

"The field drummers who maintained such a snail's pace were buried to the neck in the swamp and boiling syrup poured over their heads. If the quicksand and syrup didn't kill them . . . the insects will. Slowly."

Garnet threw out her hands, her stomach working. "*Stop.* Why are you telling me this?"

"Each man and each woman who worked in a flooded

field is having an ear sliced off even as we sit here now. They will either eat that ear or be killed."

Garnet pitched to the side of the bed and vomited into the basin on the floor. Beads of perspiration pearled on her forehead. She prayed to God that he was lying even as she knew he was not.

"This has nothing to do with me," she insisted when she had rinsed her mouth and composed herself.

"For a woman of rare intelligence, love, you are sometimes remarkably thick-headed." He met her anger with a level stare. "The Africans believe you can halt the carnage if you wished. They believe you caused the rains without pondering the consequences for your worshipers—torture and mutilation. A mountain of offerings appears on the veranda each morning."

If he was trying to frighten her, the ruse was effective. She swallowed uneasily.

"They have presented you with every tempting offering they can conceive of, short of human flesh." His gaze flickered and his jaw knotted. "But still men are dying. They want you to do something. Immediately."

A silence opened between them, as thick and uncomfortable as the humidity plastering Garnet's nightgown against her clammy skin.

"They're meeting again, aren't they?" She had heard the drums throbbing against the night.

He nodded soberly. "For the moment a state of confusion prevails. The priests are attempting to unravel the whims of the gods. Are you or are you not an impostor? Are you killing their people or not?"

A web closed about her, its silken threads pulling toward a dark, poisonous center. "What can I do?" She looked to Belaine for guidance, too weary to examine the irony of seeking his advice when minutes ago she had roundly cursed him.

"Go home to Boston," he answered flatly. "Eventually the

priests will conclude you're an impostor. It can't be otherwise. And when that happens—you're dead." His words dangled in the close, damp air. "Tell me when you want to go, Garnet, and I'll arrange your passage."

Their eyes held. Garnet was first to break their locked gaze. She swallowed against the leap of warmth in her cheeks, the sudden tingle swelling her lips. "There has to be another solution."

Jean stood, shaking his head and staring down at her. "When and if you decide to be sensible, inform me, love, and I'll get you out of here. But do it soon—I won't be in Port-au-Prince forever."

Forever. One minute he was dragging her into his arms; the next minute he was prepared to send her away. Forever. Her eyes narrowed as her heart twisted.

She wet her lips and forced herself to address directly the subject darkening her mind. "So there will be no misunderstanding, Colonel . . . the night of the storm was . . . a mistake, a foolish lapse that will not be repeated."

"Are you that afraid of your heart, love?" he asked softly.

Pride stiffened her jaw and firmed her tone. "My heart is not in question." Her green eyes flashed. "I will not be victimized again by an opportunistic womanizer. Is that so difficult to comprehend?"

"Victimized?" He grinned. "By a womanizer? Is that how you see me?" He moved to the door with a flowing, unconscious elegance. "Perhaps I have been at that." Pausing, he leaned on the doorjamb. "But perhaps I had reasons. And I certainly didn't realize I'd be held accountable for my past."

"What justifications could possibly exist for taking advantage of women?" Sparks blazed in the golden depths of her green eyes.

His own velvety stare sobered. "I don't take advantage, love. I've never had to. As for reasons, I believe in living each day to the fullest. There may not be a tomorrow."

"Nothing lasts forever," she quoted sarcastically.

"That's right."

She thought about his visit later as she pushed the food about her dinner tray, then she made a sound of disgust and moved the tray aside, sinking her chin in the quilt.

Her fever had broken and the chills were diminishing. She would feel her old self once she had washed her hair and scrubbed the stickiness of illness from her skin. What she needed was the heat of the sun. Tomorrow she would dress and ride out to see the extent of the storm damage for herself. It would give her something to think about other than the problems stacking one atop another. *Loas*, sliced ears, impostors, quicksand and insects, velvety eyes—they whirled confusion through her mind.

When a scratching sounded at her door, Garnet raised her head, grateful for the interruption of unsettling thoughts. She called for Josephine to enter, lifting her tray to be removed.

To Garnet's dismay, Tamala Philippe stepped inside and shut the door behind her, leaning against it as her ebony gaze swept the room. She wore a cotton blouse low on her smooth shoulders; a brightly striped skirt swung against bare, muddied feet.

Her dark eyes settled on Garnet's startled expression. "I think it's time we had another little talk, cousin, don't you?"

"There's nothing to discuss," Garnet snapped.

"Oh, I think there is." Tamala seated herself in the chair Jean had earlier occupied, crossing her legs and dangling an arm, calling attention to a jangling collection of gold bracelets. She touched the wide hoops in her ears and pushed back her hair. A slow, unpleasant smile curved sensual lips. "You look terrible."

Garnet's glance narrowed. "I'll survive. What do you want?"

"May I?" Without awaiting permission, Tamala poured herself a cup of plum tea in blatant defiance of custom and law. She smiled into the cup. "I think we should discuss your future."

Garnet sat against the pillows, wishing for the second time

in as many hours that she had a comb, a fresh nightgown, and a basin of soap and water. Irritation deepened by an acute awareness of her dishevelment sharpened her tone. "My future is none of your concern."

"I think it is. I'm very concerned about your future." Tamala spoke softly. She lifted the teacup with a languid movement, her posture displaying her magnificent figure to advantage. Only the malevolence in her narrowed eyes betrayed her emotion. "You see, Mademoiselle White-white, I want you gone. I want you out of Port-au-Prince."

"I've told you before, I'm not leaving." Everyone wanted her gone. She passed a hand over her eyes and drew a breath.

Tamala's voice purred, as if explaining elementary concepts to a half-wit. "Either Paul or Jean is going to give me everything I want. Which is respectability—and out of here." She held up her arm, twisting the gold bracelets. "I'll wear diamonds in my hair and have a mansion twice the size of this one."

"I hope you get everything you deserve," Garnet said dryly.

"I will." Tamala's eyes had turned viperish. "I've paid for it." Leaning back in the chair, she contemplated Garnet steadily. "Paul was coming around. I haven't given up on him yet. And Jean. Jean is the best opportunity, more immediate. And I almost had him where I wanted him." Her ebony eyes narrowed to slits. "Now I'm cast aside, just another black whore, someone to keep in reserve in case the white missy fails to open her legs."

Garnet winced. She tried not to picture Jean and Tamala together, found it impossible. Or did Tamala refer to Paul? Or to both men? "This conversation is going nowhere, Tamala. I want you to leave."

"No, my dear, it's *you* who will leave. With you gone, Jean will come back to me." Tamala spun a bracelet around her wrist, watching the golden revolutions return the candlelight. "Or . . . you may never leave at all. Your life could become very . . . dangerous."

"How amusing. Tell me, don't you have anything better to do than make threats? You overstep yourself if you believe I care what happens to you. I don't. If you're treated like a whore, it's because you've acted like one." Garnet drew herself up against the pillows. "I don't know or care where you end up, but my future is here. I won't be frightened away by childish threats."

Tamala's laugh clawed along Garnet's spine. "You stupid little fool." She stood abruptly, her fists clenching. "You can spend the next month whoring in the banana grove with Jean and it won't make any difference. You won't have him." Spinning, she approached Garnet's dressing table and scooped into her pocket both Garnet's hairbrush and the cloth that had bound her forehead. She paused at the doorway and a sullen smile crawled lazily across her lips. "You are going to regret it if you choose to remain."

Garnet stared at the slamming door, her pulse fluttering unaccountably in her throat. She could guess why Tamala had taken the cloth and the hairbrush. A hot lump stuck in her chest and her breath emerged with difficulty. But magic worked only if both parties believed it would. And Garnet Winters did not believe in magic.

She squeezed her lashes shut and tried to empty her mind. And she swore the goose bumps pebbling her flesh were the result of her recent chills and fever. And the hair rising along the back of her neck was caused by the rain.

She didn't believe in magic. Garnet stared at the empty space on her table where her hairbrush had lain, and she swallowed. She did not believe in magic.

—11—

THE MAGNITUDE OF THE DISASTER was difficult to comprehend. Not content to rely on Paul and Lille's reports, Garnet guided her horse along the muddy pathways between the carrys and observed for herself the extent of the debacle. Field after field lay beneath a foot of water, the cane juice turning to acid in sagging stalks, the root systems rotting.

And every afternoon, as predictable as Paul's rages, the rains came.

Adjusting her hat brim against the scorching midday sun, Garnet pulled on the reins and frowned at a pungent marsh of muddy water reflecting the cane stalks wilting above. Instead of assigning men to clear the clogged ditches and drain the fields, Paul had tripled the crews working in the dry carrys, trying frantically to save as much of the harvest as possible.

Perhaps his decision was the wisest course of action, perhaps not. Garnet didn't know. As she turned the horse's head toward the road, her mouth pressed into a grim line. Next year she *would* know; next year she would understand cane as well as any planter in the Cul-de-Sac. Her future depended on it.

Setting this goal foremost in her mind, she rose at dawn each morning, dressed rapidly, and rode from one end of the plantation to the other until aching muscles protested and her nose and cheeks were an unladylike sun pink.

She prowled the mills examining arriving wagons, watching the stalks squeezed and pressed between heavy rollers, asking a hundred questions, and jotting copious notes. She tracked the course of the juice down lead-lined gutters to the boiling house and into the great copper clarifiers. Perspiring profusely, Garnet suffered the terrible choking heat until she had thoroughly studied the white scum blistering to the surface of the caldrons, observing from a cautious distance as sweating, half-naked slaves swept the seething foam with scummers until the residue simmered into the fine, rich color of an aged Madeira.

Next she explored the curing house, where thick molasses dripped slowly through spongy plantation stalks into the tanks of liquid below. In the tanks the golden cane juice would ferment and mellow and mix with molasses, water, and dunder, a residue remaining after the sugar was refined, to produce a strong, straw-colored rum. Slaves added caramel to additional tanks to produce the darker rum favored for export.

She was learning.

Garnet had balanced a machete in her slender hand, had sucked the sweet juice from a freshly cut stalk, had followed the cane through every step from field to tank. And each night when she reviewed her day and her pages of notes, a dozen new questions jumped to mind. How did the sugar master know the exact moment to strike? How long did fermentation require? Was there more profit in rum or raw sugar? What was the world market for molasses? And paramount among her queries: Could the rains be more accurately predicted?

There was only one person whom she trusted to provide reliable answers. But she could not address Belaine without scarlet flooding her cheeks, without her mouth feeling as if it had suddenly filled with hot, dry pebbles. Each night, when the opportunity presented itself, she changed her mind and silently withdrew with Simone, leaving the men to discuss cane without interruption. And she despised her cowardice.

Sighing, Garnet caught her lower lip between her teeth and swung off her horse before the manor veranda. After handing the reins to a glum young boy, she sank to the bottom step of the veranda and pulled off her hat. A flaming tumble of hair sagged against her neck and she pinned it back in place, then blotted her forehead with her cuff. The shade of the vines soothed her hot skin, but not her thoughts.

What was she going to do about Belaine?

Garnet opened her bodice and fanned herself with a large leaf, her brow knit in a troubled frown. Reluctantly she admitted an undeniable physical attraction. The night the rains came had dissolved any lingering self-delusion. Jean touched her and she melted. He had only to focus those velvety eyes across the dinner table and her chest felt as if an iron band crushed the air from her lungs.

She muttered an irritated curse beneath her breath. Tilting her head back, she stared at a brilliantly tinted parrot preening itself among the vines. Another sigh of consternation fluttered past her lips. After Tamala's challenge Garnet had foolishly thought an innocent flirtation possible, but too much had happened for innocence to be possible. An expanse of beach flashed through her mind, and a storm exploding above her, around her, within her.

Had she allowed her emotions to become involved? This suspicion worried her most of all. Shameful as it was, she would prefer their attraction to be merely physical, not emotional, never emotional. "Damn." This was precisely the situation she had vowed to avoid.

Touching her fingertips to her forehead, Garnet squeezed thick lashes against her sunburned cheeks. A pair of dancing velvet eyes floated before her vision, transforming her lips into a twist of despair.

Frowning absently, she rubbed her riding crop across the dirt, obliterating a heart-shaped *vèvè*. Heartbeat. Heartsick. Heartbreak. Jean Belaine.

"Damn." Sighing heavily, she shoved at her hair with an

irritated thrust, then raised her eyes to glare at the sky. A sure intuition promised she couldn't forget Belaine as she so fervently wished. The truth was he had slipped past her emotional guard. The dark man haunting her dreams was no longer faceless—the dreams themselves had become a dismal betrayal of her convictions and aspirations.

The parrot flopped to a lower vine and fixed her with a beady stare. Its caw sounded startlingly like a laugh.

"Oh, shut up." Rising abruptly, Garnet scowled at the sea of rotting cane and listened to the distant beat of field drums. This was the future she had chosen, not impulsively, but after long thought. Cane and spinsterhood. The pronouncement emerged like a tocsin of doom. "It's what I want," she insisted aloud. She was going to learn cane well enough to succeed brilliantly; Garnet Winters would never be dependent upon anyone for her bed and board again. She would build a satisfying and profitable life without a man. It could be done. Besides, eventually Jean would return to Cap Français, thank God, and this disturbing interlude would end.

Disgusted by the ongoing mental battle, Garnet glanced at the bank of clouds expanding steadily across the horizon. Unfortunately the afternoon rains didn't cool and refresh like a New England storm. Instead the rain served to bottle the heat indoors, thickening the air and steaming tempers. Like a long-term resident, Garnet had learned to dread the darkening skies.

Inside, Rombo waited with a pitcher of strawberry lemonade. Garnet accepted a mug, then lowered her gaze from Rombo's sharp black eyes. Twice she had attempted to question him about Erzulie and blood feasts, and twice her voice had faltered to silence. And whenever the table talk turned to the troubles in Paris, her glance darted toward Rombo. The budding revolution in France too closely touched on the problems in St. Domingue. She could easily imagine Rombo wielding a knife.

"Missy S'mone be-her in parlor, Missy Ga'net."

"Thank you, Rombo." Garnet answered in flawless French, carefully scrutinizing Rombo's expression. Of course he would understand simple phrases. But how much more had he learned over the years? For an instant their eyes held, then Garnet entered the parlor, feeling his sly stare on her spine.

"Simone? Is something wrong?"

Simone sat before the window oblivious of the billowing draperies, her gray eyes staring blindly at the approaching clouds. She clutched the crumpled pages of a letter against her breast.

A trembling hand lifted to her forehead. "What?" She blinked at Garnet as if viewing her from a vast distance.

Anxiety paled Garnet's lips as she knelt beside her cousin. "What's happened?" Simone was the rock that anchored the household. Tamala was correct in labeling Simone the little mother; her presence calmed the wildest emotions, restored a sense of perspective.

Simone lifted the pages of the letter, then let them flutter from her fingers. "Charmaine-Marie—her husband is a deputy attached to the National Assembly . . ."

Garnet waited expectantly, her green eyes not leaving Simone's chalky face. "Go on."

"The news from Paris is terrible," Simone whispered. Unshed tears shone from her luminous eyes. "The king and queen, they . . . they escaped from the Tuileries, where they were being restrained like prisoners. Like prisoners!" She shook her head. "Garnet, the royal family believed they were fleeing for their lives. Imagine it, the king and queen of France in danger of their lives. From their own subjects."

Garnet nodded. French politics struck her as distant and murky, a fairy-tale epic of titled actors posturing before an audience who had ceased to appreciate them.

She covered Simone's small, cold hands, reminding herself that Simone's heart had never left Paris. "Was their escape successful?"

"No." Simone blinked at the fluttering draperies. "The

royal family was apprehended at Varennes, a few miles from the frontier. They were returned to Paris." Her fingers pressed pale lips. "Charmaine-Marie reports that Marie Antoinette's beautiful hair turned as white as rice from the shock of the ordeal. She also says the Assembly is laboring around the clock to prepare a constitution for France."

Garnet frowned. "What does that mean?"

"It means we can never go home." Simone's whisper cracked and sank. "Never." Her head fell back against the chair. She stared out at the heavy rain drumming against the graveled driveway, and her eyes brimmed with tears.

"But surely . . ."

Slowly Simone shook her head, crushing chestnut curls against the upholstery. "No. The handwriting is on the wall for those with eyes to see—written in blood. The nobles are quietly fleeing Paris, and many are leaving France. If Louis and his family are prisoners, then every member of the aristocracy is in peril. Paris is lost to us."

She brushed a tear from her cheek and cast an apologetic glance at Garnet before her smile wavered and she buried her face in her hands.

"I'm sure everything will work out for the best." Garnet's assurances sounded feeble even to her own ears. Everything in Simone's world revolved around the anticipated date of her return to Paris.

"No," Simone murmured against her fingers. "I'll never see Paris again."

"We'll go to Paris next year . . . after next year's harvest."

"Next year . . ." Simone looked at Garnet for a long moment, then turned her sorrow to the rain. She didn't notice when Garnet tiptoed from the room.

They spoke of little else for the next few days. The news from Paris added to the gloom surrounding the harvest. Cheerful topics diminished to a trickle despite Belaine's valiant efforts to enliven the dinner conversation. Additional mail packets

from Paris underscored the rising panic sweeping France; Lille's accounts translated into disaster at home.

The Habitation would recover expenses, but only just. Garnet preferred taking breakfast in her room to avoid Lille's reports, but she couldn't avoid the dinner conversation.

"It's Lille's fault," Paul snarled, scowling at a magnificent, rain-wet sunset. "He didn't work the blacks hard enough. I should whip him and send him packing."

No one disagreed. They sat in the evening shade of the veranda, sipping rum punches before dinner, no one in the mood for discussion.

"This was our last opportunity to return home in style. Now everyone who matters is scattered all over the French countryside." Gesturing Rombo away, Paul swallowed directly from the bottle, wiping his hand across his mouth. "Thanks to an ignorant crowd of filthy riffraff, we're stuck here in this godforsaken hole. Did you read Duplay's letter? People are being arrested for the crime of noble birth—imagine it!"

Simone closed her eyes and touched a tremorous hand to her forehead.

Jean stirred his rum punch. "Other locales exist," he commented mildly. "If you hate St. Domingue so much, you could emigrate to another of the islands."

Bubbles of spittle whistled at the corners of Paul's lips as he leaned forward. "You don't care that an entire way of life is being extinguished. You wear the king's uniform but your sympathies are with the common cause. Don't deny it, Jean. You supported the uprising in the English colonies, and now you cheer the French rabble."

"Regardless of my personal inclinations, I perform my duty to the king and to the uniform I wear—and no man can prove otherwise." Jean's eyes hardened to a granite challenge; his fingers tightened around his glass. "I understand your frustration, Paul, but I warn you not to push too far."

Paul's lip curled. "You always have the right answer, don't

you, Belaine? The rains came early, exactly as you predicted, and the goddamned carrys are rotting just as you said they would." A glittering hatred shone in his ice-blue eyes. "It must be very satisfying always to be correct. So pray proceed. Remind the ladies that you were right and I was wrong."

"It's over, Paul. Forget it for this year." Jean glanced at him briefly and then away, accepting another rum punch from Rombo's silver tray. His movements were a flow of controlled elegance, a marked contrast to du Casse's heavy gestures.

"Ah, the generosity of the islander. Is that it, Belaine? Or do you smugly believe the ladies already grant your expertise?" His laugh emerged harsh and ugly. "Our little cousin does. Her silence doesn't mean I can't sense her hostility."

Garnet didn't look at him. "I'm disappointed, Paul." The twitch of his mouth alarmed her, as did the congestion building in his face. His skin was the unhealthy color of rotting plums.

"You blame me. You think I mismanaged the cutting. Do you think me so stupid that I didn't guess? And you believe you could have done better, don't you?" He leaned forward to sneer through the shadows of the vines. "Don't you?" he demanded.

Tact, Garnet reminded herself firmly, use tact. It was impossible to reason with Paul when the rum bottle was empty. "I heard you order Lille to clear the ditches," she answered at length.

"But I neglected to follow through, didn't I? And you would have, is that right?" His nasty tone goaded her. He wallowed in his incompetence, alternating between self-reproach and the desire to hear his words refuted. Or perhaps it was a self-hatred scorching everything within reach.

Garnet's chin stiffened. It annoyed her that they pandered to Paul's mood for the sake of maintaining an uneasy calm. Nothing he did or said could lessen the fact of his disastrous irresponsibility. If he wished her to accommodate his frustrations or to ease his conscience, he would be disappointed. She did not excuse him. Half the loss was her own. "I hope I would have inspected something as vitally important as the ditches, yes," she snapped, losing patience.

Veins swelled along his temples and his knuckles whitened around the empty bottle. "Well, cousin, you'll have your chance. You want half of this plantation? Well, you've got it. We'll see just how well you manage. We'll see how you like making all the decisions, how you respond when everyone demands a slice of your soul, when the triumphs are few and the disasters many. You want your very own plantation to play with, cousin? A toy to amuse yourself with? Take it."

Garnet stared at him, as did Jean and Simone.

"This house sits at the center of the Habitation. Pretend we've just drawn a line running down to the road and up to the mountains. Which side do you want, cousin, north or south?" His reddened eyes burned through narrow slits; the rum bottle dangled below a lace cuff.

Jean shifted, torchlight shining through his dark hair. "Paul, you're acting in haste. May I suggest you discuss this in the morning? And may I suggest a solicitor to—"

"You may not. Stay out of this, Belaine. It's none of your affair. You, too, Simone, not a word." Small, puffed eyes fixed hard on Garnet's pale features. "Well, cousin? North or south?"

They were all looking at her, but Garnet continued to stare at Paul's bloated face. Limp strands of silver hair swung about his jowls. Fury flickered in his challenge. She couldn't imagine that she had once thought him almost as handsome as Jean.

Stunned, she tried to concentrate. She hadn't yet seized control of her own life, how could she control hundreds of others? A thousand details required resolution; she hadn't learned nearly enough about the cane, or the climate, or how to harvest coffee and indigo. She had no idea if a north-south

split was a fair proposition or if it was what Grandpère
Philippe had intended.

She licked her lips and sensed Jean's bemused glance. For
a man who had constantly interjected himself into her concerns from the beginning, he remained annoyingly silent
when she would have welcomed his advice. And she didn't
believe for a moment that Paul's admonition had silenced
Jean Belaine. No, he was waiting to watch her stumble
through this alone, or waiting to hear her beg for his assistance.

Paul drained the last golden drops in the bottom of the
rum bottle, then sent it spinning over the veranda railing into
the deepening darkness. "Changed your mind, have you,
cousin? Decided you don't know everything after all?" A slave
bent from lighting the torches and began picking up pieces of
the broken bottle.

"I'll take the south half." In a flash of pride, her future was
decided. Garnet cursed the hasty decision beneath her breath;
pride would be the ruin of her yet.

"Done."

Simone passed a slim hand across her eyes and drew a long
breath; Jean contemplated the contents of his rum punch, a
faint smile curving his lips. The crunch of a horse's hooves
filled an awkward silence. Then Tamala reined before the
house and dismounted.

"Such long faces—did someone die?" she asked pleasantly.
Accepting a rum punch, Tamala crossed her boots beneath
the hem of her riding skirt and leaned against the veranda
railing. "Ah, no, you're still here," she said, pretending to see
Garnet for the first time.

"If that's a reference to the stinking knot of rags you left at
my door last night, the answer is that I feel quite well, thank
you, but you frightened Josephine half to death."

The doll, or whatever it was, had been fashioned from
strands of red hair, stolen from Garnet's hairbrush, and dressed
in a miniature white gown. The material for the gown was no
mystery; it had been scissored from the center of Garnet's

favorite skirt. The doll was smeared with excrement and three hatpins had been stabbed through an eye, the heart, and the groin. Disgusted, Garnet had personally swept the hideous thing into a chamber pot and flung it, pot and all, down the opening of the nearest outbuilding.

"Me?" Tamala's dark eyes widened in innocence. "I can't imagine what you're talking about." She smiled into the punch as Belaine's dark gaze sobered, then swung toward Garnet.

"This is a celebration," Paul announced, swaying in his chair. He shouted at Rombo for a fresh bottle, his words slurred. "Our little cousin is now a plantation owner. Yes, indeed. Everything on that side of the house is hers and everything on this side is mine." He winked at Tamala, his gaze sliding over her throat and breast. "You are welcome to share everything on my side." Drunk, he patted the thighs of his satin breeches. "Everything I have is yours."

Simone stood abruptly. "I have a headache. If you will excuse me?" Her smile was strained, but her deep bow was graceful and dignified. She nodded chestnut curls and quietly withdrew.

Garnet's teeth ground. "I won't be frightened away, Tamala. I belong here now." Drawing a breath, she injected a purring sweetness into her next words, savoring a small vengeance. She didn't forgive Tamala for Josephine's fright or Simone's humiliation. "I will continue to share the burden of your support, naturally, by extending the charity you have come to expect. You're free to come and go on my land without begging permission. I wouldn't want anyone to suggest that Garnet Winters turned aside a penniless relative."

Tamala gasped and her body stiffened. She whirled on Paul, her riding skirt billowing. "You did this? You gave her half of your land?"

Paul shrugged. "She thinks she knows so damned much. Well, we'll just—"

"You promised you wouldn't split the plantation. You said if you ever did divide it, you would consider my claim."

Paul leered. "You know how to get what you want . . . you know what Cousin Paul likes." His palms pressed down on his thighs.

Tamala hissed, her lips pulled from her teeth in a feral snarl. "Justice means nothing to any of you, does it?" Her fists clenched. "I thought I wanted to be like you, but I was wrong. Only the Africans understand true justice. And our time is coming. When it arrives, all you white bellies will rue the day you were born."

Garnet's eyes narrowed in disgust. Tamala switched sides according to which offered her more at the moment. And she thrived on threats. But chill prickles rose on Garnet's skin when she noticed Rombo's glittering gaze riveted on Tamala's fury. His hands twitched at the hem of his white jacket and he looked as if he wished to slap Tamala into silence. Uneasy, Garnet pressed into her chair.

"You win the first round, cousin." Tamala spat venom. "But the battle has scarcely begun." Spinning, she stormed past Rombo and into the house.

"Magnificent display." Paul lurched to his feet and tucked a bottle under his arm. "All the Philippe cousins . . . temper . . . makes them wildcats in bed." He chuckled, the sound obscene, then he leaned heavily on Rombo and stumbled through the door. "Take me to the bitch's room."

Jean crossed his ankles in the silence and lit a thin cigar, blowing smoke rings toward the flaming torches pushing at the night. "Let's see," he mused when it became evident Garnet would not speak. "Paris is in the clutches of a mob; St. Domingue seethes with unrest; Paul ordered six men drawn and quartered today; Simone hides in her bedroom with a sick headache; you are suddenly the mistress of a large plantation; and Tamala has threatened us all. Another dull day, wouldn't you agree?"

When Garnet didn't respond to his teasing, he continued more seriously. "Tell me about the doll."

"Another time, Jean. I'm in no mood for *vodun*."

"It isn't going to go away, love." He refilled their cups with the last of the rum punch. And when he resumed, his voice contained more than a hint of exasperation. "Like it or not, forces are tightening all around you."

Garnet drank deeply, acutely aware that they were alone on the veranda. The sweet scent of jasmine perfumed the soft night air. She hoped the rum would relax the tenseness drawing her neck and shoulders, telling herself the tension was the result of long hours in the saddle and had nothing to do with Jean Belaine.

"What do they think I've done this time?" she asked, resigned.

"Murder, mutilation, bad temper. You aren't forgiven for ruining the harvest."

Garnet shook fiery curls in mock wonderment. "Apparently I am very powerful."

"Powerful enough to override the charms and spells of respected *mambos*."

Like Tamala. Everyone at the Habitation must be aware that Tamala's stature as a *mambo* had been diminished. "Is that so terrible?"

Jean stared. A ripple of muscle tightened along his shoulders, drawing his satin jacket. "Have you listened to anything I've said? Think what this harvest means to the Africans. Do you suppose for one instant that the whites will suffer a moment's deprivation? Will Paul budget differently? Consume less rum? Give up his club membership? Or will he cut the black's rations? Forget new clothing this year? Abandon repairs to the slave villages?"

Garnet met his sober eyes uneasily.

"The slaves are allowed an ounce of salt fish or meat a day, and a bottle of tafia a month. Plus four yards of cloth per year."

"I know that," she said.

Darts of torchlight played across the hard surface of his expression. His teeth were white against the shadows hollowing his cheeks. "Then you figure it out, love. You own approximately five hundred people as of tomorrow morning. Multiply twelve months by five hundred bottles of tafia, and how much rum are you buying for the work force? At how many livres? Multiply four yards of cloth for five hundred, and what will clothing cost you?"

Garnet wet her lips, then drained her rum punch. "Economics," she sighed irritably. She looked at his boots against the veranda floor and her own small slippers peeping from her hem. Irrationally she wondered if married people placed their shoes side by side beneath the bed at night.

"Yes, economics. If a poor harvest necessitates economic cutbacks, where do you think most of the planters will economize?"

"I won't." She listened to a sound of annoyance. "Very well—you're saying the Africans will blame me for the rum they won't receive and the new clothing they won't have."

"You're damn right that's what I'm saying." He leaned forward, elbows on knees, his dark eyes capturing hers. "Erzulie of the flaming hair and milky white skin is showing her dark side. She is punishing her subjects with an unforgivable vengeance."

Garnet felt his breath on her hands and stood abruptly, touching her temples. "I can't sit still tonight." Silently he rose and looked down at her. "Too many things are racing through my mind." Together they walked the length of the veranda, ignoring the dinner bell as neither professed an appetite. Garnet rubbed gently at the headache forming along the base of her neck. And eventually she told him about the doll in response to his persistent prodding. "I wish you would stop trying to frighten me," she said at the end.

"A little fear would do you good."

"Tell me honestly, Jean. Do the *vèvès* and the dolls really mean anything? Am I really in danger?" Frankly, she couldn't conceive of it and her smile said as much.

He leaned against the railing, and the glow of the torches spread a halo around his dark curls, flickered about the broad sweep of powerful shoulders. "In my opinion, yes." His quiet intensity caused her smile to waver. "Tamala's reputation is at stake. Unless I miss my guess, she'll be doing all she can to convince the Africans that you are an evil spirit masquerading as Erzulie. Many will believe her."

A chill drifted from the heated night, settling about Garnet's bare shoulders. "You know her better than I," she said, hating the sharpness in her tone.

"You're everything she'd like to be," Belaine replied, ignoring Garnet's sniff. "She won't forgive being made a fool of, Garnet. The doll tells you as much."

"A disgusting bit of nonsense."

Anger thinned his lips. "It's good you think so. Disbelief is your only protection."

Garnet tossed her curls. She could not comprehend how Jean and Simone could view *vodun* with any degree of seriousness. Humoring him, she asked lightly, "How do you have all this information?"

He seated himself on the veranda railing and folded his arms across his chest. "I attend the meetings."

Garnet smiled. "Ah, of course. And the *houngans* cordially invite you to the seat of honor, then calmly discuss how they plan to cut our throats while we lie in our beds." She ripped a leaf from the veranda vines and shredded it between her fingers, listening to the distant seduction of drumbeats. And wondered why she prolonged a conversation that didn't really interest her. The drums and the oppressive night heat had affected her thinking.

"Not quite." He returned her smile. "My seat is usually behind a tree trunk or in the grass."

"And no one notices you?" It didn't really surprise her that

Jean rode out to the slave gatherings. Nothing in St. Domingue surprised her anymore.

"Sometimes I think I could walk into the center of the ring and no one would notice. You'd have to witness a *vodun* ceremony to understand. There's a frenzy to the rituals that precludes noticing much of anything else."

"Perhaps I will. Perhaps I'll ride out one night and see for myself." She had considered the idea before.

Belaine sobered instantly. His boots struck the planks and he clasped her shoulders between his strong hands. "Don't even think about it, Garnet. Put the thought out of your mind this instant."

The hard warmth of calloused palms against her bare skin shot a dizzying weakness through flesh and thought. His sudden nearness rocked her senses. His cologne tantalized and moonlight chased through his black hair. His voice sounded like liquid silver in her ear.

Garnet swayed slightly, her eyes wide. When he touched her, it was as if another person emerged beneath his strong fingers. And this new person was all woman, molded in satin curves and quivering yearning. This new person moved sensuously and stared into his velvet frown with a gaze of beckoning emerald. Signaling.

Swallowing hard, she frantically gathered her wits and spun lightly from beneath the stroke of his fingers, moving hastily toward the spill of light falling from the manor doorway. After a moment he stepped from the shadowy vines and followed.

"You're a strange contradiction, love."

"How is that?" Her voice was throaty. She feared he must hear her heart thudding against her ribs. Stepping into his arms would have been so easy, so astonishingly natural. It had been a close call; sensibility had triumphed just as she was lifting her mouth. Frowning, she chastised herself for taking no pleasure in her victory.

"You accept challenge willingly, even eagerly . . . in all

areas but the most important. In matters of the heart you dare nothing." He spoke from directly behind her, softly, so near that she could feel his warm breath stirring the curls on her neck.

Dark lashes swept her cheeks as she considered denying his assertion. But nothing she could say would sound convincing. "I have my reasons."

"All the people you trusted left you."

She inhaled deeply, her nails cutting into her palms. A sudden, uncontrollable leap of tears misted her eyes and she was glad she was not facing him. Her transparency appalled her. Angrily she dashed the back of her hand across her eyes. "I don't wish to discuss this."

He caught her shoulders and turned her to face him, his eyes again the warm, deep texture of black velvet. "Dare to trust, Garnet," he murmured huskily. "Dare to risk being the woman you can be."

"And what of the pain?" she blurted out, her eyes flashing. "What do you know of betrayal? Or rejection?"

"Pain and betrayal . . . is that all you see in love?"

"We aren't discussing love. But, yes—you said yourself that nothing lasts forever."

"Circumstances change, people change. They grow, they diminish, they age and they die. But most people live full lives, Garnet. They don't hide from happiness because tomorrow doesn't come with guarantees."

A terrible, familiar anger ripped through her body. Anger directed toward the people she had loved who had vanished from her life, anger toward a world that refused permanence. And anger toward Belaine for so easily touching her vulnerability. "You see? There is no forever. There isn't even tomorrow."

She fought to wrench away, trying to understand how the conversation had veered into intimate areas, but his powerful hands held her.

"Listen to me. You want promises that love will always

remain at fever pitch, but it can't. No mortal could survive that intensity on a continuous basis. Love needs the freedom to breathe and mature, love needs quiet days and an occasional separation. That isn't betrayal. And if you want love to last forever, whatever forever means to you, then you have to be willing to work at keeping it alive and fresh. Running away isn't the solution."

"Paul was right . . . you have all the answers, don't you? Now you know everything about love, too."

"It seems I know more about it than you."

A dart of jealousy stung below her heart. "Well, you don't know what I want. You're presuming." Her blazing eyes held his and her heart fluttered and sank. His stare probed barriers no man had passed; he looked inside her and understood. The knowledge devastated her. Something intensely private had been violated. "I don't need a man." She choked, feeling the scorch of his hands on her shoulders. "I won't be a casual conquest, a new bead on some man's string." Green eyes flashed up at him.

She desperately wished to escape the compelling heat against her skin, the smell of him, the nearness of that velvet tension. "I won't be like . . . like Simone and Tamala." A New England blush fired her cheeks. And she hated herself for impulsively placing Simone in the same category as Tamala. How quickly the island corrupted thought and speech.

Jean's face hardened and his fingers tightened painfully. "You could do far worse than to pattern yourself after Simone du Casse. I will not tolerate a derogatory remark about that lady in my presence. Not even from you."

Garnet's gaze fell before his burning stare. "I . . . you know what I mean."

"Suppose you tell me."

Her head lifted defiantly. "I won't be one of Jean Belaine's women. I won't be a number in a long list." She was sure of her ground now, and her eyes challenged and accused.

"You are a fool, love. I owe you no explanations for the

women in my life before I met you. But I want you to understand something very clearly. I do not bed two women at the same time. Can you grasp that fact? Because from the moment I touched you that first day, from the moment I looked into your wonderful, lustrous eyes and twisted my hands through that magnificent hair, there has been no other woman."

She wanted to believe him. She wanted to trust what he said and believe him. If only she could think straight. But the inches separating them whirled in her awareness, his hands bruising her shoulders, his touch . . . Confusion tossed her thoughts in scattered pieces.

"I want to marry you, Garnet."

"Marry me?" she whispered, astonished. "But why? I don't understand."

"Damned if I understand it, either." Now his wide, generous mouth curved in a smile. "You're about six parts pride and four parts mule." He looked at her parted lips, at her quickening breast, and his smile faded. The warmth in his dark eyes smoldered with growing desire and his voice roughened. "But I want you as I've wanted no other woman."

And she wanted him. She'd been a fool not to flee the instant she realized they were alone. She wet her lips and found the strength to remind herself that soon he would leave Port-au-Prince. "Marriage?" she asked, her lips curling in a ribbon of contempt. "Without any commitment to forever?"

Impatience cast the hard angles of his face in lines of stone. "Do you fear the pain of loving so much that you'll deny yourself the joys as well? Are you that idiotic?"

She laughed. "Very romantic, Belaine. This is the first proposal I've received in which the gentleman, and I use the term loosely, has refused a lasting commitment, then had the effrontery to label *me* an idiot." Jerking from his hands, she gathered her skirt in clenched fists. "Well, if the offer is by any remote chance genuine, the answer is no. I want forever."

He examined her glare through the dappled moonlit shadows.

"Shall I promise never to die, love? Never to notice if you make a fool of yourself? Never to lose my temper?" His thin smile made her feel twelve years old. "You demand guarantees no man can give."

"Can't or won't?" Sarcasm iced her tone. She regarded him coolly. "Don't bother to answer. You've stated your case quite clearly already." She tossed her head and firmed her chin. "I know you, Jean. The instant I didn't meet your expectations, you'd use the event as an excuse to pursue the next pretty face."

"If you think me that shallow and dishonorable, then you don't know me as well as you suppose, Mademoiselle." Anger growled through his response.

"Or perhaps you cherish an inflated view of yourself, Colonel," she snapped.

His stare raked her blazing face before gradually softening into understanding. "The defenses fly up and you invent possibilities to protect you from even considering love. When will you be honest enough to rip away the excuses?"

"And when will your exaggerated view of your charm give way to admit you can't conquer every woman you meet?" Heart thudding, she poised to dash into the doorway. "I know what I want—and I know no man can give it." Spinning in a whisper of sapphire satin, she rushed inside, a hand pressed to trembling lips.

He was right, of course; he couldn't promise her forever—no man could. Or would. Her dreams of forever couldn't exist in reality. And she despised the lack with all her heart and soul.

—12—

GARNET SHIFTED FROM ONE FOOT to another outside Simone's door, pulling her nightdress to her throat and glancing along the silent, mirrored hallway. The clock on the landing counted the midnight hour and she nearly turned away. Then she rapped again and softly called Simone's name.

"Garnet? Come in."

"Where you sleeping?" Stepping inside, Garnet peered about curiously. In contrast to her own bedroom, Simone's furnishings were spartan. A heavy cross of hammered silver hung above a dressing area free of the pots and decanters that cluttered Garnet's table. There was only a bottle of lemon scent, a lacquered box for hairpins, a velvet cushion pierced with needles, and a small hand mirror. Muted grays and blues and quiet pastels drifted from open wardrobe doors; a single candle illuminated an open Bible atop a bed dressed in white eyelet sheets and ruffles.

"It's too hot to sleep tonight." Simone led her toward the balcony, combing heavy waves of chestnut hair back from her face with her fingers.

"Do you still have a headache?"

They seated themselves on a small balcony bench, trying to believe it was cooler outside than in. A wisp of cloud obscured the moon, and the torches below seemed bright against the deep darkness beyond. A lilt of faint song carried

193

from the manor village; Garnet strained to hear a single mournful baritone longing for death and peace and a river called the Boulang.

"Fula brought me a compress. It helped a little." Simone rested her head against the iron scrolling topping the bench. "Are you ready to take over your share of the plantation?"

"I thought I was . . . but I don't know." Garnet fanned at the heat with the end of her wrapper sash. "There are so many changes I want to make, but I keep remembering Jean's cautions . . . I don't know."

"You'll do fine." Simone's small hand patted Garnet's. "And it isn't as if we won't be here to help."

Garnet didn't want Paul's help, but she knew she would be grateful for Simone's practical advice. "Thank you." The best solution to Paul would be if she moved into a house of her own. But in view of dwindling financial reserves, a separate residence was out of the question for the moment.

"Why do you stay with him?" The rudeness horrified her; Garnet hadn't planned to ask such a thing. Still, once the offense was committed, she couldn't entirely regret it.

Simone's thin shoulders lifted in a scarcely perceptible shrug. "Where would I go? The money's gone, gambled away on cards or cockfights or harvests. Who would have me? A woman without funds or the ability to bear children." Her large gray eyes met Garnet's levelly. "Besides, I know you won't understand this, but Paul and I are friends." Sensing Garnet's resistance, she looked at her hands. "I remember when he was younger, when he still believed he could succeed at anything he tried . . ." A long sigh escaped her lips, the melancholy of loss. "If you had known him in Paris, Garnet. If you could have met him then . . ."

Listening to the soft recollections of a different age and a different Paris, Garnet wondered if they could possibly be discussing the same Paul du Casse she had learned to scorn. "You love him, then?"

A silence lengthened. "Perhaps tolerance is a more accurate expression," Simone said finally. "Love is a lightning bolt, an instant recognition. Two people look at each other and they know. Familiarity can create friendship, but not love."

A tall figure stepped onto the balcony at the far end of the house, and in a moment Garnet saw the glowing tip of a cigar. Dropping her eyes, she frowned at her hem. What had she felt when she opened her eyes on the beach and saw the sun shimmering around Belaine's black curls? A lightning bolt?

"I don't leave Paul because I can't. I won't. What God has joined, let no man put asunder. I only pray the good man locked inside will resurface one day."

Garnet considered that possibility about as likely as Colonel Jean Belaine entering a monastery.

"In the meantime, I try to be his friend."

Garnet bit the inside of her cheek, watching as Simone stood to pluck a blossom from the night-blooming vines. "Whatever you had in the beginning didn't last." She glanced toward the small, fiery point at the far end of the house.

"Ours was an arranged marriage, Garnet, nothing more. If we end in tolerance and friendship . . . it will be enough."

It would never be enough for Garnet Winters. Her appetite for life was too powerful. If she ever married, she wanted the relationship to be all-consuming, a passion that could never die. If she ever married . . . She hadn't entertained the possibility in years—why did she now? A sound of exasperation escaped her rounded lips as she stood and pushed a hand through her hair.

"I apologize for this discussion, Simone. I came to beg your forgiveness on another matter entirely. Please forgive me for not helping you address the party invitations. I promised and then entirely forgot. I haven't been much help."

"I'm having second thoughts. I've been considering a cancellation." She drew a breath. "Few planters have much to celebrate this harvest, and the shocking events at home have upset nearly everyone we know."

"Then a party is exactly what everyone needs," Garnet said brightly. The prospect sounded dismal, but she was gratified by Simone's hopeful expression.

"You think so?"

"Absolutely. A ball will cheer everyone."

Simone pressed her cheek to Garnet's, leaving behind the fresh scent of lemon. "Garnet . . . be careful of Tamala." Pulling back, she bit her lip and frowned into Garnet's eyes. "Tamala is . . . unpredictable."

Tossing her hair, Garnet shrugged confidently. "Tamala doesn't frighten me." She smiled into Simone's worried face. "After all, what can she do?"

"I don't know. I don't want to know. Just . . . be careful. And thank you for reassuring me about the party."

Later, lying in her own bed and trying desperately to blot out the provocative sensuality of throbbing drumbeats, Garnet thought about Simone's ball and decided no one needed cheering more than herself.

She punched her pillow with more force than necessary, pretending she smashed her small fist through a drumhead, then tossed on her side, staring wide-eyed at swaths of mosquito netting. She couldn't sleep.

She might as well light a candle and make a list of the things roiling through her mind. She needed to hire an overseer immediately, as retaining Lille was out of the question. And as soon as possible she wanted to ride the entire length and breadth of her land—*her* land—and judge exactly which fields needed what. At least for a time it would be necessary to share the curing houses and mills and boiling houses with Paul, and this required legal agreements as well as provisions for the future.

Flinging herself onto her back, she contemplated the canopy without seeing it. The slave villages needed fumigating and immediate accommodations for waste disposal. She'd summon a doctor from Port-au-Prince to treat the rampant cases of yaws, roundworm, and pinworm. Unless she missed her guess, bronchitis and malaria were also common in the villages.

Slave diet could be improved by granting the Africans land for larger kitchen gardens and time to work them.

And regardless of cost, she would order cloth to replace the rags most of the field laborers wore. And they should all be given sandals—bare soles invited hookworm infection.

There was so much to do that she resented the time wasted in sleeping. The cane stubble should be burned off before the week was out and melons planted in the ashes. The harvested fields needed replanting, and the sooner, the better. Ditches would have to be cleared of rubble and debris, and new ones dug. Her head spun.

Twisting, Garnet kicked at the light sheet draped over her thin gown, and she pressed her face into the pillow, hoping to smother the sound of the drums pounding against her ears, her skin, her senses.

And despite a valiant effort not to think about Belaine, his image rose against her dwindling defenses.

Marriage. He had actually proposed marriage. It was unthinkable, of course.

Then why was she thinking about it? Garnet cursed the drums and pummeled her pillow into a wadded ball. Marriage to Jean Belaine would be an exercise in self-torture. Every rapturous moment in his bronzed arms would be repaid a thousandfold in units of pain and betrayal. Every time he left her sight she would wonder what woman he went to visit. How long would it be before she began to alter her personality in an effort to please him, to avoid his disapproval? Ultimately Garnet would vanish and become a mere extension of Jean.

He insisted he cared for only one woman at a time.

Lies. Besides, soon he would tire of Garnet and seek the comfort of new arms.

He hadn't bedded Tamala that first night as Garnet had imagined.

If she believed that, she was ripe to believe his shirt concealed an angel's wings.

He was clearly concerned about her welfare; obviously he cared.

And why not? He'd claimed responsibility for her from the first.

He wanted to marry her.

But he hadn't said he loved her.

Still, he wanted to marry her.

Without promising forever.

Grinding her teeth, Garnet glared into her pillow as the unwanted conversation continued in her head. She reviewed every word he had spoken from the moment she opened her eyes on the beach to the last words murmured on the veranda. For each positive, she triumphantly presented a negative. For every admirable quality, she could offer three irritating traits.

Colonel Jean Baptiste Belaine wanted to marry her.

He was wealthy, charming, and wildly handsome.

Garnet's fist slammed into the pillow, and she kicked angrily at the folds of mosquito netting. He was charming on occasions of his own choosing. Exciting and intriguing, maybe. His mouth was generous and sensual, granted, and his eyes were velvety black and flashed from warm to cool to a smoky smolder. His jawline was stubborn and strong, a feature she liked. And she admitted he unerringly commanded respect. Women thought him fascinating . . .

What in the name of God was she thinking? Furious with herself, Garnet mopped the hem of the sheet across her brow and shook back skeins of damp, tangled hair. The drums pulsed along racing blood, sitrring craziness through her thoughts. It was the only logical explanation for such idiotic ideas.

Colonel and Madame Jean B. Belaine. Garnet Marie Belaine. Madame Jean B. Belaine.

Crazy. She was sinking into insanity.

But he wanted to marry her.

Without forever.

And without guessing how Garnet could try a man's tolerance. If he knew how intractable she could be . . . when he saw how she flung aside conventions . . . if he realized how strongly she resisted becoming a man's echo . . . when he admitted her stubborn streak of independence and self-sufficiency . . .

. . . He would turn tail and run.

She stared at nothing and reminded herself that it didn't matter. Everything had changed since midday.

Paul's drunken challenge had inadvertently rescued her from a possible disastrous lapse of good sense. She could no longer run off to Cap Français or New Orleans. Five hundred people depended on her. She had responsibilities; she had her livelihood to consider. And it was far better, far more satisfying to be the mistress of a plantation than to be the mistress of a man.

She could trust the land. The land would warm and comfort her. The land was forever.

The drumbeats laughed in her head and she groaned and pressed her hands hard against her ears. Then she turned her face into the wadded pillow and wept until she was exhausted, not understanding the helpless flood of tears.

The scream awakened her, though she couldn't identify it immediately. Garnet sat bolt upright in bed, rubbing her eyes and blinking at pearly dawn shadows. Straining, she listened to the guinea hens fussing beneath her balcony, wondering if their squabbling had wakened her. When the next scream rent the stillness, her eyes flared open and she was instantly awake. It was Josephine. Garnet flung back the netting and ran into the hallway, her hair and nightgown streaming behind her.

Something wet and solid and vile-smelling struck her in the face as she jerked open her door and rushed forward. Her bare feet skidded through a thick, gelatinous puddle.

"No, Missy Ga'net." Josephine's eyes rolled like black marbles on a white field. Clamping a hand over bloodless lips, she recoiled in horror as Garnet slipped and stumbled into the corridor. "You touched it. Lawdy, Lawd. You touched it."

The candle shaking violently in Josephine's limp fingers illuminated a row of mirrors paneling the corridor, and Garnet watched as her reflection slid and nearly fell before she halted her pell-mell rush by throwing her palms against the mirror glass. She stared at her image in stunned disbelief.

Blood smeared across her cheeks and speckled the breast of her nightgown. Clotted globules oozed between her toes. She drew back in horror, leaving bloodied handprints against the glass. Behind her mirrored image, dangling from the top of her door, swung a headless chicken, dripping blood onto the floor.

Spinning, Garnet stared at the loathsome thing, ripples of repugnance chilling her flesh. The chicken's feet were bound by a length of braided cord. Bits of red human hair and knotted ribbon and dyed feathers dangled from the carcass, nailed into place by hatpins. Two painted gourds swung on either side of the chicken, patterned over with black, nightmarish forms. The chicken twisted, and slow red drops fell on the gelatinous mound beneath.

Garnet had touched that evil thing. She bit back the scream building in her throat.

A sudden, irrational fear clutched her, and there didn't seem to be enough air in the hallway. She closed her eyes briefly and clenched her fists. This was a dead chicken, nothing more; it could work no harm. She stared at it. And a white heat surged upward from her toes and rushed into her cheeks. Shaking with outrage, she stormed past a babbling Josephine, hurling items about her dressing table until she located the small knife for paring nails. Grimly she dragged a stool to the doorway, climbed it, then sawed the knife across the cord until the chicken dropped onto the sheet she had jerked from her bed. Panting, she bent and concealed the abomination beneath the folds of the sheet. "Burn this plenty much quick," she snapped.

Josephine emitted a strangled squeak. Her eyes rolled and the candle tilted perilously before Garnet jumped to rescue it. "Missy Ga'net, Josephine no be-me touch a killing hurt. You no make me, please, please, Missy Ga'net." She fell heavily to her knees and raised clasped hands. "Please, Missy Ga'net, Josephine good girl, *oui* and *oui*." Her bulging eyes darted toward the bloody sheet and the girl's face turned gray. "Josephine do-you anything but this plenty much. Please, Missy Ga'net, *please*."

Garnet's fists clenched on the hips of her bloodied gown. Doors opened along the corridor. Jean strode toward her, tying a brocade robe over his naked chest, his black hair tumbled by sleep. Simone swung from her door. Paul stepped into the hallway, sleepily demanding to know the source of the commotion.

One door did not open.

Seeing her bloodied cheeks in the candlelight, Jean's expression tightened. "For Christ's sake, Garnet. Are you hurt? What happened?" His hand reached for her, but Garnet ducked from his grasp.

Lips pressed in a furious line, she bent and slapped the sheet aside, lifting the chicken by its bound feet. Trailing blood, she marched down the hallway and halted before Tamala's door. Her fist pounding the wood sounded very loud in the astonished silence behind her.

Tamala opened the door. The candle shaking in Garnet's fingers tinted Tamala's skin to warm shades of aged ivory, raised a plum-blue sheen to her flowing hair. She yawned elaborately, half-lidded eyes sliding over Garnet's wild hair and bloodied face and gown. Her eyes glittered ebony malice as a slow smile curled her lips. "Yes?"

"I believe this is yours." Garnet hurled the bloody chicken, smiling grimly as it struck Tamala below the breast, splattering red across her wrapper before it bumped to the floor. Garnet's voice shook as badly as her hands. Her emerald eyes were stony. "If you ever again do anything like this, I will bar you from my land and instruct my overseer to shoot you on sight as a trespasser." She trembled with the urge to assault Tamala Philippe. "Do you understand me? *No more.*"

Tamala smiled. "Your eyes ache, don't they? And there's a pain behind your ribs, isn't there?"

Garnet pressed a hand to her side feeling the scorch of each breath. "*No more.*"

"And you feel dry and useless in your woman parts, don't you? Don't you, cousin?"

"I feel nothing." She didn't believe in magic. She did not. Her stare was as cold and frozen as a New England pond. "You don't scare me with dolls and chickens." Her heart crashed painfully against her ribs and she told herself it was nerves and rage. Nothing else. "Remember what I said."

"I will do as I please, cousin. And go where I choose." The door closed.

Garnet stared hard at the polished wood, her fists opening and closing. Whirling, she stormed down the hallway, passing Simone and Paul without a word.

"Garnet . . ."

"Get out of my way." She pushed past Jean and fell to her knees at the doorway, furiously scrubbing the ruined sheet across the blood, trying to rub the spot clean.

"Garnet, for Christ's sake."

"Not now, Jean." She wiped the bundled sheet over the mirror with wide, angry strokes, obliterating her palm prints from the glass. "*Josephine.* Be-you fetch plenty hot bath hurry-up-quick."

Josephine stumbled to her feet and backed down the corridor, her wide, terrified stare not leaving the dead chicken lying before Tamala's door. At the head of the steps, she turned and fled.

"I mean it, Jean, not now," Garnet snapped when he insisted on speaking. She glared a warning, then spun and carried the sheet down the steps, through the house, and out beyond the veranda. She set it afire, watched to see that it would burn, then returned to her bedroom and stripped off the bloody nightgown.

She didn't wait for Josephine to reappear with the tub but used the basin to scrub the rusty stains from her face, rubbing until her face glowed before she felt truly clean. Then she wrapped herself in a fresh robe and flung herself onto the balcony bench and stared at the pink glow of sunrise painting the banana palms.

"All right," she muttered aloud. "All right."

If Tamala wanted a war, she would have it. *Mambo* against *loa*. There would be further incidents like the doll and the chicken; Garnet knew this as a certainty. And when they came, she would strike back in kind. Lost in thought, she reviewed all she had learned of *vodun*. She needed to know more. And she would learn it.

But first she had a plantation to attend to.

They were seated and waiting, including Tamala, when Garnet arrived at breakfast dressed in her riding skirt and a flowing silk blouse. She silently accepted the chair Rombo extended and gratefully sipped a cup of hot, bracing coffee.

Paul was first to interrupt the clink of silver and the clatter of china. Already he stank of rum. "Cousin . . . about last night. I spoke in haste. Naturally I hope you'll accept my apology. There's no need to divide the plantation prematurely."

"The south lands are mine, Paul. When you ride into town to your club, please engage a solicitor to formalize our agreement." So they wouldn't discuss the chicken. Garnet flicked a glance toward Tamala's self-satisfied smile.

Paul frowned, adjusted his cravat. "We should discuss this more thoroughly—in your interest as well as in mine. A north-south split may not be—"

"Just do it. No more discussion." Her tone and level appraisal allowed for no argument. Frowning in undisguised distaste, Garnet watched Paul swallow deeply from coffee heavily cut by raw tafia. She couldn't remember when last his eyes had been clear. "Either you engage a solicitor or I will. Today."

A purplish congestion flushed his face. "I'll see to it."

"Thank you." Garnet looked once toward Simone's pale face, then directed her attention to her plate. She didn't glance again toward the small table where Tamala put the servants through their paces.

Jean cleared his throat. His dark hair was tamed by a cord at the neck, his uniform blouse stretched taut across wide shoulders. "The ball is on again, then?" he asked Simone.

Simone's troubled gaze moved from Garnet to Jean. "It seems a shame to waste the preparations."

"I've received my orders. I'll be leaving for Cap Français a few days after the ball."

Garnet's head snapped. Her fork paused midway to her lips. Abruptly she felt Tamala's hatred crawling along her flesh, felt Paul's brooding silence. Simone's loving concern lay like a lump of guilt in her heart. For the first time it occurred to her how terribly she would miss Jean when he departed. His was the only friendly face on this unfriendly island. She stared at him, shocked to admit how strongly she had assumed his support and then leaned on it without being aware.

"André will meet me here and we'll ride back to the garrison together." Jean leaned back as Rombo removed his plate and silently poured fresh coffee. "I've imposed on your hospitality long enough."

Simone's hands fluttered above her breast. "We've been

happy to have you, Jean. You're always welcome here." She
pointedly ignored Paul's scowling silence.

"Frankly, I wonder at de Blanchelande calling us back
now." Jean's expression was sober. "The situation in the
Cul-de-Sac has worsened in the last days. More runaways—
more problems. More planters killing more Africans."

"You're damned right," Paul muttered, pushing loose strands
of white toward the ribbon at his neck. "Black bodies are
swinging along a hundred driveways. We'll teach those black
bastards not to ruin the harvest." Righteous anger pinched his
lips. "They cost a goddamned fortune and then they sabotage
the means to pay for them."

An expression of futility creased Belaine's face. "Oh, yes,
Paul. It's the Africans' fault that the harvest is rotting." He
passed a hand over hard eyes. "The torture and the killings
have got to stop or we're staring a violent rebellion in the
face. Tell the planters at your club they are courting disaster."
He pushed from the table and lit a cigar, exhaling angrily.

Paul laughed. "Insurrection? If the ignorant bastards can't
cut a simple cane field, tell me how the hell they are going to
mount a rebellion?"

Jean's eyes narrowed thoughtfully as he watched spirals of
smoke float in the morning air. "These people are experienced in the art of war, having battled for tribal dominance
in jungle terrain that would defeat the endurance of my best
men. If it comes to insurrection, Paul, we're outnumbered
and facing a formidable force."

Paul's sulky expression alarmed Garnet. He wasn't really
listening. "They have to be punished," he insisted stubbornly.

Sickened, Garnet frowned at her plate. Blame for the
harvest failure had to be laid at someone's door, and Paul
had long ago decided it wouldn't be his. She cast an uneasy
glance toward Rombo, stoic beside the archway.

And she squirmed uncomfortably at discussing a slave
revolt within Rombo's hearing. She knew he understood. It
was almost a relief when Lille was ushered into the room.

Lille yanked his straw hat from a matted shock of hair and mumbled greetings to the women's bosoms. He licked his lips and began the daily recitation before stopping short as Paul interrupted to explain sullenly the plantation's division.

Lille's watery eyes widened incredulously as he swiveled toward Garnet. Disapproval sharpened his stare. "I'm supposed to report to a woman, Mist' Paul? A woman?"

"Only today," Garnet answered coolly. She looked at him, her mouth dry with distaste. "And, Monsieur Lille, none of my people will be whipped or caged or 'hung out to dry.' Is that clearly understood?"

Lille flung out his hands. "You got to whip 'em, Missy Ga'net, you got to. Them dumb bastards are too lazy to move if you don't lay a whip to their backs. Everybody knows that."

"I repeat: If you whip one of my people, I'll have you thrown in jail before nightfall."

His little pig eyes turned sly and he winked at Paul. "I guess I understand, Missy Ga'net."

"I hope so, Lille," she said slowly, hating the taste of his name on her lips, hating the look and smell of him. "And, Lille, if you touch any of my girls, I will personally come after you with a whip."

His jaw slackened and his eyes squeezed into slits. A nervous laugh hawked from his mouth and he wiped the back of his hand across his chin. "You fooling with me, aren't you, Missy Ga'net?" He looked into her stony, unyielding expression and sucked in his breath. Ugliness compressed his features. "You best find yourself a new overseer hurry-up-quick."

"I intend to."

Jean applauded softly when Lille had stormed from the room. "Bravo."

Behind him Tamala laughed harshly. "Not one stroke of work will occur on the south side today. By tonight every idiot in the Cul-de-Sac will be laughing his fool head off."

"It's a marvelous beginning," Simone said quietly. Tears of

admiration brimmed in her gray eyes as she smiled her support.

"It's the stupidest thing I ever heard." After draining a tumbler of rum, Paul shook his head in disgust. "Cousin, you are going to be dead broke before the next harvest. If you haven't been murdered in your bed before then." He glared at Tamala's slow smile. "You think those poor dumb creatures are going to be grateful?" He snorted and leaned back in his chair. "You've got a lot to learn, cousin."

"I'm well aware of that." Blotting her lips, Garnet rose from the table, waving aside Rombo's assistance. "If you'll excuse me . . ." She accepted her riding pouch from Rombo and her hat and gloves, then asked him to order up her mare. Before she departed the dining room, however, she paused at Tamala's small table and lifted the spoon from Tamala's saucer, studying it by the window. "This will do nicely, I think." Humming beneath her breath, Garnet dropped the spoon into her pouch.

"What are you doing?" Tamala's hands leaped to her breast. Her eyes widened, fastened on the pouch, as if she could see the spoon through the heavy leather. Her voice was shrill and breathless.

"Why, nothing." Garnet smiled. "I admire the pattern, that's all." Satisfied, she stepped onto the veranda and drew on her gloves, waiting for her horse.

"You're playing a dangerous game, love." Belaine buttoned his coat and shot his cuffs, then settled his hat over his hair. "Would it do any good to caution you against being foolish?"

"None."

"Or to warn you against making abrupt changes on the plantation?"

"No."

Frowning, he released a sigh. "I didn't think so."

They waited for their horses in silence, a silence that grew more awkward with each passing second. Garnet stuffed her hair beneath a wide-brimmed hat and snapped the brim forward to conceal her face. "Are you really leaving?" she asked quietly. Biting her lip, she stared out at the gravel driveway, wishing the boy would hurry along with the horses.

"This was only a temporary assignment, love. The governor is uneasy about the mood in Cap Français." Belaine shrugged, pulling his jacket tight across his shoulders. "All the outlying regiments have been ordered back to the garrison."

Garnet nodded, not trusting herself to comment. The sky was a clear blue. Today would be as blazing hot as it was every day. The sameness of the heat battered at spirits, frayed tempers. She no longer thought it strange that confusion reigned supreme in the tropics; the constant, debilitating heat edged minds toward the rim of madness.

"Come with me, Garnet." His fingers brushed her skin as he lifted an errant red strand from her neck and wound the silky curl around his finger.

Every instinct warned her to pull from his touch. But she could not move. The familiar hated weakness sapped her strength and her breath caught in her throat.

"You aren't safe here." A finger stroked her earlobe. "How many dead chickens does it take before you'll believe what I say?" The back of his hand ran lightly along her jawline.

And she felt paralyzed by his touch, by his powerful maleness, unable to think or move. And then her hand lifted and she touched his fingers against her face, pressing their strength to her cheek. "When you touch me I can't think," she whispered. "I . . . I know what I want my future to be and then you touch me and suddenly I'm not sure anymore." She lifted her face and saw the blaze in his eyes. "Oh, Jean. I wish . . ." The sight of the boy leading their horses released her from the magic of his dark eyes. Smothering a cry, she ran down the steps and flew toward the mare, leaping on its back without assistance and bending low over the mane as she jerked the horse's head toward the manor village.

This time Belaine hadn't bothered to mention marriage.

"Come with me." And her heart had twisted toward him. Damn, damn, damn. The sooner he departed the better. Then she could restore order to her vacillating thoughts. Then she could hear the wretched drums without longing for strong, sinewy arms, without imagining the firm, sensual hunger of his mouth. Damn!

When she was sure he couldn't see her, she guided the mare into one of the carrys and flung Tamala's spoon far out into the mucky water. Had she been in a better mood, she would have invented a spell to restore her humor. Instead she watched the spoon sink without expression, then tugged her hat brim down to shade her eyes from the sun's glare. She hoped Tamala's imagination was as active as her own; she hoped the sun was hurting Tamala's eyes, too.

Guiding the mare farther into the carry, she concealed herself among the wilting stalks and waited patiently until Belaine had passed, judging his progress with a critical eye. He sat his stallion as if the two were one, controlling the powerful animal with a flick of the wrist, obviously enjoying the air and the bright sunshine.

Garnet watched until the orange dot turned onto the main road, unaware that her eyes bore the haunted yearning of deep loss.

By virtue of determined effort, Garnet put him firmly from her mind. By the time she entered the mango grove fringing the outskirts of the manor village, Garnet's thoughts had calmed and she was eager to focus on events at hand.

If the plantation possessed a heart, it resided not in the manor but in the manor village. Here the horses were shod, and saddles and bridles fashioned. The *grands blancs'* clothing was sewn and washed and ironed here. The carpenters labored in this village, and the tinsmiths and the Habitation's carriage maker. Candles, shoes, ironwork, basketry—all originated here, efficiently overseen by an obese mulatto named Juniper.

All chatter halted as Garnet slipped from the mare and

looped the reins around a post. The laundresses' singing died along the stream bed; the conversations animating the sheds broke apart mid-sentence. The noisy concerns of chickens and pigs and the parrots in the rosewood trees sounded unnaturally loud. Hammers struck wood and iron; wet breeches struck against rock. No one spoke.

Frowning hesitantly, Garnet gazed about, wondering at the abrupt absence of noise. It wasn't until Juniper hurried forward, wringing sausage hands and bowing, that she comprehended she had caused the sudden, sullen silence. Looking slowly about the sun-baked, dusty square, she realized hers was the only white face within miles. But it was enough to layer waves of tension throughout the village.

Juniper bowed low, greeting her without meeting her eyes, then he snapped massive fingers and screamed at two boys standing beneath the cotton awning shading a shed front. They stared with wide, terrified eyes at the flaming wisps escaping Garnet's hat. "Get-you cool water hurry-up-quick for Missy Ga'net. Run plenty much fast or Juniper be-him whip you black asses."

The boys bolted from the stream, the puckered brands on their buttocks sliding up and down. Garnet dropped her gaze to her hands, wondering what Juniper's veiled eyes concealed. Did he, too, believe she was a *loa*? Did he think she had killed the twin babies? Refused to save those flayed by the wrathful Paul?

Shaking her head, she accepted the gourd of water the boys offered shyly, and swallowed a token sip, repressing a shudder at the brackish taste. "I want the manor house painted. Please begin immediately."

For an instant the hood across Juniper's eyes slipped, and she saw his surprise.

"Have the carpenters fix any loose boards and shutters, and I want the splintered dowel on the veranda repaired." His woolly head bobbed. "Take as many men as you need in order to complete the work by the day after tomorrow." She wanted the painting finished before Simone's ball.

"*Oui* and *oui*."

Juniper's broad, brown face beaded with perspiration. His eyes darted across the dusty square. Garnet could almost hear him wondering if he should check first with Mist' Paul, or if that would earn him the lash from Garnet.

"And I want a container of paint for myself."

Juniper blinked, then cuffed one of the boys, sending him scurrying to fetch the paint. No hint of curiosity enlivened Juniper's bland expression, though Garnet told herself it must exist. But of course he couldn't question her. Releasing a breath, she examined the village squalor while she waited, composing a lengthy mental list. There was much to be accomplished. Juniper puffed beside her, smiling endlessly as they passed between the tannery and the smithy, both sheds silent inside.

It was a decided relief when Garnet mounted her horse and spurred forward, leaving the village behind her. She shivered despite the sun's blaze. She couldn't explain her emotions, but she felt as if she had narrowly escaped an invisible danger as real and as hot as the broiling sun.

She rode the backroads through the carrys to the plantation gate, pausing only once to observe a crew clearing ditches. Lille stood beside the road, holding the reins to his horse, his whip coiled at his belt. His dirty hands looked uncomfortably empty, but his scowl was dark and full as he silently watched her ride past. To Garnet's immense satisfaction, the work seemed to be proceeding nicely without the crack of a whip. Pleasure gleamed in her green eyes as she coolly returned Lille's slow nod.

At the main gate, she dismounted and removed the old sign, then, on a board Rombo had given her earlier, she painted a black line down the center. On one side of the board she printed HABITATION DU CASSE; on the other, HABITATION WINTERS.

When she straightened and looked toward the coffee fields marching up the mountainsides, at the rich, distant stands of mahogany and Caribbean pine, pride squared her shoulders. Her dream of independence and challenge was becoming a reality. Everything she had ever wanted shimmered in tropical sunlight.

Inhaling deeply, the pleasure almost sensual, Garnet sniffed the dusty green ripeness of the fields, smelled the pungent sweet-and-sour harvest smoke puffing from the boiler houses. Bending, she plucked a velvety cluster of cockscomb and touched it to her cheek. A butterfly meandered along the roadside, lazy in its flight, its wing span as broad as her hand. She could make a good life here, a life to view with pride at the end of her days.

So why did the prospect seem so flat and empty?

Sighing, she crossed her arms atop the fence and lifted her eyes toward the manor. And immediately gagged. Spasms cramped her stomach as she stared at the black bodies dangling from palm trees lining the main drive. Heat had bloated the torn flesh and attracted swarming dark clouds of flies.

Lowering her head, she vomited until nothing more came up. She swung atop her horse, then, instead of returning to the manor house as she had planned, she ignored the scorching midday sun and searched the carrys until she located Nesta, the field overseer who had sent the four men out of the fields with their wounded friend. She hired him as her boss overseer.

"But he's black," Paul protested later when she located him in his office. "It isn't done." Aghast, he slammed a rum bottle on the desktop and stared in shock.

"He's capable and intelligent."

"Intelligent? He's a slave, a stupid animal with less intelligence than a dog."

Garnet leaned against the desk and pushed at her hair, glancing toward the rainclouds converging on the horizon. The clammy humidity heralding the afternoon shower plastered her silk blouse to her skin. "The matter is not open for discussion, Paul. Give me the papers, please." First she would free Josephine and Nesta; the others would come later, more gradually. "I'll want someone to take the papers to town for filing."

"Have you lost your senses?" Paul's tone was chilly. "You don't know what you're doing."

"I'm too tired to argue. Just give me the papers." She folded the papers he flung across the desk. "Please cut down those bodies before Simone's party." No emotion showed in her voice or expression. She'd emptied her emotion in front of the gate, knew it to be wasted.

"Such tender feelings, cousin." His smile patronized her. "Tender, delicate feelings—for selected people."

Something in the glance sliding over her breast propelled her backward. Her green eyes swept his puffed features and the bottle in his hand, and contempt twisted her lips. "That is correct . . . cousin. Please don't confuse the people."

He leaned toward her, his face red. "And don't forget whose house you live in . . . cousin."

"Ours, I believe. Mine as much as yours."

"Ours," Paul quoted. For the first time since she had appeared in his office, his eyes warmed. "What a lovely sound." His laughter pursued her up the stairs.

Garnet stood on her balcony and listlessly watched the first fat drops smack the tops of the banana fronds. The rain steamed along the ground.

The warm flush of pride she'd earlier felt had vanished. The battle against the island seemed overwhelming. Stepping inside, she wearily flung herself across the bed, wishing for a brisk New England breeze.

From her position on the bed she could see herself in the mirror. Her body was lean and tight, adjusted to long hours in the saddle, but her eyes seemed to have aged over the last weeks. She stared into an emerald reflection and saw the weight of responsibility there, read the pain of a sickened spirit.

Pain? She sat up abruptly, shaking her head violently. No. The ache in her eyes resulted from the sun's deadly glare. The soreness behind her ribs originated from riding during the heat of the day. Dolls and chickens be damned.

Still, her fingers reached to stroke her eyelids, then slid to her stomach. As to any dryness in wasted woman parts, she could think of no method for testing. Or could she?

After stripping off her dusty clothing, she put on a light wrapper and tied it around her waist, then returned to the bed. And wished she understood why she suddenly felt like weeping.

Why did he have to leave?

—13—

"I THINK EVERYTHING IS READY." The excited flush on Simone's cheeks matched her rose gown, a Moravian muslin delicately embroidered around hundreds of tiny open stars. "I hope I haven't forgotten anything."

Garnet laughed and leaned to the mirror to adjust the diamond eardrops Simone had insisted on lending her. "I don't see how you could have." The rattle of iron wheels crunching across the gravel driveway reached the back of the house as carriages began to arrive. Her own eyes danced with anticipation as she tilted her head and listened to the faint, discordant notes of the orchestra tuning instruments in the ballroom below.

"You look beautiful." Simone puffed Garnet's ivory sleeves, adjusting them lower to display more bared shoulder. After squinting critically, she pinned a red silk rose below Garnet's breast on the band of the high-waisted gown.

"To match my sunburn?" Garnet teased.

"A pink flush looks healthy." Simone listened to the carriages. "I think we're having a successful turnout because everyone wants to inspect the lady plantation owner."

Garnet tossed a shining arrangement of glossy red curls. "Let them look." Her recent accomplishments filled her with pride. The house sparkled with fresh paint; she'd chosen furniture from the attic to flesh out the rooms; and she had

215

ordered bolts of ruby damask to replace the sun-faded draperies throughout the manor. Economics be hanged.

The phrase brought a frown. Paul had refused to cut down
the bodies rotting along the driveway, claiming they established his honor among the arriving planters. Not even the
mounds of flowers heaped through the house could disguise
the odor when the breeze shifted.

But she wouldn't think about that now. Instead she smiled
at her reflection and congratulated herself on how well Nesta
was working out. He managed the field crews as if he had
done so for years. The past week had been exhausting but
also exhilarating. Garnet hadn't squandered a minute in beginning procedures that would make Winters sugar the most
famous in the island chain.

"Garnet . . ." Simone laid a pale glove on Garnet's arm
and bit her lip apologetically. "Before we go downstairs, I
wonder if I could beg a favor?"

"Of course. Anything."

Simone's soft gray eyes dropped, then lifted in a gentle
plea. "I know how strongly you feel about certain things, but
would you refrain from making inflammatory statements
tonight?" Responding to Garnet's quick frown, she rushed
on. "We have a very mixed group and tensions are running
high." Her gloves fluttered to her throat. "I think it would be
wise to avoid discussing political issues."

"Like Africans dangling from the palms?" Garnet asked
quietly. "Like field people blown up or tortured?"

Simone pressed Garnet's hands between her gloves. "Unfortunately not everyone believes as you and I and Jean."

"I won't disgrace you, Simone." There was no escaping
restrictions. Sometimes Garnet suspected true independence
was merely an illusion. She gave Simone's hand a reassuring
pat, then squared her shoulders and reminded herself that it
was important to create a favorable first impression. Eventually she would be accepted for who and what she was, some-

thing more than a curiosity. Change and acceptance occurred slowly; these maters required time.

But some of the eagerness had vanished from her step as she followed Simone down the staircase. Stifling opinions didn't come easily, especially when she resented the need to do so.

Many of their guests had arrived from as far north as St. Marc and from as far south as Leogane. After the first glittering group had passed her in the receiving line, Garnet abandoned any effort to recall names and titles. The multitude of faces blurred into a chattering stream of jewels and silks. Her cheeks ached from constant smiling, her glove dampened and soiled beneath a hundred polite kisses.

She nodded and smiled and murmured inane pleasantries, bowed and pressed hands, then released the guests to Paul, watching as expressions shaded from curiosity to thinly concealed outrage.

"Belaine demanded my sword. Is this your doing, du Casse? Or an affront to military prerogative?"

Fat red curls bounced against Garnet's cheek as she rose on tiptoe to glance over the sea of heads. Outside, Rombo's minions assisted extravagantly gowned ladies from their carriages onto a strip of crimson carpet, unrolled along the walkways to protect dainty slippers from puddles deposited by the afternoon rain. Jean greeted the men, politely but firmly divesting them of their sidearms.

"A man isn't comfortable or adequately dressed without his sword and pistol."

Paul shrugged and forced a smile that didn't touch his eyes. A bitter satisfaction carved deep lines beside his mouth; he had predicted Belaine's actions would provoke insult. Honor, however, demanded that Paul not admit Belaine had usurped his position; honor demanded that he at least feign agreement. "I concur with the colonel's precautions, my dear *comte*," he lied smoothly. "Accidents occur when tempers are high, do they not?" He winked jovially. "And your *comtesse* will appreciate not being required to dodge your sword when the dancing begins, *oui, comtesse?*"

The couple nodded coolly, unconvinced, before gliding toward the ballroom. Bowing, Paul dutifully pressed the next extended hand to his lips, then muttered beneath his breath, "Damn Belaine's eyes. I'll never hear the end of this."

Smiling automatically, Garnet surrendered her glove to the damp kiss of a foppish gentleman wearing lavender satin and lemon-colored hose. She dismissed Paul's objections as further evidence of rum-impeded logic. After an hour of observing the hostile glances exchanged between the *grands blancs* and the *gens de couleur*, Garnet had concluded that Jean's stubborn insistence on forbidding sidearms displayed a foresight that would allow everyone to breathe easier. She thought Paul should have been grateful.

Nodding pleasantly, Garnet greeted a handsome couple with skins the warm, rich color of caramel. Forgetting herself, she extended her glove without thinking, then swiftly snatched it back in a rush of awareness, feeling a flush of heat climb her throat. The clumsy gesture served to draw attention to her lapse. Stammering, she murmured something unintelligible, midway between a greeting and an apology, then sighed with embarrassed relief as the couple stepped toward Paul, their expressions stony. Under ordinary circumstances the mulatto couple would not have been invited; nor would they have considered attending. But these were not ordinary times.

France simmered in the sauce of rebellion. Her neglected children demanded equality with her cherished favorites. A nervous king paced a prison cell as men debated his fate and their own. And the entire world watched as the pot of revolt boiled hotter.

None awaited the outcome more anxiously than St. Domingue. The bastard offspring of France and Africa had pinned their hopes on the victory of France's natural children. Despairing of local relief, the mulattoes had dispatched their representatives to the National Assembly to plead their case in the halls of revolution, seeking constitutional recognition as whole men with full human rights.

"Will they receive a fair hearing?" Garnet asked softly when the last of the carriages had discharged its passengers and Jean had joined her at the archway leading into the ballroom. She accepted a cup of champagne punch from a silver tray served by an attendant clad in snowy starched livery, her gaze straying toward the dancers. The *grands blancs* danced to one side of a crimson velvet rope; the *gens de couleur* dipped and swayed on the other. The red cord reminded Garnet uneasily of a line of blood.

"No."

She looked up at him from beneath a sweep of thick, sooty lashes. Jean had chosen to wear his full-dress uniform, a not-too-subtle reminder of law and order. White breeches hugged muscled thighs; his orange jacket was elegantly tailored to fit snugly across broad shoulders. His black hair gleamed in the soft glow of a hundred scented candles. Garnet admitted to herself that he was easily the most distinctive man in the crowded ballroom.

The crinkled lines fanning from the corners of his eyes deepened as he flicked a glance over the crush of dancers, noting the velvet rope, the separate tables on either side. "If the Assembly recognizes the mulattoes as free men, they proclaim that a fraction of black blood is equal to white. It won't happen, love. Unfortunately." His dark eyes swept the pink-and-cream glow of candlelight on her bare shoulders. "Have I mentioned how extraordinarily beautiful you are tonight?"

Quickly Garnet returned her eyes to the dance floor, silently cursing herself for the sudden sense of breathlessness. She had received countless compliments in the last hour but none had caused her heart to accelerate as his did. Uncomfortable, she murmured an incoherent response, then guided the conversation into less intimate areas. But she continued to feel his eyes slowly exploring her body. "Do you still believe a local revolt is possible?"

His eyes lifted abruptly to her serious gaze. "Absolutely. I also believe the mulattoes will determine the outcome, depending upon whether they align themselves with the whites or with the blacks."

Garnet tried to concentrate on his words instead of the smoky intensity she read in the velvet depths of his eyes. She told herself the flutter in her throat was a result of the excitement of the party and not Jean's nearness. After glancing at his rugged profile, she hastily lowered her lashes and bit her lip in irritation. "It was wise of Simone to extend this overture of friendship."

"Good lord, is that a gavotte?" Jean slapped his forehead and a boyish helplessness widened his dark eyes. "I promised the first gavotte to Countess Mornay."

Garnet smiled. She remembered Countess Mornay from the receiving line, a heavily rouged woman wearing a brocade court dress stretched across a ridiculously wide pannier. "You'll make a charming couple." She laughed, amused by the uncharacteristic vulnerability in his stricken expression.

"If I can find her among all these people." He frowned across the sea of swaying bodies but made no move to begin the search.

"Use your nose," Garnet suggested wickedly. The heat was prodigious. Garnet pitied the royalists stubbornly clinging to hot brocades and heavy damasks. Wet stains darkened the men's underarms; trickles of perspiration leaked from beneath the wigs of those women foolish enough to have worn them. She was grateful for Simone's practicality. Simone had insisted they both wear gauzy island attire, Grecian in inspiration, airy and elegant, nearly impervious to the clammy humidity left behind by the rain.

In deliberate contrast to the royalist costume, the mulatto ladies and gentlemen had chosen light materials and the colors of the French Revolution. The statement was not prominent, of course, but displayed subtly along the piping of a bodice, on an embroidered lapel, or spread across a painted fan. Seeing the small repetitions of red, white, and blue, Garnet silently applauded Jean's foresight in forbidding sidearms.

"I'd rather be holding you in my arms, love." Belaine spoke so quietly Garnet almost didn't hear.

Her heart constricted and the punch cup tilted in her hand. Would he mention the subject she had thus far managed to avoid? Edging back, she answered with a bright smile and a coquettish toss of her fiery curls. "I find that difficult to believe, Colonel, as you haven't asked to sign my card."

"I don't know if I can bear another rejection." His voice teased but his eyes did not.

Garnet expelled a sigh of exasperation. The moment she slotted him into a neat pigeonhole, he did or said something to upset her conclusions. A tiny frown ruffled her brow. It was utterly stupid to encourage him. Yet her skin glowed and tingled from his disturbing nearness. She fluttered her fan in stubborn annoyance, though she couldn't have sworn that her irritation was directed solely toward him. A tart response hovered about her lips, one to indicate she didn't care in the least if he danced with her. In fact it would be best if he did not.

But Belaine had already lifted her card from the ribbon tied about her wrist and was lettering his name beside a minuet. His heavy brows arched in surprise as he scanned the empty spaces. "I'd have wagered my sword and spurs that your card would be filled—I've noticed a steady stream of gentlemen bowing over your hand."

Garnet nodded shortly, glancing at his bold handwriting dominating her card. A flush of color warmed her cheeks as she realized she had as good as asked him to place it there. "I'll learn more about cane off the dance floor than on it," she responded.

Belaine grinned and briefly touched her chin, lifting her

face. "I think we have here a cane man." The pleasure in his expression was unmistakable.

A rush of heat tingled along her skin where his fingers touched, and she ducked away before he could notice the sudden tremble of her smile. The effect of his touch was instantaneous and deeply upsetting. Summoning a steady smile, Garnet glanced at him from beneath her lashes. "Unless I'm wrong, I believe your countess has found you." She nodded toward the heavily perspiring woman bearing down on them with a wide, toothy smile. And she experienced an odd elation that the woman was neither young nor attractive.

"Lord have mercy," Belaine muttered. He leaned into a politely elegant bow above the countess's limp glove. The countess giggled into her fan, her eyes coy above the ruffled edge. Belaine grinned at Garnet over his shoulder as the countess dragged him onto the dance floor. Before they were swallowed by the dancers, Belaine winked and rolled his eyes toward heaven.

When she could no longer see his black curls, Garnet checked her card. As planned, she had two free sets before her next promised dance. Moving purposefully, she threaded a path toward the dining room.

A staggering array of food nearly obscured Simone's best lace cloth, testing the limits of the table. Pretending hunger, Garnet examined tureens of spiced shrimp, pheasant in orange sauce, succulent turtle steaks, and the island specialties: tassot, sweet-potato pudding, and calalou, a fiery mixture of salt pork, crabmeat, pepper, onions, and okra. She filled her plate indifferently, choosing crab cakes and lobster, and ladled a helping from a black-crab pepper pot.

Next she positioned herself near the window as if by accident and nodded absently at the servants rushing in and out of the room as she pushed the food around her plate. By tilting her head toward the draperies, she could comfortably eavesdrop on the gentlemen crowding about the table of hard spirits set up on the veranda. A like bar had been provided on the far side of the house for the mulatto gentlemen. A cockfight was scheduled later behind the stables; no women would attend, of course.

The necessity of eavesdropping appalled her, but she saw no other choice. To have joined the men would have appalled everyone else, and shattered her promise to Simone. Grimacing, Garnet popped a melon ball into her mouth and leaned as near the draperies as possible without revealing her presence.

". . . another goddamned disaster. Half my profits are rotting in the fields."

"Marchant owns an Arada who swears he can predict the rains to the hour. Is that true, Marchant?"

"I didn't lose a single stalk. In fact, gentlemen, this is a banner year."

A voice growled. "This isn't an appreciative group for banner years."

"The next time a slaver docks from Dahomey, buy yourself an Arada," the voice belonging to the unseen Marchant answered.

Cursing the necessity for hiding, Garnet eased from the window as a laughing group entered. In a perfect world she could have marched out to the veranda, joined the conversation, and talked cane to her heart's delight. There was so much she needed to know. The vagaries of cane pricing remained a mystery. How many crops could she harvest before replanting? When should she burn off her fields? Her steady, resentful glare hastened the intruders from the dining room and she resumed her position near the draperies. Her green eyes flared as she realized the conversation had shifted to her. Startled, she paused with her fork midway to her lips.

"Is it true she hired a black overseer?" The speaker's sharp tone mixed contempt and anger.

Paul's voice slurred. "And filed papers on him."

A babble of shocked protest erupted along the veranda.

"Did you reason with her?"

"No one can reason with Garnet Winters," Paul answered. Garnet heard a heavy rustle of brocade as he shrugged, heard him demand lime and nutmeg for his rum. "She wants to free every black on the island. She insists on enacting her humanitarian theories to prove something to those of us who know nothing."

Garnet's eyes narrowed and she stared hard at the crab cake on her plate. Paul was putting words in her mouth that she had never spoken. She had no interest in crusading, as he was implying. What the other planters did was their business and what she did was hers. As long as she hurt no one, she could not conceive that it was anyone's concern what she did with her property.

"That stupid little bitch is going to get us all killed. Doesn't she realize she's playing with fire? How long will our stock remain in harness when they learn what she's doing? And they will. Gentlemen, we're looking at trouble."

"Exactly what I've said," Paul answered agreeably.

In the ensuing silence, Garnet listened to clinking glasses and shuffling feet. Mind racing, she stared hard at the draperies. Paul was stating idle supper speculation as actuality, which it definitely was not. Yes, she hoped the Africans would one day be freed, and she would do what little she could to hasten that day. But she wasn't so naive as to believe total freedom would be granted in her lifetime.

By presenting her as a firebrand, Paul unwittingly placed her in peril. Had he been too rum-sotted to recall the plans she had shared, gradual changes, at the dinner table? Surely Garnet had stated her position clearly; lofty aspirations had been scaled to moving slowly toward more realistic goals.

"She has to be stopped before she does any real damage." The rough voice was cold and frighteningly quiet.

"The Africans may solve our problem, gentlemen. They seem to think she's some kind of goddess, or pretending to be a goddess." Other voices concurred, mentioning the heart *vèvès* and offerings. Garnet's heart sank, then fluttered.

"Sooner or later a jealous *bocor* will order her poisoned. One night we'll hear the drums and Mademoiselle Winters will cease to trouble us further."

Garnet's fingers whitened about the edge of her plate. Silently she willed Paul's intervention.

"But the Africans may not act quickly enough," Paul offered casually. Garnet blinked and stared at the wall as if she could see him through it. "We may be forced to address the problem directly." Murmurs of agreement welcomed his words.

Fresh shock widened Garnet's eyes. What on earth was Paul doing? Didn't he realize what he was saying?

"A pity," a new voice commented above the clink of glasses and chatter. "She's a beauty." The man's voice dropped, and was followed in a moment by an explosion of ribald laughter. "May we assume you've sampled her charms, du Casse?"

"Naturally. And I'd suggest you do the same, Villiers, before we dispose of her."

Cold fury knotted Garnet's jaw. Her fingers opened and closed on the plate edge. How dare he impugn her honor. She debated rushing onto the veranda and confronting him—propriety be damned.

"If it comes to that, gentlemen. Nothing is decided. We'll give the matter more time."

"Try logic, du Casse. Talk to her. Be insistent. We simply cannot allow this stupidity—it's far too dangerous. Tell her the black overseer must be replaced immediately."

Sparks of anger shot from Garnet's eyes and high color fired her cheeks. She thanked God they could not see her, praised heaven for the wall between herself and the planters. Her hands shook with the desire to confront them.

"Ah, logic is the problem, my dear *comte*," Paul responded lazily, his voice rum-blurred. "She's just a woman. What woman responds to reason and logic?" They all laughed.

Furious, Garnet pushed her plate onto the table and fled,

stumbling blindly toward the ballroom. At the archway, she glanced into the heated crush, then veered down a deserted corridor instead, sinking abruptly to a settee placed before an embroidered screen closing off the room behind. She needed to collect her thoughts before she risked facing Paul again.

Hands shaking with anger rose to her temples and she pressed her lashes hard against her cheekbones. The planters discussed murder as calmly as they ordered the next drink. And Paul. Instead of correcting their assumptions, he had, in fact, actively incited the planters' hostility.

There had to be a reason. People did not act without reason, not even Paul du Casse. Garnet's mind skipped forward, then flew backward, knitting a thought here, an idea there. She halted abruptly when she recalled Grandpère's will. If either she or Simone died childless, their portion of the estate reverted to the survivor. Garnet's stomach turned to paste. Paul wanted her land however he could get it.

His dangerous words had not been voiced by accident, but by careful design. Her eyes flashed and her chin stiffened. No one would take the Habitation Winters from her. It was her slice of forever.

Grimly Garnet rose to her feet, gathering her skirts. Then she paused uncertainly as a low murmur approached the screen from the far side. She lifted startled eyes to the shadows against the panels of embroidered silk.

"You weren't always so elusive, Colonel."

Tamala's seductive purr was unmistakable. Garnet bit her lips and darted a quick glance down the corridor. Heat flushed her cheeks. She should leave this minute. This very minute. She stared at twin shadows against the screen and inhaled sharply as Tamala's arms circled the neck of the tall silhouette standing close to her. Very close to her.

Jean's hands lifted to disentangle Tamala's arms. "Temptation, get thee behind me." His teasing statement was gentler than Garnet wished it to be.

She smoothed her gloves over her skirt nervously. It was

wrong to remain; she'd had enough eavesdropping for one night. She darted a glance toward the profiles on the screen and an acid pang of jealousy knotted her stomach. The right thing was to leave immediately, and she would—in just a moment.

"Are you afraid your red-haired lover will discover us?" Tamala's sulky tone challenged.

Swallowing, Garnet stared at the screen. She could have sworn she felt a stab below her ribs, but she was allowing her imagination to run away with her. She really should leave, steal down the corridor . . .

"You've been a naughty girl, haven't you? Chickens and dolls." Jean laughed. "And chopped hair in my coffee? Was that your work, too?"

Tamala's shadowy hand dropped to her bosom. "Do you remember giving me this necklace?" she asked, her voice husky. "And why?"

Jean laughed softly. "I haven't forgotten."

Something twisted violently beneath Garnet's heart. She closed her eyes and clenched her teeth against the viperish coil of jealousy constricting her breathing. She had no right to feel this way. She had turned him down. Cursing herself for a fool, she dropped her forehead against her palm and listened shamelessly. And knew she should run away. There was nothing here but pain—they might step out and discover her. She would die of shame if they did.

"Take me with you to the Cap, Jean." Sensual promise wove through Tamala's husky tone. "You won't be sorry."

"I can't do that."

Garnet stared at the fingers of her gloves. Was he expressing regret?

"Not as a wife, Jean. I know the law. Just . . . just you and me, as it used to be."

"You're so beautiful," he murmured. And Garnet swayed, feeling her heart contract. "Educated, skilled in areas a man most appreciates." His voice continued over Tamala's pleased laugh. "But life with me would be half a life—is that what you really want? Wouldn't you be happier returning to the ballroom and seducing a wealthy mulatto planter, a man who can offer marriage and honor?"

"A black."

"A free mulatto. With skin as pale as your own."

Tamala's shadow quivered. Her voice lashed out, careless with emotion. "I'll not mix my blood with that of a black."

"Listen to me." Garnet watched Jean's hands tighten on Tamala's shadowy shoulders. "Can you honestly claim that you'd rather be a white man's whore than a mulatto's wife? Tamala, half of that ballroom—"

"Half."

"—is filled with men who would love you and provide you a comfortable life. If you will accept who you are."

"Don't lecture me." A blur of darkness and light flashed, then the clear outline of Tamala's lush, uncovered breast appeared exposed against the screen. Garnet smothered a gasp with her glove. "This brand is who I am. How many times did you kiss this scar and stroke it? How many times, Belaine? You weren't advising me then to seduce the sons of slaves. I was good enough for a white man then, wasn't I? I was good enough for you before *she* came."

Garnet desperately did not want to hear this. Mental images unreeled behind her stricken eyes. Helplessly she imagined them together, Tamala's long, sensual body intertwined with Belaine's powerful legs. And a sliver of pain sliced through her chest. She lowered her head, telling herself emphatically that she didn't care.

But she felt betrayed. Against all logic, she felt the poisonous sickness of betrayal.

The lilting opening of a minuet floated from the ballroom. She hastily consulted her card. Somewhere a man named Jules Barbier was looking for her.

"When she dies, you'll come back to me, Jean. You'll be rapping at my door again. And—"

"There you are. I believe I have the honor of this dance, Mademoiselle Winters." Garnet looked up in horror as Jules Barbier rounded the hallway, his broad aristocratic mouth breaking into smiles as he called her name.

The voices stopped behind the screen. Then a man's sunburned hand swept the panels aside and Jean's hard eyes met Garnet's embarrassed stare. He reached for her. "Garnet."

Cheeks flaming, Garnet ducked from his hand. A wooden smile cracked her lips as she inclined her head to Barbier. Flirting outrageously, a hint of desperation in her eyes, she accepted his extended arm and hurried him down the hall and into the ballroom without a backward glance.

Tamala's laughter rang in her ears.

—14—

THE HUMILIATION OF BEING CAUGHT eavesdropping raised circles of hot crimson to Garnet's cheeks. Trembling with embarrassment and the ache of a wild jealousy, she followed blindly as Barbier led her onto the dance floor. Bright dancers swirled around her, silk flower petals dipping and swaying. Barbier whispered extravagant compliments when he drew her near, and she smiled and watched his lips move and wondered what he had said. Simone whirled past in a billow of pink, her eyes bright, her laugh a silvery chime before she vanished within the crush.

Garnet performed the intricate patterns of the dance without listening to the music. An odd disorientation allowed her to observe herself bowing, stepping forward and back, all without the sensation of actual movement. Whom could she call friend? Had Barbier been among those on the veranda arranging her future? Had that man? Or that? She closed her eyes for a moment. It struck her as ludicrous that she could recall the plotters on the veranda with less anguish than she could recall Jean's shadow gazing at Tamala's exposed breast.

And Paul. She struck the toe of her slipper against Barbier's boot as a wave of dizziness speckled her vision. What had she done that was so terrible? Why did so many people want her dead?

Golden flecks of emotion appeared in her eyes, lightening

the deep emerald color to pale jade and causing Jules Barbier to stumble. She had stubbornly believed she could face down any obstacle—but the ranks of foes increased daily. It seemed no one wished her health and happiness but Simone. And Jean.

Jean.

"Stand aside, Barbier. This dance is mine."

Garnet stared into Jean's hard-angled face, believing for an instant that she had conjured him.

"I believe you're mistaken, Colonel. You may inspect Mademoiselle Winter's card if . . ." Barbier met Belaine's cold stare, then sniffed and wet his lips. He bowed above Garnet's glove, his cheeks flushed with angry color, his tone stiff. "If Mademoiselle does not object . . ."

"Mademoiselle does not object." Jean answered for her.

"I do object," Garnet snapped. A blush fired her cheeks as those nearest turned with curious stares. She tried to pull discreetly from Belaine's grasp, but his fingers tightened about her wrist like an iron clamp. "Let go of me!" The words came from falsely smiling lips. She nodded pleasantly to Countess Mornay, fuming at the humiliation of the scene.

"Not until we've talked." Half dragging her, Belaine strode toward the double doors opening onto the veranda, shouldering a path through the dancers. "Smile." He inclined his dark head and flashed a smile toward the aging matrons perched along the wall like crows on a fence.

Garnet cursed him through clenched but smiling lips, trying vainly to free her hand without calling additional attention to them both. "We have nothing to say."

Silently he guided her down the veranda steps, his hand like a vise, and then along one of the torchlit pathways, ignoring the strolling couples and white-coated slaves offering trays of champagne and small pastries. At the curve leading toward the stables, he departed from the path and pulled her into the dark privacy of the banana grove.

His fingers bruised her flesh, hurting, though she would

have submitted to torture before admitting as much. The smoldering anger in his black eyes triggered her defenses, and she wrenched free, whirling on him with blazing eyes. "How dare you cause such a scene. What will everyone think?"

"Why don't you eavesdrop some more and find out?" he snapped. His voice was cold, and suddenly Garnet saw the professional, unyielding soldier as she hadn't before.

Scarlet fired her cheeks and throat. As she could not defend her action, she brazenly ignored the barb. "I won't dignify that remark with a reply." Her chin jutted toward him. Whirling, she gathered ivory folds of batiste and kicked at her hem. "If you're seeking company, I suggest you return to Tamala. Obviously she's willing and, just as obviously, I am not." Her petulent tone rang with obvious jealousy. She could promise herself from now until judgment day that she didn't care what women he'd held in his arms and made love to, but she did care. The utter stupidity of caring, and the hurt of it, raised a tremble to her lips.

"Eavesdroppers merit no explanations."

"I didn't ask for any." Her sharp reply was as frosty as his. "How long were you spying on us?"

The heat in her cheeks formed crimson circles. "Long enough to watch Tamala bare her breast. Charming. But of course you've seen Tamala's breast many times before, haven't you?" Her poisonous sarcasm appalled her by its childishness. But she badly wanted to slash and wound, to inflict the same painful betrayal that lashed through her own heart. And she knew it wouldn't happen.

Abandoning the attack while she still managed to retain some semblance of pride, she clutched her skirts and attempted to shove past him. But his hands clamped her bare shoulders and held her fast, bruising her tender skin.

"I told you once and I'll tell you again: I owe you no explanations for what happened before I met you. And you owe me no explanations for your previous involvements."

The thought had never entered her head. "Explain *my*

involvements . . . to you?" She laughed, the sound shrill and approaching hysteria. "Let me go."

He released her so abruptly she stumbled, but the deep anger darkening his eyes halted her flight.

"Of course. It's laughable for me to question you, isn't it? But you are entitled to answers. Is that right, love? Do I understand our situation correctly?" His granite anger pinned her in place; the lines tightening his lips were carved from stone. "You want guarantees. You want it guaranteed that no woman existed before you and none will exist after you. You want reassurances and promises without a solitary word of commitment from you."

Her eyes flared a blazing emerald, then narrowed.

"I'm growing weary of one-sided commitments, Garnet. I can't change the past for you, nor would I. And you want the future tied in promises I'm not sure I can fulfill. You want a man without a past who is willing to mortgage his future. A man willing to promise away his life with no like promise from you." Garnet edged back from the coldness in his gaze. "I've said I want to marry you and I do. When will you trust in that and let us get on with planning a future we can both accept? If such is possible."

"Never. How can you speak of trust and marriage when I've just discovered you hidden behind a screen with a woman's arms wrapped around your neck?" She drew a breath, battling an inexplicable lump in her throat. When she saw the white flash of his sudden grin, her confusion settled into anger.

"You're jealous," he said slowly. His grin widened in comprehension, a pale curve of moonlight. "That's it, isn't it, love?" he repeated softly. "You are jealous."

His arrogant pleasure enraged her. "Of Tamala? Of your mulatto mistress?" She tossed her head defiantly and tried valiantly to sound convincing. "Of course not. You insult me to suggest I could envy a black."

They stared at each other, her words increasing the distance between them.

At the word "mulatto" his features had instantly sobered. Dark, probing eyes coolly searched her face. "How quickly this damned island infects people," he said quietly.

Threads of confusion sent Garnet's mind spinning. She had no idea why she had uttered such an idiotic remark. She who had hired and freed a black overseer, she who had deplored an uncle who refused to recognize or accept a mulatto daughter. Too late she remembered Jean's mulatto half-brother, André; recalled Jean's beliefs and her own regarding the devastation and misery of prejudice. An embarrassed bewilderment trembled along her mouth. "I . . . that isn't what I meant." She had uttered the first hateful words that sprang into her head. And she would have given anything to retrieve her impulsiveness.

"Exactly what did you mean?" Jean stepped farther into the banana grove, his bearing tall, military, and correct.

"Jean, you must know that I'm not like the others. I don't condone prejudice."

"Do I? It doesn't sound that way, does it?" His eyes locked on hers. Flickering torchlight shadowed the stony creases framing his mouth. "I'm beginning to wonder if even you know what you really think. Or if you adjust your thoughts to fit the occasion."

Garnet recoiled from his hard appraisal. "You aren't being fair."

"You're a game player, love. At the moment a poor one. You act on the instant—you don't think past the current move. For example, you dropped a ball of hair into Tamala's coffee this morning. Apart from the childishness of the act, have you considered the consequences? Now it's her move. What will Tamala do now that your impulsiveness has forced her hand? The game is heating up, love. On all fronts."

Garnet had congratulated herself on the cleverness of stealing hair from Tamala's brush. Now she felt foolish at being caught. She flushed. "I thought—"

"You didn't think," he stated flatly. "The islanders take

their magic very seriously. You've declared war on a battle-ground you can't comprehend using weapons you don't understand."

"I didn't start this." Garnet's chin steadied defensively, and her green eyes flashed. "I didn't make a stupid doll or nail a chicken over a door." Whenever she thought of the bloody chicken, her stomach cramped. Silently she swore it had nothing to do with dolls or chickens and everything to do with an overactive imagination.

"And you're doing nothing to end it, are you? You'd rather play games by stealing spoons and hair." He watched the blush deepen across her breast. "Do you have any idea what a stolen spoon represents to these people? Are you aware that chopped hair is a love potion, a ball of hair a death threat?"

Angry, they faced each other beneath the swaying banana palms. And without wishing it, Garnet suddenly thought of the last time they had been here. She moistened her parted lips and her fury departed as abruptly as it arisen, replaced by an unsettling whirlwind of emotion.

Everything he had said was correct.

She touched a shaking hand to her temple, admitting silently that she couldn't think clearly in his presence. His vivid masculinity troubled her in disturbing ways, made a foolish adolescent of a competent young woman.

His fists opened and closed beneath his cuffs. His smolder-ing stare raked her breasts, her hips, then he appeared to change his mind about saying more and turned, striding toward the pathway without a word, leaving her to the rustling silence and moist darkness of the banana grove.

"Wait!" The wind shifted and a sweet, rotting odor in-vaded Garnet's nostrils. She pressed her handkerchief to her nose and thanked God that she couldn't see the main drive-way from the banana grove. And wished she had explained herself better to Belaine. She stamped a satin slipper. Preju-dice had nothing to do with her objections to Tamala. He should have known that.

She thought of her own words and sighed heavily. There was no reason on earth why he should know what was in her mind when her mouth voiced otherwise. Damn. Slowly Garnet adjusted her shawl and stepped onto the brick pathway. Far ahead she saw Belaine, mounting the veranda steps with long strides, each step a fluid motion of unconscious grace and energy. Garnet bit the tip of her glove.

Why did such a man wish to marry? And what woman would trust his commitment? The stab of anguish Garnet had experienced when Tamala had bared her breast was but a tiny sampling of what would have lain in wait if Garnet had been foolish enough to accept him.

All right, she didn't want him as a husband—but she did want him as a friend. She badly needed a friend. Lingering on the pathway, she stooped to pluck a sprig of mirabilis and twirled it beneath her nose. She wanted Belaine's friendship and respect. Worse, she craved it. She didn't want him leaving Port-au-Prince thinking her a prejudiced, impetuous fool.

Lost in thought, she followed the sweetness of the violins, moving toward the light shining across the lawns. How to redeem herself in his eyes: That was the question. How could she prove herself worthy of Jean's admiration? She needed a heroic act, a statement.

Once inside the manor, Garnet paused at the ballroom archway, surveying the glow of candles, the heaped flowers, the throng of dancers. She didn't see Belaine on the dance floor, but she sensed his presence. Simone swayed lightly in the arms of Jules Barbier; Garnet frowned at Paul, well on his way to drunkenness, stumbling through the set with a perspiring baroness. Beyond the velvet rope Tamala danced with a handsome mulatto, an expression of boredom on her sultry features.

Simone would be pleased, Garnet thought absently, the party was a success. Watching, she tapped the edges of her fan against her teeth, her eyes sharpening. But had the ball accomplished anything? Had it convinced the *gens de couleur* of the *grands blancs*' friendship and goodwill?

After examining the blood-red divider and considering the separate veranda bars, the separate buffet tables, Garnet concluded the effort had not gone far enough. She observed no true mingling. Aside from a common roof and shared music, the whites and mulattoes might have attended separate balls.

In a flash of inspiration, Garnet saw how to win Belaine's admiration and solidify the mulattoes' support in the event of a revolt.

An excited sparkle chased the distress from her eyes as a plan formed. She could unite the two separate groups into one.

What was needed was a person of innovative courage willing to surmount the velvet divider. Why not Garnet Winters? Why not, indeed?

Gathering clouds of ivory batiste, she circled the dance floor with a firm step, a dauntless pride steeling her carriage against the thump of her heart. She hoped that somewhere Belaine was watching. At the crimson rope she halted and drew a long breath, then plunged ahead, pointedly addressing a dark young man standing on the far side, a drink in his hand. Hints of Africa shaped the mahogany planes of an arresting face.

"Monsieur Poisson?" She remembered his rich clothing and careful etiquette from the receiving line. Unfurling her fan across her breast, Garnet stepped nearer until the blood-red rope pressed into her skirts. "Are you enjoying the music?"

Raynald Poisson regarded her with ill-concealed astonishment. Uncomfortably he straightened his cravat and edged back slightly. "The music is enchanting, Mademoiselle Winters."

"Do you dance, Monsieur Poisson?" Garnet's lips curved in a dazzling invitation. Her level green eyes promised he did not misunderstand.

Shock paled Poisson's broad features. His dark eyes darted

to one side and then the other. When he spoke, his voice had thinned with emotion. "This is not Paris, mademoiselle." Briefly his narrowed gaze swept the silk roses trembling on her bosom, then instantly slid aside. "You forget where we are."

Never had Garnet been more uncomfortably aware of her flaming curls, her milky skin; never had she resented more the assumed superiority of those pale tints. The appalling injustice strengthened her position and convictions. She formed her lips into a charming pout. She wouldn't make it easy for him. "Are you refusing me, monsieur?" Forcing her voice into a light tone, she deliberately increased the pressure. "Surely you would not intentionally insult a neighbor?"

She had placed him in a double bind. No one could guess what might happen if they danced, but he would certainly end up in jail as a result of insulting a white woman.

Perspiration appeared on Poisson's brow. His reply was a hoarse whisper. "How have I offended you that you want to see me dead?" He drained his rum in a swallow, then both dark hands gripped the rope, his shoulders stiffened with anger. For a moment he stared into Garnet's eyes, then his voice sank to a plea. "Why in the name of God are you insisting on this madness?"

Garnet's wave encompassed the entire ballroom. "Because this is wrong. Because I detest everything this rope represents. Don't you?" Her simple explanation rang with the quiet intensity of truth. "Because you and I will be neighbors for many years. Not adversaries, Raynald—neighbors. People sharing the land and its resources and its heartbreaks. Must we be enemies? Must we live our lives in separate compartments?" Her eyes met his. "Why can't we reach out to each other like two caring human beings?"

Poisson regarded her as if she had fallen from the sky, a strange and alien creature.

"One dance—one courageous act of humanity might be enough to smash this damned barrier forever." Fumbling in

her earnestness, Garnet found the dance card tied about her
wrist and extended it to him, frowning as he flinched. Poisson stared at the card aghast, as if it were a viper poised to
strike. "One dance, monsieur. A gesture of conviction, and
friendship."

"Mademoiselle, you are truly mad."

"Not mad in the sense you intend. I'm angry that this rope
can exist. We're all one people, needing each other. If a
revolt shatters St. Domingue—"

A roar drowned her speech. "*Stand away from this lady.*"
Jules Barbier clamped a heavy, protective hand on Garnet's
shoulder, thrusting his body solidly between her skirts and
Poisson. A slash of velvet crimson pressed against his fawn-
colored breeches. Scarcely contained fury knotted his jaw,
shook the lace frothing from throat and cuffs. "You're dead,
Poisson."

"Jules . . ." Dancers had paused, turning to stare. Garnet
glanced at them uneasily, tasting the brackish tin of alarm
flooding into her mouth. "You don't understand."

"I understand this black jackass tried to sign your card.
He'll die for that obscenity." Barbier's hand swept to the
scabbard at his side. A surprised curse roared from his mouth
as he discovered his sword was missing. "Damn Belaine's soul
to hell."

Silently Garnet thanked Jean for his foresight. Drawing a
steadying breath, she frowned into Barbier's flushed face,
speaking quietly but firmly. "No, Jules. I asked *him* to dance.
Monsieur Poisson gave no offense, he—"

Barbier's arm enclosed her tightly, crushing the air from
her lungs, shielding her from Poisson's horrified stare. "There
is no need to distort the facts, mademoiselle. I beg you not to
allow breeding and tact to obscure the truth. I know what I
saw."

She stared up at him. Did he genuinely believe what he
was saying?

Attracted by Barbier's outrage, a circle collected on either side of the rope. Stunned murmurs passed the story; rising expressions of shock and fury dimmed the strains of a faltering minuet.

For a brief instant, Poisson met Garnet's frantic blink of disbelief, then he spoke. And the resignation dulling his tone sickened her heart. "I beg the lady's forgiveness," he said quietly. "I've recently returned from Paris. I forgot myself and where I was."

"Don't listen to him." Whirling, Garnet tugged at Barbier's satin sleeve, feeling his arm tensed like cordwood beneath her digging fingers. "This is my fault. Monsieur Poisson is blameless."

"Silence, mademoiselle," Barbier growled. Before he seized her by the waist and passed her backward through the crowd, he hissed in her ear. "You are disgracing yourself by this insane insistence. Or is it true what they say about you? That you sleep with blacks."

Garnet went limp with shock. A dozen hands clutched toward her, carrying her away from the men clustered about the rope.

Before the hands deposited her near the archway, the ballroom exploded into fighting. The eruption was instantaneous, as if every man had been waiting for the signal to begin. Garnet wrenched free, a billow of ivory swirling about her slippers, and her gloves flew to her lips.

The stanchions supporting the crimson rope crashed to the floor and men poured forward from both sides. Women screamed and fought to escape a battleground that minutes before had served as a dance floor.

Long-held grudges flared into furious memory, crossing color lines, and fists flew, avenging wrongs both real and imagined. Mulattoes and whites battered each other ferociously, whites pounded whites, mulattoes smashed mulattoes, using whatever lay at hand as weapons. A chair leg opened the head of the gentleman who had boasted the bountiful harvest. A planter renowned for especially fine molasses found himself a target for unforgiving competitors, both light-skinned and dark.

"For God's sake, stop." But no one could hear past the raucous din of screams and shouted curses and breaking furniture.

"Exactly as I predicted." Paul's rum-sweet breath bathed her cheeks as Garnet looked over her shoulder. "It's Simone's fault. And Belaine's."

Rage constricted Garnet's chest. "You idiot! You murdering idiot!" She cracked her palm across his cheek, swinging her full weight behind the blow. He staggered backward and into the path of a dark-skinned man rushing forward with bared teeth. A spray of silver hair fanned around Paul's face as the mulatto's fist slammed into his cheek. He slumped to the floor and a terrified servant dragged him out of the battle.

Good God. Garnet stared at Paul's crumpled figure propped against the wall. She wanted to shake the hand of his attacker. Instead she lifted her skirts and hastily stepped back as a body slid out of the melee. A man blinked stupidly at bleeding and broken knuckles, then scrambled to his feet with a cry of rage, lowered his head, and charged back into the battle.

Jean . . . where was Jean? Garnet's narrowed eyes searched the havoc until she found him near the far double doors. Jerking up her skirts, she plunged into the battle, weaving a path through the chaos.

Jean's spine was against the wall, his eyes a glitter of steel velvet, his jaw corded. Two men, satin sleeves torn from their jackets, threatened, one from either side. One of the attackers spun to deflect the blow of an advancing mulatto; the other, blood dripping from his nose and mouth, snarled and thrust a hand into his waistcoat. Candlelight flashed along the blade of a dagger.

Without halting her headlong rush, Garnet snatched a tray from the hands of a quivering servant and dashed forward. Clenching her teeth, she swung the heavy silver tray above her head and smashed it down with all her might. The man staggered, blinked, then crumpled at Jean's feet.

Belaine prodded the man with his boot. "Well done." He congratulated her with a quick grin. "I owe you one, love." After kicking the dagger beneath a potted palm, he surveyed the room, raking a hand through the black hair falling across his brow. His face and furious eyes frightened her. "Now be a good girl and get out of here."

"Jean . . ."

"Tell the soldiers guarding the sidearms to shoot any bastard who tries to retrieve his weapons." An urgent push propelled her toward the double doors.

Boots trampled her hem, ripping away chunks of ivory as Garnet rushed forward, then tumbled down the veranda steps toward the guard tent. After hastily relaying Jean's message, she rushed back to the ballroom, sickened by the screams of unbridled conflict.

If anything, the situation had worsened in her brief absence. Inflamed by the brawling around them, the women had joined the battle, venting long-festering envies and resentments. Two mulatto women circled each other, waving sharp hatpins; two previously dignified countesses rolled across the archway entrance pulling hair and scratching cheeks. Countess Mornay shoved her wig from over one eye and happily bashed a young beauty across the bottom, wielding a long, crusty bread loaf like a club.

"Oh, sweet heaven," Simone groaned. Sagging in the archway, she leaned a chalky forehead against Garnet's shoulder and squeezed her eyes shut, blotting out the madness. "Dear God." A chestnut curl toppled, swinging past a pink scratch opened along her arm. "Oh, my God."

Open-mouthed musicians stood on the dais, instruments hanging from their hands, their eyes as round as cymbals. They scattered toward servants huddled in the corners as the orchestra stand splintered and collapsed. Fighting raged across the ballroom, coiled fists smashed into bloodied noses, boots kicked and trampled. Bones snapped, flesh tore.

Garnet jumped as a cool, deep voice spoke near her ear. "Missy Ga'net be-her wish Rombo order up carriages plenty much quick."

Rombo's dark eyes revealed nothing but a glassy reflection of Garnet's wild dismay. "*Oui* and *oui*. For heaven's sake, don't just stand there, send someone to the stables immediately."

Rombo bowed immaculately, waiting as a body sailed through the archway, splattering red droplets across the women's skirts. Expressionless, he watched the man slide across the polished corridor and bump to rest against the far wall. The man lifted a hand, attempted to speak, then grinned and passed out. Rombo stepped over his sprawled feet and moved toward the veranda, his pace direct but unhurried.

Garnet frowned after him. Had she read mockery? Contempt? Shaking off the prickling raising her skin, she rubbed Simone's cold hands and together they watched the whirling, shouting battle, their eyes stunned. A shot exploded on the far side of the room. Showers of glass fell from the chandelier.

Belaine and two soldiers stood near the double doors, their guns leveled. "*Enough*," Belaine roared, his shout carrying above the noise in the room. "It's over now."

The shot still reverberated against the silk-clad walls, overhung the harshness of labored breathing.

"Your carriages are arriving in front. Collect your women and leave quietly." Belaine's command scraped across a charged hesitation. "My men will return your sidearms tomorrow afternoon."

A storm of protest howled through the ballroom.

Jean fired at the ceiling and waited until the silence was complete. "Anyone rushing the arms tent will be shot." His dark challenge moved slowly across a sea of belligerence. "Anyone deciding to continue this idiocy tonight or tomorrow will be jailed; no exceptions."

*　　　*　　　*

Simone slumped against the archway, wringing her hands and murmuring solicitous phrases as a bleeding stream of people passed before her in silence. Her drawn face reminded Garnet of crumpled linen.

"A pity," Jean commented, watching her. He sprawled in a ruined chair near the wreckage of the orchestra stand. The chair tilted precariously; wads of stuffing protruded where the arms had been.

"She worked on this party for weeks. She wanted so badly for it to be a success." Bowing beneath a burden of guilt, Garnet slowly surveyed the ballroom, scarcely able to believe this was the same room she had admired only a few hours ago. Awesome destruction met her gaze.

Scattered food and napkins and bits of torn clothing littered the floor. Strips of silk curled from the walls. Smashed glass crunched underfoot. Simone's porcelain lay in fragments; broken vases and candlesticks and picture frames and music stands created an obstacle course from corner to corner. A chandelier had crashed, scattering candles and wax and broken bits of crystal. The furniture lay in splinters.

Impassive as always, Rombo strode the length of the room, dragging an unconscious planter by his boots. The man's grim-lipped wife walked behind, her head held high, a nasty bruise beginning to swell beside her eye. Paul lay in a heap against the archway door, a bottle of rum thrust between his legs, his mouth gaping open in a drunken snore.

Releasing a sigh of remorse, Garnet pulled a musician's stool upright and sat gingerly. She stared at her feet, only now noticing that one of her slippers was missing. Another curl sagged, then whispered down her back.

Jean's dark hair curled loosely around his neck and ears, the ribbon having long since vanished. He had discarded his torn jacket and rolled his sleeves to the elbows. Garnet watched as he wearily flexed his shoulders, then placed a hand to his ribs with a wince.

"Are you hurt?"

"This?" His hand touched the shirt above his scar. "Only when I remember it." He pushed his hand through tousled hair, then swallowed deeply from the bottle of brandy Rombo had earlier produced. "How the hell did this fiasco start?"

Garnet bit her lip and thought it a pity that Belaine hadn't met Uncle William. Uncle William would have guessed the truth immediately. She was spared a reply as Countess Mornay approached them and extended a soiled glove for Jean's kiss.

"It appears that I'm the last to leave." She smiled. The lower portion of the countess's skirt had disappeared. Ragged edges of brocade flapped about the broken frame of her pannier. The pannier drooped like fractured wings over her hips, only partially concealing her exposed pantaloons. She kissed Jean soundly on both cheeks, then pressed Garnet's hand warmly, her face glowing. "A lovely party, my dear, simply lovely. I can't remember when I've enjoyed myself more."

Garnet blinked in astonishment.

Excusing herself, the countess skirted the debris, moving toward the archway as dignified as if her undergarments were not exposed and her wig not sliding perilously over her eyes. She paused to examine Paul's unconscious form, then drew back her slipper and kicked him smartly. "For good measure. I don't like that man." She directed a dazzling smile toward Simone. "A wonderful party, Simone, dear. *Magnifique*. I wish you'd confide your secret." A hint of envy confirmed her sincerity. "How do you manage such interesting affairs?"

Simone stared. "It's all in the guest list," she responded weakly.

"I shall be distraught unless you promise to invite me again next year." The countess swept out to the last waiting carriage. In a moment they heard the spin of iron wheels on gravel and then silence. Blessed silence.

"All in the guest list?" Jean laughed and pushed through

the broken planks of the orchestra stand until he found a stool for Simone.

Simone accepted the stool gratefully and dropped her head into her hands, a curtain of chestnut hair swinging forward to hide her face. "I've never been so humiliated in my life." She tugged aside the veil of curls to stare across the room at Paul's sprawled form. "He'll be furious," she whispered, slapping at the ragged hem of her ruined gown. Her head came up and she stared hard at Jean. "Are you all right? Forgive me, that should have been my first question. You aren't hurt? Feeling faint? Any chest pains?"

"No more than a few bruises."

She bit her lip as if uncertain whether to believe him, then closed her eyes and rubbed her fingertips over her temples. "This is all my fault. I should have listened to Paul. Now everything is worse than before—Monsieur Cabarrus believes I invited his people solely to humiliate them. Comte Duplessis is convinced every mulatto should be strung up or shot. The two groups are further apart than ever, and I caused it."

Garnet swallowed. Her hands twisted across her lap. She wished she were a hundred miles from here. "It isn't your fault, Simone. You see . . ." Confession might be good for the soul, but the first words emerged painfully.

Jean studied the paleness beneath Garnet's sunburn. He examined his fingernails. "I understand Raynald Poisson insisted upon dancing with a white woman." One dark eyebrow arched. "You wouldn't know anything about that, would you, love?"

"That isn't how it happened." Garnet inhaled deeply, then met his level gaze. "The woman asked Poisson to dance."

"Impossible." Simone lifted a tired hand in dismissal. "Women don't solicit dances."

Jean nodded slowly. He drained the brandy and dropped the empty bottle beside his chair, tilting his head to contemplate the ceiling. "Let us assume for a moment that a woman did indeed press Poisson for a dance. Why on God's green earth would she do such an incredibly stupid thing?"

A rush of heat stained Garnet's throat and face. She answered in a small voice. "Maybe she thought to unite the mulattoes and whites in an act of friendship. Maybe she hoped to prove a lack of prejudice." In light of the results, Garnet's intentions seemed hopelessly naive. She did in fact deserve the label "stupid." Pride deepened the crimson in her fiery cheeks. Her hands fluttered above her lap. "Perhaps she hoped to prove a point to . . . someone."

"I was afraid it might be something like that."

Simone glanced at them, shaking her head. "You can't be serious. No woman would disgrace herself so. Etiquette does not change. Men ask women to dance, and mulattoes and whites do not mix socially." The imprint of her teeth appeared on her lower lip. "I thought I was doing the right thing, but . . ."

"Rules change, Simone." The next words were blurted past Garnet's lips before she realized their dual impact. "Perhaps a time for new perspectives has arrived. Nothing lasts forever."

She worried her lip, avoiding Belaine's steady, triumphant gaze. She was caught in the position of straddling a fence, one foot placed on the side of forever, the other side roundly disclaiming it.

Simone patted Garnet's hand with a wan smile. "Don't tell me you believe this silly rumor, too?"

At the far end of the room, a platoon of slaves glided about in practiced silence, sweeping up the worst of the debris, laying out buckets and mops for the morning. Someone began to extinguish the candles.

Garnet lifted her hands and watched them fall. "Simone, I know the truth because I was the—"

"Well. Are you satisfied, cousin?" Tamala appeared in the archway, her fists on her slender hips, angry flecks darting about her ebony eyes. "You caused this debacle."

Simone sighed. "Not tonight, Tamala. We're all tired and upset."

Tamala's skin pulled tight across clean high bones. The pure beauty of Africa's highlands stretched across the coffee planes of her face. "She won't be finished until this island explodes in our faces. Open your eyes, Simone. Can't you see that everything was fine here until *she* came?"

Garnet jumped to her feet. "Fine? Are torture and slavery fine?"

"You know more about enslavement than I, don't you, Miss Lily-white."

"Not all tyrants are white. Three quarters of the people on the Habitation are terrified that Tamala Philippe will cast a *wanga* against them." Tamala's eyes flared and Garnet continued. "Oh, yes, I know more than you think. And is it fine to whip your personal maids, to . . ." The hypnotic throb of distant drums halted her tirade.

"Oh, no," Simone moaned. The exotic, weaving rhythms rose and fell with each heartbeat.

Tamala smiled malignantly. "You won't bother us much longer, cousin. That is a promise." Contempt curled her bright lips, then she tossed back her hair and gathered her skirts, her bow a mockery. "Good night, all."

Wearily Simone stood, her translucent smile an apology. "Forgive me, but I have a raging headache." She darted a distressed glance toward the open doors, cringing at the sensual pulse of drums and whistles and rattles. "If you'll excuse me . . ." She crossed to kneel beside Paul, brushing the silver hair away from his brow. "My poor Paul." With Rombo's aid, she hoisted Paul to his feet and they supported him up the stairs.

Acutely aware of Jean's sprawled legs, his steady stare, Garnet nibbled a thumbnail and planned her own withdrawal. A wall of shadow crept toward them as the slaves extinguished the candles, one by one. She could think of no escape that wouldn't appear a cowardly excuse to avoid Jean Belaine.

A silence stretched uncomfortably between them until Jean spoke, his expressive eyes thoughtful. "You've managed to offend nearly everyone on this island, love. But I think you try to do what's right." She looked up at him, gratitude filling her eyes with quick tears. "You simply don't know St. Dominque well enough to succeed."

"Will I ever?" she whispered.

He smiled. "Maybe. If you live long enough."

She stood abruptly, reminded of the perils closing about her like a spiderweb. For a brief instant she considered revealing the planters conversation. But he might then accuse her of further eavesdropping. Or say, "I told you so." And she couldn't have borne that. Not now. She would find her own solutions. Holding her head high, she stood and bowed, then lifted her hem to step through the wreckage, feeling his eyes on the sway of her torn gown.

"Garnet?" She turned at the archway and looked at him over her shoulder, pushing back her hair. "I hope you never go after me with a silver tray." His teeth flashed as he smiled. "You were magnificent tonight."

"In spite of . . . everything?"

"Including everything."

She met the electrifying intensity in his dark eyes and felt her stomach tighten, responding to his strong, silent call. "So were you. You were wonderful," she whispered. His stare crossed the room, penetrated areas she didn't want stirred, though she felt the weakness of needing him. She wanted to run into his powerful arms and surrender to the hungry rapture of his lips. But when he started to rise, his eyes never leaving hers, Garnet gathered her skirts and raised a palm.

"No, please. I want to, Jean . . . I want to. But I can't." A desperate confusion hoarsened her tone. "Please try to understand . . . I can't."

Before he could move closer, she smothered a cry with her fist and fled up the staircase.

—15—

A JUMBLE OF TURBULENT THOUGHTS made sleep impossible. Insects bumped against the folds of mosquito netting, and beyond their soft buzzing, enveloping the night, pulsed the hard, throbbing rhythm of the drums. The cadence swelled and faded, weaving patterns both mysteriously erotic and deeply troubling.

Garnet kicked back the sheet and sat up in bed, running her fingers through her hair. She had reviewed the party a thousand times, turning conversations in her memory, seeing the eruption of the battle.

Wrapping her arms about her knees, she stared into the soft darkness of the drum-filled night. And felt very, very alone. The planters hated her, as did most of the Africans. And now the mulattoes. Paul wanted her land; Tamala wanted her dead. And what defense did she have?

Little at best; none at worst.

She let her head fall back, staring at the underside of the canopy and listening to the steady beat disturbing the darkness. Would the Africans discuss Erzulie at their meeting? Was tonight the night that Tamala convinced them their *loa* would never show kindness again? Or was in fact a fraud?

An involuntary jerk contracted Garnet's fists; she raised them to scrub at her eyes. How could she fight speared dolls and headless chickens and vague, unnamed pains she couldn't adequately explain?

After touching the dull ache behind her ribs, she threw back the netting and slid into her slippers, wandering onto the balcony. It wasn't much cooler outside; she fanned her face with the hem of her nightgown, her brow furrowed in thought.

One by one Garnet attacked her fears. In time the neighboring planters would perceive Garnet Winters was no threat. And without the backing of his friends, Paul's ambitions would wither. The mulattoes might seethe, believing she had deliberately incited the night's disaster, but all and all they were largely impotent. Which brought her to the Africans, the silent, blank-faced Africans, whom she couldn't dismiss as easily. They were vulnerable to persuasion. They lived under conditions Garnet couldn't endure; they bent to forces she didn't understand. And then there was Tamala, who worried her most of all. Hatred was something Garnet had never experienced; she felt defenseless to deal with it.

Leaning against the balcony doorway, she stared up at a moonless sky, inhaling the sweet perfume of night-blooming vines and unconsciously swaying to the seductive magic of pulsing drumbeats. There must be something she could do to protect herself, something to counter Tamala's threats.

Jean's words floated from a corner of her mind. "You've declared war on a battleground you don't comprehend, using weapons you can't understand."

Slowly Garnet straightened in the doorway. This truth was not unchangeable. It was time she inspected her battleground, time she discovered exactly what weapons she was pitted against. For a moment she closed her eyes and tried to pinpoint the origin of the heavy drumbeats.

Then she stared hard toward the west, imagining a faint, distant glow on the black horizon. Gradually her full mouth tightened into a stubborn line. Spinning into the bedroom, she jerked her nightdress over her head and flung it aside, reaching for her riding skirt and a dark blouse.

As she wasn't going to sleep tonight, she might as well learn about *vodun*.

Under cover of the moonless sky, Garnet guided her mare into a pine forest beginning where the cultivated land ended and the slope of the mountains began. Silently she slipped to the floor of matted needles and inhaled deeply before tying her horse. She paused to gather her courage, then returned to the dim path leading upward through a tangle of wild grasses reaching nearly to her waist.

Crouching, she proceeded stealthily until her nerves demanded she step out of the path and into the surrounding brush. The precaution seemed unnecessary as she had encountered no sentries. Still, she felt safer for having left the path. She would have felt better yet had she been able to move forward without making noise. Each snapping twig cracked like thunder in her ears. She promised herself no one could possibly hear her over the wild, whirling rhythms of the drums and hammered iron and the gourd rattles. Or the chanting.

Nevertheless, she progressed cautiously, guided by the music and by a glow of light flickering through the thickening pines. Her pulse pounded in her throat as she thought perhaps this wasn't the wisest course of action. On the other hand, she had come this far and it would be cowardly to turn back now.

You're made of sterner stuff, she chided herself silently. Since when did a few drums and whistles frighten a Winters? Or a moonless night and branches that cast strange, menacing shadows? Or tall brown grasses that bent beneath the movement of unseen creatures? Garnet clenched her fists and squeezed her eyes shut. Keep thinking like this, and you'll scream at your own heartbeat, she thought.

Bending low, she stepped forward, the drums so loud now

they seemed to throb inside her head, blurring her concentration. One moment she saw nothing before her but pines and tall grass and sheltering darkness, then suddenly she stood a few short paces from a beaten-earth circle surrounded by tall trees and lush grass. And filled with whirling dark figures.

Heart leaping in her chest, Garnet dropped to the ground, hastily burrowing deep into the concealing grasses and praying she hadn't been seen. She held her breath and waited. Jean had once claimed he could walk into the center of a *vodun* ceremony undetected, but from the frenzy Garnet had glimpsed, she wouldn't have liked to try it. Flashing machetes swung from the men's belts; several of the women clasped knives between their teeth.

When she could breathe without gulping, she crawled on her hands and knees, fervently hoping no one noticed the grass bending before her. Cautiously she circled the firelight until she reached a small, grassy rise on the far side, where she could observe the ceremonies with less fear of discovery.

After giving herself a moment to swallow hard and calm her shaking hands, Garnet removed her hat and slowly raised her head, bending the stalks before her for a clearer view.

The number of dancers surprised her. She recognized Fula and Juniper from the manor village, and Caco, the Senegalese whose baby Garnet had helped deliver. There were fifty more whom she could not immediately identify. They whirled and stamped the ground, facing smoking candles fastened to the pegs of drums carved from hollowed logs. Sweat glistened in the firelight, gleaming on the women's bared breasts and on the men's faces and chests. Each danced in solitary frenzy, oblivious of the others, lost in a private ecstasy of throbbing, pounding, demanding rhythms. Men shaking pebble-filled gourds and beating iron spikes against hoe heads twisted among the dancers, swooping low, then leaping high, inciting the dancers to greater frenzy.

Garnet studied the wild scene by the light of the fire built to one side of a small, tented structure. At first glance the dancing had appeared wild and uncontrolled but harmless. However, as she observed further, her perception shifted. The throbbing tempo vibrated along her nerve endings, crawled inside her skin, and pulsed hotly along the rush of her blood. Perspiration rose on her brow as the drummers caught her heartbeat, matched it, then followed, coaxing the beat faster and faster. She discovered herself swaying on her knees to the rocking twist of the rattles, the tattoo of the drums, and she was powerless to remain still. It was impossible to watch and to hear and to sit quietly even as the chanting began to sort itself into Creole words she could understand.

> *We say, where are you?*
> *Where be Erzulie?*
> *Your horse awaits*
> *With empty saddle.*

A man spun into the center of the ring, bending and dropping low to the ground, offering himself as the horse for Erzulie to ride. He staggered and nearly fell, foam at his lips, sweat pouring from his body.

> *Listen to us!*
> *We call the sea to testify.*
> *We-be no judge.*
> *We-be no blame.*

The man rolled in the dirt before the drummers. Stumbling clumsily to his feet, he resumed dancing, his face slack, his mouth open in a silent scream of invitation and pain. His eyes rolled upward until only the whites showed in the gleam of firelight.

> *We say, where is Mistress Erzulie?*
> *Your horse awaits.*

Speak to us!
Tell us how we be-you offend!

A throaty moan issued from Garnet's lips, pulled from her breast against her will. Her fingers lifted and clawed open her collar against the heat boiling inside her flesh. A vibrant tingle raced along feverish skin, chased by the throbbing timbre of the wild chant. The dark sexuality of the music consumed her senses. Her lashes squeezed hard against her cheekbones, and she swayed, feeling herself slipping away, slipping . . .

A wild shout yanked her from the edges of a sensual abyss, confused and reluctant. Frightened, Garnet shook her head violently to clear it, and she clenched her hands until she winced as her nails cut into her palms. The drumbeat had become a part of her pulse, her breath, curling and teasing through her mind, awakening a hot urgency deep in her flesh and blood. Fighting to regain control, she bit her lip until she tasted the salty tang of blood, and she blinked rapidly. The color rushed from her cheeks and a wave of dizziness showered sparks before her staring eyes.

The man in the center of the ring had vanished. His body remained, but his soul and spirit had disappeared. In his place stood Erzulie—Garnet Winters. Someone had produced a straw wig dyed flame red and placed it upon his head. But a trick of the light—that's all it could be—had transformed the straw to fiery silk. Staring at him, Garnet swore he had sprouted breasts. Foolishly, impossibly, she saw her own breasts, full and proud. The man did not imitate Erzulie-Garnet . . . he *was* Erzulie-Garnet.

The figure moved with Garnet's walk. Open-mouthed, she stared as Erzulie-Garnet glided about the circle, the walk purposeful as hers always was, yet seductively feminine, hips swaying a subtle invitation. The hand gestures were her own, mobile and graceful. The set of the chin, the provocative tilt of the head . . . they were hers. And when the figure laughed and tossed back skeins of red hair, Garnet gasped. She was watching herself, watching Garnet Winters move and gesture. And when someone dropped a white gown over the figure's head, the illusion became complete. Garnet Winters floated about the earthen circle, smiling her own smile, swaying her own hips, and then, the greatest shock, speaking in her own voice.

"Erzulie angry plenty much." The figure pursed its lips into a pretty pout, one Garnet had practiced as an adolescent. The figure flounced about the ring, frowning and pointing at the dancers, who pretended to cringe.

A woman peeked at the figure from beneath an upraised arm. "Tell us hurry-up-quick what Erzulie's children do wrong. Why you-be punish us?"

Erzulie-Garnet tossed flowing red tresses and glowered at the drummers, who softened the beat and slid into a monotonous lower cadence. "Erzulie be-her hungry and thirsty." The demand was imperious, petulant.

Servile hands hastened to produce milk and breast of chicken roasted to a flaky white. The figure ate and drank, its motions as delicate as those of a New England parson's wife. And while the figure ate, it answered questions in Garnet's low musical voice.

A man approached in a slow, dancing shuffle. "Say-me how take killing hurt off my woman. Her-be suffer plenty much bad."

Erzulie-Garnet dispensed advice between bites, urging the services of a *bocor*, a sorcerer. Then Erzulie-Garnet castigated an unfaithful wife, and then consoled a woman whose husband's body swung from the palms lining the main drive. The figure glided among the dancers, offering advice and derision, exchanging pleasantries and gentle insults. The figure courted the audience, making a point of ignoring a moaning woman who writhed on the ground at the foot of the drums, her face slowly turning as slack and blank as the man's had been before he became Erzulie-Garnet. The woman's shoulders and stomach convulsed and she bent in on herself.

It was Tamala.

Sucking in a scalding breath, Garnet stared until her eyes ached, watching as Tamala transformed herself into a snake. Tamala didn't pretend to be a snake, she *became* a snake. She coiled and writhed upon the beaten earth, her tongue darting in and out between her lips, a hissing noise rising against the steady, deepening pulse of drums and iron. The dancers courted her as they continued to court Erzulie-Garnet, bowing, smiling, imploring. Then they stood aside as the Tamala-snake inched along the earth, slithering toward the tent. The figure coiled seductively about a log pole supporting the tent. And then, in defiance of gravity, the creature wound about the log, undulating upward toward the top of the structure, swaying, hissing, tongue flicking in and out below slitted eyes.

Garnet could not believe what she saw. Stiffening, she blinked hard, rubbing frantically at her eyes. The leaping firelight painted a rainbow shimmer over Tamala's glistening skin. The suggestion of scales was unmistakable. Her hair flowed blue-black over her scaly breasts; her head darted out from the tent pole, eyes narrowed and yellowish, tongue flickering.

"Impostor," she hissed. "You no-be Erzulie. You steal away the harvest, cause plenty much bad, very bad. You place killing-hurt on our babies and our men!" Her darting head swayed over the dancers as viperish eyes accused Erzulie-Garnet.

Erzulie-Garnet snatched a machete from the belt of a dancer and spun violently, slicing the air near the Tamala-snake in long, swishing strokes. The dancers, chanting, shuffling, stepped back to open a space between the two *loas* mounted on their human horses.

Rising to her knees in the grass, Garnet felt the tension tighten between the two, both hands pressed to her lips. Her eyes ached and a pain throbbed behind her ribs where the needles had pierced the doll. She watched the Tamala-snake slither down the log pole and coil at the base, head weaving and darting.

"Prove yourself, impostor." Hissing, spitting. "Bring back the hanged men. Breathe life into their lips . . . if you can."

A terrible silence spilled over the clearing, then the dancers fell to their knees and the drums lifted in a pounding approaching hysteria. "Zombies!" screamed the dancers, hiding their eyes in terror.

Erzulie-Garnet laughed, the sound shrill with triumph. The Tamala-snake had blundered.

The Tamala-snake swooped to the ground, licking the dirt in rage. When the head rose in a weaving frenzy, hatred glittered from viperish eyes. "Kill the whites. Kill them all. Prove your love for us. Kill the whites!"

A white-robed man stepped from the tent and lifted his arms. Rombo's voice quivered through the clearing. "The time is not right, children." He shot a look of warning toward the Tamala-snake. "But soon. Very soon."

The dancers took up the chant, spinning as the drumbeat ticked louder, hotter. "*Soon. Kill the whites—soon.*"

Without being aware that she moved, Garnet rose to her feet, feeling the blood surge through her body. Firelight raced along the hollows of her face as she stared at slashing machetes, knives stabbing invisible images. The pitch of the drums deepened, quickened, built toward a blood fever. Bare feet whirled and stamped, weapons gleamed, sweat poured.

From beneath his white robe, Rombo produced a goat, and a woman snatched the red wig from Erzulie-Garnet's head and placed it on the goat's horns. The Tamala-snake shot across the circle and her head reared back, then flashed forward and down, fangs sinking into the goat's neck. Rombo teased the Tamala-snake away from the goat, drawing her slowly to her feet, dancing opposite, his eyes never leaving hers. They moved together, in perfect step with the beat, and gradually, very gradually, the *houngan* danced the *loa* back to the nether regions. At the finish, Tamala gasped and accepted a lighted candle and a calabash of water from Rombo's hands. She poured a libation before the log pole and again before the drums. As Rombo approached Erzulie-Garnet, Tamala gave herself to the drums, spinning and panting and quivering in a wild frenzy of release.

A hand covered Garnet's mouth. One moment she was standing; the next moment she felt herself hurled to the ground.

A long, muscled form pinned her quivering body to the earth, crushing the air from her lungs.

Heart crashing, Garnet fought in blind silence. Crazily, desperately, she flailed and thrashed, kicking and hitting her assailant with fists and knees.

"For Christ's sake, *stop*. Do you want to get us both killed?"

Her eyes flared open and she stared into angry velvet eyes. She tasted fresh blood where Belaine's hand clamped her lips against her teeth. And her heart thundered as painfully loud and furious as the drums smashing against her ears, her mind.

"Jean," she panted when his hand carefully released her and he'd eased his weight from her body. She coughed, gasping for breath. "You frightened me half to death."

"You stupid little fool." He crouched in the grass, his hard stare unyielding. "You were *standing*—in full view of anyone who chanced to look in this direction." Parting the grass with his hands, he scanned the circle of dancers, then rocked back on his heels. "What in the name of God are you doing here?"

She'd been standing? A cold shudder began at Garnet's toes and trembled upward. Fear convulsed her heart. She clenched her shaking hands.

Swallowing the dryness in her throat, she rose to her knees and gripped Belaine's shoulders, feeling the hard, comforting bulge of muscle beneath her fingers. Her eyes were wide and washed of color. "Tamala turned into a snake," she babbled, "and I was there. Jean, it was *me*. He walked like me and talked like me—it *was* me." Her tone wavered at the edge of hysteria.

Jean looked at her. And when he pulled her roughly into his arms, she didn't resist. Garnet clung to him, pressing her face deep into his neck, drawing on his solid warmth until her teeth ceased to chatter and her violent trembling began to quiet.

"Don't try to speak."

"But you don't understand. Tamala, she—"

"I know."

"And they want to *kill* us, they want—"

"Shh." Stroking her hair, her shuddering shoulders, he eased her to the ground, below the tops of the grass, where they couldn't be seen. "It's all right now."

All right? When she could never again look at the people in a field without wondering if they had been here tonight? She stared at him, her eyes a drowning plea. "What are they doing now?" She had to know it all.

"Sacrificing the goat."

Darting upward, Garnet parted the grass and felt her stomach heave. Rombo stood over the fallen goat, holding a stained knife above his head. Tamala had dipped her hands into the goat's blood and smeared it across her breasts and lips. The dancers wore blood on their cheeks, their bellies, their inner thighs.

With a cry of revulsion, Garnet threw her arms around Jean's neck, burying her face against his chest and inhaling the strong, safe scent of salt and leather and man.

"The worst is over," he murmured against her hair.

Soon the drums signaled a shift in the ceremony. The low, monotonous cadence swelled and quickened. The men with the calabash rattles leaped and twirled, the gourds a dark blur in their hands. The ticking of iron against iron accelerated.

Now the drums were frankly sexual, whispering, throbbing, moaning, teasing at blood and flesh, rhythmically tormenting.

"They'll dance until they're exhausted," Jean said against her forehead.

But it was more orgy than dance. Transported by the pulsing urgency of the music, the dancers moved together, breast to breast, belly to belly. Hips ground against hips, buttocks tensed and thrust. The women, transported, lifted their skirts; men arched to display hard bulges swelling their ragged trousers.

And Garnet was suddenly aware of Jean's quick breath on her cheek, felt his powerful arms tighten around her body, felt the tremble begin deep inside. Her heartbeat thudded wildly against his chest, as loud in her ears as the beat of the drums. Slowly, her senses subjugated by the vibrating rhythms, she ceased to be Garnet Winters and became a single, frantic pulse in the music's tempo. She was but a vessel through which the pitch and pulsation flowed, firing blood and prickling flesh and scraping nerves raw with need.

She moved sensuously against him, her senses reeling, acutely aware of his body, of his flesh straining against hers, of his lips parting above her own, of his eyes smoldering down into hers like velvet stars. And when he wordlessly guided her over the rise and down the other side into darkness and privacy, Garnet followed him willingly, hypnotically, her blood afire and maddened by the pounding music. And when he turned and caught her face between his hands, a glad cry broke hoarsely from her throat, and she opened her mouth to his hard, bruising kiss, throwing her arms around his neck to pull him closer, closer, as close as the drumbeats.

"Garnet . . ." His kisses covered her ear, then swept to her eyelids, to the corner of her panting mouth, along the contours of her throat. And together they sank to the earth, lips locked in a fiery kiss as passionate as the drum sounds seducing the night.

"Yes." Her fingers flew over his face before she buried

them in his dark hair. And she could think of nothing but the
drums. They pierced her body, heated her mind. His hands
tore at her clothing and she groaned, "Yes. Hurry. Yes." And
her own hands dropped to pull at his shirt, opening it to his
waist, glorying in the sudden shock of heated skin against her
own suddenly naked flesh.

"Garnet, love . . ."

"Don't stop . . . don't stop." The clean, dusty fragrance of
crushed grass rose from beneath their bodies, gently scented
by pine. Her bones seemed to melt in a flow of pulsating
erotic rhythm, and her senses sprang into wondrous sensual
life. She tasted the smell of the grass, saw the hot color of the
drumbeats; she could feel every inch of his skin pressed along
the length of her body, could almost taste the moist flame of
contact. Her body and mind quivered into rapturous urgent
life.

"Garnet, listen to me." His hands cupping her face were
painful. He shook her. "Fight the drums, fight them!"

She couldn't. She wouldn't. She wanted Jean to fill the
vast emptiness of the spiraling night, wanted him to feed the
hot, yearning demands of her body. Writhing beneath him,
arching upward to savor the smooth, hard lines of his body,
she felt his leaping manhood, saw the perspiration glistening
on his brow, the pain of restraint in his probing eyes.

"Please," she begged against his mouth, catching his lip
between her teeth, hearing his hoarse moan.

He buried his face in her hair with a groan. "Be sure, be
very sure, love."

Her hands trailed down his belly in answer, until she
touched the strength of him and a cry of urgency broke from
her gasping lips. In a burst of exultation, she understood the
drums had released only what already existed. The wild,
racing rhythms did not create a need; they expressed it. The
frenzied music scraped away layers of inhibition and opened
the raw, dark side of nature, the hidden core that was her
womanhood, that she had always fought to repress. Her green

eyes grew wild and hot with the moist urgency to fill the emptiness with a rapture she had only too briefly sampled.

Jean pushed up on his elbows and stared down into her eyes, his body very still. "I love you," he whispered, his voice husky with desire. "I love you."

He would have said more, but her lips stopped his words. She pulled him against the molten satin of her skin. And then she felt his strong hands sliding over her breasts, guiding her knees up, teasing her thighs apart.

And she cried out in joy as he pushed into her, feeling the near-fainting ecstasy of unity. The world dropped away. No one else existed, only herself and this one man whose kisses drank her breath and fired her blood and turned her skin to flame. Nothing was left of the world but two joyous bodies. And the drums.

The drums wove between them, between arms and legs and bodies, capturing the acceleration of their hearts and breath. They moved to the ancient, arcane rhythms, and without speaking, they allowed the drums to guide them toward crescendo, thrust building upon drumbeat, heartbeats racing in tune to ticking iron and scraping rattles. And when the cadence altered, dropping before another wild building, they groaned in frustration and strained closer, their mouths burning in swollen ecstasy, their bodies meshing in perfect thrusting fit, as they approached the abyss, then retreated, only to approach once more.

Surrendering totally, Garnet abandoned herself to the wild sweetness. Waves of fiery, trembling sensation quivered along her body and his, until the need for release became a blissful agony. And when it came, finally, explosive and shattering, her eyes flew open in blind rapture and she cried his name and sobs of joy choked her throat. She clasped him tightly as his head dropped to her breast and his body contracted in a long, deep shudder before he relaxed against her. Then he rolled on his back and pulled her damp head to his naked shoulder.

They inhaled the scented darkness, waiting for the roar of their breathing to subside and for the cool night breeze to dry their bodies. A sense of well being such as she had never known crowned Garnet's heart with drowsy contentment. This memory above all others, she would treasure all the days of her life.

Belaine reached across the grass to his jacket and then lit a thin cigar, exhaling its fragrance toward the pine branches overhead. His daring astonished Garnet until she realized they were alone, the drums long since faded to silence. She heard only the rustling of tall grasses and a whisper of light wind through the pines—and his heartbeat, strong and steady beneath her ear.

His free hand stroked her tangled hair, the action as natural as if they had lain together all their lives. "Any regrets?" he asked quietly.

"None." It was true. Cautiously she probed her thoughts for the poison of guilt or blame, and found neither. She had discovered the glorious truth of men and women, and nothing in her past was strong enough to diminish the experience.

"What on earth were you doing here?"

"Trying to understand my battleground."

"That requires a lifetime of study, love. I grew up on this island and I don't completely understand it even yet."

"I have to begin somewhere."

She flattened her hand on his chest, amazed by the crisp mat of dark hair tickling her palm. He was made up of a dozen different textures. The hair on his chest felt different from the prickly stubble forming on his chin. The satiny firmness of his lower back was nothing like the hard, sunburned roughness of his arms. And what had seemed so hard and rigid had felt so velvety smooth.

"I'm leaving in four days, Garnet."

Her heart stopped, then raced. She had four days into which she must cram enough memories to sustain her for a lifetime.

"And every day I am going to ask you to marry me and come to Cap Français." Her hand clenched into a fist on his chest. "You need to understand there is a limit to how far a man's pride will bend," he continued softly. She felt his gaze on the top of her tousled head. "Once I ride out of here, that is the end of you and me. I won't be back. There won't be any letters."

She shivered and felt his arm tighten around her. She didn't want him to go. But she also didn't want to commit herself to marriage. She wouldn't succeed at marriage; nor would he. These tingling, alive feelings could only end in bitterness and disappointment.

"I was very small when my father went off to war," she said finally, wondering why she was telling him this, unable to stem the words. "He hugged me good-bye. Then he stood in the doorway and looked at my mother. He hadn't hugged her." The scene flashed behind her eyelids as vividly as if she relived the scene. "He ordered me out of the room in a strange voice, but I didn't go and neither of them noticed."

Jean didn't rush her. He smoked in silence, waiting until her voice steadied and she could continue.

"He told my mother that he was sorry. And my mother began to cry. I'd never seen her cry. She said that jealousy was a terrible disease and my father looked as if he might cry, too, but he didn't. He promised everything would be different when he returned. And then he was gone. And my mother stared at the door and she whispered, 'No, it won't be different.' Later, when the letter came, telling us he was dead, my mother wept. 'I didn't kiss him good-bye.' She said that over and over, though she was pregnant with another man's child. Within three months, she, too, was dead." Why was she telling Jean this?

Jean lifted her chin until he could look into her eyes. "You and I are not your parents or mine, love. Nor are we Paul and Simone, or any of the other examples troubling your mind. We are us. Unique and new. We don't have to replay the past. We can take whatever days remain to us and make them as wonderful as we wish them to be."

"You don't underst—"

He smothered her doubts with a kiss that flamed from lingering to passionate as he felt her resistance melt to eagerness. This time he made love to her slowly, as if time had stopped for them. He kissed the soles of her feet, ran his tongue between her toes until she gasped with laughter and kicked away. He showed her laughter in loving, and tenderness, and joys she hadn't dared to suspect. And later, when she curled against his body to sleep beneath his jacket, she had forgotten everything but him. Wrapped in his warmth, her body sated, she slept more soundly than she had in months.

She awoke smiling, turning her face for his kiss, then yelped as she discovered he was dressed and had collected their horses. She clutched his jacket against her pearly nakedness, blushing as rosy pink as the streaks of sunrise dimly glimpsed through swirls of ground fog.

Jean laughed. "Modesty, love? I like you better without it." Dropping her clothing at her feet, he sat on the rise and smoked, grinning as she cast him a mock frown.

"You could turn your back."

"Not a chance, love."

"Well, then . . ." A shy pride squared her shoulders as she dropped the jacket and presented him with her nakedness, gratified by the hard narrowing of his dark gaze.

"You should be painted exactly as you are now. With wild grass in your hair and the mist rising around you. And your eyes shining and soft."

She laughed with a quiet joy, then stepped into her riding skirt, intoxicated by a newfound power. Suspicion had firmed into confirmation. Garnet had never been a flirt, not in the true sense of the word, for she hadn't fully understood her own power. Watching him from the corner of her eye, she bent for her blouse, smiling at his sharp intake of breath.

Jean laughed and shook his head. "God help us all," he

teased. "Before the end of the week, every male in the Cul-de-Sac will be looking for a cold river to jump into."

"Except you." He would be gone.

His face sobered and for a long moment they stared at each other, hunger in their eyes. Then Garnet hurriedly shrugged into her blouse and vest and mounted her horse.

The sun had risen by the time they reined before the manor house. Garnet surrendered her reins to the boy who ran to take her horse and she slid to the ground, looking up at Belaine, shading her eyes against the hot sunlight.

"Will you come inside for breakfast?" She didn't want the magic to end even as she recognized it must.

"Tempers will be at fever pitch today. I'll be needed at the fort." Velvety eyes caressed her face, her lips.

Garnet glanced at the house, feeling the weight of reality dampen her spirits. Once she entered, she would have to face all the problems she had escaped for a few hours.

Jean adjusted his hat, watching the last vestiges of mist burn off in the bright morning sunshine. "Tell me, love . . ." When his eyes lowered to hers, she caught her breath at the sober intensity she saw there. "What exactly does forever mean to you?"

"We've discussed that before." She stroked the head of his stallion, not looking at him. "Right now I feel . . ." Biting her lip, she began again. "I want to love and be loved to the end of my life. I want a love I can count on . . . forever." She wasn't saying this well.

Jean's eyes looked inward, examining something she couldn't see. "And if this love didn't last forever—if it lasted only for a time—would the wondrous joys we've shared be lessened?"

Shock and hurt flared in her eyes. What was he saying? He had to know she had given herself to him without reservation, and now he was pushing her away by making last night something apart and separate, in no way associated with a lasting commitment.

Her hands fell to her sides and she stepped back. "I see,"

she said coldly. Last night he had said, "I love you." Now he qualified those words. The "wondrous joys" crumbled to ash in her heart. "Forever isn't a possibility for you, is it?"

"You know it isn't. Simone told you I can't promise forever."

"I know you won't," Garnet snapped. "Not because of anything Simone said, but because I have eyes and ears."

His heavy eyebrows rose. "Simone didn't tell you?"

Garnet spun toward the house, the ache in her mind blurring his words. He'd turned something magical and wonderful into something coarse and ugly. Hot embarrassment flashed across her cheeks as she hurried toward the veranda.

"We have to talk, Garnet."

But she ran up the steps and into the house, slamming the door behind her, leaning against the wood until she heard his loud curse and then the sound of hooves on gravel as he galloped toward the gate.

"Damn." She wiped at the angry tears. She'd been such a fool. After slapping her hat against her thigh, she stormed toward the staircase, running squarely into Paul.

He caught her by the shoulders and prevented them both from falling. "Good morning, cousin." Against all odds, his vivid blue eyes were not bloodshot or watery as he slowly examined her state of dishevelment, studying the grass clinging to her clothing, the tangle of wild hair spilling around her shoulders. "Are you returning from a dawn ride, or an evening ride?" The insinuation raised a guilty flush to Garnet's cheeks as she tried to decide if he mocked her or if she read jealousy in his nasty smile.

"You want my land, don't you?" she asked bluntly, her own gaze green stone. "Would you be willing to buy it? Or is murder your only option?" She didn't know where the words sprang from; she'd had no idea such a thought existed in her head. Sell her land? Impossible.

Paul swallowed from a cup of coffee oily with rum. His eyes regarded her seriously, a cunning speculation in their cool blue depths. "What do you want for it?"

"What would you offer?" This was an idiotic conversation. A waste of breath and energy.

Rombo appeared from nowhere, extending a tray of steaming chocolate. Garnet blinked at him before slowly accepting a cup. Looking into his blank eyes, observing his immaculate serving coat, she wondered if she had dreamed him standing over the goat waving a bloodied knife. In the light of day, with the familiar guinea hens chattering beneath the windows, nothing she'd witnessed last night seemed credible. She frowned as Rombo bowed and withdrew, gliding soundlessly through a bar of bright, hot sunshine.

"The value of the plantation has decreased since you took possession, cousin."

"Nonsense," Garnet snapped, her brow knitting. "My ditches are clear, which is more than you can claim. I'll begin burning off the fields nearest the forest next week. And my books are now up to date, which is also more than you can say."

He snorted. "Your slaves have turned into sloths. Not one has been whipped in a week. They're stealing you blind— everyone knows it—and they're doing as little as possible. They won't work for a black overseer."

Her voice rang with protest. "The ditches were cleared by magic, I suppose." This discussion was ridiculous, a lapse of good sense. Land was nourishing and enduring; land was forever. Garnet meant to have forever. "Never mind, Paul. Forget I ever mentioned selling." Sweeping past him, she strode down the hallway, glancing briefly into the ballroom. Simone's soft consternation drifted from the midst of the wreckage, and for an instant Garnet considered confiding in her gentle cousin. Biting her lip, she lingered uncertainly in the archway, watching as Simone tied her hair in a kerchief and set about directing the cleanup.

Suddenly she imagined Simone in Jean's arms, and the awkwardness of sharing a lover halted any impulse toward revelations she would later regret. A raw thud pulsed behind her heart as she turned toward the staircase, taking the steps two at a time.

"Lawd, Missy Ga'net. Where you been?" Josephine stripped away Garnet's grass-stained skirt and blouse, clucking her tongue, her chocolate eyes rolling in disapproval. "Josephine be-me worried plenty much sick. You no be-you in you bed when Josephine fetch morning coffee." A shudder convulsed her shoulders and she looked toward the scar on the doorjamb where the chicken had been nailed.

Garnet submitted to Josephine's ministrations, nodding gratefully when the girl ordered hot water for a bath. The scolding words flowed over and through her, and the rhythmic cadence soothed her mind. She patted Josephine's plump dark hand and settled into the scented water with a bittersweet smile, allowing herself what she vowed would be the final memories of last night's ecstasy. It had to be that way. If she allowed herself to dwell on a future alone, she would give way to confusion and despair.

After her bath, she donned fresh riding attire and rode out to the west fields, filling her lungs with hot, dusty sunshine. After instructing Nesta which fields to burn and which to fallow, she watched the crews working in the flooded fields and experienced a stubborn rush of pride. Already her people looked better fed and not as bone weary as Paul's. Surely none of them had danced around the fire last night, waving machetes and smearing their lips with goat's blood.

Returning to the manor, she caught up on her correspondence and calculated the cost of clothing and sandals for five hundred people.

And remembered a man's urgent touch on the soft inside of her thighs.

"Damn." Despite every effort, her traitorous mind drifted toward Jean, the sums blurring on the page before her. His lips had been alternately hard, then soft and teasing. She threw down her quill in disgust.

He would leave in four short days. Never to return; never

to write. She stared at the smear of ink staining the ledger pages and cursed beneath her breath.

"Missy Ga'net?"

Abandoning the bookkeeping as a hopeless cause, Garnet slammed shut the ledger and glanced up in irritation. "Yes, Rombo, what is it?" Squinting, she tried to imagine his eyes burning like coals. She could not. She must have dreamed him into the wild, heated scene.

Bowing slightly, he offered a small silver tray that held a solitary envelope.

Garnet lifted the letter in her hands, frowning at a red seal she didn't recognize. "Who sent this?"

The smallest hint of a shrug adjusted Rombo's white coat. "A rider brought it, Missy."

After dismissing him, Garnet slit open the envelope and withdrew a plain sheet of heavy linen paper.

Mlle. Winter:

Must talk to you. Meet me at midday tomorrow by the waterfall at the west end of your property.

The letter was signed with the initial P.

Poisson. Garnet tapped the letter against her teeth, a thoughtful expression sharpening her eyes. She would have sworn Raynald Poisson would rather submit to torture than see Garnet Winters again. He must hate her.

Kneeling, she touched the letter to a flame in the grate and watched the paper curl into ash. What could be so urgent that he would risk a private meeting? If they were discovered . . .

Or was it a trap?

Glancing briefly at the sunset spreading a fan of pink beneath the rim of the afternoon rainclouds, she decided there was but one way to find out.

Then she spied Belaine's horse approaching along the main drive and she hastily swept her papers into a drawer. She fled toward the staircase after leaving instructions that she would dine in her room. She couldn't face him again, not just yet.

—16—

POISSON HAD CHOSEN HIS TIME and place with care. The muffled thunder of the waterfall made eavesdropping impossible. But where was he?

Wondering if Poisson had been delayed, Garnet mopped a sheen of perspiration from her throat and brow. The midday sun, murderously hot and humid, reached even into this secluded glade, sparkling off the water, baking rocks, wilting the giant ferns rimming the pool beneath the waterfall like tatted green lace. No sensible person ventured outside at midday except those unfortunates prodded by urgent business. And the slaves. Sighing, Garnet wiped her sticky palms across her riding skirt.

A flamingo waded into a quiet pocket of water near the pool, a pink study in stately dignity. Otherwise nothing disturbed the serenity of the deserted crevice. Waving her hat before her face, Garnet urged her horse into the surrounding tropical foliage, seeking the cool shade of broad leaves and a thick overhang.

Once again she considered whether her opened collar and slim skirt were appropriate or if she should have worn her full riding habit, jacket and all. The blistering heat had governed her decision, though heat or no heat, the lack of a jacket was scandalous.

"Stupid rules," Garnet muttered, ducking her head to

avoid a low-hanging branch. "What does it matter anyway? Poisson couldn't think less of me than he does already."

"You are mistaken, mademoiselle. I admire you greatly."

Startled, she lifted her head to discover Raynald Poisson leaning on his saddle directly in front of her. "How long have you been here?"

"Forgive me for making you wait, but I had to be certain you weren't followed." Despite the heat and choking humidity, Raynald Poisson looked as if he had stepped fresh from a cool bath and donned newly laundered clothing just minutes ago. A starched white cravat lay crisp and snowy against his dark throat; his jacket fit elegantly across his shoulders; his breeches were immaculate; his boots polished to a high gleam.

Acutely conscious of limp red strands curling at her neck, of the inevitable dampness creeping beneath her arms and pasting her blouse to her spine, Garnet smiled weakly. She would have been surprised to learn her dishevelment was faintly erotic, her flushed cheeks charming. She misunderstood the slight narrowing of Poisson's gaze, interpreting his expression as one of suspicion.

"I told no one I was meeting you."

Poisson waved a hand, lace falling about his wrist, indicating they should return to the open space near the waterfall. Discomfort furrowed his brow. He scanned the heavy foliage uneasily, as if suspecting the ferns concealed a hostile army.

After spurring his horse nearer Garnet's mare, he raised his voice so he could be heard over the roar of tumbling water. "You are in grave danger, mademoiselle."

Garnet almost laughed. Danger had stalked her hemline from the moment she had washed up on the island's crystal shores. Clear green eyes smiled her amusement. "I'm well aware there are a few difficulties at the moment, Monsieur Poisson."

He stared at her. "Are you aware that my people are split into two factions regarding you? One group believes you deliberately provoked the incident at the ball. As much as we would like to forget our origins, Mademoiselle Winters, many of us still cling to the old ways in private. There are those who speak of revenge." He watched the amusement fade from her eyes. "The smaller group is listening to me. But with reluctance."

The old ways—*vodun*. Garnet swallowed. "What are you telling them?"

"That I saw your face and I heard your conviction. That I believe your blunder was innocent." His dark eyes searched hers, and a grudging admiration was evident. "What you wish to accomplish is laudable, mademoiselle. Even as we meet, men in France are placing their lives and reputations in jeopardy by arguing the mulatto's right to be regarded as an equal. You stated a similar position at Comtesse du Casse's ball. Your courage in openly displaying your convictions is highly esteemed."

Made uncomfortable by his earnest praise, Garnet studied the reins crossing her gloves. "I don't deserve such lofty acclaim, Monsieur Poisson. Ignorance played a role . . . and I had a selfish motive as well." The words emerged hard, reluctantly. "Perhaps selfishness was the primary motive."

"Does it matter? What matters is that you and you alone tried to batter down the barriers of inequality." He eyed her shrewdly. "Perhaps you did wish to prove something to yourself or to someone else. The point is that the idea of equality was in your heart."

Her gaze steadied. "*Oui*."

"The time is not right, mademoiselle." His eyes hardened. "Reason is a weak weapon against prejudice."

"I'm sorry for the difficulties I caused you, Monsieur Poisson. I apologize for the awkward position I placed you in. And I—"

"There is no need for apologies. I understand."

Looking into his level dark eyes, not hooded now but open and bright with emotion, Garnet knew he did indeed understand. As if guessing her next thoughts, Poisson touched his cravat and continued in a more formal tone.

"I am here to urgently advise you to leave St. Domingue. Eventually the *houngans* will demand your life. The *grands blancs* plot against you. The *petits blancs*, such as Monsieur Lille, resent a woman owning a plantation they cannot afford, especially one who hires a black overseer." He drew a breath. "And now, mademoiselle, a large portion of the mulatto community has aligned itself against you."

A tiny smile wavered at her lips. "Hearing it like this—it sounds overwhelming."

"It is. And your position will worsen," he continued flatly. "A slave revolt is hard upon us. Soon, very soon." Garnet examined his steady gaze, concluding he knew more than he chose to reveal. His next statement crushed the breath from her lungs. "The mulattoes will side with the blacks."

She nodded slowly. How could it have been otherwise? The pleas in Paris would not alter the mulattoes' position. Centuries of repression could not be overturned by words.

"And the blacks will win."

"There have been other slave revolts," she said slowly. "And the blacks have never won."

"They will this time."

Poisson's grim prediction was stated with such chilling conviction that Garnet found herself believing him. "And will the Africans then be subjugated by the mulattoes?" she asked crisply. "Will they exchange one master for another?"

He gazed at her with sharpened interest. "The Africans are children, unprepared for a life without guidance."

"Exactly the same excuse you can hear in any club in Port-au-Prince." Garnet passed a weary hand across her eyes. "The justification and the abuse will continue, won't it? If this revolt fails, the Africans will suffer terrible punishment, and so will your people. And if the revolt succeeds, the Africans will be tyrannized by people of the same blood." Passion fired her voice as she stared at him. "Will the Africans gain anything by a revolt, Monsieur Poisson? Or are they just cannon fodder for your people to throw at the whites?"

"I didn't come here to debate politics—I came to warn you of what will happen. Soon." His stare softened. "People will be caught up in the slaughter whether or not they deserve to be."

"Me?"

"You." He straightened in his saddle and scanned the spill of water falling from above their heads to the pool below. "Despite what every white seems to believe, all black men do not lust after white women. Many of us are repulsed by pallid skins and pale bellies. But . . ." His gaze swept toward her and pinned her in place. "Wide-scale rape will sweep this island. Not because white women are irresistible, but because rape is the act most feared by white men and therefore the most effective act of revenge." The harshness in his tone increased as he watched the blood drain from her face. "There are perhaps ten thousand white women living on this island, mademoiselle, and half a million black men will be searching for them."

Garnet wet-dry lips. "I've done nothing to—"

"You are a woman. You are white. And you will beg them to kill you long before they do."

If Poisson hoped to frighten her, he was succeeding. Garnet stared at him, her wide eyes accusing. "This is the revolt your people will support? Murder, revenge, rape? You condone this?"

A deep sadness wearied Poisson's eyes. He looked ten years older. "Violence is the only path to freedom," he answered simply. "Everything else has been tried and failed." He turned his horse toward the entrance to the glade, pausing to look back at her over his shoulder. "Your values and your efforts are admirable, mademoiselle, but this is not the time or the place for either. Leave. Leave as soon as you can."

"Wait. Can you tell me when the revolt will start?"

Poisson reined his horse and his eyes held hers across the hot green distance. "Maybe tomorrow, maybe the next day. Who can say?" He shrugged. "But I would not like to think of you still here two weeks from today," he said softly. He started to say more, then clamped his lips and touched his glove to the brim of his hat. "Good-bye, neighbor. Perhaps we'll meet again in a better place at a better time." In a moment the thick foliage had swallowed all trace of him. She was alone.

Gazing about the idyllic beauty of the pooling waterfall and the lush tropical growth, Garnet was seized by a sense of unreality. People didn't speak of murder and rape and revolt amid such timeless beauty. The threat of chaos didn't seem real; surely nothing ugly could touch this hidden crevice nestling snugly into the mountainside. But it could. And if Poisson was to be believed—it would.

Shuddering, Garnet slipped from her horse and stood on a flat rock, warming a sudden chill in the sun's hot rays. What she had to decide now was whether Raynald Poisson had spoken the truth. Or whether he was trying to drive her away. She rubbed her temples and tried to concentrate. And jumped two feet when a firm hand clamped her shoulder.

"Want to tell me what that was all about, love?"

"*Belaine*. Will you please stop creeping up on me?" Blood pounded in her ears as her heart crashed against her ribs. "Were you following me?" she demanded.

After unbuckling his sword and laying it aside, Jean sat beside her on the sun-washed boulder. "Not you, love. Poisson. If he lives out the week, I'll be surprised. Every trigger-happy planter in the Cul-de-Sac is searching for him." He tossed his hat toward a branch and ran long fingers through his hair. "Poisson is as good as dead the minute my men leave Port-au-Prince."

The day after tomorrow. "You blame me, don't you?"

"The question is, Does Poisson blame you?" He slid down

the rock and scooped a handful of water to his lips, lifting his face to the cool droplets spraying from the waterfall.

Standing spread-legged on the rocks, the roar of the waterfall behind him, Belaine was heartachingly handsome. Garnet bit her lip and frowned, gazing at his wide shoulders, tapering waist, and muscled thighs. She watched as he peeled his shirt from his body and tossed it aside, watched the flow of flexing muscle rippling his arms, saw the sparkle of mist clinging to the dark hair springing like a forest from his chest. He was the most splendid man she had seen outside her dreams. Plucking absently at a tiny purple flower invading a crevice in the rock, she wondered if emotion had colored her perceptions.

He stood before her, the scar on his side an arc of white against deeply bronzed skin, his velvet eyes probing hers. Garnet cursed beneath her breath, irritated by the flood of moisture heating secret places. Hastily she lowered her gaze from his chest and longed for the freedom to discard her own sticky shirt and enjoy the cool spray.

"Poisson understands what happened. He bears me no ill will." When she had finished relating Poisson's conversation, they sat quietly, watching the flamingos on the far side of the pool. Garnet broke into Belaine's thoughtful silence. "Could Poisson be correct? Can a revolt be imminent?" Thoughts of random slaughter raised a tinny taste in her mouth.

Belaine rose and walked to the edge of the boulder, staring down into the pool below. A hand raked back his black hair. "It all fits," he mused. "And not just for the Cul-de-Sac. Uneasy messages are arriving from all parts of the island. It's like the first warnings from a volcano. You can damn near smell the smoke." His hand slid to his chin. "Two weeks . . ."

But Garnet had ceased to think in units of weeks; her thoughts focused on days. In two days Jean would be gone. Studying him, she watched his thoughts leap ahead to the Cap and his meeting with the governor. And she knew how anxiously he anticipated discussing the situation with André, who would arrive today or tomorrow. An unreasonable jealousy constricted Garnet's heart; greedily she wanted every moment of his remaining time. He had the rest of his life to contemplate politics, but all she had was two days.

As she blotted the damp heat trickling down the valley between her breasts, she stared at the ridges of taut muscle edging the crevice of Jean's spine. She remembered running her fingers along that firm line, drawing him closer. She willed him to turn and look at her, feeling a surge of selfish anger when he did not. He stared across the sun-dappled pool, his gaze turned inward, his concentration marshaling troops, organizing lines of defense.

"Jean?"

Lost in thought, he didn't hear. And a blind, helpless anger consumed Garnet's reason. Forever or no forever, this was the man who had begged her to marry him. The same man who had reminded her of the short time left to them. A man who had now forgotten her entirely.

Standing abruptly, she lifted her skirt and hopped across the rocks until she stood behind him. She flattened her palm against his warm, smooth skin, catching her breath.

"Did Poisson definitely say that—"

"Poisson be damned." She glared at his back and remembered having wrapped her legs around his waist.

"—the revolt would take place—"

She pushed. Hard. Then jumped back from the splash, laughing as Belaine's head popped above the water. Sputtering, he tossed wet hair back from his face and roared up at her. "What the hell . . ." When he stood, the water lapped about his bare chest.

"I'm sorry. I just . . ." Garnet couldn't possibly explain the impulse. He looked so satisfyingly angry, his natural elegance for once missing, that she could not halt the laughter. It bubbled out in gusts, bringing tears to her eyes. Sinking to the rock, she wiped her eyes and grinned at him, almost envying the coolness of the water.

Belaine waded toward her, pushing the water aside with wide, irritated strokes, his face like a thundercloud.

Garnet rested an elbow on her knee and cupped her chin in her palm. Her sparkling green eyes widened innocently. "You looked so hot."

A wet hand shot forward and gripped her ankle. "So do you."

She had a second to shriek and then the water closed over her head, the coolness a shock against her hot skin. When she emerged, spitting and shoving at the hair streaming over her face, Jean was nowhere to be seen. In a moment she discovered why. Gasping, Garnet threw out her hands and clutched the nearest rock to prevent herself from being dragged beneath the water. Strong hands jerked at first one of her boots and then the other. Jean's head popped above the water as he threw her boots up onto the rocks. And then his breeches. He grinned, then dived beneath the water.

"*Belaine.*" Garnet thrust the hair out of her eyes and tried to pierce the wavering reflections dancing across the surface. Then she grabbed again for the rock as she felt his hands at her waist, roughly stripping her skirt past her hips and down over her ankles. Next came her petticoat and then her pantaloons. A cool rush of water caressed her bare skin and Garnet gave a little cry as a sensual heat flushed her face. "Belaine, this is outrageous."

He rose from the water directly in front of her, his hand reaching for her blouse.

A tiny moan scraped Garnet's throat as, suddenly helpless, she looked deep into his laughing eyes. He peeled away her blouse and tossed it toward the rocks, and her heart accelerated as his concentration narrowed on her breasts, his amusement hardening into desire. She caught a breath and held it as the water washed gently over her nipples with a coolness that belied the heat flaming upward from the pale red triangle between her thighs. A thought flashed through her mind that she had fallen a far distance from her original resolve to avoid

Colonel Jean Baptiste Belaine—but she no longer cared. Two days remained to play the wanton. Two days to store rapture against years of loneliness.

Her hands slid along the swell of his chest and she leaned forward offering her mouth, her lips parting invitingly. Then, a mischievous sparkle shooting golden flecks into her eyes, she slipped beneath the water and out of his arms, surfacing a few feet away with laughter in her throat and the delicious triumph of power in her green eyes. She had both felt and seen the urgency of his need.

"Hide and seek?" he asked, his voice husky over the roar of the waterfall. A smile curved his lips as his black eyes sought the creamy fullness of breasts bobbing gently in the water, tracing the tender rivulet ebbing and filling the cleft between. Garnet saw the white flash of a thigh and buttock as he dived toward her, his powerful arms churning the water into bubbles. He enfolded her wet body, drawing her tightly against his hard masculine heat.

Laughing, Garnet shook the water from her lashes, resting lightly in his arms as teasing kisses brushed her forehead, the corner of her open mouth, the long white column of her throat. Then she twisted away, eluding his grasping hands to dive beneath the surface, her bare bottom a tantalizing glimpse of sweet ivory. Holding her breath beneath the crystal water, she teased her fingers up the inside of his thighs and felt his satisfying shudder as the hard muscle tensed and swelled beneath her exploring hands.

When she broke the surface, lifting her arms to smooth back her hair, he had vanished. Her smile opened to a laugh as his arms circled her waist beneath the water, and then to a breathless gasp as his mouth found her stomach and slid lower. Skilled fingers guided her thighs apart and she cried out as his hot tongue invaded her, a passionate flame of heat chasing away the cool water. Her knees buckled with sudden weakness and she thrashed wildly, the thunder of the waterfall roaring inside her head. And she moaned softly when a rush of cool water replaced the burning tease of his lips and tongue.

Ducking, she swam underwater, her naked skin afire against the chill mountain waters, and when she found him, she wound sensuously about his spread legs, allowing herself to rise slowly, her breasts brushing hard against the throbbing heat of his manhood. Slowly, rubbing against him, she emerged like Venus from the sea, her mouth trailing tiny bites across his chest until her lungs demanded a breath and she stood, water streaming from her shoulders and breasts, her hair a sparkling cascade of liquid flame.

"My God," he whispered hoarsely. "You're so beautiful, so incredibly beautiful."

He captured her face between his palms and she felt his tremble of emotion and knew the playfulness had ended. His kiss bruised her lips and this time she did not pull away, but circled his neck and thrust against him with a passion that frightened her, that snatched her breath and raced through her quickened blood. And when he braced her back against a rock and guided her legs around his upper thighs, she urged him to "Hurry—please, hurry" in a throaty voice she scarcely recognized. And when she felt his first thrust, a blade of fire displacing the cool water, she cried out with joy and buried her fingers in his wet hair, opening her lips beneath his plundering mouth.

And her happiness was such that she laughed when he leaned to kiss her ear and raised a froth of bubbles to foam about her breasts. And then she didn't laugh. She grasped the slippery bulge of his wide shoulders and gasped and forgot the bubbles rising around them, forgot the thundering plunge of the waterfall, the mist of droplets clinging to their hair and lashes. She knew nothing but the fullness of him, the hot, swelling rapture spinning and soaring higher and still higher until she cried out and her eyes flew open and a rainbow burst across the sun-shot spray of water and the colors were more

vivid and shining than she had ever before witnessed because
now she was somehow a part of them.

She clung to him until her trembling body ceased to
shudder and her breathing slowed. Then she met the softness
in his gaze with a radiant smile and accepted his assistance
onto the rock. He spread their clothing to dry, then stretched
out beside her in the drowsy heat of the sun, releasing a
contented sigh.

"I could stay here forever," Garnet murmured, nestling her
wet head into his shoulder and twining her slim legs through
his. She wanted everything good to last forever.

"Not me."

"Of course you wouldn't agree with forever." Another time
the words would have been aimed to sting. But not now. The
moments were too precious for sarcasm. Instantly her mind
shied from his leaving.

"Forever has nothing to do with it." A lazy hand stroked
her hair. "Do you realize I've made love to you on a beach,
in a banana grove, on the ground, and now in a pool." She
sensed his smile above her head. "What I would really like to
do is ride out of here, find an honest-to-God bed, and make
love to you with some degree of comfort."

Garnet smiled. "Ah, yes. You admitted early on that you
were a man who liked his comforts." He pretended a great
sigh and she bit him lightly on the shoulder.

"Have I asked you to marry me yet today?"

"No."

"No, I haven't asked, or no, you won't marry me?"

Laughing, Garnet pressed her face against his sun-warmed
shoulder, enjoying his clean, fresh smell. She committed to
memory the touch of his skin, the fragrant drift of smoke
spiraling upward from the thin cigar he held between his
teeth. "Both."

"Then consider that I have asked and you have refused and
now I demand an explanation."

Her concealed smile dimmed against the arm he closed

around her. Shamelessly she shifted slightly to offer more of her body to the sun, shading her eyes to examine a creeping bank of clouds that soon would blot out the afternoon blaze. She bit her lip in the silence and knew they were no longer teasing. The quiet tension of his body signaled how serious he had become.

"I can't bear the thought of not being loved," she said quietly. "It's easier to expect nothing."

"I love you, Garnet." He rested his chin on top of her head. "Why can't you believe me?" There was no accusation in his tone, only a sober curiosity.

"Because . . . I'm not what you think I am."

"And what do I think you are?"

She frowned at the sky, glad he couldn't see her face and read how difficult this moment of honesty was. "All men see women alike. You see us as longing for a multitude of children, as centered on home and hearth. You all want a woman dedicated to anticipating and then filling a man's every need. I'm not like that."

She felt his stomach tighten against her bare back and she wanted to bite back the words. Dully she watched the clouds drift nearer the sun, casting a shadow across her heart. She drew a long, halting breath before she spoke. "If you knew me—if you really knew me—you wouldn't want to marry me." There it was, she had said it, she had told him a truth she hadn't spoken aloud to anyone but Uncle William. And she wouldn't have told Uncle William if she hadn't felt compelled to explain two broken engagements. Men didn't want independent women, women who thought for themselves. They wanted only an echo.

A brightly colored parrot soared overhead, ignored by the flamingos perched along the bank nearest the waterfall. Garnet watched through blank eyes, acutely conscious of each small movement Jean made. His stomach contracted once more and she knew she had appalled him.

"I do know you," he said in a strange voice.

Not looking at him, Garnet sat up and wrapped her arms around her knees, wishing she were dressed. The day had soured. Feeling vulnerable in her physical and verbal nakedness, she blundered on, determined to finish what she had so foolishly begun. "No, you don't," she whispered. "I would only be an embarrassment to a husband. I say and do things most women wouldn't dream of saying or doing."

"Like what? Good Lord, are you telling me there's more?"

Garnet spun to look at him, and her jaw dropped. What she had interpreted as revulsion was in fact laughter. His stomach rippled again, and then he gave up. Jean held his side as the laughter burst forth in great gusts.

"What is so damned funny?" she asked coldly.

"What else can you possibly do?" Grinning hugely, Jean ticked off the counts on his fingers. "Let's see, you jumped ship in the middle of a storm half naked, seduced me on the beach—"

"I did *not* seduce you."

"—and left me aching for a day and a half, then accused *me* of offending *you*. You have the plantation in an uproar. Half the Africans worship you—the other half are frightened out of their wits by you. You've driven Tamala to teeth-gnashing fury, and Paul is pulling out his hair. You seduced me again in the banana grove—"

"I did *not*."

"Without consulting a soul, you renamed the plantation and had the manor painted. You split the estate and operate it like you've done nothing else all your life, threatening every man in the Cul-de-Sac who believes women are only ornaments. You hired a black overseer. You attended a *vodun* dance. You have very possibly triggered a revolt. And you threw me in a pond."

Garnet stared at him uncertainly.

The flash of his grin and the velvet laughter in his eyes unnerved her. "Now that you've pointed out the obvious, am I to assume you're planning something else?" He clasped his heart in mock dismay. "I shudder to think what happens next."

Rising to his feet, Jean looked down at her as he stood naked on the flat rock, the thin brown cigar at a jaunty angle between his teeth. "Whatever you are, Mademoiselle Winters, you are *not* like other women." His eyes, sweeping the lush contours of her body, flickered with renewed desire. "For which I thank God. I love you exactly as you are." For a moment he stared into her eyes and she felt the scorch of his love against her soul. Then he smiled and pulled her to her feet, giving her a light spank across her bottom. "Now get dressed."

As she bent, slightly dazed, to step into her damp skirt, he called her name softly. "I want you to remember this conversation." Her green eyes met his level, dark stare. "And ask yourself if I know you or not. Ask yourself if knowing you has lessened my commitment, or if it might be the reason I love you."

She dropped her head, hiding quick tears behind a curtain of glowing red hair. Please, God, don't let this be a dream. Let each of the words ringing in her mind be true. When she finished dressing, she lifted shining eyes, watching him settle his hat and thinking it absolutely unique and marvelous the way he did it. Surely no other man was as elegantly handsome, as powerfully confident as Jean Baptiste Belaine.

And she knew the truth. "You love me." A sense of wonder choked her. "You know me and . . . and you love me."

He caught her in his arms and smiled down at her. "You idiot woman—of course I love you."

"And I love you." Astonishment widened her green eyes, turned them golden. Had she truly admitted she loved him? "I love you."

Grinning, he kissed the tip of her nose. "Of course you love me. No one has ever questioned your good taste. Some people even believe you're intelligent." His grin broadened. "Not me, of course, but some."

She smothered his nonsense with kisses, wanting to touch him, to hold him, to blend with him and capture forever the magic of this stupendous moment. Jean genuinely loved her. And she genuinely loved him. Wonderment filled her heart to bursting. She wanted to hurl her hat in the air and shout her love to the treetops.

A hundred disconnected thoughts whirled through her mind. "Jean. What will we do about my plantation?"

"Sell it to Paul. When my commission expires, we'll sail to New Orleans and raise the best damn cane the colonies ever bought."

A hint of suspicion ruffled her brow and she looked doubtful.

He smiled. "We. We will raise cane. Together. When the babies come, we'll hire a nursemaid and a tutor and whomever else you need to free your time." His lips brushed the swollen contours of her mouth. "You don't think I'd waste a good cane man by sentencing her to the nursery or the kitchen, do you?"

Happiness bubbled up like spring water. "That doesn't make sense—cane men and nurseries." A fat raindrop plopped against a stone, evaporating with a hiss. Holding hands, they walked toward their horses.

Garnet composed lists of things to be accomplished, discarded them and began again. She couldn't possibly finish all that would need to be done before Belaine left for the Cap. A tiny frown clouded her joy at the thought of parting with her plantation. The Habitation Winters had represented her slice of forever—a tiny corner of her mind resisted relinquishing her security when Jean still hadn't promised forever. But wasn't it implicit?

At the glade's entrance she lifted her mouth for his lingering kiss. He murmured tenderly against her hair and she felt like weeping. "I thought I could live alone," she whispered, wondering how such a stupidity could ever have seemed reasonable. "I never dreamed . . ."

"Garnet . . ." His voice emerged deep, choked with emotion.

Garnet grasped his arms tightly, her gaze intense and pleading. "Jean, promise me forever. Please, let us be forever. Promise you'll never leave me."

"There's something I have to tell you . . ."

The strange reticence in his dark eyes stabbed her heart. She opened her lips to question him when a shot exploded behind her. A sting of pain sliced along her ear, and then she felt herself thrown to the ground.

—17—

"STAY DOWN."

Jean's body covered hers, pressing her to the ground. Garnet touched her ear, then stared at the smear of blood on her fingers. The ball had whistled past, the sound like the buzz of an angry insect, tearing off her hat and releasing a sudden, warm gush across her cheek. She wiped her fingers across her blouse, then lay still, staring up into Jean's hard eyes, feeling his heart beating against her own. They listened intently to the crash of snapping vegetation as a horse retreated through the underbrush.

When the screaming birds began to settle and the glade had returned to its previous serenity, Jean shifted his weight and caught Garnet's face between his large, hard hands, frowning at the blood streaming from her ear. He pressed his handkerchief to the wound, then clasped her tightly.

"Close," he whispered hoarsely.

"How bad is it?" A calm detachment steadied her tone. A New England Winters did not dissolve into hysterics. Only a flicker in her eyes betrayed the deep cold encasing her heart.

Jean held her slightly apart to examine the wound. "A scratch, but deep. Keep the handkerchief pressed against it." Quickly, he scanned the clearing before lifting her to her feet. "Your decision to leave the Cul-de-Sac comes not a moment too soon."

Garnet retrieved her hat and poked a shaking finger through the hole made by the ball. "Who hates me this much?"

"Your enemies are legion, mademoiselle." Jean bowed with a smile that failed to touch his eyes. He boosted her onto the mare, pausing with his hands still circling her slender waist. "Garnet . . . don't wait to sell the plantation. Place it in the hands of a solicitor and come with me."

Selling her land to a hand-picked successor was one thing; abandoning it was entirely different. She bit the inside of her cheek and shifted the reins in her gloves. The slaves were no longer nameless faces. She knew many of them now, had glimpsed their lives, had dreamed of something better. Under Paul's direction her people would again be dragged to the punishment circle. They would be fed an inadequate diet, worked until they dropped. Shoulders sagging, Garnet turned her horse to follow Jean from the clearing and felt her happiness diminish. Did she have the moral right to walk away from her responsibilities?

As if guessing her thoughts, Jean halted as they entered the road running parallel to the outer cane fields. His frown encompassed the men and women bending to the dull thrumming of the field drums. "What good will you be to them if you're dead?" His leg brushed her thigh. "Or to me?"

"I know." Garnet lowered the handkerchief. Her ear pulsed hotly and the beginnings of a headache stirred at the base of her neck. "But, Jean . . ."

"Attitudes are different in New Orleans, love. We'll be able to . . ." He broke off mid-sentence and his mouth tightened into a slash of granite. "Christ!"

Garnet sucked in a sharp breath as she followed his stare. "Oh, no." The handkerchief fluttered from her gloves. She averted sickened eyes.

Raynald Poisson lay sprawled at the side of the road, partially concealed by a tangle of wild-strawberry vines. The once-immaculate suit of clothing was bloodstained and ripped. He had been castrated and his throat slit.

"My God," Garnet whispered. The taste of vomit stung her mouth. "Oh, good God."

"Damn it." Belaine's fist struck hard at his thigh. "How long were we in the glade?"

Garnet didn't know if he addressed her or if he was thinking aloud. "From midday to . . ." Brushing the raindrops from her cheek, she glanced at the cloud-dark sky. Anything to avoid looking at Poisson. A helpless shrug completed her reply. "An hour? Two?"

Jean snapped his hat brim lower against the increasing rain. "More like three. This happened several hours ago." The field drums faltered to a halt and the slaves streamed toward the paths between the carrys, their ragged straw hats pulled over their faces. Jean hesitated only a moment, then spurred his mount toward the retreating lines.

Garnet couldn't hear his shout, but she knew that asking if anyone had seen anything was a waste of time. The castration announced that whites had perpetrated this atrocity. And no slave would implicate a white. In any case, no court in St. Domingue would allow a slave's testimony. She stared into the pelting rain and knew with the certainty of indisputable truth that she had caused Poisson's death. "Forgive me," she whispered. The road turned to mud before her staring eyes. And she wished with all her grieving heart that she could relive the night of Simone's party. If only she hadn't approached Poisson. If only she hadn't insisted on the impossible. If only, if only, if only . . .

By the time Jean returned with two male slaves, one carrying a hoe, the other a spade, the rain had soaked Garnet's skirt and blouse. Her hair swung in wet strands. And she couldn't have said whether tears or rain wet her cheeks.

"You-be carry man across ditch to first pine plenty much quick." Jean slid from the stallion, his boots sinking in the mud.

The two slaves stared at Poisson, their eyes widening until they resembled black coals in a snowbank. They stood as if rooted in the roadway, their bare toes curling into the mud. Fear bubbled at the corners of their lips as they stared at Poisson's bloodied groin.

Jean pulled his pistol from his belt and leveled it. "Now. Hurry-up-quick."

As she realized what he meant to do, Garnet's eyes flared. "Jean, for God's sake. The man deserves a Christian burial."

He prodded the men toward Poisson, answering her in formal French. "Garnet, listen carefully. If the mulattoes learn about this, I can guarantee you the bloodiest uprising the Cul-de-Sac has ever witnessed." His eyes lifted briefly. "And after tomorrow my men will be gone. There aren't enough soldiers at the garrison to protect innocent planters—if there are any," he muttered. "If we bury Poisson now, he will simply have disappeared. The mulattoes may suspect what happened, but they won't know. We'll buy time."

"What's the advantage of extra time?"

"Once the governor learns of the situation here, he may dispatch extra troops. It's possible we'll arrive at the Cap only to turn around and march back."

Garnet saw the wisdom of his plan, but it made what they were about to do no easier. Reluctantly she slipped to the muddy road and shivered against the cool, steady rain, following the men up the incline to the protection of a twisted Caribbean pine. The terrified slaves held Poisson's arms and legs without looking at him.

"Dig."

The men erupted into frantic speech, the words too garbled and rapid for Garnet to grasp. One man fell to his knees in the mud and clasped his hands, imploring Belaine. Wide, bulging eyes rolled toward Poisson, then back to Belaine.

"What are they saying?"

Jean fired a ball into the earth and stared at both men above the smoking pistol. His face frightened even Garnet. "Dig!" he roared.

When both men were hacking at the muddy ground with

hoes and spades, their rolling eyes continually flicking toward Poisson and then to the ground amid moans and cries, Jean lowered the pistol but kept it in his hand.

"One of the Africans' ugliest superstitions is that of the undead."

Garnet allowed herself a quick glance at Poisson. The man was undeniably dead. And his death had been hideous. Bending, she closed his eyelids with a trembling hand, unable to bear the rain striking his opened eyes. She wished she could have closed the frozen scream drawing his lips as well.

"Unless certain rituals are performed before burial, the Africans believe the dead can be raised by a *bocor* and forced to do whatever evil the *bocor* commands."

Although the slaves did not comprehend French, they understood the word *bocor*. They broke into a high, keening wail of stark fear. Only Jean's leveled gun kept them digging.

"What rituals?" Garnet asked weakly. Her stomach heaved each time she glanced at Poisson. The sensible thing would be to keep her gaze riveted to her hands, but his outflung body drew her eyes. She kept remembering how vital and alive he had been only hours ago. How he had ridden here to warn her. She hunched her shoulders against the rain and welcomed the numbness creeping over her mind.

"In this area the corpse is bathed in orange leaves, alcohol, and soap mixed with white lime. The body is sewn into its clothes, the pockets removed so the corpse can carry nothing away. A band is wound over the head and jaw to prevent any loss of moisture from the mouth."

Garnet darted a look at Poisson. Water ran from his mouth and face, fading the bright red stains on his cravat to a watery pink.

"Even the mulattoes do these things?"

Jean nodded shortly. "Everyone on this island lives by some superstition." He continued relentlessly, although Garnet had ceased to want the answers. "Nostrils and ears are plugged. The body and head are shaved, fingernails and toes

clipped. The hair and clippings are buried with the body."
He looked at her above the gun. "In some areas a stake is
driven through the heart. These practices prevent a corpse
from becoming one of the undead."

Garnet didn't doubt it. Stomach working, she turned aside,
staring out across the vacant, rain-drenched fields. A great
weariness bowed her shoulders. She wanted to run from St.
Domingue as fast as feet and ship could carry her. Just as she
began to understand these people, an incident arose proving
she understood them not at all. Undead. A cold prickle
clawed up her spine. The concept appalled, horrified her
sensible New England spirit.

When she lifted her head, the men had lowered Poisson
into the shallow, muddy pit. But the slaves balked at shovel-
ing dirt onto the body. Not even a ball fired perilously near
their bare toes could impel them. Babbling, groaning,
clutching each other in frenzied terror, the men preferred
death to proceeding further. Jean thrust his pistol into his belt
with an oath of disgust and waved the men away. They bolted
for the road as if demons pursued their heels.

Picking up the spade, Jean heaved dirt across Poisson's
legs. "Before sunset every African in the Cul-de-Sac will
know about this," he muttered.

"Then why are we doing it?"

"They'll know we buried a mulatto, not who or where. By
the time the story reaches the right ears, I hope to God the
governor will have sent additional troops down here."

He patted the ground flat under the pine and used the hoe
to conceal the raw earth by pulling up a cover of needles and
grass. When he straightened and had thrown aside the hoe,
Jean cleaned his hands and sighed. "Poisson was a good man.
His influence will be missed. Will you say a few words,
love?"

Holding Jean's hand in the rain, Garnet removed her hat
and spoke softly above the whisper of droplets filtering through
the pine branches. At the conclusion of a short prayer, she

laid a dripping wild flower at her feet and followed Jean to the horses. Neither spoke until they had surrendered their mounts before the manor house.

"André!" After swinging Garnet to the ground, Jean bounded toward a man rising from the veranda steps, a wide grin showing teeth as white and strong as Jean's.

The two men embraced fiercely as Garnet approached more slowly. André Belaine stood an inch shorter than Jean, but his arms and upper torso were thicker, as though he had spent more time in the fields. Though André's mouth was wider, Garnet recognized Jean's smile, and Jean's warm eyes glanced at her above a nose more African than French. That André had arrived before the rain was obvious from the fact that his jacket and breeches still bore evidence of a dusty journey.

Jean grinned, holding his half-brother by the shoulders. "I'd forgotten how ugly you are. Suzanne should have married me. How is she?"

André laughed. "Pregnant again, but doing fine. So are our mothers, who both demand to know why you haven't written."

A serious expression clouded Jean's smile. "We've been busy lately."

"So I hear. We have a lot to discuss." André smiled at Garnet and she was reminded what a handsome people Africa and France had produced. "What did you do to this lady? Dunk her in a pond?"

Jean laughed. "She dunked me." His arm slipped about Garnet's waist, drawing her onto the veranda and out of the diminishing rain. Garnet warmed to the pride in his voice. "I have the honor of presenting the most beautiful creature on this island, Garnet Winters. Garnet, this is my brother, André Belaine."

André resembled Jean so closely that Garnet's first impulse was to embrace him, but of course she did not. However, had

Paul not appeared in the doorway, she would have offered her hand for his kiss regardless of rules and laws.

Paul lurched forward, extending his hand after shifting a glass of rum punch. "André, good to see you again. Rombo said a mulatto was squatting on the stairs, but he didn't say it was you. Hell, if I'd known it was you, you could have come inside."

"It was no imposition," André answered smoothly. Only someone listening carefully would have detected the slight coolness in his tone.

Paul stared at Jean, then looked closely at Garnet. "You two are drenched. Is that blood on your face, cousin?"

"An accident," Garnet murmured, covering her ear. "Nothing, really." In his drunken state Paul didn't notice as she swept her hat from her wet head and held it behind her skirt. André did. His black eyes narrowed questioningly.

Jean shrugged slightly, a gesture that promised later explanations. He drew Garnet to his side and smiled down at her. "Shall we make an announcement?"

A proud flush tinted her cheeks as she nodded, determined to concentrate on her happiness and not on the throbbing in her wounded ear. Or on the mound of earth beneath a twisted pine tree.

"Garnet has consented to be my wife."

Greed vied with jealousy in Paul's arching eyebrows. "Well, well, well. The last cousin succumbs." He raised his glass. "I congratulate you, my dear. None of the others held out for marriage."

Garnet tightened her grip on Jean's arm, feeling the bulge of straining muscle as his fingers gripped his sword handle. "Don't, Jean. He's drunk." Paul's sneering reaction was to be expected. It was André's sober appraisal that caught Garnet by surprise.

A look passed between the brothers, then André asked quietly, "Is that wise, Jean?"

Had André slapped her, Garnet couldn't have been more

shocked. She was rain-soaked and bedraggled, yes, but surely she wasn't so disreputable-looking as to be offensive. Or did he refer to something else? All her previous doubts and fears crashed in on her. André would know better than she if Jean's nature didn't allow faithfulness, if he would fail as a husband.

"Does she know?"

"Not yet, André."

"Know what?" Garnet asked. She tried to read his darkening expression as her heart constricted.

"You're shivering." Jean folded his arm around her shoulder. "Are you catching cold?"

"Know what? Tell me now."

"This calls for a drink." Paul stepped to the door. "*Rombo*. Where the hell are you when I need you? Rombo, you dumb animal, get your black ass out here."

"Jean . . ." A shower of raindrops dripped through the vines sheltering the veranda, each one falling with a sound like a tiny explosion. Dizziness swept Garnet's senses. Too much had happened in too short a time.

"We'll talk later, love. After dinner."

She looked into his eyes and told herself that he loved her. And she loved him. Whatever secret he had couldn't be all that bad. Could it? They were pledged forever and that was all that mattered. She managed a smile. "Yes, after dinner. Now, if you gentlemen will excuse me . . ." She gathered the weight of her wet skirt. "I need a warm bath and I want to tell Simone." She smiled at Jean and thought he looked pale in the spreading orange of sunset. "After dinner," she murmured, then hurried inside.

The men stared appreciatively when Garnet entered the dining room, her hair glowing about her face like a silken flame. For this special night she had chosen a flowing sprigged muslin. A pink ribbon circled her body just beneath breasts that gleamed ivory and peach in the candlelight. The smoldering leap of pride in Jean's dark eyes assured her the gown had been a fortunate choice.

Simone's slender arm slipped about Garnet's waist for a quick hug. "I'm so happy for you both," she said, her gray eyes smiling first at Garnet and then at Jean. As she slid into the chair Rombo extended, she laughed toward the smaller table, where André and Tamala sat. "I doubt we'll talk about cane tonight."

"A toast." Paul stood behind his chair and everyone rose, holding glasses fizzing with the Habitation's finest French champagne. Prodded by Simone, Paul gave the standard speech, wishing the couple health, wealth, and happiness. Before he lifted his glass to his lips, a nasty smile curled his mouth. "May New Orleans provide all you hope"—he looked at Jean—"for as long as you both shall live."

Simone bubbled with questions, bending forward to see past the elaborate candelabrum occupying the center of the table, leaning to one side as one dish after another appeared.

"How soon will you leave for New Orleans? When does your commission expire, Jean?"

"I have another six months before we can sail."

André spoke from the smaller table. "I hope you'll allow Suzanne and me to host your wedding." He smiled at Tamala, who stonily pushed her food about her plate. "Everyone present is invited, naturally."

Simone's disappointment ruffled her brow. "You won't be married here? Your mother and father were married in the ballroom. I had hoped . . ."

"Our mothers couldn't survive the trip over the mountains, Madame du Casse," André answered. "And they would never forgive either of us if we deprived them of the opportunity to organize a wedding."

Garnet returned Jean's smile. It appeared the wedding plans had been taken out of their hands. It was also clear they had much to discuss in a very short time.

"What happens to the Habitation Winters?" Paul asked

bluntly. He pushed aside the champagne in favor of a large tumbler filled with rum.

Garnet's eyes flicked to Tamala's sullen stare. Had her lush cousin possessed a kinder personality, Garnet might have surrendered to the generous impulse growing with her happiness and made Tamala a gift of at least part of the land. "I'll offer the Habitation for sale," she answered slowly.

A hiss of anger escaped Tamala's lips and she glared at André. Clearly she resented his presence at her table.

Jean tasted his wine. "Would you like to make us an offer, Paul?"

Us? Garnet glanced at him, her gaze roaming the strong set of his jaw, his black hair tied at the neck, the confident, square shoulders. Us? Was this how a husband's dominance started? How wives became echoes? Flecks of gold flashed in her emerald eyes. "I'm capable of negotiating the sale of my own property, Jean," she announced sharply.

Paul's tolerant amusement annoyed her. "These things are best left to the men, my dear." His eyes, reddened after a day of drinking, returned to Jean. "The land should remain in the family. I'll review the books and make an offer tomorrow."

Jean grinned an apology toward Garnet. "Make your offer to my bride, Paul. But I warn you, I suspect she'll drive a harder bargain than I would have."

Paul snorted as Garnet examined Jean's expression. She refused to be patronized. She was thankful she saw nothing but pride and faint amusement along the firm line of his mouth. His next words dispelled any lingering doubt.

"The wisest business decisions the Belaine men make are the women they marry. Each has been a paragon of industry and intelligence. We owe our prosperity to our women."

André agreed. "Suzanne is a marvel of efficiency and prudence." He accepted a slice of orange cake. "Without her careful management, we'd lose more money than we do."

"Didn't you have a profitable harvest?"

André nodded, turning a carefully bland expression toward

the larger table. "But a mulatto can't demand the same high prices as whites."

Simone filled the abrupt silence by rising behind her chair and smoothing her skirts with a hostess's bright smile. "Ladies, will you join me in the parlor for coffee? We'll leave the men to their cigars and cane."

Garnet arched a questioning eyebrow toward Jean and felt herself relax when he smiled and nodded, silently framing the word "later." She followed Tamala's trailing hem, surprised that Tamala deigned to accompany them.

After Rombo had served a tray of sweets and coffee in tiny china cups, Simone seated herself before the desk and dipped a quill in the ink well. "There's so much to do," she mused. "You'll need a trousseau, of course. Linens and towels and dishes and . . . or do you have a chest in Boston?"

"Yes, I have my mother's things there," Garnet answered. She sipped her coffee, watching Tamala drift about the room. Tamala's silence worried her. Tamala Philippe was not one to accept defeat gracefully.

"Have you decided upon a definite date? Madame Racine will require a minimum of three weeks for the wedding gown, and you'll need at least one good traveling suit and a dozen morning gowns and . . ." Simone's quill raced down the paper. "Have you considered the guest list yet?"

Garnet tilted her head toward the ceiling and sighed. She began to understand why most men preferred to elope. Weddings were for brothers and mothers and cousins, for everyone but the betrothed couple, it seemed. How on earth would she find time to plan an elaborate wedding and still continue to manager her plantation?

Or should she? She touched her wounded ear.

With another sigh, Garnet resolutely thrust disturbing questions out of her mind. There would be time later to worry troubling thoughts. Watching Tamala pause to plink a discordant chord on the keys of the spinet, Garnet experienced a rush of relief. She would be glad to leave this place behind, to begin afresh. With Jean. A shining glow lit her emerald eyes. Jean.

Tamala's hooded gaze slid toward her, smoky with speculation. "Will you sell *all* your land?"

Simone looked up from the desk, her gray eyes sparkling with inspiration. "Garnet, I just had a thought. This could be a wonderful opportunity to assure Tamala's future." She leaned forward, clasping her slim hands together at her breast. Her soft voice was that of the peacemaker, the little mother arranging life pleasantly. "Have you considered giving Tamala a share of your land?"

Visions flashed through Garnet's mind. A speared doll, a headless chicken, bits of hair and nail clippings fouling her food. Angry conversations rang in her memory. She stared at Tamala and remembered the Tamala-snake coiling over the sacrificial goat, heard the echo of a hoarse shriek: *Kill the whites*. A light shiver chased across her shoulders.

"I've considered such a gift and rejected the idea," Garnet replied flatly, her green eyes cool. "Tamala will not receive one stone on my land. Not a single stone."

"Bitch!" Tamala's body stiffened. Her fists slammed down on the keyboard, the crash an explosion of angry sound. "Why should I give you anything? Have you ever spoken or acted with kindness toward anyone?"

Tamala whirled in a billow of rose, her ebony eyes flashing hatred. "You aren't married yet." Her voice trembled as she watched Garnet calmly sip her coffee. "I promised you wouldn't have Belaine—and you won't."

Simone hastily interrupted. "Jean is wealthy, dear. As you don't need the income from a sale, surely—"

"Shut up, Simone. Don't beg Mademoiselle Lily-white on my behalf. I don't want her land or her charity. I don't need either!" Tamala's rich coffee-colored skin flamed pink, then paled. Narrowed eyes watched as Garnet refilled her cup from the silver urn on the tray. Then Tamala's sudden burst of laughter clawed up Garnet's spine like icy fingers. "I'm not beaten yet. If I can't have my rightful inheritance, no one else will have it, either."

"I'll be so glad to see the last of you," Garnet said quietly. "Your hatred poisons everyone near you."

"You are a fool." Tamala collected herself with effort, then inclined her head in a frosty nod. "If you'll excuse me, cousins, I have a meeting to attend." She whirled toward the arch, then spun and pinned Garnet with a hard, dark stare. "I heard a story this afternoon about a man . . ." She laughed as Garnet started, then she turned and vanished in a rustle of muslin.

There were no drums tonight, but Garnet suspected there would be. Soon. Sighing, she finished her coffee and replaced the delicate cup in its saucer. "I'm sorry, Simone . . . I'd rather abandon everything I own than give a single scrap to Tamala." The words were as bitter on her lips as the aftertaste of the coffee.

Simone bit her lip, her large eyes remaining on the archway. "I understand. But I had hoped . . ." Her voice trailed. "I thought if Tamala had a parcel of land to call her own, she might find a bit of happiness. Maybe . . ."

"Maybe she would treat her slaves with less cruelty? Maybe regard all of us with courtesy instead of contempt?" Garnet stood, hearing the men leaving the dining room. "Do you really believe that, Simone?" she added gently.

"I don't know anymore," Simone whispered. "I just know that sometimes she frightens me." She took Garnet's hands and pressed them. "I think it's best that you're leaving."

"Come with us, Simone." The words tumbled forth without prior thought, but Garnet knew the idea was right. "Leave Paul and this terrible place. Come with Jean and me."

Simone shook her head and laid a finger across Garnet's lips, her smile artificially bright as she turned to welcome the men. "I think our betrothed couple wishes to be excused." Her smile curved charmingly. There would be no cards tonight, as it would be as unthinkable to exclude André as it would have been to include him. "I received some new sheet music from Paris last week. Shall I play for you?"

André bowed from the waist. "I would be honored, Madame du Casse." Ignoring Paul's snort of forbearance, André winked at Jean and Garnet, and settled himself gingerly in a delicate chair that threatened to crash beneath his solid weight.

"I like André." Releasing Jean's arm with a lover's reluctance, Garnet seated herself on the wrought-iron bench alongside the path. Rustling banana fronds whispered against the hot night air. A lizard skittered across the torchlit bricks and darted into the darkness beyond.

"You'll like Suzanne, too. And our mothers." Jean stretched out beside her, crossing his legs at the ankles.

Garnet rested her head against his shoulder, her hair coppery in the flicking light. "Your cigars have a cherry smell." She smiled. It was a lovers' night; hot and soft and moonlit. For a while she could forget Poisson, could forget the small piece of gauze covering her ear beneath her hair. Tonight the outside world seemed unimportant. Here, in the circle of Jean's loose embrace, she was safe.

Jean smiled when she told him her thoughts. "I wish it was that simple, but it isn't." He kissed the top of her head, inhaling the fragrance of her hair. "The news is bad, love. What Poisson confided is correct—the mulattoes will join the slaves when the uprising comes."

It was no longer "if" but "when." "Even André?"

He was silent so long that Garnet wondered if he had heard her question.

"Yes. André will fight on the side of the slaves." Jean flipped the cigar into the banana grove, the glowing tip a tiny arc of light before it hit the ground. His chest lifted, then fell. "Hell, in his place I'd do the same thing. He really has no choice."

Garnet tilted her head to look into his eyes, frowning. "But this means you'll be fighting against him, doesn't it?" Although

he wore a dark brocade dinner jacket, she thought of his
uniform. The king's uniform.

"Yes."

Brother against brother. Garnet shuddered, though the
night was humid and hot. "Maybe the revolt won't occur
before your commission expires. If it happens at all."

"Maybe." His brooding tone told her he didn't agree.

Garnet kissed his chin, then snuggled deeper into his arms.
What they discussed was important and she didn't object to
discussing it in further detail, but one thing occupied her
mind. All else was merely delay.

"Jean, you promised to tell me whatever it is that . . ."

"I know." Straightening against the iron back of the bench,
Jean cupped her cheeks between his hands and waited until
she had shifted to face him fully. For a long moment his dark
eyes held hers, and she could see the reflection of the torches
burning in his gaze. Then he kissed her. A deep, searching
kiss, alternately tender and bruising. "Do you love me, Garnet?"

Breathless, she wove her fingers through his hair and tugged
playfully. But there was no amusement in her wide, serious
eyes. "I love you."

"And do you know that I love you?"

She inhaled deeply, fighting years of mistrust, years of
believing in a future that lay along an entirely different path.
"Yes."

He pulled her against his chest and held her to his heart
until she squirmed free, laughing shakily. "You're driving me
mad with suspense. What is it you're trying to say?"

Shadows deepened along the rugged angles of his face. The
intensity in his eyes flung her heart against her ribs and it
skipped a beat. "You want forever, Garnet . . ."

"Yes."

"But I can't give it to you."

Something terrible rushed toward her on wings of lightning.
She sensed impending disaster, as if she teetered on the edge
of a crevice, a murderous hand pressing against her back,

pushing her toward the rim. His sober gaze frightened her. The magic bled from the night. And suddenly she didn't want to know. Whatever it was, she didn't want to know. Her fingers tensed on his sleeves, unconsciously tightening until she felt his muscles straining. Garnet wet her lips. "Why not?" she whispered.

He pressed her fingers against his side. "You've seen this scar?"

And traced it with her lips. She nodded slowly, feeling a scald of breath against the back of her throat. "Simone said you received the wound in a duel with Paul."

"What she apparently didn't tell you is that the ball couldn't be removed."

Staring at him, Garnet swallowed. "No, she didn't tell me." Her words were scarcely audible. "What does that mean?"

"The ball is lying against my lung, Garnet. Against a very thin wall. It could shift at any time."

Gradual understanding drained the blood from her face. Shock widened her eyes. "And if it shifts . . ."

"I'll die."

She blinked rapidly, staring up at him from blind, unseeing eyes. And behind the numbing shock she saw him swinging a machete in the fields, saw him fighting at Simone's party, watched him vigorously digging Poisson's grave. She recalled him bent over the mane of his galloping stallion, remembered fragments of table conversation detailing strenuous physical activity at the garrison.

The ball could shift at any time. And he would die. This vital man, snapping with energy and life, would die.

He was a soldier, a man whose days were rife with violent physical action. Good Lord, even making love . . .

"You're committing suicide," she whispered, her eyes wide circles of pale jade.

"No." Hard fingers bit into her bare shoulders. "I'm living life. Listen to me, love. I can't exist as an invalid even if

doing so would guarantee a prolonged life. I'd die inside long
before the ball worked through my lung."

A dozen incidents invaded Garnet's shocked mind. Simone
leaning forward in the carriage, anxiety furrowing her brow as
she cautioned Jean not to enter the fields. Simone worrying
after the brawl at the party. Simone constantly inquiring after
Jean's health, questioning his activities at the fort.

"Why didn't you tell me earlier?" There was no sense of
having been betrayed in her tone; there would be time for
that later, when she'd had a chance to think. Her question
sprang from a well of bewilderment. Rejection misted her
eyes; a jumble of painful emotions turned her mind as black
as the hot night.

"Because I didn't want you fussing over me as Simone
does." His eyes burned into hers. "Because I don't want pity
and I don't want my life restricted."

Garnet's skin felt numb. Her mind spun as if a giant finger
had stirred her brain into disconnected fragments. Shaking
fingers lifted to her temples as one thing gradually became
clear, ringing over and over like a tocsin tolling deep inside
her head. He couldn't promise forever—because Jean didn't
have forever. Tomorrow was ever an uncertainty; it didn't
exist for him.

"I told myself I would never marry. I bounced from woman
to woman, never allowing an attachment to develop." Knots
rippled up his jawline. "Then you appeared, Garnet. And
everything changed. I want to spend whatever time I have
with you."

She tried to think about a life without tomorrows, but her
mind cringed from the thought. Biting her lip hard, Garnet
shook her head and stared at him, accusation growing in her
eyes. "Would you have told me the truth if André hadn't
pushed you?"

His fingers bruised her skin, neither of them aware of the
small purple marks appearing beneath his fingertips. "I know

you need guarantees—I wouldn't have married you without telling you there are none. Not with me."

Somehow they were standing, although Garnet had no memory of rising from the bench. With a smothered cry of pain and confusion, she hurled herself into his arms and pressed her face into his cravat, inhaling the scent of his cologne, smelling the unique sensual fragrance that was his alone. He couldn't die; no, it was impossible.

Blinking furiously, she clung to him with a sense of desperation, knowing she had been wrong; the world could intrude even within the shelter of his strength. "Tell me this isn't true," she begged. "Tell me it's a cruel jest."

Jean held her tightly, waiting until the tremor shaking her body had passed. "Will you still marry me?" he asked, his voice low and hoarse, urgent.

Garnet closed her eyes, glad he couldn't see her face. Her heart wrenched at his tone. He opened himself wide, his deep pride exposed to rejection and pain.

"Jean, please try to understand . . ." Her voice was muffled against his jacket. "I need time to think . . ."

His body stiffened, belying the steady hand stroking her hair. "There isn't much time. May I expect an answer by tomorrow? André and I plan to leave by midday."

"Yes, by midday." They hadn't discussed the wedding. Or selling the Habitation Winters. Nothing was important now except . . . he could die. A moment of exertion or excitement and . . . Jean could die. When he lifted her face, she averted her lips. Then saw the pain in his flickering dark eyes and cried, "Oh, Jean. It's so unfair."

"Kiss me, Garnet."

Her pale arms flew about his neck and she pressed herself against the hard length of his body, opening her mouth beneath his kiss, speaking to him with her arms, her lips, her pliant body. The kiss shattered her. It was hello and good-bye, yes and no, passion and regret. A kiss imprinted on forever, as their union could never be. When she tore her mouth from his, he buried his face in her hair and held her as if his life depended on her soft flesh filling his arms.

"I love you," he whispered, his breath warm and urgent on her cheek.

"And I love you. But . . ." Tears stung her eyes, choked her reply. "I think I need to be alone for a while."

"Whatever you decide," he said, brushing back her hair, "will be right, love." He looked into her eyes and she felt as if she were drowning in warm velvet. "I'll understand."

"I know." She wanted him to leave her now. There was no possibility of thinking with him beside her. He looked at her and her blood rushed through her veins, hot and wild. But passions of the flesh would fade in time; even with her heart pounding against his she recognized this truth. She didn't dare base her life on a transitory physical urgency. She had to be selfish about her future. Shaking, she watched him kiss her fingertips before he bowed and withdrew, walking past the torches, his back straight and unbent, his step a confident stride betraying none of the swirling doubt she had read in his eyes.

Sinking to the bench, Garnet pounded her fist against **her** knees, then dropped her fiery head into her hands. The angels played games with human fate. Her future had been so clear-cut, so satisfactorily arranged. Then the man in her dreams had sprung into vibrant life, brilliant and laughing and as much a part of Garnet Winters as her heart. In the final analysis, she could not have resisted Belaine.

Standing abruptly, she paced before the bench, watching blindly as her shadow opened and closed patterns of torch-light across the bricks. The night had changed. Now the flickering shadows seemed heavy with menace, as did the drums, unnoticed till now.

"Damn it." Tilting her head, Garnet frowned at the darkness, her skin crawling from the strident beat of palms against drumheads. Please, God, not tonight. Not with everything else. Her ear throbbed. She thought of Poisson lying in his shallow grave, his mouth silently screaming throughout eternity.

Spinning, Garnet turned toward the distant veranda, paced forward, then turned again.

Everything had changed. The drums were not sensual and erotic tonight, but threatening, dark with menace. Pausing abruptly, Garnet pushed the toe of her slipper against a drift of blossoms overhanging the path. The cloying scent of jasmine rose in a cloud. Clenching her fists, she stared at the flowers.

If she married Jean, she would abandon the security of her land for . . . for what? For a few days of happiness? A month? Maybe a year? She trailed her fingers along the back of the iron bench. The ball hadn't shifted in years; was that a good omen? Or did it mean his time was running out?

Frowning, she stared uneasily into the night. It pulsed with arcane rhythms, drums and insects and living heat and whispering leaves. Shadows darted from trunk to trunk within the banana grove, man-shaped and monstrous, giant snakes and ancient beastly forms. The stuff of troubled minds.

Shaking her head, Garnet pressed a hand against her stomach, then lifted her fingers to her temples, surrendering to the sick dizziness she had been battling since dinner. The bitter coffee, the day's events—they conspired against her.

Swallowing a brackish taste, she sat on the bench, blinking at the torches. They bobbed before her eyes. The uncomfortable darkness closed around her, as sticky hot as the thick expectancy clogging her breath.

Could she give up her land, her dream, for a love that wouldn't last? She who cherished a New Englander's love of earth and roots? A groan broke past her lips and she bent over her knees, massaging her temples. The pressure inside her head was building toward explosion.

"But I love him," she cried out. "I *love* him."

The demon of reason whispered inside her mind. One day he'll leave you. You'll stand alone beside a mound of earth.

He'll leave you. Leave you. Leave. The words pulsed with the beat of the drums. Leave, alone, leave, alone . . .

The pain in her side and in her head blurred her vision and constricted her chest. Wobbling, Garnet staggered to her feet, clinging to the bench for support. Blinking slowly, she tried hard to focus on the manor house, but the lights seemed impossibly distant and indistinct. Heart sinking, she wondered uneasily if she could walk that far unassisted. Something was very wrong. Her joints had turned to straw.

"Jean?" She groped toward a sudden shadow looming in front of her, then snatched her hand away in confusion. She squinted uncertainly as a woman's muffled voice cut sharply through the menace deepening the darkness and the drums.

"Now. Take her now!"

Nightmare faces swam across Garnet's blurred vision. Glistening ebony faces striped with white and red, nostrils pierced by shards of bone, burning coals where eyes should have been. Feathers, bits of cord, guttural voices belonging to another time, another place, another culture.

"Forever doesn't exist," she explained thickly. Shimmering torchlight rushed toward her, then receded. Dark forms raced along the path. Bare feet whispered against the bricks.

From a lucid corner of her mind, a voice screamed. "Run. For God's sake, run. Scream, shout, fight!" But when she tried to speak, Garnet's voice emerged in a fuzzy stammer; she couldn't focus her thoughts or control her tongue. She stepped forward, then stumbled, the weight of her skirt dragging at her waist like lengths of draped marble.

"I don't understand," she mumbled. "What . . ."

A viperish figure darted from the blackness. "Now!"

Rough hands seized her arms, her legs, and Garnet fell against them in confusion. Painted masks stared down at her, white and red and ebony. Moonlight flashed along the blade of a spear.

A shroud of cotton smothered her mind; slow thoughts

sank into white oblivion. "The coffee . . ." The coffee had
tasted peculiar, she remembered. Something in the coffee . . .

The drums swelled until they filled her head, pulsing
inside, bouncing off the sides of her skull, pounding, hurting,
hammering her mind clean of thought, binding her tongue
in speechless knots. A deep, warm drowsiness clouded the
sound, welcome drowsiness.

She felt herself being slung across broad shoulders like a
sack of sugar, the motion oddly slow and unreal. And she
blinked as the floor of the banana grove appeared in her
swimming vision. Her hair and arms swung limply down the
length of a gleaming ebony back. Then a curtain of blackness
closed over her and her lashes dropped. Her mind went
mercifully blank.

—18—

A SPIRAL OF FLAME ERUPTED behind Garnet's lids, hot, pulsing, suddenly shot through with jagged cracks of black. Choking, she fought toward consciousness, struggling to sit up on a narrow cot. A coarse cloth brushed her nose and she gasped as stinging fumes seared her nostrils, exploded through her head. Coughing, she discovered that her wrists were bound when she wiped at her eyes and shoved the cloth aside.

"*Fula.*" She blinked hard at the dim light filling the tent. Flickering orange shadows danced crazily across the walls, cast by the whirling figures circling the fire outside. Instantly Garnet knew where she was. Wetting her lips, she drew a deep breath, then appealed to the sullen dark girl watching her. "Fula, listen to me."

But her throat was too dry to speak above a whisper, and the unceasing menace of the drums crowded the small tent like a tangible presence, terribly loud, a sinister heartbeat throbbing against blood and bone and skin and mind. "Be calm," Garnet whispered. "Think."

She ran her tongue across her teeth and swallowed, steadying her thoughts. Almost shouting against the steady cacophony of drums and rattles and ticking iron, she tried again, staring up into Fula's broad, expressionless face.

"Fula run manor house plenty much quick. Be-you fetch Mist' B'laine. Say me *oui?*"

313

Fula looked at her, then measured a gray powder into a square of cloth. She folded the cloth into a tiny packet that slid easily into her cuff. A flick of the wrist dropped the packet into her palm. With practice the motion would be undetectable. She tried again, then placed the packet beside a row of similar squares identified by the colors of the cloth.

An apprentice *mambo*. Garnet blinked as her heart sank. Fula would not help. Swinging her feet to the ground, she glanced at the nightmare shadows flickering up the tent wall, then hastily directed her attention to the cords binding her wrists and ankles. The drumbeats snaked through her mind, coiling about her pulse, then throbbing in rhythm until her temples pounded and the flutter in her throat swelled and concentration came only sporadically. Shaking her head violently, Garnet lifted her wrists to her lips and jerked at the cords with her teeth, trying frantically to think in the brief spaces between the steady drumbeats.

Instantly Fula crossed the tent. A flash of hard ebony stung across Garnet's cheek, knocking her back on the cot. Eyes wide, Garnet lay without breathing and stared up at Fula, her face white with disbelief. Her cheek felt as if hot needles had pricked a hand-shaped pattern. The shock of the blow froze her thoughts.

The girl's heavy lips pulled back from her teeth. "You-be bad, plenty much bad. You trick us plenty much. We-be think you Mistress Erzulie, *oui* and *oui*. Real Mistress Erzulie punish us plenty much bad." Fula's black eyes accused, condemned.

"No." Garnet didn't dare move. Her eyes darted to Fula's clenched fists and she commanded herself to remain absolutely still. Inhaling deeply, she forced her voice to emerge calmly, reasonably. "This-be innocent mistake. You-be understand innocent?"

The firelight crawling over Fula's features made the girl look demented; her eyes glowed orange and red. Sneering, she reached down, hooking her fingers inside Garnet's bodice. The light material ripped away from throat to waist.

Garnet gasped and raised her arms to cover her bare breasts. They intended to kill her. The drums swelled, thudding relentlessly inside her head. They had to kill her now. She had been struck and degraded. They didn't dare allow her to live. Swallowing hard, she squeezed her eyes shut, letting the wild rhythms and shouted chanting wash through a mind gone suddenly numb.

> *We say, Erzulie!*
> *Forgive us blindness.*
> *Say-us what do with impostor!*

Garnet kept her eyes closed as Fula continued ripping her gown away until she lay naked upon the cot, her flesh rising in tiny bumps of mounting fear. The drums crawled over her body, violating her, and she felt a scream building in her throat; chanting invaded her mind. And her own voice, the voice of Erzulie-Garnet, shouted outside the tent.

> *Bury the impostor!*
> *Bury the impostor in four places.*

Garnet's lashes trembled against her cheekbones. Perspiration plastered red curls to her temples. Her heart skipped, then lurched violently. Four places. Dear God. The acrid taste of fear dried her mouth to dust.

Fula dipped a finger into a pot of red paint and scratched Erzulie's *vèvè* across Garnet's quivering stomach. Roughly she rolled Garnet over and drew the *vèvè* across her buttocks, each jabbing stroke a deliberate mockery.

Garnet's flesh shrank. The paint seared her body like a living fire, burning into her skin. Biting her lip, she cursed herself for a frightened fool and desperately commanded herself to think. Appealing to logic was futile; the Africans' logic was incomprehensible. Escape? If only the sinister cadence chipping at her mind would cease, then she could think and plan. She held her breath until her lungs scalded, then stared past Fula's skirt, scanning the tent walls for a gap, a tear, anything. She saw nothing hopeful.

Could she somehow make use of the powder packets? But she didn't know their purpose. Her shoulders sagged and her eyes flickered over the cords binding her wrists and ankles. Escape, then, was impossible.

She didn't resist when again Fula flipped her on her back. Instead she stared at the cotton ceiling, her face afire, and vowed she would not bow to the shame and vulnerability of her nakedness. Trying to vanquish all distractions, Garnet ground her teeth and blanked out the sight of Fula's curious face bending near her thighs to examine the crisp red triangle. There had to be a solution, a route of escape. There had to. be.

Garnet's heart leaped and she strained her head back as a whistle shrieked outside the tent. A pounding din concentrated before the flap, gourd rattles shaking wildly, spikes hammering on iron hoe heads, the hot, pulsating drums swelling as the tent flap flung open.

"*Tamala.*" Garnet's limbs went stiff with fear as she looked into Tamala's eyes.

Tamala was stately and magnificent in a flowing robe of brilliant crimson. A snowy turban concealed her hair. She stood over Garnet, staring at her naked beauty. Triumph glittered in Tamala's black eyes.

Garnet's jaw clenched as she saw the hatred in Tamala Philippe's hard gaze. Tamala had maneuvered toward this night from the very beginning.

Closing her eyes, Garnet tensed against the kernel of anxiety exploding through her stomach. She could die. The unthinkable could actually happen. Whistles blasting outside the tent gouged deep pockets in her thoughts, pockets that swirled in eddies of fear. She stared up at Tamala, feeling small and vulnerable and more than physically naked.

"Well, cousin," Tamala murmured pleasantly. She nudged a stool near the cot and sat, folding slim hands into the lap of the crimson robe. "You find yourself in an unpleasant predicament, say-me *oui*?"

Garnet ran her tongue over dry lips. She would willingly have surrendered ten years of her life for a scrap of cloth to cover her nakedness. "You can halt this," she whispered.

The snowy turban tilted to one side. Ebony eyes gleamed with interest. "Perhaps. Or perhaps it's gone too far to stop." A ribbon of triumph curled Tamala's lips. "The final victory is mine," she crowed softly. "With you out of the way, I can convince Paul or Simone"—a tone of contempt underscored their names—"to give me a parcel of land. Simone is ripe for the idea."

"Never. Paul will never allow—"

"And Belaine will be mine again." A hard glitter transformed Tamala's eyes to jet. "Oh, yes. He'll be back. Or I'll follow him." She shrugged, the crimson cloth adjusting around her shoulders with a whispering rustle. Her voice hardened. "But I *will* have him."

A harsh laugh forced itself past Garnet's lips. "He doesn't want you. Don't you understand that yet?"

Tamala stood abruptly, the stool toppling behind her. She stared down at Garnet, her face suddenly ugly. "Perhaps it won't matter—perhaps events will sweep the island clean. Perhaps the time will come when an alliance with a white, with any white, will be a dangerous liability." Whirling, she strode to the tent flap and murmured something to someone outside. In a moment the terrible, relentless drums dropped in volume, the cadence becoming a steady, unceasing murmur, a thread of sound weaving through blood and bone, stitching needles of muffled fear.

A sense of waiting and expectancy thickened the subdued ticking of iron, the softened scrape of pebbles inside hollowed gourds, the low pulse beat of the drums. A trickle of perspiration ran between Garnet's breasts as the heat of the night stifled her.

"What do you say now, cousin?" Loathing congealed along Tamala's pouty lips. "Do you still think I don't deserve a stone of your precious land? Or has your current position prompted you to reconsider?"

Garnet's eyes flashed a stubborn icy green. Tamala Philippe would not have the satisfaction of hearing Garnet Winters beg. Pride firmed her jaw, stiffened her naked body. "Not a stone," she answered quietly. "Not a single grain of dirt."

A purplish flush erupted on Tamala's cheeks. "If you think Belaine will save you, cousin, you're mistaken. *If* he knew where you were, and *if* he could assemble his soldiers in time, he still would not interrupt this ceremony."

Garnet's ground her teeth, but she didn't look away from Tamala's glittering stare.

"Because if he did, the Cul-de-Sac would explode. Blood would run in the manor houses and flow ankle deep in the streets. And Colonel Jean Baptiste Belaine would not risk provoking an uprising. You know it and I know it."

Something in Garnet's stomach fluttered and knocked against her rib cage. Tamala was right. A tremble Garnet couldn't control began in her thighs and spread. At the back of her mind she had assured herself that she would be missed; surely Jean would guess what had happened and somehow he would save her. Uncertainty drained the blood from her face. There wasn't time for Jean to ride to Port-au-Prince and assemble his men. And he did not dare provoke an incident that could lead to the murder of plantation families throughout the Cul-de-Sac.

Tamala smiled, knowing Garnet's thoughts as easily as if Garnet had spoken aloud. "With or without the trigger of a local incident, the cannon of revolution will fire. And soon. But not through any lack of diligence by Colonel Belaine. If Jean wasn't desperate to avert an uprising, why did he bury

Poisson?" Her smile widened at Garnet's gasp. "Oh, yes, I know all about that—by now everyone does. The *mambos* and *hougans* have been doing a brisk business this evening selling charms against the undead." She laughed softly. "There are laws, white men's laws, prohibiting unauthorized burial, and laws against concealing evidence in a murder." Her hand reached for the flap. "I think Colonel Belaine shall pay dearly."

A sick feeling prickled Garnet's naked flesh as she guessed Tamala's price.

"Wives can't testify against husbands," Tamala purred. "Certainly not mulatto wives."

"It won't work," Garnet responded weakly.

"I've won, cousin. You lose." Tamala swept through the tent flap and immediately the drums swelled, the beats counting out numbered heartbeats, assaulting the hot night air.

Fool. Garnet spat between her teeth. You silly, idiotic fool. Pride and a sharp tongue had squashed her only hope. She had driven Tamala from the tent and into the whirling, dancing madness without a word of conciliation. Instead of placating Tamala Philippe, Garnet, in her stubborn, stupid pride, had refused to bend. She should have promised Tamala everything she owned, given her Belaine and the land and whatever else the woman demanded. "*Never.*" The single word exploded from Garnet's lips. "Never, never, never."

Kicking forward, she swung her feet over the edge of the cot, ignoring Fula's warning expression. And when Rombo strode into the tent, she used the moment he spent with Fula to palm a packet of the gray powder. How she might use it, she had no idea. But she took it anyway, clutching the packet for comfort if nothing else. And she badly needed anything that offered a shred of comfort.

When Rombo turned toward her, she drew a shuddering breath and felt a scarlet shame scald her pale body as his burning eyes raked her nakedness. The pupils of his eyes dilated, flaming like smoldering coals. An enormous erection thrust at the cloth tied around his waist. A stone lodged in Garnet's throat and she shrank from his dark arms as he scooped her up against a chest glistening with sweat and banana oil.

"No—no, please. Rombo, I beg you . . ."

But he was no longer Rombo. He was someone else, a vehicle for a powerful *loa*, a human form whose spirit had withdrawn to provide space for something outside Garnet's grasp to comprehend. The wide African cheekbones were Rombo's, and the graying woolly hair, but there the resemblance ended. This person, this *thing*, was built more powerfully than Rombo. He clasped her milky body against his dark chest and she felt his unused strength trembling along the cords standing rigidly on his arms. He could have snapped her bones like twigs.

Instead he thrust through the tent flap and hoisted her above his head, lifting her by the neck and the buttocks, her long, flaming hair swinging beside his face.

"The impostor," he roared.

The drums swelled to frenzied madness. Crawling firelight painted the bodies of the men jumping and whirling around the fire, shaking their gourds, beating their iron hoes. Their eyes rolled upward until only a yellowish white gleamed in the light from the flames. Bare-breasted women, lost in a transport of wild, hot rhythms, stamped the earth and shouted mindless chants. The Erzulie-Garnet figure flounced about the perimeter of the fireglow, chewing a chicken leg, laughing crazily. Someone poured tafia into the tin cup of an imperious creature wearing a white wig and cap.

It was madness, a nightmare blackness spewing out of a malignant dream. Garnet blinked up at stars that winked like fiery diamonds from eternity's distance. Heat from the bonfire and the suffocating night bathed her body in a sheen of moisture, but nothing so hot as the searing imprint burning into her neck and buttocks.

A merciful detachment blunted her mind. She watched

from a distance as Rombo swung her down and carried her to a wooden table positioned before the fire. She struggled feebly, then abandoned the futility of resistance as black hands spread her legs and roped her ankles and wrists to the table.

Garnet watched from a point in space, removed and icy cold, when dark fingers twisted in her pubic hair and jerked away a tangle of red, displaying the marvel to shouts of amazement.

Clawing fingers scraped up her inner thighs; from her position in space she watched them withdraw. The wild drumbeats hammered her flesh; she observed the drummers' frenzy with a calm eye. A machete sliced the air above her naked breasts; she felt but didn't feel her flesh contract. She heard the chanting, listened to the drum's response, and yet she could also hear whispers telling her the ceremony would not be quick—her death would be slow and painful.

Sweat poured from the drummers' temples; their oiled bodies glistened in the firelight as they coaxed the drums into blood fever. Dancers fell to the ground and coupled before the fire, wild with urgency. And hands dared to touch the naked goddess, darting forth, then back, slapping at the painted *vèvè*, yanking at her hair until her head ached.

Garnet floated in the ashes drifting upward from the fire. Gazing down, she felt her throat constrict at the strawberry loveliness of her naked body straining across the table. Did she regret how she had used that body, that mind? Yes, a thousand times, yes. She had squandered life; she had spent the days carelessly as if she possessed a limitless supply. Foolish, foolish.

A sharp jab returned her violently to the table. Blinking, she squinted up at Tamala, who pressed a firelit blade against her throat.

Tamala smiled. She had unwound the turban, releasing waves of black hair around her face and naked shoulders. The crimson robe had been cast aside and her lush, oiled breasts reflected the firelight in shadowed flickers of peach and orange.

"No." She laughed into Garnet's flaring eyes. "This would be too easy." The knife slid into the knotted waist of her flowered skirt. "Impostors don't die easily. First they will rape you." She watched Garnet's face pale to chalk. "Then they will carve the *vèvè* into your flesh. And then they will tie stones to your tongue and your limbs, and Erzulie, the goddess of storms and water, will welcome you at the bottom of the river."

Garnet searched her dry mouth for saliva, then hawked it forward, grimacing as the spittle fell short of Tamala's ribs. "Life comes full circle." Garnet choked, her voice stronger in hatred than in fear. "You receive what you put into it. All this"—she jerked her head toward the frenzy spinning around them—"will come back to you tenfold."

Tamala laughed. Lifting a hollowed gourd, she stirred the paste within, then rapidly smeared Garnet's breasts with a stinging mixture. "Salt. To purify you."

Something was happening behind them, but Garnet couldn't see. Blinking rapidly, she watched Tamala's head snap up. And she shrank from the slow smile transforming her cousin's face into a mask of triumphant evil. The drums swelled in tempo, spiraling into a pounding, crashing frenzy until they hammered senses and skin with a physical pain, demanding, unrelenting, insistent, wild.

Then Rombo loomed before her. Powerful, naked; his eyes glittered like fiery coals. He held an enormous erection in his hand, arching back so the chanting dancers could see.

"No," Garnet whispered, her mouth parched. "Please, God—no." Frantically, she strained against the ropes, her breath bursting past her lips in scalding gasps. "No, no, no." Someone kicked smoldering branches beneath her, and wisps of smoke rose on either side of the table, bathing her in drifts of orange cloud. The stifling smoke smelled of pine and rosewood. Eyes tearing from the smoke and heat, Garnet stared blindly at the screaming, clapping figures and the edges of the stolen packet collapsed in her clenched hand. Digging nails cut into her flesh.

A blade slashed downward and her legs were momentarily freed. But before she could react, iron hands gripped her ankles. They jerked her down the table and yanked up her knees, positioning her for Rombo's assault.

The crescendo of drums soared to a feverish pitch. A wave of reddened darkness speckled Garnet's blank stare and dizziness bled her limbs of strength. Faint with fear and horror, her heart crashing in unison with the drums, she dropped her head to one side and closed her eyes, unashamed of the tears streaking her cheeks. "Jean," she whispered, "my beloved." There hadn't been enough time; an eternity wouldn't have been enough time.

Rough hands splayed out across her thighs, bruising, pulling her apart until her bones felt near cracking. A rod of heat stabbed at her flesh. Garnet tensed and cried out, her body stiff and dry with resistance, her lip bloody beneath her teeth, and then . . .

Silence.

An abrupt silence so thick and total the sounds of the night reappeared only gradually. The buzz of insects thundered, then a crackle of flames, and finally a series of exploding gasps as pent-up breath was released in strangled terror.

Panting, Garnet twisted violently against the ropes, straining her eyes until she, too, could see the ghastly figure lurching from the shadows beyond the firelight. Her heart leaped to her throat, then froze.

It was Poisson.

Each stiff, wooden step shook loose small clods of grave dirt. His face was gray white, his blank eyes wide and staring above the gaping slash opening in his throat. A dark, clotted hole marked the rip in his breeches. Slowly his dead arms lifted, the hands curving into grasping claws as he stumbled forward.

A woman screamed, her shriek a thready rasp of horror.

The silence exploded.

Men trampled women; women clawed and kicked in a frenzy to escape. People fell, others stood rooted in frozen terror. The tent toppled, a drum rolled into the fire. Screams and cries ripped the night into chaos.

Poisson lurched forward, scattering the forms like leaves before a hurricane. And each horrifying step brought him closer to the table in front of the fire.

Garnet kicked wildly, her legs freed now, and she jerked at the ropes binding her wrists until her wrists bled, twisting up her head to snap at the bonds with her teeth. Horror glazed her eyes, charred the breath in her chest. It was impossible. Impossible. She had been there; she had seen the death wounds with her own eyes, had watched that body wearing those clothes lowered into a muddy hole and then covered. Raynald Poisson was dead; she *knew* he was dead. Frantically she battled a wave of fainting blackness, her fists clenching and opening. The packet of gray powder fell into the smoldering branches below her and a burst of thick, yellowish smoke erupted around the table, blotting out the fleeing forms behind a curtain of drifting gold. Disembodied shrieks scrambled through the smoke.

Poisson's dead gray face thrust into the cloud and Garnet screamed. Incredibly, unbelievably, he grinned, his blackened lips hideous. "Nice touch, love. The smoke." A knife flashed and her arms were freed.

It couldn't be. "Jean?" Shaking lips framed his name, but no sound emerged. Trembling violently, Garnet collapsed on the table and stared up at gray paint, at smears of red above the stained cravat and surrounding the rip at his groin. "Oh, thank God." Tears strangled her whisper as Jean's hands reached beneath her and he swung her into his arms.

"Pretend you've fainted," he ordered, then, in his wooden gait, lurched out of the smoke.

Instantly, Garnet fell limp in his arms, only partially

pretending. Her heart crashed against her ribs, threatening to leap from her breast. And nothing, absolutely nothing, had ever felt as wonderful as the filthy jacket rubbing against her naked skin.

"You have the most beautiful nipples in the world," Jean murmured. Screaming drowned his voice, made it for her alone.

"Are you crazy, Belaine?" Garnet whispered. "They're all around us." Rombo and Tamala wouldn't be fooled for long. Already she could hear them shouting in the woods, attempting to halt the panicked rush.

"Thighs like satin."

Purplish bruises dotted her thighs and her arms; her wrists bore rope burns. "For God's sake, be quiet. Someone will hear you." A scrambling figure plunged through the drifting smoke and crashed into them. Jean turned stiffly, his eyes going blank, his blackened mouth opening in a ghoulish roar. The dark face went slack with terror, then the man sank to the ground and frantically crawled toward the fire, whimpering.

Jean grinned. "Not bad, huh?"

When her erratic heartbeat had steadied, Garnet opened one eye, weak with relief to discover they were but a few steps from the tall, concealing grasses and the safety of the dark woods behind.

"What in hell took you so long?" she snapped, glaring up at him.

He rolled his eyes, his painted expression grotesque. "As always, your gratitude is heartwarming, love. Actually, a simple thank you would be adequate."

She lifted her head after ascertaining that safety lay within sight and thick billows of smoke blotted out the clearing. The enormity of what had nearly occurred washed over her like ice water. "They were going to kill me." She stared at him, her eyes large and disbelieving. "And Rombo, he . . ." A shudder of loathing swept her naked flesh and she buried her face in Jean's neck, her hands flying over his chest and gray face, reassuring herself that she hadn't imagined him.

He halted, burying his lips in her hair. "I know. I know, love." Now she felt the tremor in his arms and knew the night had been an ordeal for him as well.

"This way. Over here." Stalks of grass parted around a musket barrel. André's voice barked from the darkness, "Hurry."

Jean placed her gently on her feet and André quickly dropped his jacket over her shoulders, averting his eyes. He tossed a cloth to Jean and waited impatiently as Jean scrubbed the paint from his face and Garnet shrugged into the jacket.

"The horses are waiting," he said when Jean had thrown aside the soiled cloth and hurriedly slipped into fresh clothing.

Garnet studied the discarded jacket and breeches, recognizing them. She bit her lip.

"Did you have to dig up . . ." Her tongue refused to frame the unspeakable words.

Jean's warm hands cupped her shoulders. He nodded, his eyes searching hers. "There was no choice. We didn't know who might have witnessed Poisson's murder, who might have recognized his clothing or the nature of the wounds."

Shivering, Garnet pressed her forehead against his chest and closed her eyes. Poor Poisson. He hadn't deserved any of this. None of them did. But now she knew what had delayed Jean's arrival. Lifting her arms, she clasped his wrists and he swung her up on the stallion, adjusting her slim curves to the protection of his body. They followed André, holding the horse to a walk in an attempt to make as little noise as possible.

"Why?" Garnet murmured. "Aren't we safe now?" She rapidly recalled the rescue, discovering no flaw in its execution. The Africans would think Poisson, the undead, had abducted her. They were too terrified to conduct a search; they would assume the impostor was dead. By the time she reappeared, Jean's soldiers would have captured everyone who had participated in the ceremony.

He exhaled softly, his breath warm on her cheek. "A rider appeared shortly after I left you," he said. "I discovered you were missing when I returned to the banana grove to call you inside."

Night riders seldom carried good news. Garnet caught her lip between her teeth as his arms tensed around her.

"The uprising has begun, love, three days ago at the Cap. Three hundred plantations are burning. Thousands are dead."

She twisted to stare at him, shock draining the blood from her face.

"De Blanchelande has ordered me to fortify Port-au-Prince. The rebellion is spreading, rolling over the island like a tidal wave." The kiss on her temple was gentle but his voice emerged as hard as the brittle moon overhead. "We'll stop at the manor house long enough for you to dress, then I'm taking you and Simone into Port-au-Prince and putting you both aboard whatever ship is in the harbor. I want you out of here. Tonight."

The ceremony in the woods paled to insignificance, swept from Garnet's mind in the wake of more far-reaching events. Thousands dead. Rolling toward them like a tidal wave. Her fingers curled hard over his hands. "Jean . . ." Fresh fear coated her mouth with brackish dust. He wouldn't survive the coming violence; she knew this as she knew the sweetness of his breath lifting wisps of her hair. If a machete didn't hack him down, if a flying pike didn't pierce him—the battle itself would shift the ball against his lung. As surely as she knew the steady thud of his heartbeat against her back, Garnet knew she would never see him again if she sailed from the island alone.

"I won't go," she said quietly, her voice cracking. "I want to stay with you."

"You know that's impossible, love. There are fifteen Africans for every Frenchman on this island. One hundred thousand blacks are murdering, raping, and mutilating in the Cap area alone. Within hours the same thing will erupt here. Stay and you'll die."

Knowing it was hopeless, she pleaded with him. "Then sail with me. You don't believe in slavery—you can't fight against men striking out at oppression and cruelty. Their only crime is enslavement."

"I wear the king's uniform, Garnet."

"The monarchy has toppled. Your king is imprisoned."

"The uniform represents France and France's interests."

"Are they your interests?"

He touched her cheek, tilted her face until her tears glittered in the moonlight. "In six months I'll be out of the army, love. Then we'll be together forever, for the rest of our lives."

"Will we?" she snapped bitterly. "Will we really?"

They didn't have forever. Their time together was measured in heartbeats, in one uncertain stroke after another. Didn't he care that he risked what limited happiness they might grasp by remaining on this poisonous island? Was duty more important than life?

The stallion broke from the woods and entered the road bordering the cane fields. Far ahead, André reined to one side, waiting.

"What will André do now that it's begun?" She asked the question without caring about the answer. Nothing mattered. She felt empty inside, charred by the bitterness of a betrayal she couldn't comprehend. Jean was sending her away, remaining here to die.

"He'll leave tonight for the Cap. He's worried about Suzanne and the children, our mothers." Belaine's deep voice rumbled in her ear, his breath soft and intimate. "André's sympathies are well known. I doubt his household is in danger, but he won't rest easy until he's home."

"It's good that you weren't sent to the Cap," she said listlessly. Brother against brother. Would it have happened?

"Yes." Jean reined tightly, then caught her face between

his hands, increasing his grip when she tried to wrench away. "Listen to me and try to understand." His hard eyes were black velvet, unyielding.

"How can I understand that you prefer death to life with me?" Garnet cried softly. "Why can't you choose life and sail with me tonight?"

"You are the most important thing in my world, Garnet. You have to believe that, and you have to believe in us, love. It isn't I who doubt our future, it's you." An intense sweep of velvet probed her staring eyes. "I believe in life. I believe I'll survive whatever trials the next weeks bring, as I have survived ordeals in the past. And I believe I'll live to bounce our grandchildren on my knee. If I didn't trust in this, I'd go crazy—can't you understand that? I'd live in fear of every vague ache and pain. I'd begin to fear life itself, and be no good to either of us."

"But that's a false premise." A dawn glow cast orange lights deep in his smoky eyes. "You don't have unlimited tomorrows. You have to put yourself before duty." A sudden flash of insight widened Garnet's stare. "De Blanchelande, he doesn't know, does he? The governor doesn't know about the ball against your lung." His frown confirmed the truth. "Why haven't you told him?" She could have shook him until his teeth rattled.

"It didn't matter until I met you."

Excitement flushed her face. She twisted in the saddle and her fingers dug into his shoulders. "Tell him. Once de Blanchelande knows the state of your health, he'll muster you out of the army. Jean, it's so simple. We'll sail to Boston and Uncle William will welcome you into his import business. I know he will." A cane plantation was far too strenuous an undertaking to risk, but a desk in Uncle William's quiet office . . .

Jean shook her, his face stony. "Don't do this, Garnet. Don't coddle me. For God's sake don't bury me before I'm dead. Let me live each day fully, as if I had forever."

"But you don't have forever!" Her voice caught on a sob.

Impatiently, André called from the darkness, "It's dawn."

"Dawn?" Jean's heavy brows furrowed as he glanced at the sky. "It can't be." He urged the stallion forward to André's mount and they stared at the strange glow flickering above the horizon. Sweet-smelling smoke drifted in a thin mist above the cane fields.

"Oh, my God," Garnet breathed. *"Simone."*

The manor house was burning.

—19—

JEAN AND ANDRÉ DUG IN their heels and raced toward the manor house, following the paths through the carrys rather than risk the main roads. When they could see flames licking the sky, turning the night as bright as noon, Jean pressed Garnet's head to his shoulder and shouted over her hair.

"André, this way." He urged the stallion toward the boiler house, one of the few outbuildings not yet burning, near enough that they could assess the situation yet remain undetected. Jean reined to a sliding halt and jumped to the ground, running through the deep shadows on the far side of the building. Garnet looped the reins about a pine branch, then ran to join him. Together they crouched at the corner of the sugar house and stared out at a scene of utter chaos.

The back of the house was a sheet of fire. Flames shot from the balcony doors and raced along the eaves. Fiery tongues licked upward from the windows of the ground-floor ballroom. The roof of the kitchen house flamed brightly, then crashed inward with a roar of black smoke and sizzling sparks. A hoarse cheer sounded from hundreds of ragged figures either running with smoking torches or milling about aimlessly and sucking on stalks of stolen cane. Bits of flaming ash floated in the air, drifting from the burning fields.

"Do you recognize anyone?"

331

"A few," Garnet answered, her wide stare not leaving the awesome destruction. "Not many."

Face grim, Jean looked at André. "Can we approach the front of the manor without being seen?"

"If we circle back and go through the cane fields beside the main driveway." André ran toward the horses.

Jean's hands cupped Garnet's shoulders. "You'll be safe here. Wait for us."

"No." Before he could protest, she leaped up into the saddle and reached down to assist him, knowing there was no time to argue. Glaring, Jean slapped her hand aside and swung onto the stallion's back, racing the horse away from the flames and into the shadowy fields.

Thick, sweet-smelling smoke drifted above the cane on the west side of the driveway. To the east, the fields crackled and blazed like giant bonfires, reddening the sky and spewing a heavy, syrupy smoke high in the air. Garnet slapped at the ash and glowing straw raining on her hair as they jumped from the horses and waded through shoulder-high cane stalks until they reached the edge of the field and could feel the heat scorching their faces.

On his toes, André gazed uneasily at the burning fields. One of the palm trees lining the driveway burst into flame, sizzling and hissing as fire curled up the fronds. "We can't stay here long. The road is acting as a firebreak, but"—he slapped at a fragment of hot ash burning a hole in his shirt—"the flames will jump the road very soon." He clasped Jean's shoulder. "Have a look, then let's get the hell out of here."

"Simone," Garnet breathed, her eyes pleading. "We can't leave without Simone."

"She's right." Ducking, Jean moved forward in a crouch until he reached the last thin line of stalks, then he sank to his heels and cautiously parted the cane. His granite gaze flickered as Garnet and André slid beside him.

Garnet shaded her eyes from the blistering heat and the glare. The front of the manor was a solid orange wall of fire.

The roof of the veranda crashed, curls of black smoke spiraled upward, flaming boards spilled across the graveled driveway. And there were more people here, perhaps two hundred Africans drunk on tafia and revenge. Shouting women held hands and danced, babies bouncing in slings on their backs. Men waved machetes and torches; heat and excitement oiled their bodies and wild, nightmarish faces. They ran and leaped and screamed with a raw, primitive joy.

Sickened, Garnet stared blindly at the tableau, only gradually focusing on individuals. A whip-scarred back glistening in the red light; a breast puckered by an old brand. Her eyes shifted and she sucked in a sharp breath. A pile of smoking bodies nearly covered the punishment circle. The house servants? Those who had refused to join the marauders? Swallowing back the nausea boiling into her throat, Garnet squeezed her eyes shut, looking away from the mound of sprawled forms, blotting out Josephine's frozen scream and wide, staring eyes, refusing to see the boy who had taken her horse so many times. "Oh, God." She heard the low, wailing moan and didn't know it issued from her own lips.

A small parade rounded the corner of the burning house, a parade of whistling, drumming blacks wearing Paul's brocade jackets, Jean's uniform coats. Against the roar of hungry flames, they sang and danced and applauded the women flouncing giddily in Simone's silks and Garnet's imported muslins. And inside the cage they carried on their shoulders, Lille sprawled like a rag doll more dead than alive.

Garnet's fingers dug into Jean's arm; she tasted blood beneath her teeth.

They had sliced off Lille's ears and ripped out his tongue. And nailed his ears and his tongue to his naked shoulders. They had flayed the skin from his legs up to his knees and a few inches beyond. And now they placed the wooden cage on the ground and set fire to it.

Garnet covered her eyes and cried out as Lille thrust a

clawing hand through the bars. His lips opened in a scream, the sound swallowed by the roaring crackle of the flames.

And then she saw Paul standing so near the edge of the cane that she could look directly into his cool blue eyes. Incredibly, miraculously, he was unhurt. Surrounded, but unhurt. Garnet sucked in a quick breath of the burning air. A rod of cane snapped in her hands and she felt Jean's shoulder tense in readiness, saw his hand drop to grip his sword. His body coiled in on itself, gathering to spring.

"No, my friends," Paul shouted in formal French, each word like a whip. His eyes slid deliberately past the field, coming to rest on Lille's distant agonies. "In the name of God, don't show yourselves."

André clapped a quick hand over Jean's mouth. "Don't be a fool," André whispered. "Two hundred madmen against the three of us? My brother, this is a fight we can't win. You cannot save him." The brothers stared at each other, then Jean nodded and André's hand fell away.

Paul swung a bottle of rum to his lips and swallowed steadily, eyeing the black hatred surrounding him. Half-naked men shuffled in a tightening circle, gripping long, flashing machetes, slapping wooden stakes against their palms. Even now, Paul du Casse's aristocratic confidence and icy gaze intimidated them. One man darted forward, a blade in his hand, then retreated uncertainly beneath Paul's glacial stare.

Paul's laugh was a sneer of ridicule. "*Cowards. A fatherless pack of murdering, cowardly dogs.*" He took a long pull from the bottle, then wiped the back of his hand across his mouth. "You always said I didn't know how to live, Belaine. You said I wasted my miserable life on cards and drink and self-pity. Are you hearing this?" His gaze swept the field, pausing for the span of a heartbeat, then slid past them without a flicker of recognition. "You were right, you son of a bitch. You were right. I failed at everything I tried. I destroyed everything that was important." His stare drove back a black wearing stripes of red and blue paint on scarred cheeks. "But a du Casse knows how to die. By God, I'll show these murdering savages how an aristocrat dies." He looked toward Lille and his lip curled with contempt. "If I succeed at nothing else, I'll die like a goddamned gentleman."

"Oh, my God." Garnet's teeth scraped her knuckles. Her body shook. Paul stood straight and tall, his shoulders back, his chin firm. Outlined against the orange crackle, his stance proud and commanding, he presented the finest of a dying era. Paul du Casse did not stand before them—France in all her dignity and greatness stood before them.

A machete glittered in an arc of swishing light and Paul's brocaded shoulder opened. A dark gush blackened his sleeve. Paul smiled his scorn and lifted the bottle to his lips. The black man hesitated, his fingers opening and closing about the machete handle, then he glanced uneasily at his companions and stepped back.

Jean pulled Garnet into his arms and smothered her sob against his shoulder, his eyes filled with pain as he watched Paul raise the bottle first in a toast to his tormentors and then toward the field.

"Belaine, if you're still there . . ." He paused and smiled. "Of course you're still there. You never knew when to withdraw, did you?" He ran a hand through the sugary ash sticking in his white hair. "They dragged Simone down the main driveway. If she's still alive . . ." He stared at the blazing sky and his voice cracked. Just for a moment. "Tell her . . . tell her I loved her in my own way. Tell her that I'm sorry. And, Belaine, tell her that I died well . . . tell her I finally succeeded at something she could be proud of."

One of the black men jumped forward and smashed a wooden stake across Paul's hand. Garnet heard or imagined she heard the snap of breaking bones. The rum bottle shattered against the gravel. Paul smiled at the man, his eyes like flat blue stones. Then he folded his arms across his chest and

turned his proud face to the burning manor, smiling his
terrible smile. "Go now, Belaine. Save Simone if you can."

It was an abomination, a hideous betrayal, to leave him
without a word of comfort, without a single sign they had
heard. But when Jean looked at her and shook his head,
Garnet bit her lip and nodded, knowing they had no choice.
Silently she followed André through the maze of stalks, Jean
behind her.

And this time when Jean ordered her to remain concealed
in the cane, Garnet had seen enough to obey without question.
Gulping breaths of scorching air, she crouched low, the
murderous roar of the flames filling her head as she waited
while Jean and André ran along the driveway, dodging falling
ash and fire, searching the shoulders of the road. She watched
Jean halt, bend, then stand and wave her forward.

Clutching André's jacket over her nakedness, Garnet raced
along the road, staying close to the cane stalks. Gunshots
sounded from the burning manor and she prayed one of the
balls had found Paul. It would be a quick and merciful death
compared to Lille's.

Small, sharp stones scraped the skin from her knees as she
dropped to the ground beside Simone and uttered a glad cry.
Simone was alive.

"Thank God." Garnet blinked at sudden tears as her hands
flew over Simone's white face. "We're going to get you out of
here." She crawled toward Simone's skirt, slapping at the
folds, smothering a multitude of smoking holes that smoldered where the falling ash had dropped.

Jean jerked her away. "Don't, Garnet." His eyes flickered
with a hard, unreadable expression. "She's been raped, more
than once. Don't move her."

"Thank you for pulling down my skirt, Jean." Simone
spoke in a low, breathless voice, sounding strangely distant
and removed. Beads of perspiration stood along her brow and
wet her hair to her cheeks and temples. But her large gray
eyes were calm.

For an instant, for one wild, soaring instant, Garnet dared to hope Simone was unhurt. Then she saw the silver cross clutched so tightly in Simone's palm that the bars had gouged deep cuts. Simone should have screamed at the pain, but she didn't notice; her palm closed tighter on the cross. Blood trickled steadily down her wrist. And she lay so still, so impossibly still.

Simone's serene gaze swept past Garnet, finding Jean. "They'll be back," she whispered.

"It doesn't matter," Garnet interjected hastily. She smoothed back Simone's hair, her touch reassuring, and she wondered why Jean didn't lift Simone onto one of the horses André was leading through the cane. They had to hurry. "We'll be gone." She slid an arm beneath Simone's shoulders. "Try to sit up now."

Jean's fingers bit cruelly into her shoulders and he pulled her away. "Garnet, she's dying."

Garnet stared into Simone's chalky-white face and calm, accepting eyes. "No." She stroked Simone's cheek and cringed at the chill of death against her hot fingers. "Oh, no!" Whirling on her knees, she stared into Jean's eyes, begging him to tell her it wasn't true. "She's hurt, yes, but if we can get her to a doctor . . . She can't die, not Simone . . . Please, Jean, please, we have to try!" Words babbled from her lips, as her fingers pulled and pummeled his shirtfront.

Wordlessly Jean leaned forward and lifted Simone's smoldering skirt.

For as long as she lived, Garnet would remember the shock. Red exploded in her mind. The red sky, the burning red fields, the bloody red mess of disembowelment. Screaming, she covered her eyes and fell against Jean's chest; a torrent of horror ripped upward from her soul.

Simone's gray eyes brimmed with sorrow. Wincing, she briefly touched Garnet's bowed head, then she lifted her shimmering gaze to Jean. "It hurts." The effort of her dry whisper sliced through Garnet's heart.

"I know, Simone, my little dove, I know." After taking her small hand between his large palms, Jean cast a glance at André. A look passed between them and André stepped toward Garnet.

Simone wet her lips and tried to smile. "My wild, handsome Jean." A dark trickle ran from beneath her skirts, puddled against a small stone, then overflowed it and continued into the dusty road. "We were so young, weren't we? If you ever cared for me, Jean"—she looked up at him, her gray eyes soft and imploring—"then please, please do the right thing now."

They looked at each other and for a moment the monstrous crackle of the inferno faded. For the briefest of instants, they were nineteen again and it was Paris and music and love and laughter mingled in their gaze.

"Do you understand what I'm asking, my Jean, my dearest friend?" Simone whispered.

Jean cradled her face between his hands and gently, very gently, he kissed her lips. "I understand." He raised his hand to André and his voice was gruff and hoarse. "Give me your pistol, then leave us."

"Oh, my God." Blinded by tears, Garnet collapsed against André as his arm tightened around her shoulders and he pulled her to her feet. She tried to turn, her arm stretched back. "Simone." But André whispered in her ear and held her firmly, leading her to the horses. She could hear Simone and Jean speaking in low murmurs behind her.

Waiting on Jean's stallion, her head bowed and her body shaking uncontrollably, Garnet closed her eyes against a river of silent tears. When the shot was fired, her body jerked as if the ball had been for her. She watched Jean bend and tenderly lift Simone into his arms, then he carried her into the field. The bitter sweetness of smoke and memory charred Garnet's mind. Raging, she lifted wet eyes to the blazing sky and raised her fists and screamed at God.

Then somehow Jean was behind her, his body solid and

warm and real in the midst of the nightmare, and they were flying down the driveway, skidding onto the road to Port-au-Prince, cutting through the carrys as they neared town, taking to the dark back roads as they saw leaping flames roaring through the slave quarters, crackling along the warehouses lining the wharf.

They skirted the town, galloping south until they reached the wrought-iron fence enclosing the cemetery, the one site they could be certain no African would invade. Jean reined his foaming stallion next to André's heaving mount.

For a moment neither brother spoke, each watching the bloody sky, staring at the flaming sparks and ash raining over the city; the roar of fire and the shouts of fighting reached them even here.

"Every white in the Cul-de-Sac will try to reach the harbor," Jean said. "That's where my men will be."

Another warehouse exploded, shooting clouds of black oily smoke high over the harbor. A dockside freighter had hoisted sail too late; fire raced up the canvas. Garnet could see tiny orange-lit figures racing along the decks. Fortunately the freighter was the only ship dockside; a half-dozen others rocked at anchor one hundred yards from the flaming wharf, waiting for the rowboats hauling passengers across the water to safety.

André swung his gaze from the harbor. "Don't go to the Cap, Jean. It's a slaughterhouse."

"You knew this would happen, didn't you?"

A hand crossed André's eyes, smearing the soot on his brow. "It had to happen . . . it's the only way." His dark eyes asked understanding. "And I'm part of it, for there's no choice. The whites can't win, Jean. You know that. If I side with them, I'll lose the plantation and endanger my family."

Jean nodded slowly. "In your place I would do the same. The rebellion will need leaders, André. Strong men able to withstand the pressures of savagery, men to counsel reason and sanity in the face of temptations beyond imagining. You're needed."

"Most of the insurgents reject reason—they lust for vengeance." André stared at the flaming slave quarters. "I pray reason will triumph, but much blood will flow first."

Garnet felt Jean's arms tense around her. "I've thought about this, André, about duty and career and the future. And I'll desert before I'll bear arms against you."

Quickly Garnet twisted in the saddle to look at him. She dropped her gaze from the pain in his dark eyes.

"Thank God. I've had nightmares about . . ." André closed his eyes, then said quietly, "I think we should part here. Can you make it to the harbor alone?"

"Yes."

"I have to think of Suzanne and the children and our mothers," André explained. "If I—"

Jean stopped his brother's apology by clasping his arm. "I understand. From this point we're a danger to each other. Keep our mothers safe. When this is over . . ." The cords rose along his arm. "And, André . . . avoid the wharf and the armory tonight—that's where I'll be."

"I'd rather die than raise my sword against you."

Their eyes locked and their hands trembled in a crushing grip. "Go with God," Jean whispered hoarsely.

"And you, brother. Go with God."

They leaned across the horses to embrace, then André bent forward and dug in his heels. They watched him racing toward Bel Air, the burning slave quarters, watched until he turned into a side street and was lost to view.

"Jean . . ." Garnet touched Belaine's smoky face, as sooty and sticky with sugar ash as her own. She looked deep into his hard eyes, sharing his pain, experiencing the oneness of emotions too deep and too profound to be articulated. "I love you." Her hands tightened and trembled on his face. The words weren't enough, weren't deep enough or powerful enough to express adequately what she felt in her heart.

"There may not be time later to tell you that . . . that I love you." Helplessness and anger harshened her tone. The phrase was too mild, too simplistic. "And if we don't survive tonight" —she bit her lip and felt herself drowning in the flames reflected in his dark stare—"I want you to know that loving you was the best thing I ever did." A sob choked her. "And being loved by you was my proudest accomplishment."

His teeth flashed white and strong beneath a hard, determined grin. "You insist on burying me, don't you?" His hand caught her chin and tilted her face, then his lips covered hers in a bruising kiss. When his mouth finally released hers, leaving her breathless and shaking, he clasped her tightly against his chest. "Is that the kiss of a dying man? You and I are survivors, love. It takes more than an insurrection to stamp 'finished' on us."

Garnet smiled. "Paul was right. You don't know when to admit defeat." Thinking of Paul didn't disturb her as she had supposed it would. She would remember him as he had wanted to be remembered: standing straight and proud before the flames, an aristocrat and a gentleman to the end.

Jean's thoughts obviously spiraled back too. "Take this." He closed her fist around a knife, then stared deeply into eyes pained by sudden memories of Simone. "If you must use it, use it where it will do the most good."

On herself. The echo of a shot reverberated through Garnet's memory. Nodding, she softly stroked his cheek and brushed his lips with a tenderness that told him she understood. Then she lay back in his arms as he urged the stallion west, toward the wharf.

The city reeled with chaos. If the rebellion was organized, it wasn't apparent; there was no evident leadership, no direction to the uprising. Inconsistent scenes existed side by side. Within sight and hearing of the crackling slave quarters, the Rue du Centre hosted a carnival. The street was alive with music and dancing and wild, drunken revelry.

Gathering a long, grim breath, Belaine guided the stallion into the madness, urging the horse through masses of dancers and throngs of laughing blacks, who tipped their straw hats and grinned and tossed flowers in Garnet's lap. From the next street, the Rue St. Honoré, came the screams and cries of butchery and carnage.

Leaving the insanity of the carnival, they turned left at the Rue des Champs, winding toward the wharf and the heavy clash of fighting. The Rue des Champs was quiet now, but a wave of marauders had recently passed. Two shop fronts blazed. Looters ran in the street carrying bolts of cloth and bottles of rum. A blond woman wearing a torn silk dress and one slipper with a broken heel sat on a low stone wall. She peeled green skin away from an orange above the head of the child cradled in her lap.

Carefully she opened the dead child's mouth and inserted a wedge of orange, then popped a section between her own bleeding lips.

"Come with us," Garnet called, blinking rapidly.

The woman shook ropes of tumbled hair. "I'm waiting for my husband." Wild horror widened her eyes, then she thrust away knowledge too terrible to admit. "He'll come for us soon." Smiling, her stare feverish and glazed, she waved them on and returned to peeling the orange.

Garnet closed her eyes, feeling the scorch of the blazing dock on her lids and cheeks and dry lips. When she opened her eyes, it was to a scene from hell and suddenly they were in the shouting midst of it, whipping the stallion toward the line of soldiers strung out in a fighting line along the wharf. Behind them rowboats pushed away from the dock, laden with terrified planters who had survived the bloody gauntlet.

Blacks and mulattoes, men and women, hacked and stabbed at soldiers and planters and boys not yet in long breeches. Dead and dying littered the wharf area and floated in the oily waters. The roaring din of flames and screams rocketed through Garnet's mind. She recognized faces from Simone's party and faces from the *vodun* ceremony she had escaped a lifetime ago. Teeth bared, each side fought for inches, battled for survival or for bloody revenge.

Jean's sword arm lifted and fell, flashed in the hellish orange light. Then the stallion stumbled and went down beneath them. Jean jerked Garnet free as the animal fell, and together they rushed forward toward soldiers who recognized Belaine and ran to assist.

Orange uniforms closed around them, drawing back toward the rowboats. And then Jean was lifting her, dropping her over the pier and down into a boat heavy with stunned planters and wide-eyed women.

"*Jean.*" She saw now what she had missed during their mad dash to safety. A knife or a machete had opened his thigh. Blood soaked his breeches to the knee. Garnet scrambled forward in the rocking boat, ignoring the shouted protests of the other passengers. She held to the rope securing the boat to the dock and screamed his name, watching him limp toward a junior officer, dragging his leg.

"The fight is turning toward the Grande Rue," Jean shouted to the man. "Leave a small force here and dispatch the main body forward."

"Into the boat, sir." The young officer, grim-lipped in his zeal and self-importance, glanced at Jean's thigh. "Our orders are to transport locals and wounded."

"By whose command?" Jean roared, looking at his leg as if only now noticing the wound. "*I'm* the senior officer at this garrison." He stumbled and the young officer caught him by the elbows as Garnet gasped and her knuckles flew to her lips.

"General Laborde has arrived, sir. He's taken command of the area." The officer nodded and two men jumped to take Jean's weight on their shoulders, dragging him toward the boat.

"Damn fine job Laborde's doing," Jean snapped. One hand pressed against his chest as he scanned the bloody sky, dodging a piece of flaming shingle. "Who the hell is guarding the armory?"

The young officer's head snapped toward Fort Ilet and the solitary soldier guarding the neck of the promontory on which it sat. "Christ," he muttered, his face paling. "We'll miss you, sir."

Jean protested vehemently as the soldiers lowered him into the boat, his curses dark against the crackle of flames and the din of battle. But, once he was in the boat, the fight drained from his white face and he collapsed on a wooden seat. Garnet flew to assist him out of his shirt, then ripped it into bandages with her teeth. Her shaking fingers hastily wound the shirt lengths around his thigh and she didn't turn from her task until the voice shouting Belaine's name became too strident to ignore.

Tamala Philippe crisscrossed the wharf, running, her black eyes steady on her goal, the boat Garnet and Jean occupied. The last boat at the dock. "Wait for me!" A band of drunken blacks chased after her, lust in their shouts.

At the sound of Belaine's name, the crew master hesitated with the rope, delaying the casting off. His uneasy gaze swung from Tamala to measure the approach of the machetes. The blacks outnumbered the remaining soldiers. Still he hesitated.

"No!" Garnet shouted. Jumping forward, she cut the rope with a quick, sawing motion. The boat leaped away from the pier, the tide tugging it toward open water.

Tamala skidded to a halt at the edge of the dock and fell against a rotted post, her lips twisting from her teeth in a scream. "I should have killed you when I had the chance." Whirling, she arched her back, thrusting out gleaming, bare breasts. "I'm one of you," she shouted, the words as confident as if she had always believed them. "See my brand?"

But there was no brand, only an old puckered scar where she had defaced the hated P. Some of the marauders peeled away to engage the soldiers; the others grinned and closed around Tamala Philippe.

Sickened, Garnet closed her eyes, taking no pleasure in what she had done. Flames danced on her face; fiery fragments hissed into the water beside the boat shooting toward the freighter, *Yankee Maple*. After drawing a breath, she slipped an arm around Belaine's shoulders and eased his head to her shoulder, frightened by his closed eyes and white face, by the rapidity of his breathing.

She whispered his name and when he didn't answer, she laid her hand on his chest, pressing it flat until she could feel his heartbeat. Exhaling slowly, she fixed her gaze on St. Domingue's receding shoreline.

From a distance, she could see there were fewer fires than it had seemed when they were in the midst of the destruction. Already the soldiers had begun to contain the violence.

But it wouldn't end here. The rebellion was only beginning. A lull would follow, a time of evaluation and preparation, then another uprising would erupt, and this time the fight would be to the finish. And the blacks would triumph. Garnet felt this as she felt the weight of Jean's body in her arms. The blacks had nothing to lose and everything to gain; they had numbers on their side and the will to win. The whites had only their sense of superiority.

Biting her lip, she stared up at a sky hazed over by a curtain of thick, sweet smoke. Sugar ash fell like black snow.

She had thought the land was indestructible, her future guaranteed forever, safe and secure. What a fool she had been. Her future lay in her arms, pale and breathing in halting gasps, but genuine and the only security she would ever know. Forever was nothing more than a state of mind.

She watched them hoist Belaine in a sling to the deck of the *Yankee Maple*, then she followed the men as they carried him down a flight of steps and into a long, low cavern stacked with galley supplies, water barrels, and crates of items stamped by Charleston customs, and slung with sleeping hammocks.

And she refused to leave even when the ship's surgeon poured Belaine full of whiskey and cut away his breeches. He doused raw whiskey into the machete wound, then stitched the flesh with laced catgut. Garnet heard Belaine's sharp intake of breath, and her stomach boiled.

A cabin boy appeared on the heels of the departing surgeon and offered Garnet a tin cup of brandy, which she gratefully swallowed in a single gulp.

The boy refilled Garnet's cup and shyly looked at Belaine. "Some for you, sir?"

A flush of color had returned to Jean's face and he smiled drunkenly. "More whiskey if you have it, lad."

The boy grinned. "That we do, sir. Good American whiskey."

Garnet drew a steadying breath, then stood and glanced about the cramped space they had been allotted. "Well, now, there are a few necessities we're going to require: Do you have a good memory, boy?"

The boy nodded soberly.

"Good." She raised a hand, ticking off each item on her fingers. "First we need soap and a bucket of water." She could feel the sticky sugar ash coating her face, could see it in Jean's hair. "Second, I want you to fetch the captain the instant he has a free moment. Tell him that we wish to be married."

The boy's eyes rounded and he looked slowly from Jean's whiskey grin to Garnet's cool green eyes.

"There's nothing wrong with you, Belaine, that food and a little rest won't cure." The lie had sprung to her lips with ease. With enough repetition, perhaps one day she would believe it herself.

Jean's eyes softened into a velvety glow. "I love you, Mademoiselle Winters. Have I told you recently?"

"Thirdly, we'll need privacy. I want some blankets to hang between these hammocks." She glanced absently at a woman standing an arm's length from Jean's hammock. The woman nodded hearty agreement. "I'll need fresh bandages before morning, and I want a stool or a chair." She rubbed her hands together briskly. "Oh, and I'll need a dress." She had left St. Domingue as naked as she had arrived.

"A dress, miss?" The twitch beside the boy's mouth betrayed his determination not to stare at her thighs and the long legs curving beneath André's jacket.

"A dress," Garnet repeated firmly. "And a hairbrush and shoes if you can find any."

"She's determined, ain't she, sir?" the boy muttered as he turned to depart.

Belaine roared with delight. "You don't know the half of it, lad; the woman's a terror, as fiery as her hair and just as remarkable."

"One more thing," Garnet said, ignoring them both. "Where is this ship bound?" The boy's broad Yankee accent made her homesick, raising images of autumn leaves and crisp, cold mornings, of parslied potatoes and stuffed turkey, of steeple bells ringing in a New England Sunday.

"Bound for Charleston, ma'am."

A short sail to Boston and home. Garnet squared her shoulders and drew a deep breath. "We're going to New Orleans."

" 'Spect you can get there from Charleston, ma'am."

When the boy had hurried away on his errands, Belaine opened his arms and called her name in a whiskey-warm voice. "There's room in this hammock for two, love."

Garnet smiled, eyeing the narrow sling. "I imagine we'll find out." After plumping the straw pillow beneath his dark curls, she brushed back his hair and kissed him softly on the lips. "But not tonight. Rest, my darling," she whispered fiercely. "And get well for me."

He was asleep in an instant. He didn't feel her holding his hand through the night or know when she pressed her trembling fingers on his chest. Nor did he hear her prayers as she lifted her face to the dawn and quietly asked God to grant her patience and courage and the ability to put forever out of her mind.

—20—

THE EVENING BREEZE BLEW FRESH and cool across Garnet's cheeks as she adjusted her rope sandals and stepped onto the deck. Inhaling deeply, she crossed to the oak railing, maintaining a slow, unhurried pace and pretending an interest in the changing of the watch. She heard the lazy creaking of the rigging above her head, but she could not force herself to look up.

Each morning and each evening Jean exercised his leg by climbing to the crow's nest high atop the mainmast. And each morning and each evening Garnet's heart lodged in her throat and her nerves quivered on the surface of her skin.

Resting her elbows on the railing, she gazed out at a glorious sunset washing tides of pink and lavender across the open sea. "Thank you, Lord," she murmured. She clasped each day to her heart like a miser protecting a priceless treasure. And, remarkably, she was slowly beginning to accept the unthinkable, that her happiness could end abruptly, without warning. The knowledge would never be comfortable, but she could foresee a time when worry would not occupy every waking thought. The first day Jean had climbed to the crow's nest, she had cowered belowdeck straining to hear a thud. On the second day she had ground her teeth and joined the ladies sewing skirts from lengths of canvas. On the third

348

day she had managed a wobbly smile and wished him a pleasant journey.

"Garnet!"

Now, for the first time, she turned slowly from the rail and shaded her eyes, searching the web of rigging. Her heart lurched. Then she forced herself to release a quick, steady breath and then another as Jean swung down the ropes as confidently as though he'd been born to sailing. Cheeks wind-pink and glowing, he dropped lightly to the deck, his eyes dancing.

"It's wonderful up there. Are you certain you won't join me next time?"

"No, thank you. You're the one who needs exercise, remember?" Her arms twined around his neck and her smiling eyes teased. "Sleeping double in a one-man hammock is enough exercise for me."

Laughing, he pulled her tight against his body. "Woman, have you no shame?"

Her lips parted beneath his warm kiss and she clung to him as if a dozen sailors didn't watch them and sigh. "None," she whispered, her thoughts leaping hungrily toward the night and the rapture it promised.

Smiling, Jean rested his chin atop her fiery head, and together they watched the sunset flame to shades of red and orange. "I love you, Garnet," he murmured into the fragrance of her hair.

"Forever?" The word slipped out, instantly regretted. Biting her lip, Garnet wished with all her heart that she could erase her blunder. "Fool," she muttered beneath her breath. "I'm a stubborn, impulsive fool."

Turning her in his arms, Jean gently cupped her face between his hands. His lips brushed her soft mouth, then he stared down into her eyes, his own gaze velvety warm and deep. "I will love you to the end of my days, my heart."

But that wasn't forever. Or was it? What was forever, after all, but a collection of days, one stacked upon another?

Something tight and anxious cracked around her heart and fell away. Gazing into his concerned frown, she understood she had not fooled him; he knew what she felt each time he leaped into the rigging. He knew the ball in his chest lay against their love as well as against his lung.

And this she could not allow, not if their love was to flourish, not if they hoped to find happiness together. Resting her forehead against his chest, she reached inside herself, seeking the courage to give him life. And her eyes lit with a soft radiance when she found what she sought.

Forever was not something another person could promise; forever existed within one's own heart. And because she was the guardian of her forever, she could release him to life, could give him days as vigorous and active as he chose. He would never leave her; he would always live in her heart.

She gazed at him from eyes shining with wonder. "We'll build our forever one day at a time."

Forever in units of a single day; it would be enough. She looked into his soft, dark eyes, eyes that wrapped her in velvet love. And she offered him the final gift of acceptance. "There's enough light for another climb to the crow's nest . . ."

He stared at her, then he clasped her to his heart with a hoarse cry and held her so tightly she couldn't breathe. Held her until she was laughing and crying and covering his joy with kisses.

"I love you," she whispered. "I will love you always."

Forever.

About the Author

Maggie Osborne was born in 1941 and grew up in Kansas and Colorado. After attending Ft. Lewis Junior College in Durango, Colorado, she worked on a newspaper and then as a stewardess. She currently lives with her husband, a manager with State Farm Insurance, and her son in Colorado. In addition to community activities, her leisure projects include painting and renovating old houses with her family. She is the author of ALEXA, PORTRAIT IN PASSION, SALEM'S DAUGHTER, and YANKEE PRINCESS—historical romances available in Signet editions.

Fabulous Fiction from SIGNET